Gorgeous, tall, br[...]
resist a romantic Fr[...]
you away to[...]

Latin Lovers
SEDUCTIVE FRENCHMEN

Three fabulous stories from some of our
readers' favourite authors: Abby Green,
Chantelle Shaw and Fiona Lowe

LATIN LOVERS COLLECTION

COLLECT ALL SIX!

Latin Lovers

SEDUCTIVE FRENCHMEN

Abby
GREEN

Chantelle
SHAW

Fiona
LOWE

MILLS
BOON
&

Mills & Boon, an imprint of Harlequin (UK) Limited, Eton House, 18-24 Paradise Road, Richmond, Surrey TW9 1SR

LATIN LOVERS: SEDUCTIVE FRENCHMEN
© Harlequin Enterprises II B.V./S.à.r.l. 2011

Chosen as the Frenchman's Bride © Abby Green 2006
The Frenchman's Captive Wife © Chantelle Shaw 2006
The French Doctor's Midwife Bride © Fiona Lowe 2007

ISBN: 978 0 263 88994 9

027-1111

Harlequin (UK) policy is to use papers that are natural, renewable and recyclable products and made from wood grown in sustainable forests. The logging and manufacturing processes conform to the legal environmental regulations of the country of origin.

Printed and bound in Spain
by Blackprint CPI, Barcelona

CHOSEN AS THE FRENCHMAN'S BRIDE

Abby Green

Abby Green worked for twelve years in the film industry. The glamour of four a.m. starts, dealing with precious egos, the mucky fields, driving rain…all became too much. After stumbling across a guide to writing romance, she took it as a sign and saw her way out, capitalising on her long-time love for romance books. Now she is very happy to sit in her nice warm house while others are out in the rain and muck! She lives and works in Dublin.

For Lynn and the women upstairs…

PROLOGUE

The poolside, Hotel Lézille, 8.30pm

HE NOTICED her as soon as she appeared in the archway between the lobby and the pool, his eyes drawn there as if pulled by a magnetic force. A rare excitement stirred his pulse. He told himself that he hadn't come especially to seek her out. She seemed slightly hesitant, unsure. She wasn't the most beautiful woman he'd ever seen, but she had a stunningly natural quality about her, which in his world was rare, compelling. In a simple black dress that outlined every slender curve and a generous bosom, she caught his eye *again*, and he couldn't look away. Didn't want to.

The soft waves of her dark hair framed her face. Intriguingly, she seemed to be slightly self-conscious. Or perhaps, he thought with a hardened cynicism that had been honed over years, she carefully projected that vulnerable fragility. God knew she had managed to capture his attention in the street yesterday. Her huge, striking blue eyes had momentarily stunned him, rendering him speechless. And he was never stunned, or speechless. Something in their depths had caught him, combined with that lush mouth, looking up at him so innocently, full of a shocked kind of awe.

Then, amazingly, when he had seen her on the island earlier today, he had followed some base instinct to see her up close again… She was everything he remembered, and more. He recalled how she had trembled under his hands in the street yesterday, and under his look earlier today on the island. He couldn't ever remember a woman being so blatantly responsive.

His mouth compressed when he thought of her refusal to have dinner with him. That certainly hadn't happened in a while, if ever. Was she playing some game? He wouldn't be surprised… He was constantly amazed at the lengths some women went to just to get his attention. Playing hard to get wasn't a new trick…

He mentally dismissed the bottle redhead to his left, who was chattering incessantly, oblivious of the fact that his attention had long wandered from her far too obviously surgically enhanced assets.

With a barely perceptible flick of his wrist a man materialised at his side, bending low.

'Yes, sir?'

'Who is that woman?' He indicated to where she stood.

'She's not a guest with us, sir, but I can find out if you like…'

He just shook his head and dismissed him.

The ennui that had settled over him recently was definitely fading as he took in her graceful progress through the tables to reach her companions. With a skill based on years of reading people and body language, a skill that had tripled his fortune many times over, he assessed them in seconds, focusing on the man he guessed was her date. No competition. His heart-rate speeded up pleasantly as he contemplated them from under hooded lids. He decided now that he would conveniently forget the blow to his pride when she had refused him earlier. She was definitely worth pursuing. A surge of anticipation and desire made him feel alive in a way he hadn't in months…

CHAPTER ONE

Earlier that day...

JANE VAUGHAN wandered up and down the bustling jetty with a frown appearing over the ridge of her sunglasses. She couldn't remember exactly which gate she'd been at yesterday; now there were lots of bobbing boats and people lining up to get on board. The man she'd approached had taken no deposit, nor given her a ticket, but instead had reassured her that if she came back to him he would make sure she got on the right boat...the only problem now was that she couldn't spot him anywhere.

Bumping into that stranger in the street just afterwards must have scrambled her brain more than she'd thought. She shook her head wryly. She'd never thought herself to be the kind of woman that would spend a night fantasising about someone she had bumped into for mere moments. A newly familiar heat flooded her belly, however, as his tall, powerful body and hard-boned face swam into her mind's eye, his image still as vivid as if he were standing right in front of her. She shook her head again, this time to shake free of the memory. Honestly, this was so unlike her.

She went towards a gate that looked familiar, tagging onto the end of a queue. When she got to the man at the top he seemed a little harassed. At her query of, *'Excusez-moi. C'est le bâteau pour les îles?'* he just gestured impatiently into the boat. She hesitated for a moment, before figuring what was the worst that could happen? So if she didn't end up exactly where she'd expected to then it would be an adventure. They were going somewhere, and she was on holiday, not everything had to be strictly organised. She needed to relax more.

Once they were underway she had to admit grudgingly that she was enjoying the breeze and the sun across her shoulders and bare legs. The brightly patterned halterneck dress she wore was a present from her friend Lisa, given with an order to make herself more visible.

She pushed her sunglasses onto her head, tipping her face up to the sun, and for the first time since landing on the Côte D'Azur a week ago felt a rush of wellbeing and freedom. She didn't even really miss her friend's presence. Lisa was meant to have travelled with her—after all, it was *her* family's villa that Jane was staying in. But at the last minute Lisa's father had been rushed into hospital with a suspected heart attack, and this very week was undergoing a delicate operation. The conversation she'd had with Lisa the night before her departure had been rushed, but her friend had been insistent.

'Janey, if you don't go then I'll feel guilty on top of everything else. Anyway, you'll be doing us a favour. No one has been at the house for months, and it needs to be aired, so look at it like that.'

'But I can't just leave when you might need me most…'

'Look,' Lisa pointed out, 'you know my family. It'll be like Picadilly Circus in the hospital, and we've been assured Dad is going to be fine… Seeing your little face here would only upset me, and I mean that in a good way.'

She knew Lisa was just being brave, that the outcome was anything but assured, and didn't want to put her under any more pressure.

'OK, OK.'

Jane had given in. Lisa was right; there wasn't anything she could do. With a formidable mother, four sisters and three brothers she would only get in the way. And of the three brothers one in particular was intent on pursuing Jane. Not sure how she felt about Dominic, who was lovely, if a little dull, Jane was well aware that the campaign would have been taken up with enthusiasm by Lisa had she had the opportunity.

She got up and wandered over to the railing, shades back on against the glare of the sun, the sea spray catching her every now and then.

She still couldn't help a little pang of guilt at enjoying her solitude so much. She really hadn't expected to embrace it, but for the first time in her twenty-six years she was truly alone, without the crushing responsibility she'd carried for so long.

And it felt good!

Looking up from her contemplation of the foaming sea, she saw that they were approaching an island. Something about it, rising majestically from the water, made her shiver—as if someone had just run a finger down her spine. It was a forbidding rock, softened only by the sandy beach and picturesque houses that surrounded the small harbour. The sun glinted off the water as the boat docked and they disembarked. On the jetty, as she waited with the other passengers to be told where to go, her mind wandered back to danger territory, as if it had been waiting patiently in the wings until she'd stopped thinking of other things. She tried to resist, but it was too strong, yet again she re-lived the events of yesterday…that burning moment in the streets near the harbour came flooding back.

She'd escaped the crowded pedestrian area, feeling somewhat claustrophobic, and stumbled into a charming winding street that had been blessedly quiet, with no sign of any tourists. She had looked for a street name to figure out where she was; she wanted to explore more of this sleepy part of the town.

With her map open, trying to walk and read at the same

time, she'd been unaware of the approaching corner. She had looked up briefly, there had been a flash of something, and she'd crashed into a wall.

Except it hadn't been a wall, because a wall wouldn't have reached out and clamped hard hands on her upper arms. Winded and stunned, the map slipping from her fingers, she'd realised that she'd bumped into a man. Her gaze, on a level with a T-shirt-clad broad chest, had moved up, and up again, before coming face to face with the most beautiful pair of green eyes she'd ever seen—like the green of a distant oasis in the desert—in a dark olive-skinned face, with black brows drawn together forbiddingly. Her jaw had dropped.

It had been only then that she'd become aware of her own hands, curled around his biceps, where they had gone automatically to steady herself. And with that awareness had come the feel of bunched muscle beneath his warm, silky skin. They had flexed lightly under her fingertips as his arms held her, and out of nowhere came a spiking of pleasure so intense and alien through her entire body that she'd felt her eyes open wide in shock. His gaze had moved down to her mouth, and she'd had a weightless, almost out-of-body feeling, as if they hadn't been in a side street, as if this hadn't really been happening.

The spell had been jarringly broken when a shrill voice had sounded. Jane's gaze had shifted with effort to take in a stunning blonde woman rounding the corner, her stream of incomprehensible French directed at the man. His hands had tightened momentarily before he'd dipped from view and come back up with her map in his hand. He'd held it out to her wordlessly, a slightly mocking smile on his mouth. She'd taken it, and before she had even been able to say sorry, or thank you, the blonde had grabbed the man's attention and with a scant glance at Jane had urged him away, looking at her watch with exaggerated motions. And he had disappeared.

Jane had stood, still stunned, her body energised to a

point of awareness just short of pain. She had still been able to feel the imprint of his hands on her arms. She'd lifted fingers to her lips, which had tingled…as if he had actually touched them. It had been just seconds, a mere moment, but she'd felt as though she'd stood there with him for hours. The most bizarre and disturbing feeling. And then she had remembered his enigmatic smile, as if he'd known exactly what effect he was having on her. Arrogant, as if it was expected.

Jane's reverie ended abruptly as she found that she was following the other tourists onto a small air-conditioned bus. She vowed that that was the last time she would indulge herself in thinking about that man. The last time she would indulge the fantasy she'd had of sitting across a table from him, sharing an intimate dinner, candlelight flickering, picking up the silverware and sparkling glasses. Those green eyes holding hers, not letting her look away. She quashed the silly flutter in her belly and took in the other people on the bus, leaning over to a young couple about her age across the aisle.

'Excuse me, do you know where we are?'

The woman leant across her boyfriend, replying with a strong American accent. 'Honey, this is Lézille Island—but you'd know that, coming from the hotel…aren't you a guest?'

'No!' Jane clapped a hand to her mouth. 'I'm not in a hotel…I thought this was just a general trip…'

Dismayed, she wondered what she should do, she hadn't paid for this trip… She belatedly remembered asking the man if this was the boat to *les îles*—the islands, in French, which sounded exactly like the name of this island. Lézille. No wonder he had just ushered her on board.

The other woman waved a hand. 'Oh, don't worry. I won't say anything, and no one will notice…you just bagged yourself a free trip!'

Jane smiled weakly. She hated any sort of subterfuge. But maybe it wasn't such a big deal. She could always follow them back to their hotel afterwards and offer to pay for the trip. She felt a little better with that thought.

The woman told her that they were due to visit a vineyard for some wine-tasting, and afterwards to take in an aerial display. Jane gave in and relaxed, and started to enjoy the mystery tour nature of the trip…this was exactly what she needed.

The vineyard was enormous, with beautifully kept rows of vines. They were shown every part of the winemaking process—which Jane had to admit was more interesting than she would have expected. The name on the bottles sounded familiar—as had the name of the island.

When they emerged at the other end of the buildings, they could see what looked like a medieval castle in the distance. Again she felt that funny sensation…almost like déjà vu.

'You know this island is owned by a billionaire who lives in that castle?'

Jane looked around the see the friendly woman from the bus. 'No…no, I don't know anything about it.'

Her voice lowered dramatically. 'Well, apparently he owns half the coast too—his family go back centuries… He's so private, he only allows people to visit a few times a year. There's all sorts of stories about—' She broke off when her boyfriend came and dragged her away to see something.

Jane looked back to the castle. It certainly looked as if it could have been around in the Middle Ages. On a small island like this, she guessed it could have been some kind of protective fortress.

After another short trip in the bus, along a picturesque strip of coastline, they were deposited in a big green field, full of wild flowers, with an airstrip at the far end. A dozen planes were lined up in readiness. There was a fiesta-like atmosphere, with families stretched out around the ground with picnics, stalls set up with drinks, food and handicrafts. A small stone building to the side looked like some kind of museum, and on closer inspection Jane discovered that it was. She just gave it a brief look, before wandering over to see the stalls, where she bought some bread and cheese for a light lunch, noticing that everyone else seemed to have brought picnics.

Suddenly her arm was grabbed. 'We haven't introduced ourselves. I'm Sherry, and this is Brad. We're on honeymoon from New York. You should stick with us if you're on your own.'

The woman from the bus barely allowed Jane to get a word in edgeways to introduce herself as they led her away to a spot they had picked out on the grass. It was nice to have the company as she ate her meagre lunch, and they turned out to be very friendly, insisting on sharing their wine and fruit.

After lunch Jane noticed men in flight suits walking towards the small planes from a hangar area, and the crowd got up and started to cheer. Soon there was one last pilot walking to his plane. With the sun in her eyes, he just was a shape in the distance.

A hush went around the field and, wondering at the strange reaction, Jane lifted a hand to shade her eyes—and stiffened when she saw more clearly who it was. It was the man from the street; she was sure of it. He was unmistakable. His impressive build and height set him apart.

Before she knew what she was doing she was on her feet with the rest of the crowd. He had an innately powerful grace, commanding attention as he strode towards the plane. Clearly the leader. On a gesture from him, the other pilots started up.

When he got into the plane, something in Jane's stomach fell, and she found she couldn't sit down again and relax. As they took off one by one, he being the last, she unconsciously clenched her fists. The display probably only took fifteen minutes but to Jane it seemed to go on for ever. Her eyes never left his plane, a ball lodging in her gut. She couldn't explain or fathom the completely irrational fear she felt; she just knew that nothing could move her from the spot until that plane was back on the ground and he walked out, safe.

He flew as though he had a death wish. Dizzying turns and ever increasingly daring stunts had the crowd gasping in unison and clapping. He was the last to land, watched by the other pilots, their respect obvious.

When he stepped out of the plane to thunderous applause, Jane unclenched her fists, noticing that her nails had carved half moons into her palms. Unbelievably she felt anger towards him—this complete stranger!

The sun must be getting to her, she thought, unable to tear her eyes away. As the crowd surged towards the planes, his head turned, and even though at least fifty metres separated them, his gaze caught hers. She had a freefall feeling, couldn't move. She felt as if he had reached out and touched her with those amazing eyes. With a supremely difficult struggle she turned away, and almost fell to the ground beside the American couple, who were chattering happily, oblivious to her inner turmoil. Maybe she *had* actually become delusional…conjured him up out of her rampant imagination.

When Brad and Sherry got up to check out the small museum she followed gratefully, feeling inexplicably as if she was escaping something…

She cast a quick glance back towards the planes, unable to help herself. She could just see the top of his dark head, surrounded by people—mainly adoring women from the looks of it.

She turned away resolutely and ducked inside, reassuring herself that by the time they came out all the pilots would be gone. After a few minutes she was feeling somewhat calmer, and walked around taking in the information with genuine interest. From a small plaque that was tucked into a corner she learned about a devastating earthquake at the turn of the century, which had reduced the population of nearly a thousand to a few hundred. It was only in recent decades that the island had begun to thrive again.

Apparently it had been in the hands of one family since

the time of the crusades. They were called Salgado-Lézille, and had come originally from Spain. That would explain the hacienda-like houses Jane thought, remembering seeing them dotted around the harbour and elsewhere. And in retrospect there was something vaguely Moorish about the shape of the majestic castle.

She had turned to follow the crush out the door when the light was blocked momentarily and someone came in.

It was him. Even before she saw his face she knew. He scanned the room as people passed by him, and Jane held her breath. Slowly his gaze came to rest on her and stopped. Immediately her heart started to thump and her legs turned to jelly.

He stared at her.

Jane shook herself mentally. This was crazy. How could she be reacting like this *again*? She turned away and looked back at a document behind the glass, but she could see his shape reflected. He wasn't moving. She forced herself to walk around the exhibit again and admonished herself. She was going to have to leave sooner or later, and there was no way he would have come in just to stare at her.

But he was. She could feel it.

All she had to do was walk past him. Easy.

She followed the chattering line of other tourists heading out, drawing ever closer to the door, looking anywhere but at the disturbing man and his large, broad-shouldered body leaning insouciantly against the wall. She sensed his dark gaze, hot and heavy upon her, like a physical caress, and trembled.

Now there were only two people in front of her. Why had they stopped? She dampened down her irritation. Her reaction was completely over the top. She just needed to get back out into the fresh air. That must be it, she comforted herself—the heat. As if to prove her point, she felt a trickle of sweat between her breasts.

She could see his long legs crossed at the ankles. She focused on the back of the heavy loud man in front of her. Maybe she could pretend she was with him, ensuring a smooth passage past. She had no idea why it was so important; she just felt it deep in the core of her being.

She was almost beside him now, the breath hitching in her throat. He took up her peripheral vision. She didn't have to be looking at him to know what he was like. Despite only the brief moment the day before, and her distant view earlier today, she knew she would be able to describe him in detail.

Thick dark hair, swept high off a strong broad forehead. Harsh, vitally masculine face, lines broken only by an aquiline nose, sensually sculpted lips. And those mesmerising eyes, the eyelashes visible even from a distance. His flight suit enhanced his commanding physique.

'Oh, my God, he is gorgeous.'

You don't say, Jane thought wryly at Sherry's indiscreetly loud whisper behind her. Without looking she could feel his sardonic smile. He had heard and understood; he must speak English.

She was almost at the door, almost home free, when her wrist was captured in an electrifying grip by a familiarly strong lean hand. The people behind her jostled, and to avoid a crush she had to move closer, go with the pull of the hand. Her blue eyes huge, she looked up at him.

He drew her in, close to his body, the people pushing past her inadvertently moving her in even closer. She could feel the heat of his thigh, hard against her own through the thin material of her dress.

What was happening?

She looked up, the question on her face, captivated by his gaze, which looked back down at her, lazily assessing. This man who had dominated nearly her every thought since yesterday.

'What are you looking at?' she croaked.

'You,' he answered with deceptive simplicity, and the word rocked through Jane's body.

'Who…who are you?'

He didn't answer, just kept a loose, yet immovable grip on her wrist. She could feel her pulse thumping against the warm skin of his hand like a captured bird. Something in her blood leapt, and excited anticipation built in her belly. The part of her that he had reached yesterday, unknown and alien, was coming to life again…just under his look. He smiled indolently, before his eyes left hers to look her up and down so thoroughly that she felt naked, exposed. A flush spread from her belly all the way up to her neck. She tried to yank her wrist away to no avail; his grip only tightened. He couldn't possibly remember her, could he?

Nerves made her blurt out, 'Who do you think you are? How dare you look at me like that…?'

His eyes bored into hers, the green becoming darker, making him look dangerous, 'You pretend to not recognise me?'

He remembered.

'No…well, that is, yes. I saw you yesterday in the street… when you bumped into me.'

'As I recall it was the other way around, *n'est ce pas*?'

His voice sounded as though it had been dipped in honey treacle, deep and dark, with only the barest hint of an accent, his English flawless. She was finding it hard to concentrate.

'I was just reading a map. Surely you saw me…' She cursed the breathless tone in her voice.

He ran a quick glance up and down again. 'Oh, I saw you all right.'

She saw the amusement lurking in his eyes and she tried to pull away again. This time he let her go, and she felt inexplicably bereft.

'You should have been looking where you were going. You could have collided with a more…immovable object.'

From what she could remember, all too well, *he* had been

like a wall…a wall of hard-packed muscle. She felt her legs weaken. More than disturbed by the effect he was having on her, she looked at him incensed,

'The street was empty…it's hardly a crime to divert one's attention for a moment.'

He inclined his head in a surprisingly old-fashioned gesture. 'Maybe we can agree that we were equally to blame.'

She huffed slightly. 'It's no big deal.'

'Yet you are the one who seems to be upset about it,' he pointed out, picking up on her discomfort.

Jane looked around then, and saw that they were alone in the building. Everyone else had disappeared. When had that happened?

She looked out through the door and sighed with relief when she saw the bus, where the others were embarking. She turned to find him right behind her, and stepped back hurriedly.

'I have to go…that's my bus leaving now.'

He caught her hand just as she turned away. Her pulse leapt again.

'Would you do me the honour of being my dinner guest tonight? To…foster a truce and allow me to make amends for my part in our collision.'

He was smooth, and practised, and too, too seductive. Jane shook her head, slightly dazed. He was asking her out for dinner? Her eyes met his. *No way, no way*, went through her mind. This man was so out of her league that he might as well be from another planet. She didn't have the wherewithal to sit across a table from him! She'd dissolve in a puddle within minutes. And the way he was looking at her…as though he wanted to have *her* for dinner!

'I'm sorry,' she said stiffly, pulling her hand free. 'I…I have arrangements made already, but thank you for asking.'

His eyes probed hers for an uncomfortably long moment, and then he shrugged lightly, a shuttered look descending over his face. 'Very well.'

Now she had offended him, she thought miserably. Without knowing what to say or do, she stepped away and half ran, half walked back to the bus.

She sank into her seat breathing heavily. She felt hot and bothered, her hand still tingling where he had caught it. Jane evaded Sherry's very pointed look and stared out of the window.

All the way back to the mainland she veered between feeling as if she had made a lucky escape and extreme self-recrimination. Since bumping into him she had thought of little else, even fantasised about having dinner with him, but when she was offered the opportunity what did she do? Refused point-blank.

She didn't deserve a date with such a man if she couldn't even handle being asked out. And *why* had he asked her out? She couldn't fathom it. She could tell that he was mannerly—perhaps it was a pilot thing, a code of conduct? Although somehow he didn't look like just a pilot. Her brain began to throb. She couldn't help but feel as though she had let herself down in some way. She could well imagine Lisa's reaction.

Back on land, she sighed to herself, trying to catch a glimpse of the island which was too far away to view in the late-afternoon haze. She would just have to put it down to experience. A man like Lisa's brother Dominic was obviously all she could handle…maybe this was a sign.

When she saw the others get on the bus for their hotel she followed them on board.

Fifteen minutes later they pulled off the road and into a resort. It screamed extreme wealth. Immaculate lawns and manicured gardens led up to a beautiful hacienda-style building, all in white. In the early dusk lights shone from the windows, gauzy curtains fluttering in the breeze. She read the name of the hotel carved discreetly into a low stone wall, and only registered then how well dressed her companions were.

She had tagged on to a day trip from one of the Lézille Hotels. No wonder the name had sounded familiar. The owner of the island obviously also owned this very well-known string of resorts dotted all over the world in prime locations and renowned for their discretion, luxuriousness, exclusivity.

She followed the others into the lobby and they split off in different directions. Just as she went to look for the tourist office Sherry stopped her. 'Hey, Jane, why don't you come back here for dinner tonight? You said you were on your own, and we've made friends with a guy from Washington DC who works in town… We could make a foursome; he'd love your accent.'

Jane opened her mouth on reflex to say no, and stopped herself. Had she learnt nothing from her recent experience? Here she was, being offered another chance. She smiled at Sherry. 'I'd love to.'

'Plus, I want to hear all about your conversation with Mr Gorgeous!'

Jane's smile faded. They would most certainly *not* be discussing that. She made a mental note to make sure the conversation never strayed into that area.

Once she had sorted out payment for the trip with a very bemused tour manager she made her way back to the villa.

A few hours later Jane was in a taxi on her way back to the hotel. She hoped that her mystery date was tall. She was five foot nine herself in flats, and if he wasn't they would look ridiculous. Unlike *him*—she knew she could wear the highest heels and would still have to look up. Her heart started to thump, just thinking of what it would be like to be on the way to meet *him*… *But you were a chicken and turned him down.* As if she needed to be reminded…

The taxi pulled into the front courtyard and Jane made a last-ditch effort to erase his image. She made her way out to the poolside buffet, where she had arranged to meet the others, and Sherry's madly waving arm caught her attention easily enough—along with the sparkly half-dress she was wearing. She weaved through the tables to get to them, completely oblivious of several admiring glances on the way. And one in particular from the other side of the pool.

CHAPTER TWO

'JANE! Meet Pete—he split up with his fiancée back home a few months ago and moved here to lick his wounds.'

Jane had to hold back a smile at Sherry's effervescent indiscretion, and stuck out her hand to the other man. 'Pleased to meet you. I'm Jane Vaughan.'

He was pleasantly attractive, with nothing overpowering about him—brown hair, brown eyes, nice smile. No chemistry whatsoever. Jane relaxed, and they settled into a light easy conversation. When the band struck up a slow jazzy tune Pete stood and asked her to dance. As she went into his arms on the dance floor she had to admit that it was all very agreeable. This was much more her scene than the messily overwhelming attraction she had felt for the stranger. Heat induced lust. This she could handle. That… She shivered at the thought.

Pete tightened his arms around her. 'Hey, are you cold?'

Jane immediately recoiled, surprised at the strength of her reaction. 'No!' she said, far too quickly, amending it with a smile. 'No…just a little tired. Maybe if we could sit down again…'

As they approached the table another woman was leaving and waving gaily at Sherry, who turned gleaming eyes on Jane as she sat down. 'You'll never guess what I just found out.'

Jane obediently supplied, 'What?'

The men took themselves off to the bar, muttering something about women and gossip. It made Jane cringe a little, but Sherry was leaning over the table, saying with a loud whisper, 'That guy…the gorgeous hunk from earlier…well, don't look now, but he's behind you on the other side of the pool, and he's been looking this way.'

Immediately Jane's back straightened, and she started breathing faster. She just managed to stop herself from turning around, but Sherry was doing it for her, looking over Jane's shoulder. A frown marred her pretty features,

'Shoot—he's gone. Oh, well…anyway, wait till you hear what I found out from Tilly Brown. He's Mr Island!' She looked at Jane as if to say, *Don't you get it?* Jane just looked back blankly. What on earth did she mean?

Sherry sighed exaggeratedly. 'He owns the island we were on today. *He's* the billionaire. His name is—get this for a mouthful—Xavier Salgado-Lézille, and he owns this whole complex too. Can you believe that? To think that we saw him and didn't know. I'm so dumb…'

Jane sat there stunned as Sherry chattered on. It made sense now—his presence, the authority he commanded. She recognised that he must have assumed she was a guest at the hotel. His reaction to her refusal earlier didn't surprise her now. She doubted that many women would turn down someone like him.

'And the best thing is,' Sherry continued, pausing for dramatic effect, 'he's a bachelor. Well, actually a notorious playboy, incapable of commitment some say—they call him the Prince of Darkness because he's so dark and brooding and—'

'You really shouldn't listen to idle gossip you know.'

The deep voice beside them could have cut through steel. They both looked up to find the object of their conversation beside the table. The epitome of wealth and sophistication in an impeccable tuxedo. The man who had loomed large in

Jane's imagination for two days now had a name—and an island, a hotel chain, a wine label, a reputation. Her head swirled. Sherry didn't even have the grace to blush, but Jane did, horribly aware of how they must have looked, their heads close together like conspirators.

'Why, Mr Salgado-Lézille—why don't you join us?'

'Please, Mr Salgado will do. The full name is such a... *mouthful*...if that's the right term.'

Jane cringed, going even pinker with embarrassment, and she marvelled at Sherry's hide, which was as thick as a rhinoceros. He flicked Sherry a dismissive glance and turned his attention to Jane, holding out a hand in a clear invitation to dance. She couldn't refuse. Especially after what had just happened. Wordlessly she put her hand in his much larger one and felt a tingle go up her arm as he lightly guided her onto the dance floor.

Drawing into his arms, Jane fought for composure. The difference between this man and Pete from only a few moments ago was laughable. This was what she had been afraid of—this melting feeling, a hyper-awareness of every part of her skin, an acute consciousness of the way her body seemed to want to fuse with his. His scent was clean and crisp, with a hint of some indefinably erotic element. The man himself, she guessed.

One arm held her securely, high across her back, his hand curving around to just beside her breast. His other hand held hers lightly against his chest. They said nothing, swaying together in perfect unison. When the song ended he held her fast when she would have pulled away until another number started up.

'Don't you think you owe me at least one more dance?'

Jane lifted her head and looked up into his eyes. 'Of...of course.'

His eyes glinted in the flickering light of the candles all around them, a small hard smile playing around his mouth.

As they started to move again she felt she had to say something, blurting out, 'I'm sorry about Sherry... That is, I don't even really know her. I'd hate for you to think that you were the subject of our...' She trailed off, reminding herself that she *had* been listening to Sherry with bated breath. 'I thought you were just one of the pilots...'

Even as the words came out she wanted to grab them back. But it was too late. She couldn't mistake the cynical edge to his voice,

'Ah...I should have known. It is much easier to accept a dance, or dinner for that matter, from the owner of a hotel rather than just a pilot.'

She pulled back as far as he would allow, every line in her body indignant. 'I didn't mean it like that...that had nothing to do with anything, Mr Salgado. The reason I declined your invitation earlier was because—' She broke off. As if she could tell him that the reason she'd turned him down was because her reaction to him had scared the life out of her.

'Well?' he prompted softly, one dark brow lifted.

'I...I, well, as you can see I had made arrangements with Sherry and Brad.' She crossed her fingers, hating the lie, but self-preservation was more important. 'I'm not actually staying here...I'm alone, staying at a friend's villa on the hill. I ended up on the day trip by mistake earlier, and they invited me for dinner.'

It wasn't a complete lie, she reassured herself. Their invitation had just come after his.

He frowned slightly. 'The tour manager told me about someone who had inadvertently ended up on a trip coming in afterwards to pay...was that you?'

'I guess so...unless there was someone else.'

'Quite an enigma, aren't you? Miss...?'

'Vaughan. Jane Vaughan.'

He stepped back for a moment and made a courteous bow, taking her hand. 'Pleased to meet you, Miss Vaughan.'

And then he kissed her hand. She could feel his lips firm and yet soft against her skin, and the fluttering excitement grew stronger in her belly.

'Let's start again,' he said, in a low seductive voice, tucking her into him even closer than before.

Jane fought an internal battle for a few seconds and then gave in. It was too strong…this…whatever it was that she was feeling. She allowed her head to fall into the crook of his neck and shoulder, closing her eyes. A perfect fit.

His hand on her back was moving in slow sensuous circles, grazing her bare skin. She could feel her breasts grow heavier, sensitive against the material of her dress. When he shifted subtly she could feel the thrust of his arousal low against her belly. She pulled back for a second, but Xavier felt it and caught her even closer, growling into her ear, 'You can't move now. Everyone will see what you're doing to me.'

Jane blushed scarlet to the roots of her hair. The next few minutes were an exercise in erotic torture. She had never felt anything like this in her life. Completely unaware of everyone around them. Burning up.

Finally, when she feared her very legs weren't capable of holding her up any more, he pulled back, but held onto her hand. Dark green eyes glittered into blue ones.

'Let's get out of here.'

She nodded mutely. She was being swept away on a tidal wave of feelings and sensations. Sanity tried to break through her consciousness but she pushed it aside. She couldn't let this second chance slip away.

They were in the alcove that led outside to the front of the building and the gardens. Muslin drapes fluttered around them, acting as a shield between the lobby and the main entrance. Jane stopped suddenly. 'Wait!' She turned horrified eyes to his. 'I can't just leave…I'm with people…Pete.'

How could she have forgotten and be so unquestionably rude? No matter what wild spirit seemed to have taken her over, there was no excuse for leaving so abruptly. And, more to the point, the fact that this man had made her take leave of her senses so easily caused a panicky sensation in her belly.

Xavier's eyes narrowed as he looked down at her and took in her expressive face. He had forgotten about her companions too…all he had been aware of was getting her out of there to some private place where he could explore that lush mouth and—

'I'm sorry, Mr Salgado—'

'Xavier, please…'

She couldn't bring herself to say his name. 'I'll have to go back to the others. I really can't just run out on them like this.'

She hoped that the regret in her voice didn't sound too obvious. But the heavy disappointment in her chest dispelled any panic. He'd wouldn't indulge her again. No doubt he thought she must be playing some game with him. She watched with dismay as he seemed to concur.

'You are right. It would be remiss of me to take you away. But be under no illusion that if you weren't obliged to return then right now I would be doing this…'

Before she knew what was happening he had pulled her close, one arm around her back, the other cradling her head, covering her mouth with his. Taking advantage of her startled sigh, he expertly plundered the moist interior, exploring, tracing her lips. When his tongue sought and found hers, stroking with sure mastery, a white-hot flame of desire raced through her body. Her hands clenched on his shoulders in reaction. She was lost in the moment…and in him.

Reluctantly Xavier lifted his head to look down. She took a second to open glazed eyes, lashes long against her cheeks, her lips swollen and parted slightly. He felt the tremor in the body held tightly against his. She would be his, of that he had no doubt. He had branded her.

Jane stepped back and tried to control her breathing, just

managing to stop herself from bringing a hand up to feel her lips. Crazily, she felt as if he had just marked her in some way. She had heard about kisses like that, and thought it was some pathetic fantasy, or Lisa waxing lyrical about her latest obsession…but it wasn't. If he hadn't stopped when he had…

She had been reduced to mush by little more than a kiss.

'Yes…well…I…have to…'

'Have lunch with me tomorrow.'

He still wanted to see her?

She looked at him helplessly. She felt like a moth that was being attracted to a flame with danger written all over it, but the pull was so inexorable that she couldn't help herself. She took a deep breath. The new Jane. Quash the panic. She felt shaky.

'I'd like that.'

'Which villa are you staying at?'

She told him the address.

'*Bien.* I will pick you up at midday…till then.'

He strode back into the lobby and got into the lift without a backward glance.

Jane wandered back out to the poolside table in a daze. Sherry squealed when she saw her arrive. Remarkably, the men still hadn't returned from the bar. Jane felt as though whole lifetimes had passed since Xavier had asked her to dance.

She fielded Sherry's questions, being as vague as possible. When the men arrived back poor Pete didn't stand a chance. He tried to press a kiss to her lips before she left at the end of the evening, but she gave him her cheek. Somehow the thought of anyone else kissing her where Xavier had was anathema.

She didn't see the look of triumph on the face of the man watching from his penthouse suite overlooking the pool.

Back in the villa, Jane couldn't settle and went up to the terrace which overlooked the twinkling lights of the town below, still feeling slightly dazed. Her thoughts drifted to her mother, who she hoped was enjoying much the same view. She was on her honeymoon in Cyprus, with Arthur, the man she'd met a year previously. Jane thought of the recent wedding day with a smile. How proud she had been to give her mother away to such a kind, gentle man. If anyone deserved another stab at happiness it was she.

Since her father had died at just thirty, leaving her mother penniless, with Jane still a baby, it had been a monumental struggle. Her mother had changed overnight from a relatively carefree newlywed to a woman who had had to seek work to make ends meet. Sometimes she worked three jobs at once, just to put food on the table and get Jane through school and then college, despite Jane working too to help out.

Even when Jane had finished her degree and had begun working as a teacher her mother had refused money, insisting that she build up a nest egg for herself.

Years of worry and work had sapped her mother's joy and increased Jane's concern. But now…now she was allowing herself to feel love and happiness again, and if she could embrace a new lease on life then so could Jane.

Starting tomorrow.

With a shiver of anticipation snaking down her spine she finally left the view.

CHAPTER THREE

WHEN she woke the next morning Jane couldn't believe she had slept at all—much less for... She consulted her watch in disbelief—ten hours straight. Which meant, she realised with a lurch of panic, that she had exactly one hour before Xavier was due to pick her up for lunch.

She sprang out of bed and after a quick shower regarded her wardrobe, plucking a pair of white culottes from the messy pile, and a striped white and black halterneck top. She smoothed her hair behind her ears, and with espadrilles and a pair of hoop earrings was just about ready to go downstairs when the doorbell rang.

Already!

She took a few deep breaths and walked to the front door, trying to calm the butterflies in her belly.

Be cool, be calm, be sophisticated.

She opened the door, the smile on her face fading and her mouth going dry when she took in the man in front of her. Pure devastation. He was leaning against the doorframe, arms folded across his broad chest, showing his muscles off to perfection. He wore a casually faded black T-shirt and jeans, scuffed deck shoes on his bare feet. She could feel her face colour as she brought her eyes back up. She had just examined him...and blatantly!

She couldn't see his eyes, as they were hidden behind

dark shades, but she saw all too well the way his mouth quirked.

'I hope I pass inspection?'

What could she do? She had been caught out beautifully. She had to smile, revealing small, even white teeth and a dimple in her cheek.

'You'll do.'

She bent down to pick up her bag, where she'd stuffed her bikini and a sarong among other bits and pieces, not sure what he had planned, and pulled the door behind her, careful to lock it securely. He took the bag from her and led the way to his car. She was glad to see that although it was a convertible it wasn't one of those tiny low-slung things that she privately thought looked ridiculous.

As he negotiated his way down the small winding streets with casual expertise she started to relax and look around. She was very aware of his tanned hands on the wheel, moving to the gear-stick near her leg, and of the long fingers with short square nails. She swallowed and quickly put on the shades that had been resting on her head in case he caught her staring again.

'How long are you here for?' he asked idly.

'Just another week; I've already been here for one. This is such a treat.'

'What is?'

Nerves made her babble. 'To be taken out…driven around. I have a hire car, but this place is like a labyrinth… The first day it took me an hour to find my way back up the hill from the town.'

'I know…it is getting crazier, with more and more tourists… We're hoping that they'll make the centre of the town entirely for pedestrians only; it's small enough, so it could work.'

His comment reminded her who she was dealing with. He wasn't just a local, he was *the* local. She felt intimidated all of a sudden.

He cast a curious glance her way. 'Cat got your tongue?'

She shrugged lightly, honesty prevailing. 'I know this might sound silly, but I keep forgetting that you are…who you are. You own that entire island…that hotel chain. I guess it's just a little overwhelming. I bump into you in the street two days ago and now here I am in your car.' She gave a nervous laugh.

Xavier looked over at her sharply, but she had her face averted. Well, this was a new approach—and one that he hadn't encountered before. Was she for real? More or less hinting that she'd be more comfortable with him if he were just a pilot? He'd never had to reassure a woman before by playing his status down…normally they wanted him to play it up! Well, if this was a game that she was playing then he would play along. She was intriguingly different from any other woman he'd ever known. Whether it was artifice or not he didn't much care. He wasn't planning on getting to know her too well…just well enough.

His glance took in the long shapely legs beside him. He could imagine how they might feel wrapped around his naked back. He grew hard there and then, much to his chagrin. He wasn't used to being at the mercy of hormones he had long ago learnt to control. A woman hadn't had the power to ignite his desire so forcibly since…*ever*, he realised. He focused on the road, hands gripping the wheel. Only one way to exorcise this hunger raging in his blood.

He forced himself to say lightly, 'Ah, so you admit now that you were the one who bumped into me?'

Jane cast him a quick glance, relieved to see him flash her a teasing smile.

Lord, but he was gorgeous. She couldn't answer, nervously touching her tongue to dry lips.

'I thought we'd take a little trip on my boat. I know a cove near here that's usually deserted. We can swim and have a picnic.'

She was going to forget everything and enjoy this moment

for what it was. She was being given a second chance…her fantasy was coming true…and she was smart enough not to sabotage it again. She hoped.

'That sounds lovely.'

After he had parked the car and lifted out a hamper, he led her into a private marina, where yacht after yacht was lined up, bobbing on the water. His was a small sleek speed boat, with a tiny cabin down below.

'This is how you get to and from the island?'

'Yes…or I use the helicopter. This takes fifteen minutes.'

Of course…the helicopter!

It was hard to keep her intimidation at bay when he threw out such admissions of extreme wealth. She forgot everything, though, as he helped her into the boat, big hands curling around her waist to steady her, just under her breasts. Suddenly breathless, she moved away quickly to the other end and looked anywhere but at him. She could see the tourists in the distance, lining up for their day trips. That had been her yesterday, and if she hadn't tagged onto that particular queue…

He showed her where to sit back and relax as he started up the engine and they pulled out into the open water. The breeze felt wonderfully cool on Jane's skin, and she closed her eyes, lifting her face to the sun.

When she opened them again she found Xavier staring at her from behind the wheel, shades on his head. He didn't look away. The gleam in his eyes was explicit, and Jane's pulse started to speed up and throb through her veins. That kiss last night came back in vivid Technicolor, the feel of his chest against hers… She was the one to break contact first, putting on her sunglasses again. His mouth quirked in a mocking smile, the same one he had smiled in the street, aware of his effect. She tried not to let it unsettle her.

Leaving the harbour and marina behind, Xavier hugged the coast for a while. Jane was enthralled by the view of all the huge estates visible from their vantage point. They couldn't really talk over the sound of the engine, but she was happy to drink in the sight of him when she was sure she couldn't be caught. She'd never been reduced to this level of carnal feeling before. Didn't know how to handle it.

She could see a small cove come into view, and Xavier negotiated the boat towards it. It looked empty. She was bizarrely both disappointed and excited not to have company, but if she was honest with herself she knew which feeling won out.

When he had anchored a short way from the shore he indicated the cabin below. 'Why don't you change into your swimsuit here? That way you can leave your things on board.'

'Sure.' Jane feigned a nonchalance that she was far from feeling.

Down below in the small cabin, she changed with awkward haste, half terrified that he'd come down the ladder. Her bikini had felt perfectly adequate up until today, but now she pulled at it ineffectually and tried to stretch it out. Had it shrunk? Somehow it felt as if it had become the skimpiest two-piece on earth since she had last worn it, and she was very conscious of her skin, still pale despite a slight tan. She chastised herself. He was no doubt used to seeing women baring a lot more, especially in this part of the world.

When she emerged from the cabin her skin was still gleaming from an application of suncream. Xavier's breath stopped in his throat as she was revealed bit by bit. Like a lust-controlled youth, he couldn't take his eyes off her chest, full and generous, yet perfectly shaped. She had tied a sarong around hips that flared out gently from a small waist. She looked shy and uncertain, as if she couldn't bring herself to meet his eyes, which were hidden behind his dark lenses. Unbidden, and as swift as his physical response, came a desire to reassure and protect. Alien and unwelcome emotions when it came to him and women. Especially ones he'd known for less than forty-eight hours.

He masked it speaking more brusquely than he'd intended. 'The water should only be waist-deep here, so you can wade ashore.'

He had to stop himself staring when she took off her sarong to reveal a curvy bottom and those never-ending legs... Her self-consciousness was at odds with her body. A body made for pleasure. *His* pleasure.

When Jane hit the water she welcomed the distraction from the fever racing in her blood. Tried to block out the potent image of the man leaning over the edge.

'OK?'

'Yes...fine.'

She half-swam, half-waded to the shore, grateful for the moment to herself. However impressive she had thought his physique while under clothes, it hadn't prepared her for seeing him half naked. He should come with a health warning. He was the most perfect man she had ever seen. She'd tried to avoid looking, but it was impossible not to take in that expanse of bare, toned, exquisitely muscled chest. A light smattering of dark hair led down in a silky line to where his shorts... She gulped as she rested on the sand.

He was wading towards her, with the hamper held aloft in his arms, dark hair gleaming wetly against his head. Strong-muscled legs strode out of the water towards her. She had spread her sarong out on the sand, and was glad of the need for sunglasses and the protection, however slight, they afforded her. She brought her knees up to her chest, wrapping her arms around them in another unconscious gesture of protection.

To her relief, he was businesslike. Coming to rest beside her on the sand, he opened up the basket, taking out a light blanket. He spread it out and started to take out a mouthwatering array of food. Olives, bread, cheese, houmous...sliced ham, chicken wings, pâté.

'There's enough food here to feed an army.'

'Well, I don't know about you, but I'm starving.'

'I wouldn't know where to start.'

'Why don't we start here?' he said, uncorking a bottle of champagne that came in its own encasing to ensure it stayed chilled. He filled two glasses and handed one to her.

'To…meeting you.'

'To meeting you.' She echoed his words, not sure what to say.

A funny feeling lodged in her chest as she took a sip, the bubbles tickling her nostrils. As he busied himself preparing her a selection of food to pick from on a plate, she couldn't help but shake the feeling that this was all a little too smooth…practiced, even—as if he had done it a thousand times before.

'Do you come here often?' she asked lightly, trying to make it sound like a joke.

He stopped what he was doing and looked at her sharply. 'Do you mean have I brought women here before? Then the answer is yes.'

She was taken aback by his honesty. He hadn't tried to temper his words, or make her feel better. Somehow it comforted her. Although the thought of being the latest in a long line of undoubtedly more beautiful women caused some dark emotion to threaten her equilibrium, which she was barely clinging on to as it was.

'I can tell you, though, that it hasn't been for some time. And there probably haven't been half as many as you seem to be imagining. I've come here since my teens, and it's a favourite hang-out for friends of both sexes…not some place purely to seduce women.'

'Oh…well, of course. I never thought for a second—'

'Yes, you did—but I suppose I can't blame you.'

A blush crept up over her face and she turned her attention to the food, hoping to distract him and get off the subject. She could envisage a neon sign above her head with an arrow pointing downwards saying—*Gauche!*

She crossed her legs and helped him to put out the food.

If anything had ever helped her to take her mind off things then it was food. She tucked in healthily. After the first few mouthfuls she looked up to find him staring.

'What?' She wiped her mouth with a napkin. 'Have I got some food somewhere?'

He shook his head, taking his glasses off. 'I don't think I've ever seen a woman eat the way you do. You look like you could keep going until everything is gone.'

She smiled wryly. 'My appetite is legendary, I'm afraid. You've probably met your match. I've never been a delicate eater...'

He nodded towards her. 'Keep going, please—I'm enjoying the novelty of watching a woman relish her food.'

Suddenly self-conscious, she took a sip of champagne to wet her throat and forced herself to keep eating as nonchalantly as possible. But now his attention was focused on her it was impossible. He seemed to be fixated by her mouth. She swallowed a piece of cheese with difficulty.

'The history of your island seems fascinating...what I read of it in the exhibit space. Has your family really been there for centuries?'

Thankfully he finally took his gaze away. 'Yes. They were given the island as a gift by the French royal family in the twelfth century. We originally came from Aragon, in Spain. The royals in the north wanted to establish allies in the south. We took the name of the island and added it to Salgado... hence my name today.'

'And are there many in your family now?'

His voice was curiously unemotional. 'No, just me left... Hard to believe that the line could very well die out with me. I was the first born, and my mother passed away when I was five...my father never married again, and he died when I was in my early twenties.'

Jane pushed her glasses up onto her head, her eyes wide and sympathetic. 'I'm sorry...he must have loved her a great deal…and to lose both parents so young… My father died when I was small too—a baby. But at least I still have my mother.'

Xavier looked into her eyes and felt an unfamiliar sensation, almost like losing his footing. How had they got onto this subject?

She gazed out to the sea and shook her head.

'I just remembered what I read about the earthquake…it must have affected your family?'

He followed her look. 'Yes, it did…all of them perished apart from my great-grandparents…not to mention many of the islanders. Whole families were wiped out.'

'That's awful. It must have taken generations to begin to forget, rebuild lives…'

He nodded. 'We built a commemorative grotto to their memory on the island some years ago. There are hundreds of names inscribed.'

She turned shining eyes on him, stunning him again momentarily. 'That sounds like a lovely thing to do. I wish I'd seen it…how come the tour didn't go there?'

He shrugged. 'It's small, and wouldn't mean much to anyone else. It's a very personal space for the islanders.'

He regarded her profile. 'If you want you could come back there with me tomorrow and I'll show it to you.'

'Would you really?'

She couldn't control the surge of excitement that took hold at the thought of seeing him again the next day.

He nodded. They didn't speak for a few moments, and then he started to pack away some food but refilled her glass. He avoided her eye.

'I'm going for a quick swim, but you should let your food settle for a while.'

She had to smile inwardly at his arrogant assumption that he was somehow immune to cramp after eating. Which, she had to admit as she watched his powerful back and legs walk away from her, he probably was. Immune to banal mortal complaints.

She lay back on her sarong, feeling deliciously relaxed and replete. The sky was hazy, the sun blissfully not beating down with full force. The lapping of the waves lulled her into a light sleep.

A while later she woke with a start… She looked to her side, to see Xavier stretched out beside her. The basket was gone and there was nothing between them. His eyes were closed, lashes long and dark against high cheekbones. He really was beautiful.

'Do I pass inspection again?' he asked, opening one eye, fixing her.

She sat up quickly to hide her mortification. 'I think I'll go for a swim now…'

'I'll join you.' And with lithe grace he stood up beside her and held out a hand. She looked at it warily for a moment before taking it.

The initial cool of the waves lapping against her feet woke her up better than a pail of water over her head.

She extricated her hand from his, and once in far enough dived headlong into the first big wave, swimming underwater for as long as her breath held out.

She popped up to the surface some way off and shook her head. The sun glinting off the water was dazzling. She looked around and could see Xavier's sleek head, arms gracefully scissoring through the water as he swam powerfully towards her. She trod water, breathing far more heavily than was normal after what she had just done.

He came within a couple of feet of her. They just looked at each other. Simultaneously his arms reached for her, and she felt herself gravitate towards him as if being pulled by a magnetic force until she was in his arms. It felt completely right…inevitable.

He brought her arms around his neck and instinctively she wrapped her legs around his waist to steady herself. She was out of her depth…in more ways than one.

Seduced by the place, by him, and her resolve to embrace the moment, she gave in to a powerful desire. Slowly she dipped her head towards his, eyes closing as she felt the hard, sensual contours of his lips. His arms were like a steel band around her waist.

With naive boldness she explored his lips, feeling their shape and texture. One of his hands moved up to the back of her head and he angled it, his tongue sliding between her lips to taste and explore. Hesitantly she allowed him access.

A molten urgent feeling was building between her legs, the centre of her desire. She could feel the friction against his chest, and just below her bottom she could feel a hard ridge. Realizing what it was made her gasp.

He tore his lips from hers and looked down. Her nipples were two hard points thrusting against the wet material of her bikini.

He brought smoky green eyes up to hers and shifted her subtly, so that now he carried her in his arms and out of the water.

Jane knew that if he had put her down her legs would have given way, and was thankful he didn't as he walked up the beach and laid her down on the sarong, stretching out his long length beside her. He looked down her body, a hand resting possessively on her stomach, its gentle feminine swell.

'So beautiful…'

'So are you,' she said shyly.

The sun was blocked as his head dipped again to take her mouth, slowly, languorously. As if they had all the time in the world to touch, explore. She arched herself towards him slightly, a hand reaching out blindly to rest against his chest, revelling in the feel of the surprisingly silky hair, finding a hard nipple, circling it experimentally before flicking it accidentally with a nail.

He tore his mouth away with a moan. 'Let's see how *you* like that.'

Before she could question what he was doing, he had lowered his mouth to one jutting peak, sucking through the wet material of her top. An exquisite burst of pleasure made her cry out. He was relentless, and she gasped when he finally pulled the material aside to reveal the dark peak, raw and aroused. The feel of his tongue on her bare skin made her almost pass out with pleasure, and then he moved to the other side.

Jane barely recognised this wanton version of herself. Her hands tangled in his hair, holding his head in case he might pull away. She was caught up…caught up in uncharted territory…powerless to do anything but feel…respond.

She could feel him drifting a hand down over her belly, to rest near the top of her briefs. Toying with her, moving in slow sensuous circles, before his fingers moved down…under the elastic, over the mound of soft hair…down further, until…

She held her breath, her body tensing as his fingers dipped into her most secret place, exploring, rubbing back and forth over the most sensitive part, which she could feel getting slicker, harder. It was too much. No one had ever touched her there.

Her legs came together, trapping his hand, but he gently manoeuvred them apart again.

A very strident child-like squeal made them both tense.

In a haze of pleasure that was fast receding Jane became aware of Xavier reacting quicker than her, adjusting her bikini back over her body, which felt acutely sensitised.

'We have company…pity,' he drawled, making sure she was decent again, and then he looked down into her shocked eyes.

Sure enough another boat was pulling into the small cove, and a gang of children were starting to jump down from a yacht into the water, splashing and swimming towards the beach. Thankfully they were far enough out not to have seen anything…she hoped.

She wanted the sand to rise up around her and suck her

down. A mortified flush burned her skin as she thought of what would have happened if they hadn't arrived. He must think her so…easy. Bring her to a deserted stretch of beach, ply her with a little champagne and food, and she was a possessed woman in his arms, with little or no encouragement. The worst cliché of a tourist looking for a quick holiday fling.

She thrust herself away from him and sat up, gathering her sarong around her waist and tying it in a knot.

'This has been…lovely…but we probably should be getting back. I'm sure you have lots of important things to be doing.'

She couldn't even look at him. She stood up awkwardly and a soft gasp escaped her lips as she felt him whirl her around to face him. She couldn't escape his eyes, which probed far deeper than the surface. They were oblivious to the people arriving onto the beach only feet away from them.

'Lovely…?' He shook his head incredulously. 'Correct me if I'm wrong, but if we hadn't been interrupted, right about now I think you would be fast approaching a climax.'

She blanched at the starkness of his words.

'*Lovely* is a little bit of an understatement, don't you think, for what two people seem to be able to ignite in each other within seconds or with just a look?'

'I…I…well, maybe…'

His eyes were hypnotic. 'The most important thing on my mind at the moment is exploring this attraction between us.'

'It is?'

'Yes.'

'Look…Xavier…we hardly know each other, and I'm not normally—'

'So responsive? Well, neither am I.' His voice sounded harsh.

She had been about to say *easy*, and amended her words. 'That is…I mean…I want you to know that it wasn't my intention to come here just for some kind of holiday…thing.'

He moved her closer to him, looping deceptively loose

arms around her waist, ignoring the chatter around them. She came in contact with the still semi-hard evidence of his arousal. Immediately an answering liquid heat pooled in her groin.

'And, contrary to what you may think, I'm not in the habit of pursuing random tourists…I'm not sure what this is either, but don't you think it might be fun to explore?'

Fun. Explore. The words resounded in her head.

He stepped back, putting her away from him gently. 'I'll take you back now, but I have a proposition…' He trailed a long finger down one cheek. 'I promised to bring you to the island tomorrow to show you the memorial.'

He lifted a brow as if to ask if she still wanted to do that.

She felt herself nodding slowly, trying to focus just on his words, not on the finger caressing her heated skin.

'I'd like you to come and stay there as my guest for the rest of the week… We could get to know one another… explore this…attraction.' His finger left her cheek. 'It's up to you.'

He looked at her for a long moment, before shading his eyes again with the dark glasses and starting back towards the boat. He hadn't meant to ask her to stay, the words had surprised him, but now, having asked, it felt right. One thing was for sure. An afternoon picnic wasn't enough.

A few seconds later Jane followed blindly, her mind churning furiously. She would never see him again after this week. She would have it to hug to herself for ever. What did she have to lose? Could she really be contemplating this? Could she indulge the fantasy?

They were silent on the boat back, and during the car journey up to the villa. He was detached and polite. At her front door they looked at one another for the first time since they had left the beach. He tipped up her face with a finger under her chin.

'So, Jane Vaughan…I'll be here to pick you up at ten a.m. It can be a simple day trip to see the grotto, or you can come and stay for the next few days… Like I said, the choice is yours.'

And then he was in his car, the purring sound of the engine growing fainter before she drew in another breath, still looking at the spot where he had stood. She knew without a doubt that he would let her go at the end of the next day if she so desired. He was far too proud to push her. It was, as he'd said, up to her.

She mechanically went into the house, and before she knew what she was doing she realised that she was packing her things, tidying up in readiness to leave for a few days. Her body was ahead of her brain. She sat on the couch in the living room, an excited, nervous, shivery feeling in her belly.

Be careful what you wish for because you just might get it. The words popped into her head. Well, this was what she had wished for, wasn't it? The start of something new. Letting go of the old reliable, sensible, mature Jane. It was time for her to have some fun for a change. And when someone like Xavier Salgado-Lézille wanted you…then surely it went against the flow of the universe to say no? She was being offered a taste of something that she knew many women would not hesitate for a second to experience.

The only thing was…she had a sneaking suspicion that more than her body was in danger of falling under his spell. Was it a risk she was prepared to take? A resounding voice in her head said *yes*. Throw caution to the wind. She caught sight of her reflection in a mirror. I mean really, she asked herself, how involved could she get in one week? She turned away before she could see the mocking glint in her eye.

CHAPTER FOUR

By NINE forty-five the next morning Jane was having second, third and fourth thoughts. In the cold light of day things were more stark. She would get burned. And not from the sun. She knew it. She heard an engine outside. He was early. As if he could hear the doubts that were in her private thoughts. Which was ridiculous.

She took a deep breath and waited for the doorbell to sound. She was wearing simple shorts, flip-flops and a plain T-shirt. If he wanted her then he could have her as she was, unadorned.

She lifted the small weekend bag that she had brought to carry home gifts, and suddenly it felt as if it held rocks instead of clothes and toiletries for the next few days.

The doorbell rang. Her heart stopped. She could see his tall dark shape against the glass. The Prince of Darkness. The name made her shiver.

When she opened the door his sharp eyes took in her slender figure in the plain clothes, and the bag clutched in one hand with her knuckles showing white. Instinctively he schooled his features, not allowing the surge of triumph he felt to show on his face. For once in his life he actually hadn't been sure which way a woman was going to react, and had been prepared for her to reject his offer. But the bag told him that she was saying yes. He needed to tread carefully. She was as skittish as a colt. He bent to take the bag from her grip, and left her to lock up.

Jane had sent a text to Lisa that morning, wishing her all the best for her dad's operation and saying she was taking a small trip. Just in case Lisa rang and got no answer from the house. She wasn't going to go into any details about Xavier yet. If her friend thought for a second there was a man in the picture she'd be like a dog with a bone.

And, as Jane could barely quantify to herself what was happening, she could hardly begin to explain herself to someone else.

By the time they reached the island, and Xavier had guided her to a waiting Jeep, she had pushed any last dissenting voices out of her head. He was being a complete gentleman. Charming, funny, insightful. She hadn't felt this kind of connection with anyone before—almost as though they'd known each other for years.

A couple of times when they'd locked eyes the heat had flared, swift and intense, reminding her of what was not so far from the surface.

He paused in the Jeep, turning towards her in his seat. 'We'll have to go to my home first…an unavoidable conference call I need to take. My penance for taking some time off…I'm sorry.'

'That's OK…I don't mind.'

'So, what I was going to suggest was this…as it's nearly lunch, why don't we eat, you can get settled, and we see the memorial tomorrow?'

This was it. Even though he was assuming that she wanted to stay, he was giving her the opportunity to back out now. But she didn't want to. She had to take the chance, knowing that in her acceptance, should she choose it, he would read her total acquiescence. She took a deep breath, feeling as though she were stepping over an invisible line drawn in the sand.

'All right. That sounds good.'

He looked at her for a long moment before leaning over and placing a feather-light kiss on her lips. 'It will be, Jane…are you sure?'

She looked at him steadily. 'Yes, I'm sure.'

With a spurt of dry earth, he turned the Jeep towards the castle in the distance. After they came to a stop in the courtyard outside, Jane couldn't hide her reaction. It didn't look like a castle, in the sense of turrets and moats. It had two higher wings on either side, huge, imposing archways, and intricate carvings on every stone. She had never seen anything like it before.

'It's amazing… Sorry—I'm sure you get that all the time. But really it is beautiful.'

Xavier had stepped out of the Jeep and looked up, hands on hips. 'Yes, I guess it is…the Moorish influence probably makes it a little less austere.'

'I thought that was what it was, when I saw it from the distance the other day, but I wasn't sure.'

He lifted out her bag and took her hand, leading her into a huge open-plan flagstoned hall covered in complicated mosaics. Numerous green plants stood against the walls, and the open spaces were light-filled and indescribably foreign and exotic. Tall pillars led to an inner roofless courtyard.

Jane looked around in awe, taking it all in. She could almost imagine an ancestor of Xavier's reclining darkly on a divan, voluminous folds of silk covering his body, being attended to by lustrous haired beauties. She blushed at her imagination. Xavier reached out a finger and trailed it down her cheek, leaving a line of fire in its wake.

'You blush so easily…a rare phenomenon these days.'

'An embarrassing one, you mean…it tends to come at the most awkward moments, when the last thing I want is for someone to guess I might be unnerved.'

'And are you…unnerved…here, now, with me?'

'Well…a little.'

'Your honesty is refreshing. How have you managed not to lose it yet?'

'That's a very cynical thing to say.'

'I've come to learn it's a very cynical world we live in…but you might prove me wrong.'

Her eyes widened, a vulnerable light in their depths. That and any other thought flew from her mind as his large body closed the distance between them and he claimed her mouth with a kiss full of pent-up passion, his hands moving over her back. She found herself responding, instinctively matching his passion with her own.

Before she knew what was what, she felt herself being lifted into strong arms, and hers automatically went around his neck as he walked back into the hall and up some stairs which were obscured behind material moving gently in the breeze.

She took in an upper level, corridors, more open spaces, before Xavier shouldered his way through an imposing oak door and into a vast room, with a huge king-size bed in the centre. She barely had time to take in the rest of the room before he put her on her feet. Sudden panic gripped her. This was happening too quickly. She backed away, breath coming hard and fast.

'Wait…do you think we could just…take things slowly for now?'

He stood back from her and ran a hand through his hair. When he saw the look on her face he said quickly, 'I never planned on dragging you up here like some teenager…I just lost control…which seems to happen more and more frequently since I saw you.'

He gave her a rueful smile. He held out a hand and she took it.

'Come on. Let's have some lunch, and I promise not to manhandle you again.'

'That's OK. It's not that I don't *want* to be manhandled by you. I'm sure that'd be perfectly nice—'

'Jane.'

'Yes?'

'Stop talking. It's fine, you don't have to say anything.'

'OK.'

He paused at a door almost opposite his bedroom, opening it to reveal another equally stunning room.

'This is your room. I'll bring your bag up after we've eaten and you can get settled.' He turned towards her. 'I'm sorry again, Jane. Believe me, I didn't just assume that because you're staying falling into my bed is a foregone conclusion, but I won't lie to you…I want you. I'm perfectly happy for us to take it slowly, get to know each other…I'll wait until you're ready'

Her heart flipped over. Danger. She looked up into his eyes, feeling a drowning sensation, 'Thank you…'

He needed the space as much as she did. The truth was that he had never before felt such an overwhelming urge to take a woman to his bed… His plan, as he had told her, had been that they would have lunch, get to know one another a little better, have dinner in the evening and then…who knew? But within mere minutes of coming in the front door he had been overtaken by his hormones.

People called him the Prince of Darkness. Because in business he was ruthless and brilliant—even cold, some would say, but always fair. He had that necessary detachment. It was the same with women. He was the one in control. Always. Without exception. Until now.

Jane sat back a while later, in her chair at the lunch table Xavier had set up in the inner courtyard. He had made a light meal of gazpacho soup with a summer salad and crusty bread, all washed down with a crisp white wine.

'That was delicious…I don't think I've eaten as well in months.'

'Like I said yesterday, it's a pleasure to see a woman enjoy her food, and I like cooking.'

'You'd better be careful or you might be rolling me out of here in a few days.'

She smiled easily, but the words reminded her that this *was* only for a few days. A mere interlude. Xavier would never remember someone like her when this was over. He would be moving on to the next exquisite beauty. Someone much more his equal, in every way.

'You have such an expressive face…'

She groaned with a lightness she suddenly didn't feel. 'That along with the blushing…it must be an intoxicating mix for someone used to a more sophist—'

He shook his head, cutting her off. 'Don't even say it…you have more innate grace in you than half the people I deal with every day.'

'Th…thank you.' Her tongue felt heavy in her mouth. She wasn't used to compliments. Wanting to change to subject, she asked, 'Do you have any staff? Surely you can't look after this place by yourself.'

'Yes, I do but they're on a few days' break.'

She couldn't help a silly flutter of fear.

Xavier read the look on her face effortlessly. 'They go on holiday this time every year. It's pure coincidence that it happens to be this week.'

'Oh…of course.'

The fact that he seemed to be able to read her better than anyone she knew made the flutter come back. That was nearly more disturbing than the thought of being alone with him in this huge castle.

'Come on, I'll show you around.'

He stood and held out a hand again, and she found herself taking it without thinking.

Every corner they turned made her exclaim anew. It was full of nooks and crannies, and secret courtyards overflowing with plants and eclectic furniture. She could imagine it being a children's paradise…and immediately stopped her wayward mind. What on earth had made her think of that?

He brought her to a swimming pool at the back. It was surrounded by trees and flowering bushes, in idyllic seclusion from the rest of the house.

'Why don't you go for a swim and relax for a bit? I've got that call to take.'

'OK…why not? If I can ever find my way back here.'

'There are cabins just behind the trees.' He indicated to the other side of the pool. 'Help yourself to a bathing suit and towels; there are robes as well.'

She should have guessed.

She chose a modest one-piece in dark blue, and went back to the pool to choose a lounger. After a quick dip and drying off she succumbed to the peace, which was broken only by the sound of birds and crickets.

A couple of hours later there was still no sign of him, and Jane felt she wanted to wash and get rid of the stickiness of the day. She gathered up her things and tied a robe securely around herself, wandering back through the house until she eventually found the stairs. She whirled around at the sound of a door opening. Xavier stood framed in the doorway. She could see a vast room behind him, with all manner of hi-tech office equipment.

'I'm sorry, but I'm still caught up with this call… Make yourself at home. I shouldn't be much longer.'

'Oh, don't worry about me,' Jane declared airily.

Up in the bedroom, she found her bag and padded barefoot to the *en suite* bathroom. She looked at the huge bath. The bath of her dreams. Filling it almost to the top, and adding copious amounts of the oils and scents that she'd found in a cupboard, she sank blissfully into the bubbles. Along with food, baths were her only other fatal weakness. This one was so huge she could have almost done a length.

But before she could turn into a prune—or, more disturbingly, have Xavier come looking for her—she stepped out. She smoothed on some body lotion and wrapped a towel around herself. Despite it being her own room, she went out cautiously. She couldn't hear any sounds…he must be busy still.

She caught sight of her reflection in a mirror and stopped for a second. She nearly didn't recognise herself. Skin glowing a light golden, her hair drifting around her face in waves, softening the harsh bob it had been when she'd first got it cut. Her eyes shone and sparkled, and her cheeks were flushed rosy from the bath.

In the mirror behind her a figure materialised in the doorway. Her eyes lifted, and she froze and watched as Xavier crossed the room to stand behind her.

Their eyes met in the mirror. There was only the sound of their breathing in the room. His hands were on her shoulders, dark against her skin. She watched, barely able to breathe, as they moved down her arms. She brought her eyes back up to his. Her whole body seemed to be pulsating in time with her heart, goosebumps making her skin prickle in anticipation. Right at that moment she wanted nothing more than for him to read her mind, undo her towel, let it drop to the floor, baring her to his gaze. She wanted him to take her breasts in his dark hands, weigh them, feel their heaviness, she wanted him to take off his clothes so she could lean back against the naked length of him…

But he didn't. His hands came up to her shoulders and rested there heavily.

'I'm sorry it took so long… When you're dressed come back downstairs and I'll cook us some dinner.'

She nodded at his reflection in the mirror, wordlessly watched as he stepped back and away. Thank God he *couldn't* read her mind, she thought shakily as he disappeared. Talk about waking a hitherto dormant sexual desire. Where had those images come from?

She went to close the door and whisked off the towel abruptly, studiously avoiding her own reflection again. In the space of a few hours she had morphed from shrinking virgin to mentally stripping him…but he was taking her at her word, holding back, letting her get comfortable. Well, she'd asked for it. She just hoped that he would take the initiative again, before she had to drum up the courage to let him know that she was ready!

A while later Jane sipped from a glass of deep red wine in the open-plan kitchen as she watched Xavier prepare a simple pasta dish. He was dressed casually, in jeans and a loose shirt, and she was equally casual, in a loose pair of linen trousers and a crossover short-sleeved top. She enjoyed watching him move dexterously around the kitchen.

'Where did you learn to cook?'

He glanced up briefly. 'In my teens I rebelled against the role my father wanted me to take up in the family business—namely the island—and ran away to the flight school on the mainland…I worked as a cook in a restaurant to help pay my way.'

'That's why you took part in the display?'

'Yes…I allow the pilots to do it here every year. Since my father died, we've incorporated it into a summer fête. It's a day out for everyone, and it's good for morale—and it allows me to indulge my love for flying.'

Jane had to suppress a slight shudder when she remembered his death-defying stunts.

'You were better then any of the others…you had some edge that they don't.'

He looked at her, but instead of finding a look of false flattery on her face saw she was busily picking at a salad. She had merely stated a fact.

'Thank you… I do miss it, but it was never going to be my destiny. Once my father died, I had to come back and take over the reins here. It used to be just the vineyard, but I developed abroad into the hotel chain and various other investments…mainly property.'

'Did you see your father before he died?' she asked softly.

'No.' It was curt, and Jane knew she'd hit a nerve. She deflected his attention.

'Well, this all looks more than fabulous—if that's possible. You'll have to let me cook for you, maybe tomorrow…'

He placed a swift kiss on her lips. 'For now, I'm quite happy to cook and enjoy watching you eat.'

For a moment he seemed as shocked as she was at the impulsive kiss that had come so naturally, but he recovered himself quickly.

Jane coloured as he had known she would. How was it that he felt as though he could read her like a book?

They sat out on a veranda at the back of the house. Soft jazz was coming from a speaker that was artfully hidden. Low lights from the house and candles illuminated the scene outside. Steps led down to a beautifully manicured lawn, teeming with exotic flowers. A clear sky glittered with stars and a full moon hung low in the horizon. It was magical.

The conversation flowed as Jane told him about her mother, the marriage, her job…her life. Instead of a glazed look of boredom passing over his face, as she had feared, he seemed genuinely interested.

He cradled his glass of wine. 'It's a strange connection to have…'

When she lifted a quizzical brow he elaborated.

'You growing up without a father, me without a mother.'

Jane nodded and shrugged lightly. 'I know…I wish I'd known him. But you can't really miss what you never had. I think for years Mum immortalised him as the perfect husband, but the truth was that he left us with nothing, and that…that was hard.'

'The truth usually is…'

She was surprised by the bleak look that crossed his face but then it was gone.

He leant forward to top up her glass of wine. 'Enough of this maudlin talk…'

He deftly changed the subject and she found herself forgetting about his enigmatic look as he effortlessly charmed her. After they had exhausted several topics, she couldn't remember when she had enjoyed talking to anyone as much. When she could forget for a moment the intense attraction that was always humming between them…

Later, when he stood and held out a hand to lead her inside, she took it easily. She followed him upstairs to her bedroom door. In the moonlit hallway she could just make out his eyes, feeling them rove over her face. Surely he would…?

She wanted him to take her, mould her to him, kiss her senseless. Her hands itched to pull his head down to hers. But she was too shy to show him. He bent his head and pressed a friendly kiss to her forehead…she felt a crushing disappointment.

'Goodnight, sweet Jane… I'll see you in the morning.' And he firmly turned her towards the bedroom and pushed her gently in.

Hours later Jane lay in sheets that were a tangled mess around her overheated body. Overheated because of all the images that wouldn't abate. Because of the knowledge that that man was mere feet away, probably naked, just lying there… All she had to do was get up, walk over…

She veered between just about getting up and sinking back into the pillows. At one point she cursed him. He probably knew exactly what he was doing, was so tuned in to the female psyche that this was a tried and tested technique… He was probably sleeping like a baby. As the first fingers of dawn crept into the sky she gave up and admitted defeat. She was a coward. Tomorrow, after all, was another day. And it was her own fault. She finally fell into a deep, dreamless sleep of exhaustion.

* * *

Jane woke to a gentle prodding, opening up one eye to see a cleanshaven and impeccable Xavier looking down at her. Both eyes snapped open.

'What time is it?'

'Almost midday…couldn't you sleep last night?'

She eyed him suspiciously from under her lashes, was that a mocking smile? She as good as had *sexual frustration* tattooed on her forehead.

'Fine, thank you, actually…and you?' she asked sweetly, making sure the sheet was pulled all the way up to her neck. Did he *have* to stand so close to the bed?

'Oh…like the proverbial log. I've made a picnic. There's a nice route we can take on the boat to get around to the memorial. We can take a gentle hike up to see it. It's a little more demanding, but ultimately rewarding.'

With a glint in his eye and his lip twitching he took his leave to let her get ready, before she could make a smart comeback to his none too subtle *double entendre*.

Gentle hike…? Some gentle hike, she thought about two hours later, when her legs were aching and sweat was running in rivulets down her brow, between her breasts and down her back. Her shorts and vest clung to her body like an indecent second skin, and all she could do was focus on Xavier's feet ahead of her, making sure to take exactly the same steps as him.

They had come around to the other end of the island, with Xavier pointing out landmarks, interesting birds and fauna along the way. There was so much more than she had seen at first. It was vibrant with the colour of thousands of wild flowers, cared for laboriously by the islanders who grew them to sell on the mainland.

They had docked the boat at a small cove, not dissimilar to the one he had taken her to the other day. He'd pointed up at what looked a perilously long way away to an overhanging rock. She hadn't been able to see the memorial, but he'd assured her that it was up there.

They had left their picnic in the shade on the beach, and now she was following Xavier up the hill, which was fast becoming her personal Everest.

Finally, just when she was about to beg for a break, his feet disappeared. She lifted her head to see his outstretched hand and took it gratefully, allowing him to haul her up the last couple of feet. He didn't let go of her hand, waiting until she had her breath under control, but the view was threatening to take it away again. They had emerged at the highest point of the island, the southernmost tip, and falling away from them and to the north they could see everything…the mainland shimmering faintly in the distance and the castle a small speck up at the other tip.

'This is…words fail me,' she breathed when she had enough to spare.

'I know…it's beautiful, isn't it?'

'Beautiful doesn't do it justice. It's epic…and it's yours.' She shook her head. 'How must it feel to come up here and know that all you survey is yours and yours alone?'

'Not everything…'

She turned her head to see him looking at her. Words crammed her mouth, wanting to come out, but she couldn't say them. She was tongue-tied, wanting to make some flip comment…but it just wasn't her.

He drew her attention to the grotto-like shrine a few feet to their left. It was a simple altar, with some candles, and vases with flowers that looked a few days old. It was sheltered on three sides by walls and a roof, facing out to the sea. She felt immeasurably honoured to be shown this special place. She took the small backpack off her shoulders and reached in, pulling out some flowers she had picked on their way up the hill, placing them in one of the vases. Around at the back, Xavier pointed out where the names were inscribed in clear and simple black paint.

'Thank you for showing me this…it's very special.' Her voice was husky.

'My pleasure.'

He made sure she drank some water, and after a few minutes of companionable silence he took her hand again and started to lead her back down the rocky path.

When they reached the beach Jane saw the water glinting and shimmering, and it was the best thing she'd ever seen. She tore off her shorts and vest, thankful that she had thought to put her bikini on before they left, and ran into the water, relishing the first cool sting and freshness over her sticky body.

Xavier did the same, and she squealed with delight when he emerged from underneath the water only inches away, pulling her down playfully. She silently urged him to kiss her, as he had done that first day, but he was still being the consummate gentleman—much to her growing frustration.

When they were cooled down, he led her back to the beach and spread out a delicious feast. Jane relaxed back and watched him talk…not even hearing his words. She couldn't remember a time when she had felt so full of delighted expectation. She was aware of every part of him—his hands, his mouth, legs…that chest. She was burning up just thinking about touching him, having him touch her. Her skin itched to be next to his. She wanted to reach over, stop his mouth with hers, run her hands over his muscles. But she didn't.

It was as if there was a silent communication going on between them on a subliminal level:

Come on, touch me if you dare…you're the one who wanted to go slowly…

I know! I just don't know what to do…how to make the move.

The atmosphere that surrounded them was thick with it.

That evening her skin felt hot after the sun…or else her imagination was just keeping it overheated. In bare feet and a plain shift dress, she padded down to the kitchen where she could hear Xavier making dinner. She paused at the door, drinking him in as he worked. He wore a white T-shirt and faded jeans, feet bare like hers. His hair was still wet from the shower, like hers, and a crisp fresh scent intoxicated her nostrils as he moved. He looked up then, and caught her staring. She didn't even blush…she was beyond that…just smiled.

His eyes boldly appraised her as she came towards him. She was completely unconscious of the provocatively innocent sway to her hips. He poured her a glass of wine and lifted his to hers. They clinked glasses.

'À nous.'

She nodded jerkily in response.

All through dinner they talked, but it had a hushed, frantic quality. A breathless anticipation was building in Jane's belly.

When he stood to take her hand under the stars at the end of the evening she was trembling, unable to speak. They stopped once again outside her door. She turned her face up to his. Wordlessly she tried to communicate with him. Couldn't he tell? Surely he had to know how ready she was? She watched as he brought her hand to his mouth and pressed a kiss to the delicate underside of her wrist. She closed her eyes and felt a weakening in her body, her blood slowing to a deep throbbing pulse.

'Goodnight, Jane. Sleep tight.'

CHAPTER FIVE

GOODNIGHT, Jane…Sleep tight?

Her eyes flew open. *No!* her mind screamed…he had let her hand go. A dark, bottomless pit threatened to suck her down. She had to do something. But even as she thought this, she could feel herself turning away, sudden doubts assailing her. Maybe he didn't find her attractive any more? Maybe he was regretting having asked her to stay? Surely he would have tried to make love to her again?

Then she stopped. She realised that she hadn't heard him move behind her. She turned around slowly and saw his face. It told her everything she needed to know. Raw masculine arousal was stamped into every line. She felt every cell in her body jump in response.

'Xavier—' Her words were stopped as he hauled her into his arms. The relief made her dizzy as she locked her arms around his neck.

'I swear if you had gone into that room I was going to come after you, ready or not…'

'Thank God…because I nearly did…'

'I couldn't have spent another night in that bed, knowing you were only feet away.'

'I nearly went to you last night, but couldn't work up the nerve…'

'What? Do you know how hard it's been for me to keep from touching you all day?'

He groaned and bent his head to hers, finding and taking her lips, tasting them as if they were succulent fruits. His control was fast slipping as his hands smoothed down her back, down to her buttocks, moulding their peachy firmness, cupping them and drawing her up into the cradle of his lap, where he felt her gasp against his mouth when she felt his arousal.

In one graceful move he lifted her against his chest and kicked open his bedroom door, bringing her inside. He brought her over to the mirror, where he stood her in front of him. She looked at him in the reflection, a question on her face.

'This is what I thought of last night, the image that kept me awake.'

She felt his hands at the top of her dress, fingers grazing her skin as he slowly started to pull the zip down. Immediately she knew what he meant, and the thought of him imagining the same scenario made her knees weak.

She felt the slight night breeze on her skin, and shivered in reaction as he gently but firmly pulled the dress from her shoulders and down, past her breasts, past her waist, over the swell of her hips, until it hit the floor with a muted swish. Her bra quickly followed, and she was standing there naked but for a pair of very brief briefs. She brought her hands up to cover her breasts, feeling shy, but he came close behind her and brought them back down.

'Look at how beautiful you are.'

His head lowered and he pressed a hot kiss to where her neck and shoulder met, causing a shudder to run through her body…and then began to shed his own clothes behind her. She could hear the whisper of his T-shirt dropping to the floor, a button being snapped, jeans falling. An unbearable tightness began to build in her abdomen as she continued to watch through their reflection, until he stood behind her completely naked, his dark form a contrast to her much paler one.

Her head felt light. She watched in the mirror as his hands came around her to cup her breasts. They looked full and heavy in his palms. Her eyes widened as she saw her nipples growing harder, puckering, felt the ache that escaped as a guttural moan when his hands closed over them, her nipples caught between his fingers. She could feel his arousal against her bottom and instinctively moved back and leant against him, delighting in his own low moan.

He turned her to face him, bringing her into intimate contact with his whole length, taking her mouth with his. His hands were under her panties, slowly tugging them down until they fell at her feet.

She started to shake uncontrollably with reaction as he lifted her into his arms and walked over to the bed.

He gently laid her down, following her, leaning over her with strong arms. He bent to take her lips, the kiss starting out gentle, rapidly becoming more heated and passionate. Jane's hands stretched out blindly, searching for and finding his chest, his shoulders, smoothing, touching every part she could reach.

He groaned softly as her hands reached lower, coming dangerously close to his rock-hard erection. He couldn't remember ever being so aroused. He shifted to lie down beside her, lifting his head for a moment, watching her reaction as his fingertips closed over one nipple, how her back arched, her eyes closed and her breathing became fractured. Noticing how her skin had flushed to a dull red. He bent and took the jewel-hard peak into this mouth, his own control fast slipping as he suckled and nipped gently, first at one, then the other.

'Xavier… I can't… God!'

Her hands clutched at his shoulders, and her body writhed as he moved a hand down over her belly to feel how ready she was. The wetness he felt at the apex of her thighs almost pushed him over the edge, and he'd hardly touched her! Or she him…

As his hand explored, stroked, Jane felt herself bucking.

She'd had no idea it could be like this. Had had no expecta-tion…certainly hadn't expected this hunger in her blood that was consuming her to the point where she was no longer herself. She had become…someone else? Or perhaps the person she was meant to be… All these incoherent fevered thoughts raced through her head at the same time.

Xavier's fingers were pushing her to a point of no return, his mouth was on hers, then on her breast. It was too much…her whole body stilled for a moment before she felt herself crashing over the edge and tumbling down, her body contracting and pulsating in the aftermath. His hand cupped her mound, waiting until her tremors had stopped. She looked up into his face, her eyes wide with shock… Words trembled on her lips, but then he claimed her mouth once more, with a hot, drugging kiss, and she felt him move over her body. He lifted his head, his eyes glittering in the half-light, pupils dilated with barely contained passion. She sucked in a breath of anticipation as she took in the daunting size of him, moisture beading at the tip.

His voice was hoarse with need and restraint. 'Jane…I can't wait.'

Moving instinctively, she nudged her hips up towards him, silently encouraging him. A sheen of light sweat covered their bodies. Slowly, so slowly, he started to enter her. Jane felt no pain. Her body seemed to recognise him and welcomed him in deeper and deeper.

'Oh…that feels so good.'

Was that low, husky voice hers?

When he drew out again she whimpered, until he thrust back in all the way. She wrapped her legs around his back, as if to draw him in even deeper, tighter. His strokes were long and hard and assured. She felt the anticipation build once again. After what seemed like an eternity of sensation, building and building until she thought she'd expire, his pace quickened and his movements became less controlled, as if he couldn't hold on. And she couldn't either.

She felt herself tense. Xavier was thrusting so deep that she bit her lips to stop from crying out at the exquisite pleasure of it... And then she came, fast and strong, only dimly registering Xavier's final thrust as his whole body went taut and she felt his own orgasm deep inside her.

They lay locked together for some time. Xavier shifted slightly so that his heavy weight was off her, his hand drifting idly up and down her back. Jane couldn't help a feeling of serene completion from stealing over her. As if she was now whole. He was still part of her, hadn't pulled away yet from her body's tight embrace.

He opened his eyes, that brilliant green pinning her to the spot.

'Are you OK?'

She nodded her head, incapable of speech, her eyes drawn helplessly to his. They lay face to face, her hands captured against his chest, his arms around her. She was mesmerised by every part of him—his eyes, nose, mouth. She reached a finger up to trace his lips wonderingly. He gently pulled himself from her body and she blushed.

He shook his head wryly. 'You're the first virgin I've slept with since my teens...I suspected, but wasn't sure, and when you didn't say anything—'

Jane coloured, wanting to hide. Her virginity had been the last thing on her mind.

'If I'd known...'

She felt herself tense slightly. 'If...if you'd known, what?'

He wouldn't have pursued her? He preferred his women more experienced?

His hand drifted up and down her back, relaxing her again. 'It doesn't matter now. To think I'm your first lover is actually the most erotic thing I've experienced in...'

He didn't finish, just bent and kissed her mouth with aching tenderness. What had she expected after all? The man was sinfully gorgeous, powerful and rich. Of course he was experienced, used to women falling at his feet. She locked her misgivings away somewhere deep inside her.

He curled her into him more tightly, and finally she drifted off to sleep, enclosed in his arms, his strong heart beating under her cheek.

Jane woke the next morning to face an expanse of naked chest. Lifted her eyes slowly to meet green ones looking back. A heavy, possessive arm lay across her hip, the hand moving in slow circles.

'Morning,' she said shyly, wanting to duck her head as the previous night came back into her consciousness. She felt a pleasurable ache in every muscle.

'Morning.' He pressed a kiss to her mouth.

She could feel some tension in the air, and his eyes took on a serious light, making a finger of something skate up and down her spine.

'I didn't use protection last night. I never usually forget, but…' A strange expression came over his face, but it was bland again in a second, making her think she'd imagined it.

'I'm guessing you're probably not on the Pill?'

Reality crashed in on Jane, waking her sleep-muddled brain up in a second. Of course he wouldn't want any complications from this…holiday fling. Because that was all it was. She tried to remain unaware of his naked body stretched close against hers, where she could already feel the stirrings of his arousal, and felt herself responding, with heat unfurling in her lower body. She struggled to focus on his words, not the response of her body.

'No, I'm not…but it's a safe time of the month for me…'

It wasn't strictly accurate, but she did a quick calculation in her head. She was sure it would be fine. Seemingly content with her assurance, he relaxed and drew her in tighter against his body, where she could feel the full strength of his hardness as it pressed against her.

'I think you owe me at least a day in bed…to make up for making me wait…'

All previous thoughts fled as her pulse threatened to strangle her words. She was already breathing faster as his hand caressed the globe of her bottom. 'You knew better than me…you must have known the torture I was going through.'

'No…I was going through my own… In fact it's happening again—something you can help me remedy…'

He drew her on top of him, running his hands down her smooth back, cupping her bottom, bringing up her legs to either side of him. He drew her head down to his, and as she closed her eyes she thought that she'd never get enough of him.

Over the next two days they made love, talked, ate. Xavier revelled in teaching her how much her body could respond to his touch…and how he could respond to hers.

Jane shut out the outside world. Even when they went beyond the confines of the castle and he took her on a sightseeing tour of the rest of the island, it felt as though the island itself was the perimeter of this world, that nothing could intrude. He brought her to the small village, with exactly two hundred and seven inhabitants. It was a bustling, thriving community—largely thanks to him. The people considered themselves markedly different from the mainland, with their Spanish heritage, and it was reflected everywhere. The locals welcomed him as if he was their king…the children shy, men respectful, young women blushing.

Jane knew that without his presence there was no way the island would have retained its unique heritage.

Xavier had promised to show her his favourite childhood spot for swimming, and as they drove there another Jeep approached them on the small narrow road. When it drew alongside the driver was gesturing. Xavier stopped and got out. Jane followed. A stunning brunette, clad in an exquisite suit, was embracing Xavier energetically, speaking fast and furiously.

Jane walked around to join them, feeling very mussed-up and plain next to this vision of chic. Xavier pulled her close and cut through the other woman's stream of words. 'Sophie Vercors…meet Jane Vaughan.'

The woman halted with comic surprise as Jane was revealed, her eyes widening, and then a mischievous look dawned, an undeniable warmth in her face.

She replied in English, 'Xavier, you dark horse…entertaining on the island? Why, I thought you never—'

He cut her off with a warning look in his eye. 'Sophie, Jane is on holiday from England. She goes home in two days.'

Jane felt the brusque comment like a physical slap. He was very tacitly stating the extent of their involvement…

She held out a hand and smiled, ignoring an ache somewhere deep inside. 'Nice to meet you.'

'You too, Jane.' Sophie's smile was wide and unaffected. She had obviously decided to drop any further probing, and launched into a long and hilarious explanation of how she had to race to the mainland to meet her husband, who had forgotten something. She left after a few minutes with a friendly wink to Jane, a flurry of kisses and a cloud of dust in her wake.

Xavier didn't elaborate, beyond telling Jane that she was a Parisienne who had married one of his oldest friends. He, like Xavier, worked primarily on the mainland. It was obvious that she and Xavier were very good friends, easily affectionate with each other.

After a short drive, they pulled in off the track and made their way on foot to the secluded cove. They left the picnic Jane had prepared under a tree on the edge of the beach and raced each other into the water. All thoughts of the future, and her looming departure, were gone, and Jane strenuously focused on the present moment.

In the water, their horseplay quickly turned into something more serious, and afterwards, under the shade of the tree,

Xavier laid out the blanket and stood before her. Hair slicked against his head, the tang of the salty water on his skin, Xavier removed her bikini, kissing every exposed piece of flesh until he came to kneel before her. Her hands were on his shoulders, and her legs were threatening to buckle under waves of intense pleasure as he held her bottom. He wouldn't allow her to fall as his mouth and tongue did wicked things between her legs. Finally, when she thought she couldn't bear it any more, with words pleading for release on her lips, he laid her down and stretched over her, his body long and lean, every muscle clearly delineated, his erection jutting proudly, majestically between their bodies.

Jane felt a primal possessiveness as she looked into his eyes. *This man is mine…*

And it scared her to death. She drove it away, reaching up, her lips seeking and finding his, saying his name on a moan. 'Xavier…now, please now.'

'What…what do you want?'

She urged her hips to his, but he went with her, thwarting her efforts. She bit her lip in frustration.

He took a second to slip on protection, and the knowledge that he hadn't failed to do so since that first time was all too clear in Jane's head. But the throbbing of her body drowned that thought out as she felt him position himself between her legs in one fluid move.

'Tell me what you want…is it this?'

He started to enter the heart of her, just with the tip, and pulled out again.

Jane was nearly mindless with need, barely coherent. 'Yes…yes! Please, Xavier, I can't…hold on…'

He continued to torture her, focusing his attention on her breasts, taking each peak with a hot mouth and stimulating them unbearably, and then his mouth found hers, tongue stroking hers, igniting an ever-climbing fire of need that raced along every vein and cell.

Finally he entered her again, a little deeper, but this time Jane wanted to frustrate *him* and she pulled back. Much as it pained her, it excited her unbearably, this erotic dance.

'Two can play that game…' she breathed with a new confidence.

'Oh, really…?' Xavier growled low in his throat. 'We'll see about that.'

He cupped her bottom, tilting it upwards, laying her bare to his gaze, not allowing her to move, and with one deep thrust entered her so completely that she cried out with pleasure. He didn't allow her any quarter as he drove in and out with a relentless rhythm, sometimes shallow, sometimes deep, until at last they tipped over the precipice of extreme pleasure together, and down into a state of such bliss that it was some time before either one could move.

For the rest of the afternoon, as the light fell, they ate and watched the sun set over the horizon. Jane couldn't help but feel that this was possibly the happiest she had ever been in her life, and she tried to keep it from her eyes, fearing it must be blatantly obvious every time he looked at her.

The next morning she woke in the bed to find Xavier already up. She rolled over onto her side and tucked her head into her arm. Her last day on the island.

With a heavy heart she got up and dressed. She went downstairs and found him in the kitchen, sipping from a cup of coffee. She tried to project a light front, when inside she felt as though she was shrivelling up.

He looked up, a dazzling smile illuminating his face when he saw her in the doorway.

'I have to go to the mainland for a couple of hours today…you could stay here, or come with me if you like?'

Jane poured herself a cup of coffee, praying that he wouldn't notice the tremor in her hands. Delay the inevitable? One more night? Was is so self-indulgent to want to hang on to the fantasy?

A rogue dark part of her answered, 'I'll stay here, if you don't mind…'

He frowned for a second. 'When did you say your flight was?'

'Tomorrow night…I'll have to get back to the villa first thing in the morning, to clean it up and make sure everything is tidied away…pack my things.'

He thought for a second. 'Well, look, why don't you come back to the mainland with me today? You can do your things at the villa, pack and lock it up while I'm busy, and then we could spend the night at the hotel. You could leave from there tomorrow.'

Her heart twisted at his matter-of-fact tone. He was obviously having no qualms at the thought of her leaving. She had an irrational fear that once they stepped off the island, all this would fade as if it never happened.

But what he was saying made perfect sense. Perfect practical sense. He wouldn't understand if she said she'd prefer their last night to be here…to hang on to the dream for as long as possible. No, it was for the best. The break would be easier surrounded by the hustle and bustle of the real world.

Maybe he wanted them to be surrounded by people, the town, in case she became clingy, refused to go. Was he used to women acting that way? She wouldn't be one of those women—couldn't have him suspect for a moment how deeply involved she'd become.

'Yes…yes, of course you're right…'

CHAPTER SIX

AN HOUR later, bag packed and ready to go, Jane waited by the front entrance of the castle. She turned around and drank in the view, committing it all to memory, sucked in the air deeply. The morning sun was gathering more and more heat. In late June its potency was powerful, and the distinctive smell of sun-baked earth wafted over her. The cicadas' incessant chatter stopped, and then started further away every time she moved to try and catch them out.

In the space of just one week she had come to really love this island. That first forbidding view had hidden something much more complex. It had a heart and a vitality that was artfully disguised by its appearance. Completely unique. Much like the man who was striding through the doors towards her now. Every line of his physique screamed dynamic…independent…successful. He reminded her of a lone wolf. Who would get to tame him in the end? Could any one woman do it?

She schooled her features as he approached, and let him take her bag to swing it into the back of his car, which would take them to the boat.

As they got close to the private marina at the harbour on the mainland, Jane could see someone waiting for them. It was the beautiful blonde woman she had noticed that first time she had seen him in the street.

She was waving gaily as the boat approached, but Jane could see her arm falter slightly when she noticed Xavier had a companion.

As they climbed out Jane took Xavier's helping hand, a familiar tingle travelling up her arm, slightly breathless when she came to stand beside him. The other woman didn't even glance Jane's way as she unleashed a torrent of French at Xavier. She was stunning, her perfectly proportioned petite figure and deep tan set off by white jeans and a tight white shirt, artfully tousled blonde hair cascaded down her back.

Xavier drew Jane in to his side with a possessive arm, and when he could get a word in edgeways interjected in English. 'Sasha, don't be so rude. I'd like you to meet Jane. She's been my guest for the past week. You haven't been able to get me because I made sure I was unavailable. Jane, this is Sasha— one of my assistants.'

His tone, while light, held a steely undertone. Jane shivered, and felt a little sorry for Sasha. Any hint of which was swiftly gone when the girl turned her exacting gaze on Jane. Pure venom. She sneaked a look at Xavier, to see if he had noticed, but he had let go of her to rope off the boat, and had moved away a few feet. Jane was acutely conscious of her added inches and bigger frame as the woman sent a scathing glance up and down, summarily dismissing her. Her accent when she spoke was captivating, her English impeccable.

'So nice to meet you…thank you for entertaining Xavi for me…he works far too hard. Tell me, England, is it? You're a tourist?'

Jane nodded warily, feeling hackles that she'd never known she possessed rise.

'Ah, I thought so… Xavi is incorrigible—such a weakness for the—'

But whatever she'd been going to say was halted when Xavier came back to stand beside them.

'Jane, I'll give you a lift to the villa. Sasha, will you arrange for a car to pick Jane up this afternoon? Say around four p.m.'

Jane was still slightly stunned from Sasha's words, not sure where she had been going and not sure if she wanted to know. She looked at her uneasily. Her beautiful smile didn't go near her chocolate-brown eyes. Jane didn't want anything to do with this woman, and remembered belatedly with relief, 'I still have my hire car. I have to get it back anyway, so I'll make my own way to the hotel later.'

These words earned positive waves of radioactivity from the other woman. Jane avoided her eye, relieved when Xavier said, 'Fine. Sasha, I'll see you in the office in about an hour.'

Back in the villa, after Xavier had dropped her off, Jane wandered around disconsolately. She went through the motions of cleaning up and packing. She felt as though she were empty inside, and tried to shake the feeling off.

She made a light lunch for herself, and carried it up to the terrace, remembering back to the night she had stood there, dreaming about him—the night after she had bumped into him in the street. Wandering back to take in the view, she had to smile a little sad smile to herself.

Well, her fantasy had come true. Spectacularly. It had come to life...*he* had come to life...brought *her* to life in ways she would have never envisaged. He had awakened her. Been her first lover. Opened her eyes to a sensuality she had never imagined herself to possess. Helped her to own that sensuality. He had been her gift for the past week...and tonight would be their last night.

She would have to let him go. Be strong. She wouldn't fall at his feet, weeping and wailing. He belonged in this world of unimaginable wealth and beauty. Every day blessed by the benediction of the sun. And she belonged... She didn't belong here.

God knew what it was that attracted him to her...but he

was offering her one more night. And she would take it. Savour it. And somehow find the strength to walk away tomorrow with her head held high.

Later, when Jane walked into the hotel lobby after dropping the car off, she felt a little more in control of her emotions. Xavier had told her to give her name to the receptionist, who would be expecting her. She did so, and a bellboy came to take her luggage and show her up to the penthouse suite.

When she got up there she couldn't see any sign of him, and her heart slowed to a regular beat again. She spied a bottle of champagne in an ice bucket, with a note and pristine white rose resting against its side. With trembling fingers she opened the note after smelling the rose. The handwriting was big and curt. She smiled, imagining his impatience.

> I'm sorry I'm not here to meet you. Have a glass of
> champagne while you are waited on hand and foot, and
> I will be there to pick you up at 7.30. *A bientôt.* X

For a minute she wondered if the X meant a kiss or was just his initial, before trying to figure out the rest of the message. A knock came and she went to answer it, still puzzling over his note.

At the door were three women, all carrying various accoutrements. The light dawned when they came in and told Jane they were there to do a massage, pedicure, manicure, facial, her hair…in no special order. Her mouth dropped open, but they were too well trained to make any comment when it became apparent that they were dealing with a novice. Having never indulged herself like this before, Jane, after a moment of trepidation and the old haunting guilt, gave herself over to the experience. And went to heaven and back.

A couple of hours later, when they'd left, she went to one of the mirrors and stared incredulously. Another creature looked back. A relaxed, buffed, shining version of herself, with sleek hair that fell in a smooth wave to just below her jaw. They had tinted her eyelashes, which she had never had done before, and now her eyes seemed huge in her face, framed by thick luxurious lashes.

Before she could lose herself in uncustomary narcissistic bliss, she spied the clock out of the corner of her eye and saw that it was almost seven-fifteen. In a panic, she realised that she hadn't even unpacked—and what could she possibly wear that he hadn't already seen by now? With dismay, she pulled her bag into the bedroom and stopped when she saw the bed. A huge white box lay there, with another note and a red rose this time.

Just in case. X

She opened the box with clumsy fingers and pulled out a dress from the folds of tissue paper. And what a dress. It slid through her fingers when she tried to hold it. She gathered it back again, and stared in shock. It screamed *designer*. Sure enough, the label confirmed her suspicion. She mightn't be a fount of knowledge when it came to celebrity and celebrity lifestyles, but even she recognised the famous name. It must be worth a fortune. She spied more in the box, and opened up the paper to reveal a matching set of silk and lace underwear. Silk stockings. Even shoes.

Against every penny-scrimping sensibility that had been drummed into her, she couldn't resist. She allowed the hotel robe to drop from her shoulders and she pulled on the underwear before stepping into the dress. It was strapless and tight-fitting. She looked at herself in the mirror. Was it meant to cling like that? Especially around her breasts? She looked behind…her bottom looked so…round.

She heard the door and her heart thudded to a stop, before starting up again at twice the speed.

'Jane? Where are you?'

'In…in here… Wait! I'll come out.'

She felt suddenly panicked at the thought of him coming into the bedroom. With a deep breath, and squaring her shoulders, she opened the door and went into the suite.

Xavier was pouring himself a glass of champagne, and he looked up, his hand stilling in the action. He put the bottle down slowly as his gaze raked her up and down from under his lashes. He had to put his hands into his pockets in a reflex action, to stop himself from reaching out and hauling her against his chest and crushing that soft kissable mouth under his.

She looked…stunning. The dress showed off her figure to perfection, emphasising her hourglass shape, exactly as he had imagined. And her eyes… Lord, those eyes…with their innocently sensual promise—they made him want to lock all the doors, take her and bury himself so deep inside her that she'd never want another man again.

He shook himself mentally. It was a nice dress. No need to go over the top about it. He'd seen plenty of women in far more revealing dresses. Taken them off too. And he would again in the future. Jane Vaughan was going home tomorrow, and it was a good thing… He'd been far too uncomfortably aware of alien emotions all week. Time to say goodbye and get back to normal. He had one more night. To get her out of his system for good.

He dropped heavy lids over his eyes and bent to pour another glass of champagne before strolling over and passing it to her.

Jane still hadn't moved—had been rendered immobile under his very thorough inspection. She covered up her insecurity by taking a gulp of the sparkling vintage wine. The bubbles made her nose screw up, and she immediately felt silly for worrying. She was going to enjoy this last night, be free and easy.

Xavier said throatily, 'To you…you look beautiful tonight.'

'Thank you…so do you.' And he did. Darkly handsome in a black tuxedo. The snowy white shirt making his eyes stand out, that glittering phenomenal green.

'Thank you for…laying on the massage and things today and this…' She indicated the dress shyly.

'My pleasure…' And it would be, later, he vowed, struck again by her charming politeness. He was used to women expecting…taking from him. 'I've booked a restaurant on the seafront for dinner…it's not far. We can stroll, if you think you can in those shoes.'

'I'll be fine…' Jane vowed that even if her feet were bleeding she wouldn't say a word; she didn't want a moment of the evening to be spoiled.

He took her glass, and they were almost at the door when she stopped in her tracks by his side in sudden embarrassment.

'I didn't put any make-up on… I can't go out in a dress like this with no—'

Xavier put a finger to her lips, silencing her. He looked at her carefully and came very close, one hand on either side of her face. Then he bent his head and brought his mouth to hers and kissed her.

Taken aback slightly for a second, Jane quickly forgot everything—where they were, where they were going—as the kiss deepened, and she brought her hands up to steady herself on his chest, the beat of his heart starting up a throbbing in her own pulse. With masterful expertise Xavier plumbed the depths of her mouth, and then, achingly slowly, traced her lips with his tongue before delving back in and stoking a fire that had heat travel from the molten centre of her all the way up to where she could feel her breasts aching heavily against their confinement.

He lifted his head, breathing harshly. Jane opened her eyes reluctantly. He saw her cheeks flushed with a burgeoning arousal, her eyes glittering like stars under long black spiky lashes, and her lips… He almost kicked the door closed behind him, painfully aware of his own arousal… Her lips were full and swollen and moist, like two crushed petals.

'There…' he said gruffly. 'You don't need any make-up.'

Taking her hand firmly in his, he pulled her behind him. Jane stumbled to keep up, bringing a hand up to sensitised lips. What did he mean by that?

When she caught her reflection in the elevator mirror a few seconds later she saw exactly what he had meant, and blushed from her toes to the tip of her head.

The restaurant was exclusive. When they arrived the bouncers fell over themselves to be the one to admit Xavier and his guest. The maître d' fawned and fussed as he led them to a table tucked away from the main floor by an open window. Strategically placed plants ensured the kind of privacy that allowed them to see the rest of the room and yet not be observed themselves. A white tablecloth, sparkling silverware, gleaming glasses. Candlelight. Jane sighed and smiled. She couldn't have done better if she had actually written it down on paper.

'What's so amusing?'

She looked at him across the table, so at ease in these surroundings, supremely confident. He would never understand where she was from…where she had to go back to. How special this was for her.

She shrugged lightly. 'Nothing…I'm enjoying the spectacle of all the minions tripping over themselves to impress you.'

'But not you, Jane…you didn't trip over yourself to impress me. You're different.'

Different… Which made reference to all those other women…

A short, sharp dart arrowed its way into her heart. She spoke lightly to disguise it.

'Well…my cunning plan worked, didn't it?'

'Ah…as I thought. You're as mercenary as the rest of them…'
See?

'Yes…' A brittle laugh came out of somewhere. 'You see, I've actually been stalking you for months, and I devised the best, most effective way to get your attention.'

'I thought you looked familiar in the street that day.'

He wagged a triumphant finger at her. Even though they were joking, she felt sad. Though he hadn't let it appear too often, she knew he harboured a well-worn cynicism.

The waiter appeared and took their order. Jane pushed aside all reservations, judgements, fears, and focused entirely on the moment—and Xavier. All too effortlessly she succeeded, and the conversation flowed like a burbling stream. Joyfully, easily, and far, far too seductively to resist.

She barely noticed the courses being delivered. She must have eaten, but for the life of her she couldn't remember what. She found herself watching him talk, committing every part of his hard-boned face to memory. The way his eyes crinkled ever so slightly when he smiled, the glimpse of bright white teeth. The way he inclined his head, encouraging her to go on when she faltered during a story.

All too soon it was time to go. The last drops of wine had been drunk, the espresso cups were taken away. A bare tablecloth sat between them. Xavier stood easily and held out a hand. She allowed him to pull her up, a little unsteady with the effects of the wine. He slipped an arm around her waist and together they walked out. His scent was heavy and potent in her nostrils. She had to stop herself from turning into his chest and breathing deeply.

Instead of going back the way they had come, he led her down by the beach. She hesitated for a second, before taking off her shoes and then reaching up under her dress to pull down her stockings.

'Wait.'

Her hands stilled as Xavier crouched down in front of her.

They were sheltered from the main promenade by a tree, the sound of the sea only feet way.

'Let me.'

Jane stood and closed her eyes as she felt his hands come up under her dress to encircle one thigh, fingers stalling, and slowly snagging the stocking top to bring it down. Exquisite pleasure. Especially when his hands seemed to take far too long to travel their way up her other leg. She was shaking, her hands heavy on his shoulders by the time he reached his destination and pulled the other stocking down, trembling with the unbearable desire for him to keep going up…fingers reaching higher until they found…

He stood up lithely, dangling her shoes and stockings with one hand. On impulse she reached up and tugged at his bow tie until it came loose and free, then undid his top button, tongue between her teeth when it proved stiff and unwieldy.

When she had finished she looked up to find him staring down at her, eyes fixated on her mouth. She innocently moistened her lips with her tongue.

He took her hand with urgency, and led her onto the beach. 'There's a quick way back to the hotel from here…'

Jane barely took in the magical view as they made their silent way across the beach, the moonlight bathing everything with a milky glow, sounds of laughter and muted music coming from the strip on the other side of the bushes.

Soon they were at the steps that led up to the gardens at the back of the hotel. They stood there looking at each other, lost in the moment. Then he handed her the shoes and stockings and disappeared—before she felt an arm coming under her legs and herself being lifted and held against his broad chest.

'Xavier…you can't.'

'There's gravel on the ground up here, and I can't wait for you to put your shoes on… As sexy as you are walking in them, it'll take too long…'

'Too long for what?'

'To get you where I want you…on my bed…under me.'

She buried her head in his shoulder as they approached the hotel, arms around his neck. She felt extraordinarily cherished and protected and desired. They avoided bumping into anyone, and took the service elevator all the way up, coming in to the penthouse from another entrance. He didn't put her down until they reached the bedroom.

Shoes and stockings fell from nerveless fingers as he slowly lowered her down his body. When her feet touched the floor they were standing so close that she could feel his heart beating against her chest.

In what felt like slow motion, her zip was pulled down, buttons popped open, catches undone. There was the whisper of clothes falling to the floor, skin meeting skin, soft and hard and silky, tongues touching and tasting, legs buckling, falling onto the bed in a tangle of limbs. Jane shut her eyes and ears to the voices in her head, concentrating on Xavier's hand as it glided over her breasts and down across her belly, down further…

When Jane woke the next morning she was alone in the bed. Just then the bathroom door opened and Xavier emerged, with an indecently small towel around his waist. She felt a blush coming on when she remembered the previous night… To think of how wanton she'd been…had become in the space of a few days. Where on earth had she ever got the nerve to do those things to him?

He watched the expressions flit over her face. Did she have any idea how beguiling she looked? How much it turned him on to think that he was the only lover she'd ever known? She looked at him, sleepy eyes, flushed cheeks, biting her lip, pulling the sheet up. He strode over to the bed and came down on his arms beside her. Her eyes widened, the pupils dilating. It firmed his resolve for what he was going to ask her. But not yet. Later. He pressed a quick kiss to her lips and straightened.

'Morning, sleepy. I'm sorry about this, but there's an emergency with the hotel in Malaysia and I have a crisis meeting to attend… Stay put, and I'll be right back. We can have breakfast together.'

'OK…'

Jane watched dry-mouthed as he let the towel drop and unselfconsciously pulled on his clothes. What a body.

When she heard the main door close she rolled over, burying her face in the pillow. She had to face it. Couldn't block it out any more. Especially after last night. He had brought her to the height of something so beautiful that she knew without a doubt that she would never experience anything remotely close with another man.

She had fallen in love with him. Hard and deep and fast. Irrevocably. Unbelievably. Needless to say he had made no indication that to him this was anything more than a brief diversion, which was ending today. She wouldn't allow her thoughts to fly ahead a few hours, when she would have to think about leaving. As if ignoring it would make it less of a reality.

Forcing herself to block the dangerous thoughts, telling herself she had to be crazy, she got up and went to have a quick shower, noticing faint marks on her body and colouring when she remembered herself urging Xavier to go harder, how she had assured him that he didn't need to be so gentle. She groaned under the powerful jet of water.

After towelling her hair and donning a voluminous robe, she wandered into the suite and opened the windows, looking out over the pool area and the sea beyond, breathing in the warm morning air.

There was a knock on the door. That was funny—didn't he have a key? Jane went and opened the door, a ready smile on her lips.

'Missing me already?'

CHAPTER SEVEN

HER smile faded fast when she saw who it was at the door.

Sasha.

His assistant looked sparkly and bright. As if she'd been up for hours. Before Jane knew what was happening, Sasha had sidled past her and into the room, looking around with interest.

'If you're looking for Xavier, he's gone for a meeting—'

She turned and fixed Jane with cold eyes. 'I know *exactly* where he is. I *always* know where he is.'

'I'll tell him you called…' Jane stayed by the open door and hoped she would take the hint.

'Actually, I came to see you.'

Sasha sat on the couch, crossing one elegant leg over the other. Where was this going?

'Did you enjoy last night? The pampering….the restaurant?'

How did she know about that? Jane felt a stillness come into her body, as if it were preparing for some kind of attack. Her hand gripped the knob of the door.

'Yes, thank you,' she said faintly, dimly thinking to herself, Well, maybe she booked it for him, so she'd be bound to know…

'Oh, yes! I nearly forgot about the champagne and everything else…'

A dull roaring sensation was beginning somewhere in her head as Sasha continued.

'I hope I organised it all to Xavier's satisfaction. I thought I'd check with you to make sure I did a good job...'

'You...you organised everything?'

She knows about the dress?

Sasha threw back her head and laughed. 'Of course, silly! You don't think someone like Xavier has time to go around booking restaurants and making facial appointments do you?'

Jane's brain was barely taking in her words any more.

And the notes? Surely not those...

Holding onto the door as if it were a lifeline, she fought for composure. 'Sasha, why don't you say what you want to say and get out...I have to pack.'

'I wouldn't be doing my job if I didn't make sure that *all* of Xavi's women were looked after.'

She stood up and sauntered close to Jane, who held her breath, just wanting the other woman gone.

'I have to admit, it gets a bit boring after a while. I keep telling him not to be so predictable, to vary things a bit...' Sasha smiled indulgently. 'But I guess he's just old-fashioned. That's why I'm here, Jane. I can see the type of woman you are. You're not like the others.' She looked at Jane closely before a cruel smile twisted her lips, 'You've fallen for him haven't you?'

Jane said nothing. Couldn't move a muscle.

'You poor thing... It'll be someone else next week, you know...the same thing all over again. Like I said, you seem nice, and I'd hate to see you get hurt. He hates clingy women. *Au revoir.*'

And just like that she sashayed out of the room.

Jane felt as though she'd been punched in the stomach. She actually couldn't suck enough air into her belly for a minute, and had to take calming breaths to prevent working herself into a panic attack. She stumbled over to the mini-bar and pulled out a bottle of water, taking a deep gulp. She felt shivery and nauseous. She sat down on a chair and stared blindly in front of her.

Stupid, stupid Jane. Allowing herself to fall in love with him. If Sasha had picked up on it, then who was to say he hadn't either? Utter humiliation rose up and swamped her. Words that Sasha had said dropped like stones into Jane's numbed brain: *So predictable...someone else next week...all of Xavi's women...*

She stood suddenly. Well, she wouldn't be waiting here for him like a lame duck. She tripped over the robe in her haste to get into the bedroom, and packed quickly and feverishly, throwing on trousers and a shirt, uncaring if they matched or not. The dress lay on the floor, where it had landed last night, a cruel reminder. She didn't bother to call for a bellboy in case they alerted Xavier.

She was outside the hotel and hailing a cab, sitting in it with the driver looking at her expectantly before she could function. She still had hours to go before her plane that night. She directed him to the villa. It was the only other place she could think of. She'd wait there until she had to leave.

Up in the villa, she felt as though she could breathe again. Despite all her brave ideas, notions, how had she ever thought she could walk away unscathed? Sasha hadn't told her anything she hadn't suspected on some level, she had just pointed out the truth...showed her the proof, so to speak. And it hurt like hell. But better that it hurt now. Better than if she'd been waiting in the suite for him to come back. Better than if he'd seen something in her eyes. She could well imagine the panicked look that might have crossed his face, the pity in his eyes as he gently had to tell her that it had been fun...but it was over. No, Sasha had done her a favour.

She heard the low rumble of an engine, which got louder before finally stopping outside the front door. She jumped up. The unmistakable sound of a door being slammed came, and a large shape appeared on the other side of the front door, a harsh knock on the glass.

'Jane! Jane, are you in there? Open this door now. I know you're there…'

Xavier.

She stood behind the wall for a moment, her heart thudding so loudly and heavily that she felt a little faint. The nausea was returning with a vengeance.

She went on shaky limbs to open the door, pasting what she hoped was a bland smile on her face.

He stood there bristling, dark glasses covering his eyes, hands on hips.

'Xavier…'

He pushed his glasses onto his head, and with the sun behind him Jane was blinded for a moment. He took advantage and walked into the open-plan hall. Jane stayed by the door.

'Well? Are you always this rude, or is it just with me?' he asked with deceptive calm.

Every line in her body screamed from being held so tightly. 'What's the big deal, Xavier? I wanted to come back here to collect some things I'd forgotten, and was hoping to get to say goodbye before leaving…'

He came and stood far too close. 'Liar. You were planning on leaving. Sasha told me.'

'What?'

'When I went back to the room and you were gone, I went looking for you. I met Sasha in the lobby and she told me she'd just seen you get in a cab—said you'd told her that you were leaving.'

'But she—' She stopped. What could she say? That Sasha had told her exactly how it was…what his little routine was…how she had organised everything, made it all too easy for his holiday *fling*?

She would not humiliate herself.

'Well?' he asked softly.

Jane wasn't sure what Sasha was playing at. Maybe she

wanted him for herself…maybe she already had him… The thought made Jane feel sick again… Maybe she was tired of accommodating his long line of women. But what did it matter anyway? It didn't change the fact that he would be entertaining someone new next week. Why didn't he just let her go? She looked up into his eyes and felt her equilibrium falter, tried to remember his question. Looked away.

'Nothing, Xavier… Look, I have to leave in a few hours, so what's the point? We're never going to see each other again.'

His hand reached out and caught her under her chin, forcing her face to his. The warmth of his fingers made her want to lean into him. She clenched her jaw.

'I wanted to talk to you about that.'

'What…?' She was having trouble concentrating on what he was saying.

'Never seeing each other again… Forget about this morning. Why don't you stay on for a while? You said yourself you're subbing at the moment, without a permanent teaching position. You're free to do what you want.'

The confusion showed in her eyes as she gazed up into his. She hadn't expected this. Her mind, trying to make sense of what he was saying, seized on the banal.

'But…but I can't just stay here… I've got a mortgage…bills to pay.'

'I could take care of all of that,' he dismissed arrogantly.

The treacherous wings of something that had taken off in her heart were fast crumbling. Jane reached up and brought his hand down. 'So…effectively you would pay for me to stay here?'

He shrugged. 'Yes. I could make it easy for you.'

Jane tried to make sense of it.

'You would keep me here as some sort of…paid woman…a mistress? For an affair?'

'Well, it wouldn't be exactly like that.' His hand sliced the air impatiently. 'You make it sound almost sordid.'

He took her hand and lifted it, not letting her pull away. One thumb rotated in her palm, making slow circles. She could feel herself responding. Her body and head going in completely opposite directions.

'Jane…I haven't had enough of you yet…and I know you feel the same way. Stay…for as long as this lasts.'

For as long as this lasts… That was the problem. It wouldn't last for ever for him, and when it was over he'd move on, desire sated and she knew she'd be feeling about a million times worse than this very moment. *He's used to doing this.*

Jane pulled her hand out of his with a jerky movement. The nausea that had diminished rose again, making her feel light-headed, and dirty, tainted, when she thought of how Sasha had set up last night's date for him, as if Jane were some kind of concubine. It lent a harsh quality to her voice.

'No, Xavier. I don't want to be your mistress. You'll find a replacement soon enough. This week has been more than enough for me.'

She'd had enough? Who was she kidding? She'd never get enough of this man. A lifetime wouldn't be enough…and anything less wouldn't do. And he was not in the market for lifetime commitments. How could she have forgotten that first night by the pool? Sherry had told her about his reputation.

She could see the muscle twitch in his jaw, knew she'd made a hit. She held herself erect. His ego might be wounded, but that would be it. He'd get over it. She, on the other hand…wouldn't.

'I'm not interested,' she said, as if to drive the point home.

He took a step back and Jane felt a rush of air between them and a wave of desolation washed over her. The shuttered look descended. A look she hadn't seen since that first time they'd spoken. It made her want to reach out and touch him. He backed away again and put on his shades.

'If that's what you want.'

She nodded miserably, trying to maintain a look of bland indifference. He turned and went through the door.

And then he was gone. The engine gunned fiercely, and with a spurt of gravel it died away into the distance. Jane couldn't keep it down any longer, and just made it to the toilet—where she threw up violently.

Xavier forced his hands to relax their death grip on the wheel as he sped away. What a fool he'd been, allowing her to get under his skin so easily. How dared she turn him down? His hand slapped the wheel. She thought she was too good for him.

An utter fool. That was what he was. She was nothing but a tourist, looking for a story to bring home. The sooner he put the last week and her out of his mind for good, the better.

CHAPTER EIGHT

Nearly Four Months Later

JANE shouldered her way through the door of her one-bedroom ground-floor flat, shutting out the noise of the traffic and wailing sirens. She was soaked. Autumn was here with a vengeance. She dropped the bags of shopping and kicked off her shoes with relief, taking off her layers and leaving them to drip dry in the bathroom. She ran a quick hot bath and afterwards wrapped herself in her dressing gown, feeling a little better. She would have to be more careful. She sat gratefully on her sofa, placing a hand on her belly. She still couldn't believe she was pregnant. But she was.

She remembered the shock of that day when, after weeks of relentless nausea on her return from France and then no sign of her period, dread had settled in her heart. Finally, one day after work, she had worked up the nerve to buy an over the counter test. A positive result. Confirmed by the doctor.

She hadn't told anyone yet. Not even her mother. Even now she was barely able to contain her heartbreak. It was far, far worse than she had imagined. She had fobbed Lisa off when asked about the holiday, being vague, and Lisa thankfully had responded with her usual exasperated roll of the eyes, before launching into the latest adventure of her own love-life.

Her hand moved abstractedly over her belly. She had never contemplated not keeping the baby. That wasn't an option. She sighed heavily as the object of her every waking and sleeping thought intruded.

Xavier.

She knew she couldn't live a lie, couldn't have the baby and not have the truth known. She had to let him know. But how to tell him? How to get in touch with him? How to be prepared in case he got heavy-handed and demanded...what? Jane remembered him telling her that he was last in his line. No doubt an heir figured somewhere in his future. Just not with someone like her.

But would he demand she hand over the baby? She felt a sliver of fear. She didn't think he would be capable, but then he was so powerful. An heir to his fortune was important, necessary for the survival of the island...

She would have to be strong and not let him bully her. She doubted he'd want to be saddled with a small baby anyway. It would seriously cramp his lifestyle.

She grimaced. She'd gone from a world where Xavier had never existed to one in which, since she'd come home, every paper she opened seemed to have a picture of him. In New York, Paris, Milan... In each place a new fortune being made, a new woman on his arm. Each time like a knife in her heart.

She got up wearily and went through the motions of cooking dinner, eating it and tasting nothing. Afterwards she went into the bathroom and saw the pool of water on the floor under her dripping clothes. She went to get the Sunday papers she was about to throw away, opening them out on the floor to soak up the water.

For a second she didn't even notice that she'd stopped breathing, then shook her head as if to clear it. The photo and the words didn't disappear. It was the business section. His face stared at her starkly from the page under a headline:

FRENCH BILLIONAIRE IN UK TO SAVE AILING HOTEL CHAIN

Xavier Salgado-Lézille, the French entrepreneur, owner of Lézille island and the exclusive hotel chain of the same name, is in London this week in negotiations to save the once luxurious chain of Lancaster hotels…

In recent times they have deteriorated…

Has his own offices in the City…

Other companies interested in his expertise…

Why do we have to look abroad to be saved…?

The words swam up at her from the page. She sank down oblivious to the wet floor. Checked the date. Yesterday. That meant he was here this week. Incredibly.

She read it again. He had offices in the City. She went to her phone book and checked with nerveless fingers. Sure enough, there it was, the address and phone number. Why hadn't she thought of that before? She checked the clock. It was still business hours. Just.

Before she could think or lose her nerve she dialled the number from the book. A crisp voice answered. She asked to be put through to Xavier's personal secretary.

'Hello, Molly Parker here.'

'Hello…are you Mr Salgado-Lézille's personal secretary?'

'Yes, I am. May I ask who is calling please?'

'It's…my name is Jane Vaughan. Could you tell him please that I'd like to make an appointment to see him?'

Her heart was beating so hard and fast she was surprised the other woman couldn't hear it. Her hands felt slippery with sweat.

His assistant sounded suspicious. 'Very well—please hold for a moment.'

After a couple of agonising minutes she came back on the line. 'Mr Salgado will see you at ten-thirty tomorrow morning. He's very busy, you know—'

'I'm well aware of that. I won't take up much of his time, thank you.'

Jane put down the phone with a shaking hand. Automatically she placed a hand on her belly and sank into the sofa. The phone rang again, shrill in the room. She jumped violently, picking it up warily, as if it would bite her.

'Oh, Mum it's you... No, I wasn't expecting anyone else—don't be silly.'

In the course of the conversation Jane decided it was time to break the news. Now that she was going to see Xavier and tell him. After all, she was beginning to show.

Her mother was disappointed that Jane was going to have the baby on her own, knowing all too well how hard it had been for her after Jane's father died, and she was worried because she and Arthur were going to be leaving England, but Jane made sure to reassure her on that score. The last thing she wanted was to be responsible for Arthur not being able to take his new bride away to their new life. He had grown up in South Africa, and after the honeymoon he had persuaded her mother to emigrate to the warmer climes of Cape Town.

Jane knew her mother was stubborn and that Arthur would do whatever she wanted. They were due to leave in three weeks, and Jane was determined that they go. She hoped she had done the right thing in telling her.

As if the telephone wires were buzzing, the phone rang again shortly after. It was Lisa. She decided to tell her too, feeling a little more weight lift off her shoulders. She refused to say who the father was, only that she was going to see him the next day and that, no, he wouldn't be a part of her life.

After the initial screech Lisa was for once stunned into silence. Jane managed to see the humour and appreciate this uncustomary role-reversal. It was nice to have the support of a friend, but she declined her offer to come with her. She had to face Xavier alone.

* * *

The following morning in the cab, Jane tried to quell the mammoth butterflies in her stomach. She felt nauseous, and knew it wasn't morning sickness. She hadn't had that in a few weeks now. The thought of seeing Xavier again had her blood running cold through her veins. Then hot. How would he look in this climate? Somehow less? As if! She knew all too well that he would stand out like an exotic hothouse flower.

Luckily, after an intensely busy period with work, the teacher she had been subbing for had returned from sick leave, and Jane as yet hadn't been placed anywhere else. She couldn't contemplate it right now.

The cab drew up under an ominously grey sky outside a huge gleaming building.

Salgado-Lézille Enterprises.

After she got out she fought the urge to turn around, step right back into the cab and tell the driver to go back to her flat. Instead she put one foot in front of the other.

Inside the building there was a hushed reverence more in keeping with a cathedral. No doubt because the boss was in attendance, she thought darkly.

At the reception desk she gave her name and got a security tag. Then she was directed to the top floor. The lift was entirely glass, and she could see the ground floor slip away. The panic rose again.

After agonisingly long seconds it came to a stop and the door swished open with a little ping. She stepped into a luxuriously carpeted hall. A pretty girl behind a desk took her name again, and told her where she could wait on a comfortable couch just outside some huge imposing oak doors. Jane had dressed down, in jeans, sneakers and a sweater. She didn't want him to think she was coming here for anything else. And she was protective of her small telltale bump.

The door opened and her heart jumped into her mouth. It

revealed a matronly woman with a neat grey bob. She emerged, holding out a hand.

'Hello, dear, you must be Jane. I'm Molly, Mr Salgado's UK assistant. Please come through.'

Jane stuttered a few words and followed her into an office where Molly took her coat and stopped outside another set of doors. It was like Fort Knox. She rapped lightly on the door, and opened it before turning to let Jane pass through. She felt a hysterical moment of wanting to bury her head in this woman's chest and have her tell her it would all be OK. But she didn't.

When she walked in she couldn't see Xavier at first, the office was so big. She felt at a serious disadvantage. The door clicked shut behind her.

Then she saw him. Standing with hands in his pockets in an exquisite suit before a huge window that took in the whole of London, or so it seemed. His tall dark shape was silhouetted against the skyline. Master of all he surveyed.

The blood rushed to her head and there was a roaring in her ears. He was saying something, coming towards her. She could feel herself swaying for an interminable moment, but just before she fell strong arms came around her and then she was half-sitting, half-lying on some sort of chaise longue. Xavier was crouching down beside her, holding a glass with some dark liquid.

'Here—take a sip of this. You're whiter than a ghost.'

In such close proximity every cell jumped to zinging life. So much for hoping that any attraction might have diminished. It was still there, like a plug going back into a socket. The energy running between them was palpable.

She moved to sit up. 'I'm sorry, I don't know what happened…'

'When was the last time you ate?'

'What?'

'Food—you know, we use it to stay alive. You look as though you haven't eaten a square meal in weeks.'

Jane stifled a defensive retort. She knew she'd lost weight since she'd got home, but she just hadn't had time…and the doctor had reassured her that it was quite a normal phenomenon to actually lose weight when first becoming pregnant.

'I'm fine…it's isn't any concern of yours what I eat or don't eat.'

He left the untouched glass on a table beside her and stepped away. 'Of course not… To what do I owe the pleasure of your visit?'

Jane stood, not liking the way he was towering over her, and was relieved that the dizziness had dissipated somewhat.

'I've come to tell you something.'

His gaze slanted down at her, no trace of warmth on his face.

'Ah…could it be that you're having second thoughts about my offer? Back in the cold, grey reality of England you're realising what an opportunity you passed up?'

She looked at him blankly for a second before exploding, nerves making her reaction stronger. 'Unbelievable…how arrogant is that? You know, I never thought you had such an inflated sense of self, but obviously I was wrong.'

'Well, then, why are you here?' he sneered. 'Hardly to catch up on old times, eh? As I seem recall you were only too eager to see the back of me that morning…couldn't even wait to say goodbye.'

Her head started to pound. This wasn't going to plan. First almost fainting, and now he thought she wanted to be his mistress after all.

'No…I mean yes. Look, I really do have something to tell you, and it's not easy…' She looked at him beseechingly.

She breathed a sigh of relief when she saw him sit down behind his desk. Space. She sat down on the other side, her hands held tight together in her lap.

'The fact is…I know I said that I thought it was OK, but I was wrong…the truth is…'

'Yes?' he bit out impatiently.

She squared her chin and looked at him unflinchingly. 'I'm pregnant.'

The words dropped into a deafening silence. He didn't react. His face was like a mask, Jane had a moment of clarity when she knew that was why he was so successful at business—a perfect poker face. He got up and went to stand at the window with his back to her.

'Xavier…'

'I heard you,' he said, in a curiously flat voice. Then he turned around abruptly, green eyes pinning her to the spot.

'It's mine?' A slight inflection made it a question.

She stood angrily, her whole frame quivering. 'Well, of course it's yours…how dare you imply that you might not be the father? I haven't had time to do anything since I got home much less find a new lover and try to get pregnant in the gleeful anticipation of tracking you down and trying to pass the baby off as yours.'

He ran an impatient hand through his hair, and for the first time she noticed lines on his face that she didn't remember. He looked tired.

'Look, I'm sorry…it's just a bit much to take in. How much…when are you due?'

'In March.'

'It must have been that first time.'

'Yes.' Jane felt a blush ascending from her chest all the way up to her face. Couldn't stop the torrent of images that were all too frequent, haunting her imagination. She tried to avoid his focus. She started babbling. 'Ah…look, I just wanted to let you know. The last thing I want is for you to feel that you have to be responsible for anything…I don't expect anything from you at all. I'm going to bring the baby up myself. Of course you can come and see him…or her…whenever you want. Why don't I let you get used to the idea?'

She placed a card on the table. 'That's my address and number.'

She was practically at the door before he seemed to break himself out of his stupor. 'Jane, wait…we need to talk about this.'

Just then the door opened, and Molly appeared with some men behind her.

'Not now, Molly, please.'

Even Jane balked at the barely leashed anger in his voice, but Molly seemed to have weathered worse, and stood her ground.

'Mr Salgado, it's the men from Tokyo…remember, they only have one hour in London before they have to fly to New York? You yourself specifically requested this meeting.'

Jane took full advantage of the opportunity and fled before he could stop her, grabbing her coat, mumbling a goodbye to Molly.

Xavier tried to keep his mind on the meeting after Jane left but, the truth was that he was blown away. Everything was distilled down to her and the fact that she was pregnant. He still felt remnants of the pure elation that had surged through him when he had seen her again. Then the concern that had ripped through him when she had gone so white and almost collapsed. The feel of her slender body in his arms…his inappropriate response.

Alone again in his office, he held her card in his hand. The truth was that he had been in possession of her address for a couple of months now. It hadn't been hard to trace her. He wasn't sure if he'd really planned on getting in touch with her. But one thing was for certain: he hadn't been able to get her out of his head. Oh, he had tried. With various women. But when it had come to it, he just couldn't. Her face, the smell of her body…the way she had responded to his touch…would flash into his head and render him more or less impotent.

Him…impotent!

He obviously just hadn't had enough of her—needed to get her out of his system once and for all. When he'd heard she had phoned he had thought it was because she'd realised the same thing. But it wasn't.

Pregnant. The word fell heavily into his head. It brought up images, memories… A dark emotion threatened to rise up. His fists clenched. He wouldn't think about that now. Things were complicated. However, he knew what he wanted with a fierceness that surprised him. He didn't want to look too closely at his reasoning yet, or why it was so strong, he just knew it was the only solution. And he knew exactly how to get to her to comply, whether she wanted to or not. Uncomfortably he was aware that it was more than likely *not*. And he didn't like how that felt.

That evening Jane tried to relax. It was impossible. Her whole body felt as though it had received an injection of some vital life force energy. When she had got back to the flat she'd changed into tracksuit bottoms and an old baggy sweatshirt.

Xavier was in the country, and as long as he was she couldn't rest easy. She hoped that he would just leave her alone. Let her get on with things.

The doorbell rang.

It couldn't be…could it? She went towards the door, her hands balled into fists, opening it warily.

'Dominic.' She breathed a sigh of relief, but also felt a stab of disappointment. Lisa's brother stood on the doorstep. She hadn't seen him since she'd got back, had avoided his persistent calls.

'Come in…what are you doing here?' She ushered him into the sitting room.

He was shy, as usual, not really able to meet her eye. 'Look, I won't beat around the bush…Lisa told me about your…being pregnant.'

A blush stained his freckled cheeks, and Jane's heart went out to him, but she didn't interrupt.

'The thing is, Jane…well, you know how I feel about you.

I came to say that I'm here if you need someone to lean on. That is, if you'd have me, I'd marry you.'

A lump came into her throat. 'Oh, Dominic…that's so sweet. I'm very flattered that you would offer to marry me, but the truth is—'

The doorbell rang again. Jane muttered an apology and went to open it.

Xavier.

Standing on the doorstep, crowding the small doorway.

The breath was driven from her lungs and her body reacted spectacularly, a million miles away from what her head was trying to impose on it. She felt a tremor start in her legs.

She had completely forgotten about Dominic until she heard him behind her. 'Janey, love, are you all right? Do you know this man?'

She came out of her reverie.

'Yes.'

She let Xavier pass her to come into the small hall, feeling a hysterical giggle bubbling up from somewhere deep in her belly.

'Dominic, this is Xavier Salgado-Lézille. Xavier, this is Dominic Miller—an old friend of mine.'

The men looked at each other with deep suspicion. Jane knew she had to put Dominic out of his misery. She threw a quelling look at Xavier and showed him into the sitting room, shutting the door behind him.

Leading Dominic away from the door, she said, 'Xavier is my baby's father…and it wouldn't be fair to take you up on your offer because…' her voice gentled '…I'm not in love with you.'

'Are you in love with him?'

She nodded her head mutely.

'Is he in love with you?'

She shook her head. 'But he will take care of me and the baby if I so wish. I know that. You don't have to worry about me.'

She pressed a kiss to his cheek, making him colour again.

'Are you sure you're OK…? I can stay if you want.'

Jane shook her head, ignoring her rapid pulse. Dominic was no match for Xavier.

She let him out, the difference in the two men comical as they passed in the hallway. At the sitting room door took a deep breath before going in.

Xavier was pacing the small room, dwarfing it with his size and presence.

'Who was that?'

She bristled at the proprietorial tone in his voice, hating the effect he was having on her.

'He's my best friend's brother.'

'What did he want?'

'It's none of your business what he wanted.' She sat down to disguise the trembling in her legs, then contradicted herself, saying disbelievingly, 'As a matter of fact, he asked me to marry him.'

'Did you say yes…*Janey, love*?' Xavier's voice was sharp.

She looked up. His face was shuttered, his eyes giving nothing away. Her heart twisted at the mocking way he repeated Dominic's friendly endearment.

'What's it to you? I can marry whoever I want.'

He hauled her up against his chest so quickly that she didn't have time to protest before his mouth descended and his lips found hers. After a second of shock she was like someone dying of thirst who had found water in the desert. With a small whimper she wrapped her arms around his neck, and their tongues collided in a heated feverish dance.

Time stood still.

She was home.

Then he thrust her away from him.

'*That's* why it's my business. You're carrying my baby— and don't tell me you react like that with everyone.'

Shocked blue eyes clashed with blistering green.

'That's why, if you marry anyone, it'll be me. No one

else. Our baby deserves to be brought up within a marriage. He is going to be my heir, and as such will be afforded the necessary ceremony for his inheritance.'

The shock of what he was suggesting rendered her speechless for a moment.

'I will not marry you just for the sake of an heir. Don't be so ridiculous… It would be a sham…and anyway it could be a girl,' she pointed out somewhat pedantically.

He threw off his overcoat and jacket, loosening his tie. He was like a panther in a confined space. Hands on hips.

'Boy or girl… You would deny our child—possibly the only child I may ever have—its inheritance?'

Jane gasped. 'Are you threatening me? That if I don't marry you then you will effectively deny its existence?'

'It won't be up to me… Before my father died he added a codicil to his will stating that should I have any children outside marriage they wouldn't be entitled to anything. It was his way of ensuring the line would continue in our family's name, ensuring that the island stays in the family.' He shrugged. 'He was very conservative, and there's no way around it.'

She had a sudden memory of the numerous pictures of Xavier with countless women in the press, and words tumbled out, barely coherent to her muddled brain.

'You've had to check that out already? Maybe you have other children dotted around the world—Milan, Paris—?'

He took her by the shoulders. 'No, I don't. I don't make a habit of jumping in and out of bed with countless partners, and I always make sure I'm protected…. Just with you…with you something happened.'

His hands were biting into her shoulders. Something had happened, all right, and she could see how much he hated to admit it. It was in every strained line in his face. He had been taken over by the lust of the moment, whereas she had been taken over by much, much more. She could remember all too well what had happened. She had let good sense out and madness in. She tried to avoid his probing gaze.

'OK...maybe you don't, but what you're suggesting is positively medieval. Surely in this day and age—'

'Did you really think I'd just walk away? I'm offering you everything on a plate...security, respectability, a name for our child.'

Everything but yourself... This heir is everything to him... as important as she had suspected.

She sought for rational words in a brain that was fast becoming fuzzier and fuzzier. 'He or she could still take your name, if it's that important. I can't...please don't make me...'

'There's no need to go green. It doesn't have to be a completely unpleasant experience. We're still attracted to each other—you can't deny feeling it too, the minute you walked into my office today.'

He didn't have to remind her of that mortifying fact. She brought huge wary eyes up to his. 'Yes, but that's all, isn't it?'

His face was expressionless. He shrugged negligently. 'It's more than a lot of people start out with. Jane, I'm thirty-six. It's time I got married and produced an heir.'

She felt a hysterical laugh bubble up again. 'It's almost as if I've fallen in with some cosmic plan to save your family legacy.'

The lines in his face were harsh, and suddenly she didn't feel like laughing. This was all too real.

'Don't mock me, Jane. There aren't many women who would turn down an offer like this.'

Even though his words reeked with arrogance, she didn't doubt for a second that what he said was true. She just happened to hold the ace. His seed inside her belly. Lucky her. She had pipped all the contenders to the post. She tried another tack.

'Yes, but most people start out with love, however misguided...at least it's there to start.'

'And where does it leave them in the end? At least we would be going into this with eyes open—without the illusion of love to cloud things. I believe we have something we can work on, Jane. I wouldn't suggest it otherwise.'

She shifted out from under his hands and sank back down onto the couch, feeling hunted.

Something we can work on...

She knew all too well what he meant. It saturated the air around them.

He hunched down before her, not letting her evade his compelling gaze. 'Jane, the future of Lézille is at stake if I don't provide an heir. This could be my only child.'

She looked at him, helpless.

The doorbell rang again. Xavier went to answer it. She didn't even notice. But she did when she heard the voices. Her mother and Arthur. She closed her eyes. It couldn't get any worse.

Her mother came into the room with one brow arched so high that it almost met her hairline.

'Hello, Mum.' Jane hugged her, feeling the onset of tears in her maternal presence.

She quickly made the introductions, without saying precisely who Xavier was, but she could see that her mother had deduced exactly what his role was.

Unbelievably, Xavier offered to go into the kitchen to make some tea, leaving them alone for a few minutes and making her feel even more confused. How could he come in here and take over so effortlessly? Her mother and Arthur were certainly looking after him with barely disguised awe.

'So that's…?' Arthur nodded in the direction of Xavier's retreating back.

Jane nodded miserably.

'Well, darling, you don't look very happy about it,' her mother whispered.

I'm not!

Her mother and Arthur looked at each other before linking hands. The lump grew in her throat again.

'Dear…we've had a long think, and we came to tell you that if you're still determined to go it alone…we're going to stay here in England.'

Jane started to protest and her mother shushed her, holding up a hand. 'Now, I know what you're going to say, but it's decided… There is no way we can leave you here on your own to bring up that child, and that's final.'

Despite the encouraging smiles on their faces, she could see how hard it had been for them to make this decision. And there was no way she could let them. Her Mum's happiness involved Arthur too. And right now they came first. She could mess up her own life, but not the life of this woman in front of her, who had sacrificed so much already.

She heard Xavier's step approach the sitting room and knew what she had to do. She went with her gut. In that split second she knew she was about to make a choice that was going to change her life. She hoped and prayed that it was the right one. She didn't have time to consider the ramifications.

He came in to the room with a laden tray. Jane waited until he had put it down and the tea was passed out before speaking, and tried to keep a steady voice.

'Mum, Arthur…I really appreciate what you want to do for me, but you see there's no need.'

She glanced at Xavier's ever unreadable face. She wasn't going to get any help there. She took a deep breath.

'You don't have to stay here because…you see…I'm not going to be here.'

Her mother and Arthur looked at each other blankly, then at Xavier and then at her.

'What are you talking about, dear?'

Jane mentally crossed her fingers and took poetic licence with her recent conversation with Xavier. 'Xavier has asked me to marry him…and I am going to say…yes.'

She could hear a splutter of tea come from his corner of the room. Then she was enveloped in hugs and tears and congratulations. Xavier joined in and answered questions vaguely. She was very aware of his sharp, assessing eyes on her all the time.

She knew she had done the right thing, however, when she saw the badly disguised relief on their faces at the prospect that their dream would be fulfilled after all.

Finally, after what seemed an age, they were gone. She went back into the sitting room to find Xavier standing at the window. He turned around and fixed her with hard eyes.

'I gather that little charade was for the benefit of persuading your mother that she and her husband could emigrate after all?'

'Well, it's not going to be a charade unless you won't marry me.'

He approached her softly, coming dangerously close. 'If you were trying to call my bluff then it didn't work. We *will* be getting married. I suppose I should have thanked your mother for helping you to come to your decision…' He gave a short harsh laugh. 'You couldn't have made it clearer that it's the last thing you'd be doing otherwise.'

'You're right. I hate you for this.' Her chest felt tight and restricted, her hands clammy.

A savage intensity flashed over his face so briefly that she might have imagined it before it was gone, and he drawled, 'That hate will just fuel our passion…because it is still there.'

She vowed there and then that there would be no passion. If he so much as touched her, she wasn't sure that she could contain her feelings—and if he guessed for a second…her life would be hell.

He left with a promise to return and discuss things in the morning, and after the door shut behind him Jane sagged against it, the stuffing knocked out of her.

Despite everything that had just transpired, somewhere

within herself she felt curiously at peace. Was she so straight that once she had agreed to doing 'the right thing' she felt good? It couldn't be. What was more likely, she feared, was that she was such a masochist that even though being married to Xavier spelt certain heartbreak, it also meant she got to be with him…and seeing him again had proved how completely he held her heart in his hands.

The baby. How could she deny this little person access to his or her father? To their birth heritage? Especially one so rich—and not just in monetary terms. She knew instinctively that Xavier would be a good father.

Her mind went a more incendiary route. Would he be faithful if she refused to sleep with him? A man as virile and highly sexed as Xavier would not stand for a celibate marriage. How could she hope to live side by side with him and resist him? All she knew was that she had to, for now. Her emotions were too raw…too close to the surface. Maybe in time, when they were more under control, she could… remain detached. As if there ever could be such a time.

She went to bed with a heavy heart and slept fitfully.

The next morning when she opened the door to admit Xavier he took in her pinched face and the dark smudges under her eyes. The pang that struck him when he realised that he was the one who was making her look this unhappy gripped him unawares. He quashed it ruthlessly.

Jane eyed him warily with crossed arms as he effortlessly commanded her small flat again. He was dressed in a suit that hugged his frame, making him seem even more powerful, dynamic. He looked exotic and foreign, his tan standing out against the grimly grey backdrop outside. Stupendously gorgeous.

'I've arranged for us to be married here in London in just over two weeks time at a register office. It's the earliest I could arrange… Also it should be easier for your mother and Arthur to attend before they leave for South Africa. If there's anyone else you want to witness it…'

His efficiency and ability to make the powers that be fall into his plans stunned her—and his unexpected sensitivity to accommodate her mother.

'Well, yes…' She thought of Lisa. 'There's one or two people, maybe…'

'*Bien.* I have to go to New York today, and will be gone until the day of the wedding, so I trust that will give you time to pack up here, tie up any loose ends and inform your work. Molly can arrange to have this place let or sold, whichever you prefer.'

She spoke quickly. 'Let…that is, I don't want to sell it.'

Somehow the thought of severing all ties was too much just now.

He shrugged as if he didn't care.

'Fine. As you wish. I'll let her know she can go ahead with arrangements and find a suitable agent?'

Jane nodded dumbly.

'After the wedding we will stop over in Paris for a short honeymoon. We can replenish your wardrobe there.' He eyed her casual attire critically. 'You'll have a certain role to fulfil as my wife, and will need to be dressed suitably.'

His bossy tone was too much.

'I think I know how to dress myself, thank you very much… You don't have to spend your money on me.'

'Very commendable, darling, but somehow I don't think you could afford even the price tags on the kind of clothes I'm talking about,' he drawled, with infuriating arrogance.

'Fine…' She threw her hands up. 'If you want to spend thousands on making me into something I will never be except on paper, then go ahead and be my guest.'

He came and stood right in front of her. She could feel his breath warm on her face. Her heart lurched as he drifted a finger down one cheek and underneath to her neck, where her pulse was beating crazily against her skin.

'Oh, but you will, Jane...you will. Trust me on that.'

CHAPTER NINE

Two weeks later Jane was trying to contain herself as she felt an increasing sense of panic threaten to overwhelm her. Lisa and her mother fussed around her as she got ready to go to the register office, their chatter skimming over her head:

'…and poor Dominic is heartbroken, but he happened to mention that Xavier is gorgeous…'

'Oh, he is, dear—wait till you see him…'

'And he really owns a whole island?'

'That's nothing…his hotel chain…'

'Still waters, eh, Mrs V? Who would have thought our little Janey had it in her? And to think of all those holidays spent with him under my nose—the time I wasted on those waiters…'

Jane cut in with wry exasperation. 'You know, I *am* here, guys.'

'Yes, dear, don't mind us…now, let's have a look at you.'

She was wearing a fitted cream silk jacket and a matching skirt that was cut on the bias and fell in soft swinging folds to her knees. The material clung to her curves, and the buttons on the jacket closed under her bust, with a lace camisole just visible in a slightly darker shade of off-white. An effective camouflage for her thickening middle.

Her mother hadn't grilled her too much since her revelations and announcement. She assumed she and Xavier had

had some sort of lovers' tiff, and was blithely unaware of the circumstances—which Jane was quite happy with.

She contemplated the rest of the outfit—sheer tights, and high heels covered in the same material as the suit. It wasn't bad for the last minute. Lisa had secured her hair with a flower, and stood back to regard her subject, resplendent herself in a vibrant hot pink dress that clashed magnificently with her red hair.

'Janey, you look like a model… Honestly, what I wouldn't give for your height and figure… When I get pregnant I'm going to be the proverbial whale from day one.'

Right now Jane would have given anything to switch places with Lisa. But of course she couldn't. She had to do this, for the baby and to ensure her mother and Arthur's future. And if she was honest she had to acknowledge the dark part of her that *wanted* to go through with this—wanted to tie herself to Xavier, whatever the cost.

When she saw him standing at the table in front of the registrar she faltered for a moment, her nerve failing her, but in that instant he turned and saw her. They hadn't seen each other since that morning in her flat. It all fell away. Some intensity in his eyes held her. Didn't allow her to break contact. She looked neither left nor right, just went towards him as if he was some kind of homing beacon in a fog. Then she was next to him. It was only the voice of the registrar that brought her back into room and their surroundings.

The words were meaningless. She hoped she made the appropriate response at the right time because she felt disembodied from everything. Before she knew it Xavier was taking a ring from his pocket and placing it on her finger, his hands cool and steady. Then, remarkably, Lisa was handing her a ring—where had that come from?

Jane put it on his finger, it slid on effortlessly. He didn't let go of her hand until the end of the ceremony.

Once it was over they went outside. Xavier told her that

he had arranged for a celebratory breakfast to be held at his London hotel. He led her to a waiting chauffeur-driven Bentley. She could see that there were more people than she had initially noticed, and that there were cars lined up for everyone. He had organised all this?

In the back of the car they were alone once he indicated to the driver to raise the partition. He brought a couple of glasses from a hidden compartment and poured them both some sparkling water. She couldn't help but be aware of his huge frame encased in the dark grey morning suit. The material stretched over hard thighs only inches from hers.

'A poor replacement for champagne, but necessary.'

Jane didn't want him to guess how her insides were churning, the confused anger and frustration she felt at his matter-of-fact tone.

'Let's drink to us.'

'A bit of a lie, don't you think? There's no one around to fool.'

'Let's drink to a truce, then, because we're sure as hell not going to last one week if you stay in that filthy mood. You've looked like you were going to your own funeral since you arrived.'

Hot tears threatened. She clinked his glass and took a sip, feeling like a fraud.

'I'm sorry…it's just a little overwhelming… Within weeks of seeing you again I'm married and about to emigrate…'

He surprised her by taking her hand in his and lifting it to his mouth. The heat of his lips pressed to her skin made her insides melt. Along with the look in his eyes.

'Don't think about it now…let's just get through the next few days. It's not exactly been easy for me either, you know.'

For a moment they shared an intense communication. There was something in his face…but then it was gone. A bland expression replaced whatever it was, and Jane couldn't help but feel he was talking about being forced into a marriage he didn't want. She reminded herself how single-minded he was. He hadn't even made an attempt for them to talk about things, get to know one another again. He'd taken off as soon as he knew she'd comply with his demands, spent the last two weeks in New York, and come back only at the last minute. Arrogantly sure of her response.

The car drew to a smooth halt outside the hotel, and they were ushered out and into the melee.

Jane was introduced to so many people that they were soon blurring into one, and her cheeks ached from smiling. Her feet ached too, and for the first time since becoming pregnant she felt exhausted. She was ever conscious of Xavier, and where he was. Whenever she caught his eye he held it for long moments, until she began to get flustered and looked away.

She had just seen off her mother, Arthur and Lisa, whose own parents had come too. Jane had been delighted to see Lisa's dad, looking so well after his scare. Her friend had promised to visit soon, and her mother was planning on coming when the baby was born.

Standing alone in the doorway of the function room, she felt awkward with all these unknown people. Some of them were friends of Xavier's and seemed perfectly nice; others were business acquaintances.

Suddenly he materialised at her side, slipping an arm around her waist, and for once she sank gratefully into him, glad of the support.

'Let's get out of here,' he murmured into her ear.

'Yes, please.' She couldn't disguise the relief in her voice.

He brought her up to the penthouse suite. The staff had left out a bottle of champagne and there were rose petals all over the bed.

What a waste…

She turned to face Xavier as he closed and locked the door. He came towards her, pulling off his bow tie and opening his shirt. She could see his eyes darkening and saw the intention in them. It reached out and caressed her across the room, and she could feel every part of herself respond. It was too much. Her feelings were too raw. She backed away.

'Xavier…please. I'm tired…I want to go to sleep.'

He kept coming. 'So do I. With you.'

'No!' She hadn't meant for her voice to come out so strident. 'Just…I need a little space, and I am exhausted.'

She had been exhausted earlier, but now an excess of energy was causing her body to hum, making a lie of her words. Since seeing him again an ache had settled into every cell, an ache that she knew only he could assuage. He stopped in his tracks and she wanted to throw caution to the wind, throw herself at him with an animalistic instinct…rip off his clothes, have him take her right where they were. The strength of her reaction shook her.

'I don't know what you're playing at, but I'll give you the benefit of the doubt for now. I'll go back downstairs for a while. You take the bed…I'll sleep on the couch.'

'Xavier, there's no need—'

'Save it, Jane. If you think we can share that bed tonight without anything happening then you're lying to yourself.'

The door closed ominously quietly behind him.

Jane began to get ready for bed, feeling even more miserable. As if she had somehow cut off her nose to spite her face. Her body still hadn't cooled down since that electrifying look.

She sped through her toilet in record time, and was soon under the sheets, breathing harshly and feeling very silly. After waiting as long as she could, she finally gave in to her exhaustion and slept, not hearing her bedroom door open or Xavier come in and spend long moments looking at her.

The next day on Xavier's private jet, as they flew to Paris, she tried to control her conflicting emotions. She studied him covertly from under her lashes, and twisted the slim white-gold band on her finger as he looked through some paperwork in the seat across the aisle from her. He looked totally at ease, with not a care in the world. Unlike her. She looked out of her window and tried to force herself to relax.

What seemed like only moments later she felt someone shaking her gently. It was Xavier. His face was very close to hers. She could see the darker flecks of green in his eyes. It brought back a vivid image of his pupils dilating as his head descended to hers before he took her mouth with his. She hunched back in the seat to escape the potent memory.

He frowned at her movement. 'What...what is it?' she asked, her voice strained.

'We're here...in Paris.'

She looked out of the window. Sure enough they were on the Tarmac; she could see a waiting limo just at the bottom of the steps. None of the usual Customs or red tape for Xavier and his wife.

Once in the limo, it wasn't long before they were in the thick of traffic in the city. Jane looked out with undisguised awe.

'Have you never been here before?' Xavier asked incredulously.

She shook her head. 'Never had time...or the money. When I left school I worked straight away through college. I wanted to start paying Mum back for all the years that she'd worked her fingers to the bone.'

'If I didn't already know you I'd say that was a line...'

Jane looked at him, shaking her head. 'So cynical...how can you bear it?'

'Not everyone sees the world through rose-tinted glasses.'

'Well, mine are rapidly turning more opaque.'

She could feel his sharp look of enquiry, but didn't elaborate.

She picked out the Eiffel Tower, Notre Dame...and before long she could see that they were going over an ornate bridge on to what looked like an island in the middle of the river.

'Wow...' she breathed.

'This is the Île St-Louis—one of a few islands on the Seine…it's mainly residential.'

I'll say, Jane thought to herself. Chic, immaculately made-up women walked their beautifully coiffed dogs. And she had thought that image of Paris was such a cliché!

They drew to a smooth halt outside one of the buildings and were effusively greeted by the doorman. Jane was fast becoming accustomed again to the bowing and scraping people did in Xavier's vicinity. In the lift she wasn't surprised to see that they went all the way to the top floor. Nothing but the best.

The doors opened straight into a hall with one door, which Xavier opened.

'This is where I come and stay when in Paris on business or for stopovers on long haul journeys—have a look around.'

Jane tore her eyes away from his and did as he asked. It was the quintessential bachelor pad. The age of the building meant that the shell and windows were still of a certain period, but the whole of the inside had been remodelled. The colours were dark, and it was full of sharp corners, with abstract art on the walls, state-of-the-art sound and TV systems. The kitchen was worse, all gleaming steel and not a hint of homeliness in sight. She hated it.

He stood back, arms folded, and watched her face with amusement. She couldn't hide a thing. He felt a sharp, uncustomary burst of pleasure, remembering her refreshing honesty, and became aware of just how much he had missed it…

'You hate it, don't you?'

'I'm sorry…' She blushed. 'It's just so cold and charac-terless.'

And he became aware of how he'd missed her blushes.

'I suppose I'd be offended if I'd actually had a hand in the decoration, but thankfully for my ego I didn't. I allowed a friend who was trying to build up his interior design portfolio the run of the place. I'm here so infrequently that it doesn't really bother me.'

He thought of the women that he had brought here. He couldn't remember one who hadn't oohed and ahed delightedly over every room. Either they had all loved it or, more realistically, said what they thought he wanted to hear. Now he could see it through Jane's eyes he hated it too, and vowed to rip it all out and do it up again.

Her heart hammered when he suddenly took her hand. He led her to a bedroom, where he faced her again.

'What…what are you doing?' she asked desperately, hating the effect just holding his hand was having on her, but determined not to pull away and reveal the extent of her discomfiture.

He indicated with his head round the room, starkly decorated in creams and browns. 'This is your room.'

The relief on her face was comic. 'Thank…thank you.'

He rested heavy hands on her shoulders. 'Your hands-off signals are loud and clear. Rest assured, Jane, I've never forced myself on a woman and I'm not about to now…but you know you're fighting a losing battle, don't you? This scared virginal act is wasted on me. We both know you're no virgin.'

He brought his face down to hers, his mouth close to her ear, and she closed her eyes weakly. His breath tickled the sensitive part of her neck just below her ear. The fine hairs standing up.

'But if you think for a second that you can hold out for ever…then you're very, very mistaken. It's only going to be a matter of time. It's there, vibrating between us like an electric current, and it's not going to go away. Do you know what happens when you suppress something? It just gets stronger and stronger.'

He straightened up, his eyes taking in her flushed face, the bead of sweat on her brow, the pulse hammering against the

base of her neck, and he had to use every ounce of his will-
power not to pull her into him, mould her body to his and
make her acquiesce—which he knew he could do.

He would wait until she was shaking with longing, weak
with desire. Until she could barely look at him because of it.
He wanted her. Badly. But that was all it was. Sheer, unadul-
terated lust. Nothing else. This was why he'd been unable to
get her out of his head the past few months.

'Settle in, and I'll get lunch ready.'

He walked out of the room. Jane pressed her hands up
against flaming cheeks. That was her reaction after mere
words! What would she do if he kissed her? Or if she lost
control and grabbed him? Which seemed more likely right at
that moment. She'd go up like tumbleweed to a lit match on
a dry day.

All the more reason to be strong.

And what then…?

One day at a time. That was the only way she was going
to handle this.

CHAPTER TEN

THE next morning Xavier insisted on a day of sightseeing.

In the early evening they emerged from the Louvre. Jane was bone weary, even though the ever-present limo had whisked them from place to place.

Bone weary because at every opportunity during the day he had touched her—usually just the slightest glance of physical contact, a brush of a hand here, a light touch on her waist or shoulder…pressing close against her in the crowds. But it had been enough to set her nerve-ends jangling, almost as though he knew exactly what he was doing. His face each time she'd sneaked a look had shown pure innocence.

By the time he took her hand outside the great museum she was worn down from trying to escape him, and just left it in his without a word. That contact, chaste as it was, was torture in itself.

'I let Pascal go home… There's a restaurant near here I thought might be nice for dinner. We can get a cab later.'

'I'm not dressed properly…' She indicated her jeans and sneakers.

'Don't worry, it's a low-key place.'

She shrugged and allowed him to lead her through the streets. They came to a charming little bistro, tucked into a small side street, with only a few tables that were already full.

Xavier was greeted like a long-lost son by the proprietor,

and when he introduced Jane as his wife there were shouts and a woman came running out. Jane was enveloped in hugs and warm kisses, and couldn't help but be charmed. The older woman at one point looked at Jane's ring finger and unleashed a stream of French at Xavier that Jane couldn't follow. He looked shamefaced after it.

Once they were seated at a free table that had appeared as if by magic, Jane had to ask, 'What on earth did she say to you?'

'Madame Feron pointed out that you don't have an engagement ring.'

Jane lifted her hand stupidly. 'Oh…I hadn't even thought about it myself.' She looked back to him. 'I don't need one, you know…it'd be silly just for the sake of it. Plenty of people nowadays just wear a wedding band.'

'Nevertheless, she's right. We will do this properly. I'll buy you one tomorrow.'

His tone brooked no argument. His businesslike attitude reinforced her will to resist him at all costs. This was nothing more than a mutual agreement, each having their own reasons: him to secure his heir and its future, her for the baby's sake and to secure her mother's future in South Africa.

But maybe down the road when the baby was born they could negotiate a separation? Surely by then any inheritance would be safe? Jane knew in her heart of hearts that sooner or later her will would break, or Xavier would succumb to another woman, and either scenario would be untenable for long. She knew that now, as she looked at him across the table.

Her appetite still wasn't back to normal, but she forced the food down, not wanting to insult the couple who couldn't stop beaming at them.

That night when they got back to the apartment Jane fled into her room as soon as she could. She rested against the door, breathing heavily with eyes closed. She heard Xavier's step pausing outside her door and her mouth went dry, her pulse tripping.

'Goodnight…' he called softly through the door.

But he may as well have said *coward*. It was what he meant.

She got under the covers a short while later and pulled them over her head, as if that would block out the images, the vivid memories that played like a home movie every night in her dreams. Her body felt as though it had a fever. What was wrong with her? She was pregnant…how could she be feeling so…so…*sexually aware* of herself and him?

She slept fitfully. Again.

The following morning Xavier informed her that they would spend the day shopping and return to the island that evening. When he saw the less than enthusiastic expression on her face he frowned.

'What is it? Are you feeling ill?'

'No…it's nothing…just that I've always hated shopping. The crowds…trying things on. It bores me to tears. But as you say, I have to keep up appearances now.'

He shook his head, once again struck dumb. Reminded of how different she was from the women he was used to.

An hour or so later, when they approached the door of a designer shop, Jane caught his hand and dragged him back. The memory of years of scrimping and saving rushed back in lurid humiliating detail, her mother's face lined with worry and strain as she struggled to let down another hem, trying to get another year out of a school skirt.

'We can't go in there…those clothes cost a fortune. Look, why don't you just let me go off for a few hours? I'll find some high street stores and kit myself out. Honestly, you can trust me…'

'Woman!' he exploded, stunning her into silence. 'I'm normally dragged on these expeditions, reduced to nothing more than a walking credit card, but you—' He shook his head. 'You have to have morals. Jane, without insulting your intelligence too much, will you please trust me when I say that if I let you go off and *kit yourself out*, as you put it, within weeks we will be at some function where it will be horrendously obvious to everyone that I can't afford to dress my own wife. This isn't just for you. As much as I agree with your sensibilities, unfortunately society hasn't caught up with us, and I have a certain standard to maintain.'

Her mouth opened and closed ineffectually, a red-hot poker of pain striking her at his reference to what must have been many other trips like this…with other women he had indulged. She walked into the shop without another word, hoping to distract him from her hurt.

By that afternoon she'd lost count of the shops… Dresses, casual clothes, shoes, underwear—which thankfully he had absented himself for—and last but not least maternity wear. She had worked very hard at putting images of other women out of her head, and berated herself for not expecting as much in the first place.

Xavier had arranged for everything to be sent straight to the plane and loaded up. Once they were on it themselves, later that day, Jane felt a pang of guilt mixed with fear. Xavier saw the look on her face.

'What is it?'

She shook her head rapidly. 'Nothing…nothing at all.'

Everything!

She averted her head and looked out of the window. When she thought about the afternoon she had to admit that she had enjoyed it on some level. Who wouldn't have? Assistants fawning all over her. Well, over Xavier's credit card, to be accurate. And what on the surface must have looked like a doting husband indulging his new bride. The covetous looks of the other women hadn't gone unnoticed. At one point she had even felt the old warmth creep up, when one of the women had been particularly sycophantic. Jane had looked to Xavier and caught his identical look, and a bubble of delighted communication had almost transformed her face, made her forget why she was there. But that would be far too dangerous. What they had shared in the summer was not who he really was. She had to remember that.

Once the small plane was cruising, and the seat belt signs were off, she saw Xavier turn towards her from the corner of her eye.

'Jane, I have something for you.'

She turned to look.

'More? What could you possibly—?'

She went silent when she saw him reach into the inside pocket of his jacket and pull out a small box, which he offered her across the aisle. She looked at him and her hands shook slightly as took it. When she opened it she gasped. Nestled in a bed of cream velvet was the most stunning sapphire ring in an antique square setting of tiny diamonds and white-gold. It was beautiful. How could he have picked exactly what she would have gone for herself?

'How did you know…?'

'I remembered something you told me once about sapphires being your favourite stone…'

She couldn't help but be touched that he had remembered.

'We can change it if you don't like it,' he said stiffly.

She looked up quickly. 'I lo—' She stopped herself and amended her words. 'It's beautiful.'

She put it on her finger with a tremor in her hand. A perfect fit.

He went back to his papers; she went back to looking out of the window, with the sting of tears in her eyes at the sterility of the exchange.

They landed at the private air strip on Lézille in the early evening.

Xavier's four-wheel drive was parked nearby, and he expertly negotiated his way out of the tiny airstrip and towards the castle, silhouetted on the horizon against a darkening sky.

This time it wasn't empty. A retinue of people were lined up to welcome them home. Most of the names and faces were a blur as Jane struggled to hang onto them. A gardener, cook, maid...and at the head of the queue Xavier introduced her with obvious affection to Jean-Paul and Yvette who, he told her, had run the castle since he was a baby. They had the same dark distinctively Spanish features of the rest of the islanders.

Before she knew what was happening, Xavier had lifted her up to carry her over the threshold. When he put her down again she stood back, trembling and breathing hard...disconcerted. Another tear threatened....for about the third time that day. She told herself it must be her hormones, emotions too close to the surface. She couldn't read his face, searching desperately for some indication that his motivation wasn't ironic. Or an act purely for the staff, who were looking on delightedly. She had to admit that was more likely. But his face was shuttered, expressionless. She controlled her wayward reactions.

Yvette shyly led Jane upstairs to the master bedroom. It all looked familiar, and exactly how she remembered it. Little had she known that she'd ever be back...married and pregnant. She sank onto the side of the bed and looked around, feeling a little removed from everything. Her life had changed so completely within just a few months, a total one-hundred-and-eighty-degree turn. Goosebumps prickled across her skin and she wrapped her arms around herself, feeling a sudden chill.

She went to look out of the window. The scenery was as vividly breathtaking as she remembered, just slightly less lush than it had been in the summer.

A movement out of the corner of her eye made her look round. Xavier had appeared in the door, holding one of her bags.

With sudden panic and clarity she realised something. 'Xavier...this is your room.'

'Yes. And now it's your room too.'

He walked in, closing the door behind him, coming uncomfortably close. Jane wrapped her arms tighter around herself, forcing herself to remain calm. But it was difficult. The bed in the corner of her eye loomed large and threatening; the memories were rushing back.

'We are not sleeping together.'

'Yes, we are.' He enunciated each word with chilling softness.

'No.'

He ran an angry hand through his hair and Jane could feel the energy crackle around them. 'Jane, we are going to share this room if I have to lock us both in here every night. If the staff see us sleeping separately, word of a fractured marriage will spread before morning. And I will not have that. We may as well not have bothered getting married.'

Jane threw her hands in the air and moved away jerkily, pacing back and forth. 'Don't be ridiculous. If I sleep in the other room I can make sure the sheets are pristine every morning…I'll—'

'Now you're being ridiculous. Tell me, Jane…why the great resistance? Don't you remember how it was between us?'

Didn't she remember?

Her stomach dropped with sudden panic under his narrowed gaze. Resisting him…and this overwhelming desire…was the only way she knew how to protect herself. He *couldn't* ever know…and if he started to look at her motives…

She wouldn't even contemplate that scenario. She placed a protective hand on her belly. It might as well have been over her heart. She mustered up a look that would have frozen boiling water, her blue eyes chips of ice,

'This baby is the only thing I care about. I'm pregnant, Xavier, I don't feel those…*urges*.'

She hated using the baby like this, but she needed all the armour she could get. Anything that would keep him at a distance. She knew that he would not step over the line…

unless she gave the word. Which she was determined not to—until she knew she could stay detached, if such a time existed.

A savage intensity flashed over his face. The hell she didn't feel those *urges*. Every part of her quivered lightly before him; she was taut as a bow, just waiting for his touch. His eyes dropped to the hand over her belly, before they took in the rise and fall of her chest. He wanted to walk over and shake her, and call her a liar to her face. He caught her darting a glance to the bed, the slight flush under her skin. He moved closer.

She backed away.

He gestured to the bed, taking in her reluctance to follow his gaze with something akin to triumph. 'It's a king-size bed. Plenty of room for two people on opposite sides to never come close to touching.'

'I don't trust you. No way.' She eyed him warily from under her lashes, arms back around her body.

'Oh, Jane, be honest…it's not me you don't trust, it's yourself.'

Of all the conceited…!

Jane's blood boiled; her arms dropped. 'Fine. If you can keep your hands to yourself, then I certainly won't have a problem keeping my hands off *you*.'

'Good.' He smiled smugly. 'I'm going to catch up on some calls. Yvette will bring the rest of your things up shortly, so you can get settled in.'

When he left the room Jane could have kicked herself for allowing him to goad her. But she couldn't back down. Somehow she knew it would be more dangerous if he suspected for a second what she suspected herself. That he was absolutely right about her not trusting herself to share his bed. He was playing a game with her, she knew. She would not be the one to crack.

But in a deep, dark corner she was very much afraid that she would indeed be the one to crack…

CHAPTER ELEVEN

'I PRESUME you won't mind me leaving you to make some calls, as you've barely said two words over dinner…?'

Jane looked up sharply. In contrast to her tense form, spine as straight as a dancer's, he lounged at the opposite side of the table, long legs stretched out, a brow quirked mockingly.

'Not at all…' she replied sweetly.

The heavy potent atmosphere was giving her a headache. She was more than uncomfortably aware of him. His scent, his large body mere inches away across the table. During dinner she'd been transfixed by his hands, until she'd realised she was staring. Still in a state of shock to be back here…with him…again.

In a way, she reflected when he'd taken his leave and her pulse had finally returned to normal, it would be easier to have people around. It would have been too much to have the slumberous heat outside and the entire place to themselves. Things were more formal with the staff here. There was none of the seductive easy intimacy of the summer…making dinner in the kitchen, eating outside. The outer changes just reflected their own inner reality. Everything was different.

She went up to the bedroom and changed into the most un-revealing nightwear she had—a pair of silk pyjamas—button-ing them up as far as possible, and automatically went to the side of the bed that she'd used before, aghast at how natural it felt.

Scooting down under the covers, she felt her body rigid with tension, and she lay like that for at least an hour, until she heard his footfall and the door open. She stopped breathing, her eyes shut tight as he came into the room.

Forcing herself to take long shallow breaths, it was torture as she heard his movements and tried not to imagine what he was doing. The whisper of a shirt sliding off, a belt buckle opened, a button being popped. When she heard his trousers hit the floor, and the barely discernible sound of his underwear being tugged down, a corresponding heat flooded her lower belly. She had to bite her lip to keep back a moan.

She heard his footsteps pad to the bathroom and water running, being turned off, and then the footsteps come back to the bed. She felt the dip as he pulled the covers back and got in. She was curled in a ball, as far away from him as she could get, the covers tucked around her like a wall.

She only fell asleep once he'd stopped moving and she heard his deep breaths even out.

When Jane woke the next morning she was in the same position she'd fallen asleep in, and she could feel how the tension had cramped her muscles. With a wary look over her shoulder, she breathed out when she saw that Xavier was already up, the sheet pulled neatly back. She took advantage of the solitude and got up, taking a quick shower and dressing before going downstairs, meeting Yvette on the way.

'Oh, *madame*! You should have stayed in bed. You must be tired...I was going to bring you breakfast.'

Jane smiled warmly at her. 'There's no need. I'm sure you have enough to be doing...I'll come and get something in the kitchen myself.'

She looked up over Yvette's head and saw Xavier at the bottom of the stairs, watching her intently. She could see a muscle work in his jaw from where she was. Had he slept well last night? She searched his face for signs, but he looked remarkably well. Vibrant. She proceeded down the stairs, fighting to look cool.

'Morning.'

'Morning.'

'Did you—?'

'I hope you—'

They both spoke at the same time, and Jane took the lead, saying airily, 'Oh, like a log. I didn't even hear you come in. Was it late?'

He took her arm and led her across the hall before leaning down close and breathing into her ear, 'Liar.'

Before she could react, and quell the butterflies he'd set off in her stomach, he straightened and said in a normal voice, 'We have visitors to see you, darling...' He looked back to Yvette. 'The Vercors are here. Bring some tea and a selection of things please...' He dropped his voice again as he walked her to the door of the sitting room. 'I remember what a large appetite you have, even if you don't want to.'

Her mouth was open and her face pink when he manoeuvred her into the bright room. He smiled benignly down into her face.

'Darling, do you remember Sophie Vercors? And this is her husband Paul.'

Jane forced herself to tear her eyes away from his mesmerising pull and looked at the couple. She immediately recalled the glamorous woman from that day when they'd bumped into her on the road, on the way down to the beach. The sudden memory of it had her cheeks flame red.

She stood to greet Jane warmly. Xavier's hand on her back propelled her forward.

'Jane! It's good to see you again...I had a funny feeling I might.'

Sophie's eyes twinkled with mischief, and Jane found herself responding to her warmth gratefully.

'And this is my darling husband, Paul.'

She pulled the man forward. He was quite a bit older than Sophie, balding and with a definite paunch, but he had the kindest eyes and a look of mischief to match his wife's. It was clear, despite their mismatched appearances, that they loved each other deeply.

'Shame on you, Xavier, for getting married in London… and the baby! What great news…'

Xavier slanted a privately mocking glance down at Jane. 'What can I say? It took four months before I could win her back.'

Sophie clapped her hands. 'Jane…you *are* the one for him. I knew it. No other woman would have run rings around him like that!'

Jane smiled weakly, wanting nothing more than to swing for Xavier, who was still clamping her to his side. They settled down to chat, Sophie clearly delighted to have another woman of similar standing on the island.

'It can get so boring sometimes…especially in the winter.' She winked at her husband cheekily. 'But now you're here we can do all sorts of things. Though you'll probably spend a lot of time on the mainland, with Xavier when he's working…'

Jane was quite happy to let her prattle on, horribly aware of Xavier's thigh pressed hard against her own on the small couch. What would they say if they knew that their marriage was a sham?

Before long they were in the hall, saying their goodbyes. Sophie embraced Jane. 'So don't forget the Winter Ball will be coming up next month. That calls for at least a few shopping trips… You lucky thing—at least it's in Xavier's hotel, your home from home.'

When they were gone, Jane turned to Xavier. 'How can you deceive your friends like that? Let them think that you're happily married?'

'What makes you think I'm not?'

Jane frowned at his obtuseness. 'But of course you're…
we're not. How can you say that?'

His eyes narrowed on her face, a shuttered look descending, making a chill run down her spine.

'Jane, I am very happily married, believe me. I've got the most important thing I always wanted and expected to get out of a marriage. An heir.'

She staved off the ice that settled around her heart at his words. 'How can you be so cold?'

He smiled, but it didn't reach his eyes. 'You call me cold? You're in this for your reasons too, or have you conveniently forgotten them?'

A stillness came into the air around them. Nothing moved; not a sound came from anywhere. She found her voice and it sounded remarkably calm. 'No, I haven't. I'm doing this for the baby. And I want my mother to be happy. They are the only reasons I said yes. Certainly not for anything else.'

Liar…

She felt her throat close over and wanted to get as far away as possible right at that moment, but she forced herself to stand strong.

He brought a large warm hand to her neck, caressing, and the pulse thumped crazily against her skin and his. Every muscle tensed as she fought against reacting, against closing her eyes. When, oh, when would she be free of this debilitating desire for him?

'You'll never be free of me, Jane. You'll come to me. Sooner or later. I'll wait. And until you do we will share our bed. We both know you curled up in that tight ball beside me to stop yourself reaching out and experiencing the passion you know is still there.'

Her eyes widened as his words echoed her thoughts, as if he had read her mind. Belatedly she remembered his uncanny ability to do just that. But his arrogant assumption helped to dampen her clamouring body. She tore his hand away from her neck.

'It's good to clarify things and know that at least we agree on our motivations for the marriage. It'll be a cold day in hell, Xavier, before we make love. I'm going for a walk.'

And she stormed out of the house, feeling as though the hounds of the Baskervilles were at her heels.

Xavier watched her go and felt rage surge upwards. He stormed into his study and poured himself a shot of whisky, gulping it back. His hand was a white-knuckle grip around the glass. How was she able to enrage him so? He'd never allowed any woman to affect him like this... How could she stand there so coolly and say those words?

A bleak expression crossed his face and he rubbed a weary hand over his eyes. It was nothing less than he'd said to her.

Why should it bother him that she felt exactly the same way? That she wasn't what he had imagined all those months ago? He had allowed himself to imagine for the first time ever something elusive, ethereal. A glimpse of fulfillment—what he saw Sophie and Paul share...he'd stupidly hoped that perhaps he too could have that sense of coming home...

He crushed the empty feeling. A foolish daydream, that was all it had been. He'd been wrong...it existed for others but not him. Never him.

A newly familiar surge of guilt rushed through him, and he swallowed back another shot to drown it out... Guilt was an emotion he had little time for. He conducted every aspect of his life with ruthless precision...so why should he feel guilt that maybe he...what? That he'd bullied her into marrying him? As she had just told him, she had her own very concrete reasons for entering the marriage. He shook his head. No way would she have given in unless she'd wanted to.

But she needed to...not wanted to. She told you she hated you for doing this to her, for not offering her another way...

He cursed the voice that mocked him.

It was just physical frustration. That was all. He'd never been denied a woman he desired before now. Her and her damned insistence that she didn't feel those *urges*. She hated the attraction. This was just her way of claiming control over the situation... The guilt rose again like a spectre. He swallowed another shot.

It had taken all the strength and will-power he possessed not to reach across the bed and pull her into his arms last night. Her achingly familiar sweet scent had tantalised his senses as he lay there, his body aroused to the point of pain, testing him beyond endurance. But he wouldn't do it...he couldn't. She was his *pregnant* wife, dammit. She would have to come to him.

When that day came...when she did come to him...maybe then that voice would disappear.

Another shot didn't help.

A few days later, a wan-faced Jane came into the dining room where Xavier was finishing breakfast. She eyed him warily. She'd had the most vivid dream last night. That he had pulled her close and tucked himself around her so completely that she'd felt unspeakably comforted, safe and cherished. She'd even felt love from it. And then she'd felt his hardness against her back, and it had started up a throbbing need that had woken her with its intensity. When she'd woken with a start, the bed had been empty. Xavier hadn't yet joined her, and the loneliness that had lodged in her chest had been so heavy that she still felt it this morning.

He looked at her over the rim of his coffee cup, and Jane hid her churning emotions behind a mask of bland happiness.

'Morning. Did you sleep well? Are you going to the mainland today? Isn't it lovely outside? I might go for a drive later, explore a bit.'

He frowned at her inane chatter, clearly not taken in.

'We're having some people over tonight—business colleagues, friends. A small dinner party. About ten people. Sophie and Paul, and Sasha will be there too. So you'll know a few.'

At the mention of Sasha's name, Jane nearly fell into her chair, her face paling. She'd managed to put the other woman out of her head, but now that awful morning came back vividly. Her own humiliation.

'Oh…that sounds nice.'

What else could she say? Don't you dare invite that woman?

'You'll act as hostess, of course.'

She just nodded her head. Still thinking about Sasha, distracted.

'I have to go to the hotel…I'll be back around seven p.m. The guests are due to arrive at eight.'

He drained the last of his coffee and got up to go. Just as he did Jane felt a flutter of something in her belly, and gasped audibly. Xavier came around to her side quickly.

'What is it? Is something wrong?'

Jane shook her head, her hand on her belly. 'I think I just felt the first kick.'

She turned to face him, smiling, her eyes gleaming with excitement. He crouched down beside her chair and she had the irresistible urge to reach out and take his hand, place it on her belly. The air around them grew heavy. She couldn't take her eyes from his. She saw his hand come out towards her, and suddenly checked herself. The feeling that he had read her mind was too strong, that he might have seen something on her face.

She flinched back. A tiny movement, but he saw it. His hand stopped. She saw his eyes harden. His face was inscrutable. A muscle twitched in his jaw.

'So you're all right.'

Jane gathered herself together. God, she was so transparent…she had to control these impulses.

She forced her voice to be light. 'Yes. It's nothing. It's probably not even the baby at all.'

She felt the acute disappointment that she couldn't share the moment with him. But she was far too vulnerable and weak in his presence; she had to maintain her guard at all times. Looking at him with welcoming eyes, wanting him to feel the baby move—that would have led her down a very dangerous path...

After helping Yvette and Jean-Paul prepare for the dinner, despite their remonstrations, Jane took a drive all the way up to the memorial at the other end of the island. It was bitter-sweet to be back there again and remember that day in the summer. She placed some flowers in the vases and lit a candle that was sheltered by the wind.

As she looked out to the sea, churning in a grey froth, she asked herself yet again what she was doing. Did she really have the strength to go through with this?

And then she felt the flutter again, barely perceptible, low in her abdomen. She turned and contemplated the view to the north. The view she had contemplated that day she'd come up here with Xavier, so full of optimism and joy, delighted expectation. And that night...that night was when this baby had been conceived. She unconsciously rubbed the bump beneath her jumper. That was why she was here. Loving Xavier was unfortunate, incidental, and not giving in to his potent seductiveness was her main priority. She had to remember that.

She was dressed and ready that evening when Xavier returned. His sharp, assessing eyes took her in. A long indolent look up and down that left her breathing faster. She cursed his ability to weaken her.

'Very nice.'

'Thank you,' she answered tightly.

She had tied her hair back in a loose knot, and was wearing a midnight-blue silk button-down dress. Demure and classic.

He reached into his pocket and pulled out a small box, handing it to her. She looked from him to it, a small frown creasing her forehead as she took it. When she opened it she had to hold back a gasp. Sapphire drop earrings glistened against the velvet background. They were stunning. Priceless. Her eyes flew up to his.

'But…what's this for? I can't take these; they're far too expensive.'

His voice was almost harsh, his face closed. 'Just take them, Jane. I got them to match your ring… You'll be getting plenty more jewels in time, and I'll expect you to wear them.'

Of course he would. She had a certain standard to maintain, didn't she? As his wife, she would be expected to wear jewels, compete with the other women in their society. The rush of pleasure she had felt initially at receiving such a gift was quashed.

As he'd said, they were to match her ring. He hadn't put any more thought into it apart from that.

She could be just as closed. She took them out of the box and put them in her ears, feeling as though they were piercing her heart, not the lobes of her ears. They felt heavy. She handed him back the box.

'Thank you for the gift. Excuse me. I have to help Yvette get the dining room ready.'

And with a straight back she walked away, barely hearing him take the stairs two at a time.

Jane threw herself into helping get the dining room ready to take her mind off their exchange, and it was just before the guests were due to arrive that Xavier appeared again downstairs. She was putting the finishing touches to a vase of flowers she'd picked herself on her excursion earlier, and looked up, her hands stilling of their own accord as she took him in.

He wasn't formally dressed, but had changed into a dark grey suit and a snowy white shirt with the top button open, giving a tantalising glimpse of dark skin and hair just under-neath. Jane could almost feel the heat emanating from his chest as he paused on the bottom step. He took her breath away. Literally. Cleanshaven, hair swept back, sardonic eyes taking her in.

She burned up with colour at how she'd been caught staring to intently. Had she lost her mind? She was meant to be keeping him at arm's length, not drooling over him—and certainly not so obviously.

'Still blushing, Jane…? How remarkably sweet.'

Before she could answer, the doorbell pealed and Xavier took her arm.

'Time to act the loving wife.'

She smiled her way through the introductions as everyone seemed to arrive at once—Sasha being the last. She came in and threw her arms around Xavier's neck, pressing an eager kiss to his cheek. Jane couldn't take her eyes off the display, the way Sasha looked so sexy draped in his arms, blonde con-trasting with dark. Xavier caught her eye and pulled himself out of Sasha's arms.

'Sasha, you remember Jane…my wife?'

Was there a subtle possessive inflection there? Jane wondered. Or was it just wishful thinking on her part?

'Sasha, how nice to see you again,' she said, lying through her teeth. 'Please come through. What would you like to drink?'

Sasha avoided Jane's eye, clinging on to Xavier's arm as they went into the main drawing room, where the rest of the guests were enjoying their aperitifs.

By the time they were on coffee and desserts, Jane's cheeks ached from smiling. Thankfully Sasha was at the other end of the table, beside Sophie, who had thrown Jane a few pained looks during dinner. At least now she didn't feel as though her dislike of Sasha was just in her own head.

Back in the drawing room afterwards, she rested on the arm of a chair, talking to the very friendly wife of one of

Xavier's older colleagues. She felt a prickle of awareness, and looked up to catch him staring at her from across the room.

The weight and intensity of his gaze caught her by surprise and, not having the time to react and school her features, she felt her body responding to his look, crying out for fulfilment. Her breasts grew heavy, and she felt her nipples harden into tight points, and that treacherous all-revealing flush stain her cheeks. She was unable to tear her gaze away from his, as if he'd put some kind of spell on her.

Sophie finally broke it, when she rolled her eyes and said to the room at large, 'Newlyweds! What is it the Americans say? Oh, yes! Get a room! We didn't come here to see you two devour each other with looks.'

Everyone laughed, and Jane blushed even harder. How had she ever thought she could handle this enforced celibacy?

And it was about to get worse.

Xavier, taking full advantage of the situation, strolled over and caught Jane up to him with one graceful move. He bent his head, taking her mouth with such a sweet kiss that a wave of longing made her shudder in his arms. His action was so swift that he took her off guard, much as he had with his look.

When he pulled away, her mouth clung to his, reluctant to let him go, and with a dazed look she realised that they were still in the room, and it hadn't been some dream. She couldn't let go of the feeling that had surged through her body, every point sensitive to his touch, his presence…the sheer sexiness of it, her breasts crushed against him.

She looked into his eyes and saw them flicker around the room. Reality crashed around her. An act…that was all it was. An act to unnerve her and for the guests.

She spoke quickly to hide her vulnerability, afraid he might read something into her easy acquiescence. 'I hope that was convincing enough for you?'

When she tried to pull out of his arms, they tightened. His

eyes flashed down at her. 'If I'd known you were going to be so happy to comply and act along then I'd have taken advantage a lot sooner...but rest assured I'll remember next time.'

And with a casual kiss on her wrist, he calmly strolled back to the other side of the room.

Xavier watched Jane from under hooded lids. She was studiously avoiding looking anywhere near him. He was only half taking in Paul's conversation, glad that there was a third person so he could watch her without appearing rude.

The kiss had unsettled him. How quickly he'd become aroused, like a flash fire. Rapidly devouring any sense of reality except what he felt when he touched her. He had felt how ripe and lush she was, more curved, rounded. The feel of her belly, pressing low against his groin... The intense possessiveness he'd felt had nearly floored him...she was *his* woman...carrying *his* baby. The thought of other men looking at her blooming beauty, the burgeoning curves, made his hands curl into fists.

Only registering the presence of their guests had held him back from hauling her up into his arms and out of the room...much like the caveman impulse he'd felt when he'd first brought her into this house. Amazingly, after all this time, he still felt the same out-of-control desire—if anything it had grown even stronger, and with it he felt...weak. Like Samson and Delilah, he thought with a small hard smile to himself. As if she was sucking his strength. Taking his power.

He could see how her chest rose and fell with uneven breaths, the V of her dress giving tantalising glimpses of her breasts, which pushed against the silk. He'd felt them through the fabric of their clothes. He wondered if they looked different now she was pregnant. Were they already fuller, harder?

His erection grew again, and he shifted uncomfortably. Then he remembered that morning, in the breakfast room.

When she'd turned that innocent gaze on him, so full of delight at the joy of their baby. Her hand on her belly, feeling something that he could only imagine. He'd ached with the sudden need to reach out and share what she was feeling, share the experience, and he had been sure the invitation had been in her eyes, her face. But then…just when he'd reached out…she'd flinched back, and the icy cool look had come down. Something inside him had shriveled up. He had done that to her. She could barely bring herself to look at him.

That the baby could bring such effortless joy to her face but not him… He resolutely turned away from her and back to the conversation, a heavy feeling in his heart. A place he'd never given much thought to…until now.

Finally the last guests left, and Jane closed the door wearily. She'd told Yvette and Jean-Paul to go to bed long ago. Thank God that was over. She rubbed a hand over her tired eyes and pulled her hair free at the back of her head, massaging her scalp.

Xavier stood in the doorway of the drawing room. 'Care for a nightcap? Non-alcoholic, of course,' he added dryly.

She had a sudden overwhelming urge to walk over, run her hands under his jacket, lean into his tall body and say, *Take me to bed. Make love to me until we can't move any more.*

As if that scenario existed in some parallel world. A world where he loved her as much as she loved him.

But it didn't. She quashed the seductive daydream and instead moved towards the stairs, every cell in her body screaming to go in the other direction.

'No, thanks. I'm tired.'

'Of course. Wouldn't want you to miss out on any sleep. It mightn't be good for the baby.'

She looked at him warily as she got to the bottom step, saw him tip his glass back and drain the contents with something savage in his movements.

'Goodnight.' And she fled.

CHAPTER TWELVE

A MONTH later Jane was getting ready for the Winter Ball, which was that evening. Her hands shook as she put earrings in her ears, smoothed back her hair and flicked some lint off her dress.

Her nerves were wound so tightly now that she jumped at the slightest sound or movement. The last few weeks had been an exercise in torture. Self-inflicted torture. On the outside she was the picture of a glowing pregnancy. The sleepless nights, waking with muscles cramping from tension, hadn't yet told on her face, apart from faint dark circles. Xavier hadn't touched her again since that devastating kiss in front of their guests, but she could hardly look at him for fear of him seeing the naked desire on her face. She avoided him whenever she could. Slept late or got up early. Whatever was required.

He spent some nights on the mainland, and those were the only ones she slept. On a rational level she welcomed this, but on every other *honest* level she missed his presence with a physical pain that was almost unbearable. One day he'd brushed past her, barely touched her, and it had caused such an intense spiking of desire to rush through her that she'd had to restrain herself from grabbing him.

That was just what he wanted. Her to give in, beg him for release.

And…in weak moments…she had begun to entertain treacherous thoughts of doing just that. But each time she did, she'd remember why she couldn't… What if she couldn't keep her feelings hidden?

She sighed loudly in the empty room, and turned side-on to check her reflection. She smoothed the black empire line dress over her bump. It was growing every day, still neat, but now very evident.

A sound made her jump. Xavier stood against the doorjamb nonchalantly, devastating in a tuxedo. A memory of the first time she had seen him like that, by the pool in the hotel, came rushing back with such sudden force that she felt faint, and grabbed on to the table beside her to stay steady.

In two quick strides he was by her side, a hand curling around her arm.

'What is it?'

She shook her head, warding him off. 'No…nothing. Just a dizzy moment. I'm fine.'

He dropped his grip as though burnt, and ran an angry hand through his immaculate hair, leaving it tousled. 'For pity's sake, Jane, would you expect me to leave you lying there if you'd collapsed? I haven't laid a hand on you in weeks. Your startled jumps and fearful glances aren't exactly arousing me to passionate heights.'

He was furious, his pulse beating erratically against the skin of his neck. And all she wanted to do was reach out and press her lips against it. Feel the flutter under her mouth, taste his skin, see if it still had that musky tang…

She closed her eyes. 'I'm sorry. Of course I don't expect you to jump on me.'

The way she was feeling, she was more likely to jump on him.

She was a mess. A mass of churning frustrated emotions and desires…he was the cool one.

'The helicopter is ready; the Jeep is waiting. I'll be downstairs.'

He left the room.

Jane turned back to the mirror. Noticed her cheeks burning up, the fever-bright glitter of her eyes. Her breasts pushing against the fabric of the dress felt heavy and full. It was herself she needed protection from, not him. She closed her eyes at her reflection in despair.

By the time they got to the hotel she was calm again. Relatively. It was her first time back there since returning to France, and the memories rushing up were kept down with difficulty. She'd had plenty of opportunity to go to the mainland before now—Sophie rang nearly every other day to check in and ask her out—but Jane kept begging off. Somehow she knew she wouldn't be able to cope with Sophie's easy friendliness. She was just holding it together for herself. The island had become something of a sanctuary.

She followed Xavier to the main ballroom. He stopped her just before entering, the muted sounds of an orchestra coming from behind the doors.

'Ready for the performance of your life?' he drawled.

She nodded jerkily, avoiding his eye. She suddenly felt exhausted, as though she was conducting an impossible immense uphill battle.

'I am if you are.'

'Oh, I've been ready for some time.'

She ignored the implication in his tone. He took her hand in his and led her into the huge main ballroom, the crowd and sounds stunning Jane for a second after the peace of the island.

She nodded and smiled her way through the crush. With the help of Yvette she'd been picking up more and more French, and was now able to converse haltingly at Xavier's side.

A couple of hours later, after speeches and auctions in aid of charity, Jane was trapped by a very boring colleague of Xavier's. Some sixth sense made her realise that they'd become separated. She looked around and found him on the other side of the room. It wasn't hard. He stood head and shoulders above everyone else. His dark head was inclined towards someone. Jane couldn't see who, but then the crowd cleared and she had an unimpeded view. It was Sasha, in a stunning cream backless gown that showed off a smooth, tanned expanse of bare back. She was holding Xavier's arm, her head thrown back, throat exposed, laughing at something he'd just said.

Jane felt a red-hot poker right through her heart, and shook with the desire to march over there and rip every tousled blonde lock out one by one.

'She's a piece of work, isn't she?'

She looked around suddenly, aware that her heart was racing and shocked at the intensity of her feelings. To her relief she saw that the man had gone and Sophie was beside her.

They kissed each other's cheeks in greeting. Jane tried to make sense of her comment.

'What do you mean...piece of work?'

Sophie nodded her head towards Xavier and Sasha.

Jane feigned uninterest. 'Oh, that...'

Sophie flicked her hand in a very gallic gesture. 'Sasha...she's nothing. No, my dear. The women you need to watch out for are the ones giving you dagger looks.'

'What?' Jane followed Sophie's gaze and saw all the beautiful women dotted around the room, and she did indeed catch some looks that were none too friendly.

'Who...who are they?'

'They're the ones who thought they had a chance, who want to be where you are—married to Xavier and expecting his child.'

Sophie caught her husband gesturing at her from across the room and winked at Jane, 'My man wants me... I know what you might think, chérie, but you're quite welcome to your Alpha man...I'll take my pot-bellied version any day!'

Jane had to laugh at Sophie's outrageous sense of humour as she disappeared into the crowd.

Her smile faded, though, as she took in the women who had just been pointed out. More than a few speculative looks *were* coming her way, and she suddenly imagined them all shooting come-hither looks to Xavier.

She felt a huge surge of possessiveness and jealousy. So strong that she shook with it. Her first time out in public with her husband and she wanted to rip the head off every woman in a ten-mile radius. This didn't bode well.

She looked across the room again. Sasha had now been joined by two other beauties. They surrounded Xavier. Vying for his attention. A cold rage filled her body. Acting purely on some primeval instinct she was barely aware of, she started to walk over to him, not even thinking about what she would do when she got there.

She kept getting bumped and jostled by the crowd. Suddenly a tall man appeared in front of her, didn't move. She looked up…for a second her brain stopped working and then cleared.

'I don't believe it…Pete?'

'Jane!'

She kissed him on his cheek. 'You're still here! It's so lovely to see you…'

It all rushed back—her blind date with Pete, the night she'd met Xavier properly for the first time. She remembered his easy, unthreatening presence, and it was like a soothing balm to her soul. She smiled up at him widely.

'I was due to return home in September, but I met someone just before I did…and decided to stay on.' He blushed endearingly. 'We're getting married in the spring.'

'Oh, Pete, I'm so happy for you. That's wonderful news.'

Impulsively she reached up to kiss him again, a silly jealous dart rising unbidden at his exuberant happiness. When she stepped back, he had a funny look on his face.

Jane frowned. 'What…what's wrong?'

But she knew. She felt the familiar prickle of awareness.

An arm snaked around her waist, holding her firm. Xavier held out a hand to Pete. Jane could feel the tension radiating off him in waves.

'I'm Jane's husband…and you are?'

Pete visibly swallowed. 'Pete Sullivan.'

Jane couldn't believe Xavier was being so rude. Pete mumbled something and made a quick escape—Jane barely had a chance to say goodbye properly. She rounded on Xavier, pulling herself out of his embrace, but he had other ideas. He clamped a hand around hers and pulled her into an alcove where they were hidden from the room.

'Who the hell was *that*?' he snarled.

'Well, if you'd been acting like a human being I could have introduced you properly.'

'You were all over him.'

'Hardly, Xavier.'

'Well?'

She crossed her arms in front of her chest. 'I'm not going to dignify your behaviour with an explanation.'

'Oh, yes, you are…' A funny look came into his eyes. She recognised that darkening, that intent as he bent towards her, and instinctively pulled back, her hands coming up.

'Xavier…no.'

Hard hands took her arms. 'Yes, Jane. If you can kiss perfect strangers in front of the whole room, then you can kiss your damn husband.'

'He's not a stranger!' she cried desperately.

It was the worst thing she could have said. All she had was a glimpse of flashing green before the light was blocked and Xavier's mouth slanted over hers.

Her drew her in close to his body and kissed her with raw, unchecked passion. She tried not to respond, but her hands weren't obeying the order to push away…they rested between them, ineffectual.

The fire that had been simmering for weeks turned into an inferno…and on a deep sigh, she gave in. It was too strong for her to fight. And she was so tired of fighting it.

When he realised she wasn't resisting him, his arms relaxed and one hand moved to cup her bottom through the silk of her dress. The other threaded through soft hair, tilting her head, allowing his tongue to delve deeper.

Her hands uncurled and with sweet hesitancy climbed up his chest, until they were around his neck, holding him tight. She traced his lips with her tongue, her breath coming in short, sharp gasps, fingers tangling in the silky strands of hair that curled over his collar. He didn't allow her any quarter. His hand moved up, skimming, touching her more rounded curves, over her belly and up, until she felt him cup the heavy weight of her breast.

She'd never felt as womanly, as desirable. She tore her mouth away with a moan as his thumb found a jutting nipple and flicked it through her dress. With her increased sensitivity everywhere, it nearly pushed her over the edge.

His head dipped and he took her mouth again, remorseless, until Jane was weak and clinging to him with a powerful desire pulsing through her entire trembling body.

He finally tore his mouth away, both of them breathing hard.

She pulled back, and this time he let her go. Through the haze of desire that pounded in her blood, Jane couldn't believe she'd let him kiss her like that. Or that she'd kissed him back. All of her precious barriers, so carefully in place to guard her weak heart. Torn down with a kiss. And it was blatantly obvious that her so-called *urges* were very much there.

She shook her head dumbly, suddenly remembering seeing him surrounded by that bevy of beauties. He was just staking his claim. On his property. In case she was getting any ideas.

Xavier looked at her, colour high on his cheeks, his lips curled derisively. 'Don't look at me like that, Jane…you wanted it as much as I did.'

She turned quickly and half-ran, half-walked back through the room, praying that he wasn't following. She muttered apologies as she crashed into people, unseeing. All she wanted was to get out of there. Suddenly she felt more claustrophobic than she'd ever been in her life.

Finally she stumbled out into the lobby on unsteady legs, breathing hard. Xavier was right behind her. She backed away.

'Xavier, please leave me alone.'

'Jane, you were with me back there every step of the way…you were very responsive.'

So responsive, in fact, that his body tightened again just at the thought.

Her eyes flashed and the possessive rage coursed through her again. 'Only half as responsive, I'm sure, as Sasha…or any of the other willing ladies in there.'

Someone walked out of the room and Xavier grabbed Jane's elbow, leading her to a quiet corner.

'What are you talking about?'

'I'd like to know exactly what is going on with you and Sasha.' Fire spat from her eyes.

He frowned for a second. 'What on earth do you mean?'

'I saw you with her…it didn't exactly look innocent. Every time she sees you she jumps all over you, and hisses at me like a cat.'

And what about the other women?

He took her shoulders and she tried to break free, but he wouldn't let her. 'I've known Sasha since she was a baby. She's had a crush on me for years…a stupid crush.'

He paused and looked at her assessingly, dangerously.

'Jealous, Jane? You won't let me touch you, but can't stand the thought of other women?'

She snorted, hiding the panic. *What was she thinking?*

'Hardly…don't flatter yourself.'

But the words sounded weak to her ears. She tried to evade

his gaze, but it was impossible. She realised that what he said was true. She didn't want those other women near him with a passion that scared her.

His hands tightened. 'Who was he?'

She looked up, feeling sudden relief that his attention had been taken from her disastrous admission of jealousy, from her raw emotions.

'Pete?'

Jane could feel him barely reining his temper in. His heavy-lidded gaze bored into her.

'Yes…who is he?'

She contemplated not answering him, but knew it was futile. And she certainly didn't want him focusing on her reaction to Sasha again.

'I met him the night I came here for dinner after the day trip. He was my blind date… He's living here, working in town. He was just telling me about the girl he's getting married to.'

She looked into his eyes, something twisting in her heart. 'What a coincidence, both of us finding our true loves here…'

Her sarcastic comment bounced off him. She could see his rapier-sharp mind make the connection, recognition drop. He straightened up to his full intimidating height and let her go. She swayed precariously. It was all too much…the crowds, the other women, Sasha, the kiss…and underneath it all this all-consuming, still raging desire for this man who just wanted her for the baby in her belly.

She felt herself being lifted against his chest and closed her eyes, a blessed numbness taking over. Felt herself being carried through a door and then carefully put down. She realised she was sitting on the edge of the bed in the penthouse suite.

Xavier was at her feet, taking off her shoes. 'What are you doing?'

He shot her a quelling look. 'Relax, Jane. You're obviously exhausted; you need to rest. Lie down for a while and I'll come back to check on you.'

He pushed her down onto the bed and drew a cover over her in the darkened room.

But then, instead of moving, he rested on his hands over her for a timeless moment. Jane looked up, transfixed by his eyes. It was as if time stood still. She saw something in the green depths, some expression of desire and blatant need that connected with the deepest part of her so strongly that she felt energy course through her system, exhaustion forgotten.

Xavier closed his eyes for a split second. She could see the pulse throb in his temple. Then he stood and straightened, looking down from his great height. Distant and remote, he stepped away from her.

He opened the door, about to walk out, and stopped. Jane's breath stopped too. He shut the door again and rested his hands on it, his head bent. Then he turned around with a sudden savage movement and strode back towards the bed, taking off his jacket as he did so. Jane's eyes widened, the breath coming jerkily in and out of her mouth as he came back and leant over her on his arms.

'Xavier…what are you…?' Her hands came up automatically between them when she saw the feral glitter in his eyes. He kept coming down, closer and closer. Her hands tried to push but he was immovable. She could feel her blood throbbing through her body, that energy pulsing through every cell.

'I want to sleep with my wife…I've waited long enough, and after that kiss…' His mouth tightened. 'God, Jane, how can you deny us this?'

He came closer, his torso practically touching her chest. She could feel her breasts swell against her dress, the nipples peaking into hard points. Her hands still pushed ineffectually at the hard wall of muscle.

Closer and closer.

She shut her eyes as she felt his mouth near her ear, his lips a breath away from touching. She was trembling all over.

'If you push very, very hard, push me away, I'll go back downstairs and leave you alone. But know this. I need you, Jane. I want you so much it hurts.'

His words resounded and echoed in her, through her. She hurt too. All over. The heat from his chest enveloped her, his scent arousing her beyond anything she'd ever felt. But she couldn't do this…had to resist. She pushed. Nothing. He didn't budge. Pushed again, harder.

Xavier expelled a harsh breath and started to pull away. Suddenly Jane had a vision of him walking out through the door, back downstairs to all those predatory women. Saw an aching lonely void when he left the room. It was the same as the kiss…she was suddenly tired, so tired of fighting herself, him…*this*.

Her hands stopped pushing. He stopped. She looked into his eyes and knew with fatal clarity that she could not let him walk out. She needed him with an aching, craving desire that obliterated all coherent thought and washed through her with such force that she shook.

Her hands moved up and around his neck. She pulled his head back to her.

On a mutual sigh of relief his arms came around her tightly and his tongue entered her mouth with one igniting stroke that mimicked another form of penetration so vividly that Jane moaned deep in her throat, her tongue meeting his, melding and mating and dancing.

She couldn't think beyond the here and now. She was too far gone. She'd worry about it later. Their kiss quickly got out of control as her hands roved over his chest, back, wherever she could reach. It was heaven to be able to finally touch him…and she wanted him to touch her…all over.

He drew back, breathing harshly, and pulled her up to a sitting position. His hands ran over her shoulders, glanced down over breasts that ached against the confines of her clothes.

'Take it off. I need to see you…'

She pulled the dress over her head awkwardly, feeling suddenly shy. She hadn't been naked before him since the summer. Xavier gazed at her wonderingly, a hand reaching out to cup her breast. They strained against the lace cups of her bra, bigger, the veins visible under the translucent skin, and then his hand moved down to her belly, the proud hard swell. He bent his head and pressed a kiss to the skin, his hand visibly shaking as he traced the smooth contour. She felt immeasurably moved.

He flicked open the front clasp of her bra, letting her breasts tumble free. The clamouring of her pulse got louder and she sucked in a hard breath, her head thrown back as his hot mouth bent and suckled there. A throbbing heat pulsed between her legs.

'You…I need to see you too,' she muttered thickly, coming up on her knees to pull off his bow tie, and open his shirt, her hands trembling. A button popped, and then she was smoothing it off his shoulders, baring him to her hungry gaze. How had she survived till now without this?

He sat back for a moment, watched as she bent forward, pressed her mouth against his skin, found a hard flat nipple, nipped gently. His hand threaded through her hair, holding her head, and she heard the whistle of his sucked-in breath.

Hands on her shoulders, gently he put her away from him, and she watched with a dry mouth as he stood and kicked off the rest of his clothes.

His body was even more beautiful than she remembered. The long lean lines, every muscle and sinew taut, the warm olive gleam of his skin rippling as he stepped back to the bed. Her gaze travelled down and her pulse ratcheted up a few notches when she saw his erection. It was bigger and harder than she remembered, and she felt a liquid burst of desire in response.

He caught her look and said wryly, 'It's been a while.'

He must mean since getting married, Jane thought dimly.

And then couldn't think as he took her shoulders and pressed her back down onto the bed. He rested over her on strong arms, the muscles bunching. She reached up, revelling in the feel of him, the satin warm skin, the musky scent. The strength of his body poised over hers made her quake with the need to take him into her, know him again.

His mouth was hot on her neck, on her pulse, beating out of control. He rested on his elbows over her, careful to keep her shielded from his full weight. She could feel the entire length of his body against her, his hardness against her belly. She writhed in response, a small moan escaping when his hair roughened chest stimulated her breasts unbearably.

He pulled back slightly, brought a hand up to skim over her shoulders, down over her breasts, before his mouth dropped and paid homage to each hard thrusting peak in turn. She was not herself any more. She sucked in jerky breaths, arching against him. His breath tickled as his mouth finally moved down, over her belly and lower, where she felt his fingers hook around her panties and pull them down, stockings following.

When she was naked, he pulled her into his body, torso to torso, legs entwined around hers, every part of their bodies touching. Jane could feel the tremors run through her. It was too much, too heady after so long…her breathing was laboured. She needed him, wanted him so badly.

He spoke her thoughts out loud. 'I don't think I can wait…or go slowly…'

'Me neither…' She arched as his hand caressed between her legs, fingers finding the moist centre of her desire. Stroking back and forth.

'You're so ready.'

She was half crazed with the need to feel him inside her, and instinctively lifted her leg over his hip, bringing her into intimate contact with his erection. It jumped and pulsed against her body. Xavier moved down slightly, keeping her leg lifted, and with one smooth thrust entered her. Jane cried out with the sensation, her walls tight around him after all this time.

'Have I hurt you?'

He went to withdraw and Jane grabbed him. 'No...don't stop.'

He started to thrust upwards, one arm around her back holding her steady, the other on her leg, holding it over his hip. And all the time came that delicious building, tightening, as they climbed and climbed, his strokes going deeper, harder, filling her exquisitely. She blindly sought his mouth and kissed him, unable to contain her instinctive drives any more. She arched towards him and felt every part of herself clench as with one last thrust Xavier sent her into a huge explosion of stars that left her quivering around his body just as he joined her in his own climax. She felt his power spill into her, deep in her body.

It was unbearably, exquisitely intimate, lying like this, still joined, face to face, their breath mingling, every inch of skin in contact, legs entwined.

When they were finally breathing normally Xavier shifted himself free of Jane's embrace, causing her to gasp again, her body still painfully sensitive.

He turned her gently, so her back was tucked into his chest, pulled a sheet over their bodies and pressed a kiss to the back of her head. A heavy, possessive arm lay around the swell of her belly, a hand stretched out to cover it.

She felt a kick in her belly under Xavier's hand and stilled.

'Did you feel that?'

It came again, stronger, and she turned a shining happy face up to him, holding his hand firm against her belly. 'Oh, Xavier, did you feel that?'

As he looked down into her face and felt the baby kick, he felt something inside him close off. Shut down.

He had to get away. Now... He couldn't trust himself here with her. He felt raw, exposed. They had just shared the strongest climax he could ever remember experiencing, and he'd been pretty sure it was the same for her, and yet…it was the baby that was giving her that glow of happiness, that smile as she looked up into his face.

Images and sensations rushed through him…the red mist of anger that had settled over his vision when he'd seen her talking to Pete…the feel of the baby kicking under her smooth skin…her happiness for that but not him—and the fear. The fear that he was falling into some place that he'd never find his way out of again…

She was just giving in to carnal desires—desires she had been resisting. She'd almost pushed him away; he'd almost left the room. It was laughable. Instead of the mocking voice in his head stopping, now it was all he could hear. He had to get out.

Jane felt the tension in Xavier's body, tried to gauge the look on his face.

He pulled his hand away from under hers and pulled himself out of the bed. She drew the sheet up over her chest, feeling a sudden chill. Xavier was stepping back into his clothes, a million miles away from the man who had just tucked her into his body. A cold look of detachment on his face, the angles harsh in the dim light.

'I should go back downstairs in case we're missed.'

He picked up his jacket and cast her a quick glance as he left the room.

'I'm glad you've decided it's time to be my wife. *Properly.*'

CHAPTER THIRTEEN

JANE lay in the bed, tucked into a curled-up position, for some time. Until the air began to chill her skin and she had to pull another blanket onto the bed to stop her teeth chattering.

This was exactly what she had feared. Sleeping with him had opened her up, taken the scab off the wound…and now she was afraid there would be no way to stem the flow of blood. This intimacy had cracked her heart open completely. And there was no going back. No closing it off again. After this…she couldn't.

What had she done…?

The next morning when she woke she was in the bed alone, and knew that Xavier hadn't joined her at all. Her body ached with a betrayingly pleasurable ache as she got up and belted a robe firmly around her waist. When she went out into the suite she paled visibly when she saw him standing at the window, pristine in a dark suit. He ran a cool look over her as she emerged, feeling sleepy and tousled in comparison. Her heart hardened when she saw the lack of anything on his face.

'Morning.'

'Morning.'

'I have to go to Paris for a couple of days…something's come up.'

She exuded what she hoped was an air of extreme uninterest, fighting the reaction of her body to the musky scent
that reached her nostrils, the smell of which was bringing last
night back to vivid life. Her voice sounded strained to her
ears.

'Fine...I'll go back to the island later on. Sophie said
something about meeting for lunch, so I might do that.'

Xavier was very still as Jane helped herself to coffee and
a croissant. She moved over towards a chair at the other end
of the table and had to walk past him. He blocked her way,
and she nearly jumped out of her skin. He took the cup and
plate out of her hand and put his hands on her arms. She carefully schooled her features before looking up, but started
trembling when she took in the green eyes, smoky like last
night, took in his mouth and quickly returned to his eyes. His
mouth was far too potent.

'Jane...no more of the startled rabbit. We can't go back
after last night.'

He took his hands away and ran one through his hair impatiently. 'Hell, Jane, you stopped pushing me away. I
almost left...'

Every self-protective mechanism kicked in. She shrugged
negligently. 'It's no big deal, Xavier. I'm quite aware of what
I did. We both got what we wanted.'

A hand came to her jaw, forcing her face up to his. She
flinched inwardly at the hardness in his face. The lack of
emotion.

*The voice in his head would stop. He'd make it...and this
was how.*

'Good. Because when I get back we are going to be man
and wife...properly...from now on.'

Jane refused to give in to the desire to run as fast as she
could, stood her ground. She had got herself into this and
there was no way that he would ever know how much it was
going to kill her to be intimate, how much she feared her heart

was going to break with every encounter, every time he left her so dispassionately afterwards.

Why, oh, why had she been so weak? She'd hit the self-destruct button. Spectacularly. And she couldn't even blame him! As he had pointed out, she had pulled him back to her, had made the choice.

Xavier held her jaw in a light but firm grip and bent his head, his breath tickling her face for a moment before he touched his mouth to hers. Even now, despite her pain, the pull was too strong, the desire overwhelming to just sink against his body, pull him close, allow him full access.

'I'll see you in two days…'

Two days later, back in the castle, Jane was like a cat on a hot tin roof. Listening out for the helicopter or the Jeep. Trying to read and giving up. Watching the TV and giving up. She knew she was irritating Yvette by getting under her feet, and took herself out for a walk to burn off the excess energy.

As much as she dreaded seeing Xavier again, she hungered for him now in a way she never had before. She had convinced herself in the past two days that she could do this…maintain a physical relationship and keep her feelings back. She couldn't fight him again. If she did, that razor-sharp mind would focus on her motivations and not let go until he'd found the beating heart of her.

And that weak heart, so brimming over with love for him, was what she had to guard against. She had nearly revealed it that night, when she'd felt the baby kick. And that was what had driven him from the bed. She was sure of it. She had seen the dawning horror on his face, the cool detachment as he had firmly extricated himself from her embrace.

She wouldn't make that mistake again.

When she returned to the castle there was still no sign of him. She tried not to worry, and picked up the phone countless times only to put it down again. He'd love that, wouldn't he? No doubt he'd laugh at her attempt to be a concerned wife. But the truth was she *was* concerned. She paced back and forth in the sitting room, looking out of the window at the skies that looked ominously grey.

Yvette appeared at the door, an indulgent smile on her face. '*Madame*, don't worry…he will be here. You should go to bed.'

Jane smiled weakly and nodded. 'Maybe you're right.'

It was a relief not to have to hold back her feelings with the other woman. Yvette assumed, of course, that Jane was madly in love.

She climbed the stairs and once in bed eventually fell asleep, despite the niggling worry.

Xavier walked into the bedroom, every bone and muscle in his body screaming with fatigue. Two days of intense negotiations and then he had flown himself back to the island on the plane. Ordinarily he would have stayed overnight in Paris. He had never had the overwhelming desire to come home before…

But now he did. And the reason was curled up under the covers. Her hair was fanned out on the pillow, lashes long against her cheek, and he could imagine the hidden curves. Her arms were bare and his body hardened in an instant at the thought of her naked.

He stripped and got into the bed, pulling her body close into his, breathing in her sweet scent. He felt the flimsy silk of her slip. She'd never worn this before…was it because she'd been waiting for him? The thought made him harder. His hand was firm on her belly, just under the weight of her breasts, and he cupped one full heavy mound, delighting in the way her nipple sprang to hard life in his palm.

He couldn't shut out the thought: She might want this for now…but you know she would resist if she could…she's going to hate you for this…sooner or later…

He blocked it out with every ounce of will-power, pushed it into some dark recess. It was too heady...too seductive... being here, having her in his arms like this...

Jane was half asleep and moaned softly in her drowsy state. She couldn't believe it. She was having that dream again. When would it stop?

She wiggled to try and force herself to wake up, but instead of the feelings subsiding as she became more awake, they got stronger. The pulse beating between her legs was all too real, as was the hand on her breast, the nudging of a very aroused man low at her back.

She came to full tense alertness. Her head falling back. 'Xavier...'

His mouth was busy trailing a hot blaze of fire down the back of her neck. Relief coursed through her. She tried to stay coherent for a moment, not in this all too dangerous dream-like state where anything could happen, anything might be said...

'Xavier...where were you?'

He lifted his head and she could just make out the glittering green in the darkness. His voice was sardonic, but didn't quench her desire, which was fast spiralling out of control.

'You missed me...?'

She blustered, 'No, of course not.'

He was pulling up her silk slip, up over her thighs. She hesitated for a split second and then lifted them to help, and felt his moan of approval against her back as he slipped her free of the flimsy garment entirely with one swift move.

Had she somehow subconsciously picked it because, if she was honest, she'd imagined this very scenario...?

She turned her head so that her lips were close to his. His mouth hovered over them for an infinitesimal moment and then he took them with a drugging, heated kiss, his tongue invading, exploring, plundering her weak, non-existent defence.

His hands on her breasts roused them to hard, engorged

points, and she gasped when he took his mouth away from hers. Keeping her back to him, he brought an arm under one leg, lifting it slightly, opening her up for him to explore with long fingers, feel the telling wetness, arousing her to even further heights.

She bit her lip to stop from crying out as she felt him guide his hard length into her tight passage, his chest pressed close against her, his hand holding her in place as he smoothly thrust in and out.

She was fast being borne away in an ever tightening need, the eroticism of the position, the hunger with which they both sought to reach the pinnacle, something almost animalistic in their movements helping them to reach a simultaneous climax of such strength that Jane felt everything go black for a split second…and then came back down on the shuddering waves of her orgasm, her body clenching and pulsating around Xavier for long moments.

How was it that they could reach this intoxicating peak every time without love? Words trembled on her lips. She turned her head and blindly sought his mouth…every buried wish and desire naked for him to see…if only he could.

Then she tensed abruptly. This was what she had to fight. This uncontrollable awful need to blurt out her feelings.

Xavier felt her distancing herself and pulled free from her body. He needed no further indication. They had scratched their itch.

He lay on his back by her side, and didn't pull her into his arms as she curled away from him. Jane lay for a long time staring into the dark. Long after Xavier had turned away on the opposite side and his breathing had slowed and deepened.

Two weeks later…two long weeks of similar nights…nights of blinding, all-consuming passion followed by each of them turning away from the other…Jane walked into the dining room, the toll now obvious on her face. Dark circles were evident under her eyes, and no amount of make-up could disguise the puffiness. She knew she couldn't keep going on like this. Despite her grand justifications to herself. She had hit the wall of as much emotional pain she could take.

Xavier took in her appearance with a sharp look.

'You don't look well.'

She bristled at his tone. He didn't have to point out to her what she knew herself. The bloom had gone. In the past few days she had even begun feeling nauseous again.

'It's called being pregnant, Xavier. I'm sorry, but not everyone feels amazing all the time. And I certainly don't at the moment.'

'You didn't seem to be feeling unwell last night…'

'Well, you wouldn't have exactly noticed, would you?' she snapped.

'Are you saying you didn't want me? Correct me if I'm wrong, but from what I recall you were a very willing partner—couldn't even wait for me to get out of the shower.'

She flushed a dull red, her body reacting to the image his words evoked, a tide of humiliation burning her up inside. A muscle twitched in his jaw. His face was hard.

'Xavier, it's just desire, purely physical, and, yes…I feel it too. Believe me, if I could switch it off I would.' The ringing bitterness in her tone surprised even her, and she stopped, avoiding his eyes.

He got up with a sudden violent movement, his chair scraping back, loud in the silence of the room. Jane flinched.

'I have business to attend to in the hotel. I'll be back this evening.'

A huge lump grew in her throat and tears blurred her vision as she sat there, miserable after he'd stalked out, unable to take even a sip of coffee. They were no better than bickering children…and it would only get worse. She knew the barbs would get sharper, cut deeper.

She blinked back the tears and hid her face when Yvette

bustled in and clucked like a mother hen. She went up to the bedroom and tried to take a nap, but it was impossible to sleep. She went down and helped make lunch, and prepared for dinner later as it was Yvette and Jean-Paul's night off, but her mind still churned, her stomach feeling acidy. In the afternoon, feeling as though she was going to go out of her mind, she made her escape and fled. She took the car on a drive, not knowing where she was headed.

She found herself arriving at the small cove where they'd spent their last day together in the summer. Grey skies and pounding waves reflected her mood effortlessly. She remembered the sweet happiness she'd felt that day…feelings that had long been submerged by now.

Her thoughts went inward. All along, since they'd met again, Xavier had professed to being motivated by nothing other than wanting this heir. The warmth they had shared in the summer had been the smooth, urbane playboy part of him. The seductive man beneath the cynical, ruthless businessman. She only had to remind herself of how, once he had taken the decision to marry her, he'd gone to New York for two weeks, not to see her again until their wedding day. Supremely confident that she'd acquiesce.

She had thought she was doing the best thing for the baby, for her mother…but all along she had to admit that she had harboured a deep fantasy that maybe things would change, that he would look at her with the same tenderness she remembered from the summer.

She knew it was that that had prompted her to give in to her overwhelming desire…an effort to recapture some elusive dream, maybe change the status quo… But she'd made things worse, not better. And she knew, sadly, even if she could go back to the penthouse suite and that night, she still wouldn't have the strength to watch him walk out through the door. That had been inevitable, a force of nature.

But, because of it, all that stretched ahead for now were

long, lonely days. Nights filled with passion, maybe. But afterwards he would pull away from her, exactly as he had each night up till now, and she would stifle the words that begged for release... She knew it was only a matter of time before she revealed herself, and to do it in a moment of weak passion would annihilate her.

She knew then what she had to do. With a clean, clear certainty in her heart, she felt relieved for the first time in weeks. She would go to him and tell him. She would tell him she loved him, calmly, with dignity, not in a moment of passion.

If there was any way he thought he could feel anything at all beyond a purely physical attraction, then she would stay and try to make the marriage work. But if he couldn't...and that thought made her feel weak...she would leave. As much as it would kill her to do that, it was the only way she could hope to survive.

She could go to the mainland, stay in Lisa's villa, figure out what to do. After all, they were married now, surely the inheritance had to be merely a formality? She wouldn't even insist on a divorce for now, if he didn't want it. But she was sure he would one day...he would meet someone else. How could he not?

Jane got back into the car, a nervous knot in her belly, wanting nothing more than to finally be honest with him...and herself.

By the time she got back to the castle it was much later than she had realized—early evening, the light darkening in the sky. Xavier's Jeep was back already, and Jane felt her stomach plummet. Her hands felt clammy as she gripped the wheel after she'd come to a stop. Could she really go through with this?

Then she saw him at the door, his tall body tense. He strode towards the car, pulling the door open.

'Where the hell have you been?'

Her churning emotions, what she had to do, made Jane

match him in anger. 'I went for a drive. Is that permissible? Don't worry, Xavier, your precious cargo is still safe.'

He frowned down at her as she got out, barely allowing her enough room to move. She clenched her jaw as she brushed against him.

'Cargo…what on earth are you talking about?'

Blue eyes blazing in her face, she looked up after slamming the door shut. 'The baby…the reason we're here.'

His mouth compressed. 'Of course. How could I have forgotten.'

He took her by the elbow and pulled her inside.

'Xavier, let me go. I'm perfectly capable of walking by myself.'

He dropped her arm and rubbed a hand over his eyes. Jane suddenly noticed that he looked terrible, and there was a slight smell of alcohol on his breath.

'Have you been drinking?'

Hard green eyes regarded her as his head came back, nostrils flaring slightly. 'Yes, dear wife. You're driving me to drink…happy now?'

Jane walked towards the kitchen. 'You need a cup of coffee.'

He grabbed her arm and swung her around, bringing her into intimate contact with his whole length. He looked and felt dark and dangerous, dressed all in black. She closed her eyes at the dismayingly predictable way her body responded to his heady proximity. With an effort she held herself stiff as a board in his arms and slowly opened her eyes.

She shook her head at him. 'Xavier, let me go…we can't do this…'

This just firmed her resolve for what she was going to do. Their passion, if unchecked, would soon make them bitter with their need for each other. It was already happening. She pushed herself out of his arms with effort, more from her own self than Xavier holding onto her.

'You're right.' A bleak look crossed his face and he stepped away. 'I'll go and make some coffee. I came home early to talk to you...and then when you weren't here...'

'I...I wanted to talk to you about something too...'

'I'll get us both coffee and bring it into the sitting room.'

He went towards the kitchen and Jane took off her coat, hanging it up and going into the sitting room. She felt ridiculously nervous, pacing up and down, biting her lips, wrapping her arms around her body, sitting down and then standing up.

He appeared at the door silently, with two mugs in his hands. She took the one he handed her. She wrapped her hands around it as if to pull some of the heat into her chilled body. Take some comfort where she could.

She sat on the couch while Xavier stood pensively by the fire.

'Jane, I—'

'Look, Xavier...'

They spoke at the same time. Jane put down her mug and stood up, feeling at a disadvantage sitting down. She locked her hands together to stop the betraying tremor. She needed to calm herself before launching into the hardest confession of her life. She needed time.

She gestured to him. 'You go first...'

He stood for a minute, looking into the fire, before turning towards her. She'd never seen him look so serious, and so distant that it scared her a little. She felt an awful foreboding trickle down her spine.

'Tell me, Jane, does the sight of me really disgust you so much that you can't look at me without your body being rigid with tension?'

'Of course not...how can you say such a thing...?' Her eyes widened in reproach, confusion in their depths, her body going even more rigid despite his words.

'Because ever since we got married you've been like a deer

caught in the headlights…flinching whenever I come near you…rigid like you are now, with that cool icy look in your eyes. Oh, I know how to make you relax—' he laughed harshly '—it's very apparent to both of us how we can make the tension disappear. But then afterwards you can barely wait until I've pulled free of your body before you shut down again.'

Jane blanched at his crude words, remembering all too vividly the night in the penthouse when *he* had been the one to pull away, get out of there as fast as he could. And her humiliation and self-derision rose again like bile.

'It seems to me to be mutual.' She couldn't disguise the bitterness lacing her voice.

He noted it with a look, and emitted an audible sigh. 'I've been thinking all day today about…us. And not just today, if I'm honest. It's something I've tried to avoid thinking about.' He looked into the fire for a moment before looking back at her. 'There's something I should explain, though.'

'Go on.'

She marveled that she sounded so calm.

He thrust his hands into his pockets. 'My parents weren't happily married. By the time my mother died when I was five I was being used as a pawn in their relentless bitter feuds with one another. That's why my father never remarried; he was bitter his whole life, and he took it out on me.' His lips thinned. 'Everyone assumed he never remarried because he loved my mother so much, but it was the opposite. And…I'm afraid that I can see the same thing happening with us. Jane, this morning we were sniping at each other like…exactly how they used to.'

He looked at her, his eyes fixing her with their green luminescence. She took in his words, dimly remembered every time she'd brought up his father, only to have him change the subject, the look that would cross his face. It made sense now. She had to focus when he spoke again.

'I won't bring a child into that again…so that's why I'm

prepared to give you a separation if you want. At least if we're apart, we might be able to maintain respect for each other.'

She stopped breathing. 'What…what do you mean…?' she asked faintly.

'I think we both know this marriage isn't working. You went into this with the clearest of motivations, intentions… and I took advantage of that. The inheritance is assured by our marriage. I shouldn't have brought you back here…'

She couldn't understand how everything wasn't crumbling around her, disintegrating. She sank down onto the couch behind her, her eyes unseeing, unfocused on the ground in front of her.

Xavier's voice continued, like a relentless battering ram against her heart,

'Believe me, I'm tempted to do the cowardly thing, indulge our physical attraction, keep going as if nothing is wrong—and I know you might too, up to a point. I thought it would work…that it would be possible with just…just what we had. But it's not. We're becoming bitter, and that will poison any chance of a civil relationship.'

He was talking about their attraction being the only thing he thought they could have worked on…and even that wasn't enough now.

He paused and took a deep breath. She knew he hated the admission with every bone in his body. It would be hard for him to admit to any frailty, weakness, and their marriage not working would fall under that.

She found herself nodding her head. It was the worst-case scenario. Even knowing that this had happened, *was* happening, she could feel the tiny part of her that had clung to treacherous hope…die.

Just don't make me speak… I can't speak, can't breathe.

'I can set you up wherever you want. If you want to stay

here, I'll go to the mainland. You'll be taken care of... I would just ask that you consider staying in France, so I can have more access to...our child.'

He sounded so cold, so clinical.

She forced herself to stand again, not wanting him to see the devastation on her face, in her body. Well, now she knew. He'd done her the unwitting favour of allowing her to keep her dignity intact. He'd never know how much she loved him.

She looked up, focusing on a point just beyond his shoulder, the lines in her face rigid. He came towards her, she backed away.

'Jane? You can't tell me you're happy...you're not the same person I knew in the summer.'

Neither was he...

'No...I'm not happy.'

That much at least was true.

They faced each other like strangers. A gaping chasm between them.

'You wanted to tell me something?'

She looked at him then, and she had to keep back the slightly hysterical laugh that threatened to bubble out of her mouth. 'Would you believe it was to ask for a separation, too...?'

He sighed heavily. 'Yes, I would. At least it seems we're agreed on this.'

She turned blindly and walked out of the room, just managing to stop herself from running out through the door.

'Jane—wait. We should talk about this now...what we're going to do.'

She turned with huge effort at the door, her face white, her eyes huge blue pools. 'I'm very tired. I'd like to lie down for a while.'

'I'll take the spare room tonight.'

That was all she heard as she walked across the hall, her

singular desire right then to get away to some private space where she could be alone with her pain.

Just as she approached the stairs she had the strangest sensation of not feeling her legs—before a blinding cramp seized her middle and she doubled over in pain. It was so intense that she couldn't breathe. She was vaguely aware of someone calling her name, arms supporting her…and then she collapsed.

She came to for a second, was only half aware of Xavier picking her up into his arms, and then she thought of the baby. Completely forgetting the recent conversation, the uppermost thing in her head with crystal-clear clarity was this baby—and what the future would hold if anything should happen to it

Nothing.

He would send her away, let her go. She clutched his jumper in a white-knuckle grip.

'Xavier…the baby. Nothing can happen to the baby… I need it so much… I love…' And she passed out again.

CHAPTER FOURTEEN

JANE opened her eyes slowly and realised that she was lying on their bed, dim light casting shadows into the room. Then she saw Xavier standing at the base of the bed, talking to some man in a suit. That was weird. Why was she on the bed? And what was that man doing in their room?

She tried to speak and a croak came out. The men turned to face her. The older man hurried to her side. He lifted her hand and took her pulse.

'Hello, my dear, you gave us quite a fright…'

His words meant little to Jane as she struggled to take things in.

'What…what happened?'

She looked from Xavier to the man with a frown on her face.

He sat on the bed and kept her hand in his. 'Jane, I'm Dr Villeneuve. Xavier called me when you collapsed a short time ago. Luckily I was here on the island, doing my rounds, and was close by…otherwise you would have been taken to the hospital on the mainland.'

Suddenly it all came back—every single second of what had happened. Her hand went straight to her belly, her face white.

'The baby…?' But even as she felt her bump, she knew it was all right. The relief she felt made her feel giddy with light-headedness. She caught Xavier's eye, but his face was immobile, shuttered.

Dr Villeneuve patted her hand and looked at Xavier. 'If you'll excuse us for a moment, Xavier? Now that she's awake I'll need to do a thorough exam, just to make sure she's safe to rest here for the night. But she will need to go to the hospital first thing tomorrow.'

'Of course.' Xavier's voice was terse and he left the room.

The doctor helped Jane to undress, and examined her for any signs of anything more serious than a cramp. When she had changed into nightclothes, he came back and sat beside her on the bed.

'Jane…I'm happy enough that nothing is wrong. It's clear that this is stress-related, and it can be common enough, although very frightening. I know it's your first pregnancy, and it can take a lot out of you. You need to take care of yourself…is there anything bothering you?'

She looked into his kind, jovial face and felt like crying.

Only that Xavier doesn't love me and wants to separate…

She shook her head. 'No…don't worry, Doctor. I'll take care of myself and the baby.'

He gestured to the door with a smile. 'And that man out there, wearing a hole in the floor! I've never seen him so frantic. He pulled me out of my car before it had stopped moving. I shudder to think what he would have done if I hadn't been passing. He's asked me to stay for the night, and I'll come to the hospital with you in the morning…he's a very persuasive man.'

She smiled weakly. Xavier's concern for the baby was admirable, but not exactly a soothing balm to her spirit. The doctor left her, and when he was gone she heard his and Xavier's steps echo down the hall.

She sank back into the pillows. The last thing she remembered was Xavier wanting to talk things through, and then that awful pain. She focused on her breathing and staying calm. She wouldn't think about what they had said now…knowing very well that her cramp had been brought on by the sheer shock of Xavier informing her he wanted a separation.

Thank God she hadn't spoken first. To have to separate and have Xavier know how she felt would have made him look at her with such pity…at least this way she could leave, dignity relatively intact.

The door opened and he stood framed in the doorway. Jane's breath stopped, and then quickened as her heart leapt.

'Xavier, the doctor doesn't have to stay. The poor man probably wants to go home to his family.'

'I'm not taking any chances. He's staying, and that's that.'

His tone brooked no argument. He closed the door behind him and came further in, shedding clothes as he did. Jane's mouth went dry as she watched him.

'What are you doing? I thought you said you were going to sleep in the spare room.'

'The doctor is using the spare room.'

'There are at least five more,' she pointed out, an edge of panic strangling her voice.

'And they're all the other end of the house…I won't have the doctor that far away, and you are not sleeping on your own. Anything could happen.'

She averted her face, closing her eyes to his naked body climbing in beside her, her hands clenched under the covers. The doctor had said to stay away from stress—surely this qualified as stress? She could feel her pulse skyrocket.

She lay on her back, eyes closed, and heard the light click off, felt the darkness surround them. Their breathing was unbearably loud to her ears in the quiet room. She could feel a heavy cloud of need and desire hover over them, felt her body coming alive against her will.

Suddenly a gravelly cough from across the hall broke the spell. The doctor. Imperceptibly Jane breathed out a sigh of relief, and turned on her side, willing her body to calm down.

She sank into a deep, dreamless sleep, half waking during

the night to feel herself tucked into Xavier's chest, his head resting on hers, arms tight around her belly and chest, spooning her lower body. In blissful half-consciousness, able to ignore reality, dangerous thoughts, she snuggled in tighter and drifted off again. She told herself this contact was inevitable if they were in the same bed. She knew well enough that morning was just around the corner. And perhaps it was the last time she would ever share a bed with him.

When she woke, sunlight was streaming into the room. Jane took a moment to remember the previous night's events. When she did, a hard weight lodged in her heart. No more hope…no more maybe….no more possibility that perhaps he could come to feel something…

She pulled herself out of the bed, feeling a hundred years old. A small reassuring kick deep in her belly focused her thoughts and reminded her of how close she'd come to nearly losing everything. At least with the baby she'd always have a piece of him.

A movement caught her attention, and she looked up to see Xavier come into the room. He was carrying a tray, and looked smart and cleanshaven, but there were lines around his mouth and circles under his eyes. She willed down the concern that rose up.

'Here's some breakfast. Dr Villeneuve is downstairs, ready to go when you're dressed.'

'I feel much better today. I'm sure I'll be fine. There's no need—'

'Jane. We're going to the hospital.'

He left the tray and walked out. He'd hardly even looked at her.

She forced herself to eat something small, but it tasted like chalk in her mouth. She washed and dressed in jeans and a simple smock top before making her way downstairs.

In no time they were in the chopper, landed, shown to a

waiting car, and then Jane was being settled into a private
room at the hospital. The whole thing happened so fast it
made her head spin. The nurse left, and then it was just the
two of them.

A heavy silence settled over the room. Xavier crossed his
arms and rested back against the sill of the window.

'Tell me, I'm interested to know why you were going to
ask for a separation…you never did say.'

Her hand stilled on the sheet. The conversational tone he'd
used, as if it was as innocuous a comment as asking about
the weather, made her see red. The pain and anger she'd been
holding in since yesterday evening, the pain that had caused
her to cramp, rose like acid bile on her tongue, and she wanted
to lash out. Lash out at his cool façade, his reserve, his perfectly articulated reasons why he thought they should
separate. As if he was in supreme control, capable of these
rational judgements. She wanted to smash through that
control…say something to make him squirm…run out
through the door and perhaps finally leave her in peace.

She hitched up her chin, looked him in the eye, and with
an unwavering voice she was proud of said, 'Would you
believe that I was going to ask for a separation because…?'
She faltered. Faced with those devastating eyes, her brave
façade crumbled, her heart skipped a beat.

'Well…?' he taunted softly, quirking a black brow over
cool, sardonic eyes.

It was all the impetus she needed. White hands clenched the
bedspread. The full weight of her heartache settled over her
like a dark cloud. She felt her voice quaver but didn't care. The
words came stumbling, rushing out, tripping over each other…

'Because…Xavier…I love you. I love you so much I can't
breathe with it. Every time I look at you I want to make love
to you. I hurt all over, but especially in my heart, because
you don't love me, and if we don't separate then I'm afraid
that by the time this baby is born there won't be anything

left of me. Because I just can't bear to be in the same room as you and want you so much, and know that it's only physical attraction you feel, and that you only want me for this baby…' She paused for a second, drawing in a gulping, shuddering breath, too distraught to see how he had straightened and paled. 'And that you don't, can't, *won't* ever love me…that's why…and it's just as good a reason, if not better, than yours.'

Tears blurred her vision and she fought to stop the wobble in her lip, feeling more raw and exposed than she'd ever felt. In shock at what she had just said.

She turned her head away, closing her eyes, the tears trickling down her cheeks as she waited to hear the click of the door. Waited to give in to the huge sobs she could barely hold back, her chest heaving silently.

Instead of the door opening and closing, she felt the bed dip beside her, and a warm hand under her chin, turning her head around. She kept her eyes shut tight, bringing a hand over her face in a pathetic attempt to hide her anguish.

Xavier brought her hand down. The sobs were threatening to break free. She choked them back, opening pain-filled streaming eyes. 'Just go, Xavier…please, leave me alone.'

He was intense, his eyes roving over her face. 'Jane, it's the baby you love, not me.'

How could he do this to her? Humiliate her? Wasn't it enough that she had laid her heart bare for him, and now he had to trample it into the ground? Why wasn't he walking away?

'Xavier, if you can't handle the truth, then leave. This is why I want to separate.'

'But, Jane, all along you've said…' He stopped, started again. 'When you collapsed it was the only thing you mentioned before passing out…'

She pulled his hand down from her chin, saying with a choked voice, 'Of *course* I love the baby…but, like it or not, I love you too. I was scared because this baby is my only link to you. There—are you satisfied? Now, just go and leave me be…*please*.'

He still didn't move. He dropped his head, his hands fists on the bedspread either side of her body. She wiped at the tears on her cheeks and waited for him to stand up and leave, a little hiccup escaping her mouth.

He brought his head up and fixed her with a look of something indefinable that she'd never seen before. Her breath caught in her throat. She couldn't escape his eyes, pinning her to the spot, their brilliant green reminding her of their first meeting.

'Jane…I did think it might be best to separate because of what I told you about my parents. But the stronger reason was that I couldn't live with myself any more for making you so unhappy. Because every time we slept together you were hating me a little more…every time I saw joy in your face for the baby I felt jealous…'

A numbness was taking her over. She recognised it as a form of self-protection. What was he saying?

He went to reach for her hand, but she drew back. He could see the trepidation in her eyes.

'Jane…let me explain. Ever since that night in the penthouse—'

She cut him off, her body taut with tension. 'You were the one who left. And the next morning…you were so cold…'

'I left because…sleeping with you again blew everything out of the water. My feelings didn't go away, they got stronger. And I was jealous…insanely…of your joy in the baby when…when we had just shared…' He stopped himself, a rare vulnerability in his eyes. '*You* were so cool, so blasé about it. As if you'd decided sleeping together was nothing more than giving in to our overwhelming physical urges. I told myself I didn't need feelings to be involved…' He gave a short sharp laugh. 'You were handing me exactly what I thought I wanted, and suddenly it wasn't enough.'

'All *you* want is this baby…'

'I told myself that at the start. I used the baby to justify how much I had to have you, no matter how it happened. When you came to me in London, so self-contained and full of independence, I followed the strongest instinct I've ever felt and did all I could to make you marry me, sure that you'd fall into my bed and we'd pick where we left off and I wouldn't have to examine my feelings.'

'But you— Feelings? You weren't even *thinking* about me...'

'Wasn't I?' He lifted a brow, a rueful look on his face.

Jane still clung onto the protective shield.

'I had your address for two months before I saw you. I had you traced a month after you left... I'll admit I wasn't sure if I was going to get in touch, but I know that I wanted to...and believe me, I didn't like feeling like that.'

She frowned, shaking her head. 'But how...? What about all those women? I saw the papers, all the models...'

He hung his head and groaned before coming back up, his gaze on her mouth, her eyes. 'I took them all out...wined them, dined them...even kissed a few—and as soon as I did the memory of you would break through and any desire I felt disappeared. It happened with infuriating regularity, and no woman...*ever*...has had that effect on me.'

She resisted the pull...dampened the spark that wanted to erupt in her chest.

'But when you asked me to marry you...you left me alone...didn't come back until the wedding.'

'I couldn't be near you. It was too intense. I was terrified of losing you again, and so in denial about how I was feeling that I went as far away as I could...'

He looked away for a moment, then back, a sad light in his eyes. 'After witnessing my parents' fighting, my father's bitterness, I never dared believe I could feel the real thing...I didn't know what it was. This summer you reached a part of me I didn't know existed...then, when you left...'

He looked shamefaced. 'I think on some level I wanted to

tie you to me, sate my desire, which I told myself was the root of all my feelings, and punish you for making me feel so vulnerable. I was so sure you felt nothing for me. But then…it was slowly killing me inside to know how unhappy I was making you. It was the hardest thing I ever did, telling you that you could leave.'

'What…what exactly are you saying?'

She had to be strong. His words still didn't necessarily mean what she thought, hoped. It could just be pity…guilt… and that would kill her all over again.

His eyes stunned her with their intensity. 'Jane, I have not stopped thinking about you since that day you…*we* bumped into each other. It was a *coup de foudre*—love at first sight. I know that now, but it's taken me the longest time to just give in and admit it to myself…'

He grew blurry again through her tears. The spark grew; her heart cracked open.

He tenderly wiped her cheeks with his thumbs, his hands warm around her jaw. She put her hands over his.

'I've been in love with you for so long. I couldn't believe I'd fallen for you that week…' She hiccuped again. 'So stupid.'

'Shh, you don't have to say anything…'

'But I do. I didn't stay in June because I couldn't bear to be just your mistress, especially after Sasha—' She stopped, the pain of that morning still vivid.

Xavier frowned. 'After Sasha, what?'

'She came to the suite that morning and told me that she had organised everything for our date… She told me that it was your usual routine—the pampering, the champagne, dinner…that she did this for all your…women.'

His whole body tensed, his hands dropped. 'No wonder you left… She must have seen that you were different. You have to believe me, Jane. She must have heard me on the phone… I'll bloody kill her.'

He looked so fierce that Jane took his hand. 'I do…I do believe you. I know now that she's no threat.'

She looked down at her hand on his, still not really sure if she could believe. She wanted to tell him…everything.

'When we got married, I didn't sleep with you because I thought you'd guess straight away how I felt. I was so raw and emotional with the pregnancy, and seeing you again…but of course you were right.' She smiled a watery smile, 'What I suppressed only got stronger—the *urges*—God, how I hated using that word—were always there. But using the pregnancy was the only way I knew to try and keep you at a distance. At the ball I wanted to rip the head off every woman there…'

He shook his head ruefully. 'Not sleeping with me was the smartest thing you did…it forced me to face myself. And as for the ball, when I saw you with Pete…he's lucky he got to walk away.'

He looked at her, his face suddenly serious. 'Jane, do you really mean what you said? Are you sure it's not just the baby…?'

'My darling, I loved you long before I found out about the baby…'

He brought his hands up to frame her face again. Jane could feel them tremble. 'When you collapsed in my arms…' He closed his eyes, his skin suddenly ashen. 'If anything had happened to you, I don't think I could have lived. I love you so much that it terrifies me…'

'I'm not going anywhere… I love you, Xavier, with all my heart and soul.'

'And you and this baby—' he bent and pressed a kiss to her belly '—are my heart and soul, *mon coeur*. Without you, my life would be over.'

Then he took her lips in a sweet, healing kiss, a kiss of benediction, and with such reverence that fresh tears streamed down her cheeks—just as the door opened and the doctor walked in.

'What's this? I said no stress.'

They couldn't take their eyes off each other. Jane smiled. 'Everything is just fine.'

Six months later, at the annual summer fête, the island was celebrating. Xavier tucked Jane into his side and held Amelie against his shoulder while she cradled Max against her chest.

Jane's mother and Arthur bustled over. 'You young people need to have fun and relax. We'll take care of the little ones.'

Giving in to a greater force, Jane chuckled as she handed over her son, and watched as Xavier handed over his daughter with comical reluctance and care.

'Will they be OK?' he asked, looking anxiously after the doting elders holding their precious bundles.

Jane slipped her arm around his waist, pushing a hand into one jeans pocket and cheekily squeezing his firm behind. 'Yes, darling, they're taking them for the day—which means I have you all to myself.'

He managed to drag his worried eyes away and brought Jane around to face him, drawing her in tight against his body. She blissfully laced her fingers around the back of his head and moved sinuously against his pelvis, exulting in his low, appreciative groan.

'As I'm not flying in "one of those death traps", as you so succinctly put it—this year or ever again if it reduces you to the terror that you told me it did—then why don't we go somewhere a little more private?'

'Yes, please.'

They walked towards the castle, which wasn't far in the distance, arms wrapped tight around each other.

'Do you think we can find out well in advance if there's any likelihood of twins again? I don't know if I could handle the shock.'

Jane had to laugh out loud as she remembered the moment

that day in the hospital when, during a check-up scan, they had discovered for the first time that she was carrying twins. The doctor had informed them that it was rare, but nevertheless quite possible, for one twin to mask the other until relatively late in the pregnancy.

She pretended to think for a second. 'You know, I must ask Mum. I'm nearly certain there are triplets somewhere on her side…'

He lifted her up into his arms. 'You witch…you just want to see me go into Neanderthal protection mode again…'

'But you did it so well…' She batted her eyelashes up at him.

He claimed her mouth in a hot and desperate kiss. All joking fled from her mind as her pulse speeded up and a familiar throb of desire pulsed through her veins. By the time they got to the front door they were both breathing heavily, with flushed cheeks.

He looked down into her face with such naked love and desire that her heart sang.

'Do you have any idea how happy you've made me?' he asked huskily.

She brought a tender hand up to caress his face. 'If it's half as happy as you make me every day, then we have enough happiness to last a few lifetimes.

THE FRENCHMAN'S
CAPTIVE WIFE

Chantelle Shaw

Chantelle Shaw lives on the Kent coast, five minutes from the sea, and does much of her thinking about the characters in her books while walking on the beach. She's been an avid reader from an early age. Her schoolfriends used to hide their books when she visited—but Chantelle would retreat into her own world, and still writes stories in her head all the time. Chantelle has been blissfully married to her own tall, dark and very patient hero for over twenty years, and has six children. She began to read Mills & Boon® novels as a teenager and throughout the years of being a stay-at-home mum to her brood found romantic fiction helped her to stay sane! She enjoys reading and writing about strong-willed, feisty women, and even stronger-willed sexy heroes. Chantelle is at her happiest when writing. She is particularly inspired while cooking dinner, which unfortunately results in a lot of culinary disasters! She also loves gardening, walking, and eating chocolate (followed by more walking!).

PROLOGUE

August

'OF COURSE WE didn't *bribe* Jean-Luc to marry you!' Sarah Dyer said crisply, 'although I admit there was some financial incentive.'

'Oh, God.' Emily swung away from her mother as a wave of sickness gripped her. Sarah always spent a few weeks of the summer with friends in Hampstead and, although mother and daughter had never been particularly close, she was the first person Emily had turned to in her hour of need. But rather than sympathising, Sarah had unwittingly added the final nail to the coffin. She couldn't stay with Luc now.

'Darling, you have to understand that Jean-Luc Vaillon isn't like other men. You don't amass a multimillion-pound fortune without a ruthless streak, and your husband is first and foremost a businessman.'

'I know,' Emily murmured dully. She didn't need anyone to remind her of Luc's dedication to work, but she was prepared to put up with the endless business trips and the long hours he spent shut away in his study if she thought there was any hope that he might love her.

'The trouble with you, Emily, is that you're a romantic,' Sarah went on, after another glance at her daughter's pale face. 'Perhaps Jean-Luc is having a fling with his personal assistant, but you're his wife and it's in everyone's best interests that you remain so. Pregnancy can place a marriage under huge strain,' she added, eyeing Emily's swollen abdomen, 'and, to put it frankly, I imagine your husband is an extremely virile man. Once the baby's born, everything will return to normal, you'll see.'

But what constituted normal? Emily wondered bleakly as she trudged across the heath, after assuring her mother she would do nothing rash. She had realised soon after her marriage that her role in Luc's life was designated almost exclusively to the bedroom. The fierce sexual attraction that had existed from the moment they had first met was their only real form of communication. Their passion for each other had made them equal but without it they had nothing.

It was busy on the heath. The air rang with children's high-pitched laughter as families took advantage of the late summer sunshine, and as Emily watched a man and a little boy flying a kite, something snapped in her head. She gave a low moan, like an animal in pain, and swiftly covered her mouth with her hands as if she could push the sound back inside. She couldn't fall apart now, not here, but her legs gave way and she sank onto a bench as she faced the reality that her son would never enjoy such an innocent pastime with his father.

She could stay, she thought desperately. For the sake of the baby inside her she could turn a blind eye to the fact that her husband was an unfaithful liar. But Jean-Luc did not want their child any more than he wanted her. His look of horror when he had learned of her pregnancy still haunted her, and his coldness towards her ever since only reinforced her belief that he viewed their marriage as a mistake.

How long had his affair with his personal assistant been going on? she wondered miserably. Robyn Blake had worked for him for years and right from the start she had never missed a chance to emphasise the special relationship she shared with Luc. She was his brother's widow, not just a member of his staff, and Emily had tried to banish her feelings of jealousy at the obvious affection that existed between her husband and his PA. But now she had irrefutable proof that Robyn was Luc's mistress and her sense of betrayal was unbearable.

What about her baby? her mind argued. Her excitement when the ultrasound scan had revealed she was carrying a boy had been overshadowed by misery that Luc hadn't been with her. Of all the hurt he had inflicted on her, that had been the worst, she acknowledged bitterly. He hadn't even bothered to turn up at the hospital to see the magical, grainy image of their child, and she had to face the agonising truth that he just didn't care. Even if she told him he was going to have a son it would make little difference to his attitude. He seemed to grow more and more distant with each passing day and his polite indifference tortured her. Surely it would be better to go now, before her baby was born, and envelop him in her love rather than let him suffer the pain of realising his father had a lump of ice where his heart should be?

Leaving Luc would break her heart, Emily accepted bleakly, but to stay with him now would kill her, and with a muffled sob she stumbled towards the road.

'Where to, love?' the taxi driver asked cheerfully as she climbed into the cab, and for a split second she was torn by indecision, the address of Luc's Chelsea penthouse hovering on her lips.

Maybe she should give him one more chance? Maybe there was a rational explanation why he had spent the night he'd arrived back from Australia with Robyn, rather than returning home to her? But she could not dismiss the images that tortured her mind of Luc making love to his beautiful assistant, and despair overwhelmed her.

Face it, it's over, she told herself savagely, biting down on her lip until her mouth filled with blood. Luc didn't love her and, to give him his due, he had never pretended to. Her mother's revelation that his proposal had been part of a shrewd financial deal only emphasised that fact.

She loved him so much, maybe too much. He was her life, her reason for living, but at that moment the baby kicked and she felt a determined little foot push against her stomach. Now there was a new reason, she reminded herself fiercely, and lifting her chin she relayed the address of her friend Laura's flat to the waiting driver.

CHAPTER ONE

A year later—San Antonia

'ARE YOU SURE you've got everything? Passports, tickets, keys to the flat?'

'Everything's under control—stop fretting,' Emily bade her friend cheerfully. 'You've got enough to worry about. The coach is here.'

Arrivals day was always hectic, she mused as she followed Laura out into the courtyard. The farmhouse at San Antonia had once been a quiet refuge for Laura's boyfriend and his crowd of artist friends. All that had changed when Nick had persuaded Laura to join him in Spain and she had opened up her cookery school. The business had been an instant success, catering for tourists eager to take lessons from an innovative chef who had earned her stars at a top London restaurant. Emily was pleased for Laura and glad she had been able to help out by organising the guests' living and sleeping facilities, but the time had come for her go back to England and take control of her life.

'I hope you'll manage,' she murmured as she joined her friend on the front step and watched the party alight from the coach. 'I could be away for a couple of months while the lawyers sort out the divorce.'

'From bitter experience, I'd better warn you it could take a lot longer than that,' Laura replied grimly. 'Mine took over a year to finalise and cost me a small fortune.'

'I'm not anticipating any problems,' Emily said with a shrug. 'Luc will be as pleased as me to see the end of our marriage.' Especially if the recent photo in one of the British tabloids was anything to go by, she thought bleakly. Seeing his dark, handsome features again had momentarily caused her heart to stop beating. She had been shocked to discover the effect he still had on her, even after more than a year apart, but it had been the sight of his companion, the stunningly beautiful Robyn Blake, that had been the catalyst for her decision to bring a legal end to their farcical marriage.

It was time to put the past behind her, she thought resolutely. She had a baby, a burgeoning new business of her own and the freedom to live her life the way she chose. She enjoyed her independence, she reminded herself fiercely. She had fought hard to rebuild her self-respect and it was time to sever the legal ties that bound her to Jean-Luc Vaillon.

'How do you think you'll feel about seeing your husband again?' Laura asked.

'With any luck, I won't have to. I don't want anything from him, certainly not money,' Emily added fiercely.

'You're entitled to demand that he make proper provision for Jean-Claude,' Laura pointed out. 'Luc is his father after all, and it won't hurt him to dip into the Vaillon millions.'

'No!' Emily instantly refuted the suggestion. 'I'm responsible for my son and I'll provide for him. Luc never wanted a child. Jean-Claude's conception was an accident and I refuse to use him as leverage for financial gain. I'll manage,' she assured her friend brightly when Laura frowned in concern, 'but I won't take anything from Luc.'

In theory it all seemed so simple. She would make contact with Luc through a third party, and if he expressed any interest in seeing his son, the lawyers could thrash out the access arrangements along with the divorce. She wasn't expecting any complications but as she glanced over to where Jean-Claude was sleeping in his pushchair, shaded from the sun by a parasol, she was filled with a sense of foreboding. Nothing about Jean-Luc Vaillon was simple. He was a man of secrets and despite the fact that they had been married for two years, she didn't really know him at all.

'Someone's arrived in style.' Laura's voice broke into her thoughts and she glanced across the courtyard at the sleek black limousine that had swung in behind the coach. 'I hope they appreciate that this is a working holiday. I won't have time to run around after some spoilt millionaire's wife who can't boil an egg. The coach driver is quite happy to take you to the airport,' she added as she stepped forward to greet her guests. 'He's finished unloading now so you can give him your luggage before you have to disturb Jean-Claude.' She gave Emily a brief kiss on the cheek. 'Take care. We'll celebrate your new life as a single woman when you come back.'

A quick glance at the buggy revealed that Jean-Claude was still sleeping soundly and Emily decided to leave him for a few more minutes while she loaded her cases.

'How are you, Enzo?' she greeted the coach driver, who regularly made the journey between San Antonia and the airport.

'*Hola, Señora,* you're looking pretty today.'

Conversation about Enzo's huge extended family took another five minutes and when Emily looked back at the pushchair, it was empty. Laura must have taken Jean-Claude into the farmhouse, she thought, a prickle of unease threading along her spine. Something made her turn her head towards the car parked at the further end of the courtyard.

For a few seconds she thought it must be a trick of the light, a mirage brought on by the heat of the midday sun, but when she blinked she realised he was no illusion. Handsome was hardly an adequate description of him, she acknowledged numbly. This man was awesome, the power of his broad shoulders beneath his superbly tailored jacket so formidable that a trembling started deep inside her.

The air in the courtyard was still and sultry but she could not suppress a shiver as her eyes travelled up to the visitor's face and locked with his cold, grey stare. His eyes were hooded, hiding his expression, but she was struck by the hardness that emanated from him, the air of arrogance, of ruthlessness and sheer power, and she gave a cry as the world spun.

'Luc!'

Confusion made her close her eyes, as if by doing so she could rid herself of the unwelcome vision, but when she opened them again he was still there, larger than life, taller and more imposing than anyone she had ever met and her hands flew to cover her mouth, forcing back her cry.

'What are you doing here? What do you want?' she demanded tremulously, shock almost robbing her of her voice. He smiled, his mouth stretching to reveal his teeth so that she was reminded of a wolf preparing to devour its prey.

'I've already got what I came for, *chérie,*' he taunted softly, and she stared at him in confusion. 'It's up to you whether you choose to join us.'

'Us?' Emily parroted, her brain moving as sluggishly as

treacle. 'I don't understand.' She felt breathless and disorientated as he towered over her. Her heart was pounding and it took every ounce of her courage to lift her eyes to his face. If anything he was even more devastatingly good-looking than she remembered, leaner and harder than the man who regularly haunted her dreams. Looking at him caused a peculiar feeling inside, like a knife being thrust between her ribs, and she quickly tore her eyes away, blinking under the brilliant glare of the sun.

Luc's arrival at the farmhouse was so unexpected she didn't know what to do, what to say. 'How did you find me?' she croaked at last, and his expression hardened.

'You wrote to your solicitor, requesting that he start divorce proceedings,' he reminded her coolly. 'I must commend him for the speed with which he contacted my legal firm to set the wheels in motion.'

'Mr Carmichael has taken care of the Dyer family's legal matters for years,' Emily faltered. 'I specifically asked him to withhold my whereabouts and I don't believe he would have willingly handed you that information.'

'No, but his very pretty junior secretary proved much more amenable,' he murmured silkily. 'The evenings spent wining and dining her proved highly profitable—in more ways than one,' he added dulcetly, and the sudden gleam in his eyes sickened her.

'I really don't want to know the details of your grubby love life,' she snapped, hurt coursing through her, 'although from past experience I imagine *love* plays very little part in it. But I still don't understand why you're here,' she continued stonily, refusing to acknowledge that the familiar tang of the aftershave he favoured had evoked a host of memories she wished had remained buried. 'Presumably you read my letter explaining to Mr Carmichael that I would be returning to England to sort out the divorce. Why didn't you just wait for me?'

Luc inhaled sharply, his nostrils flaring as he sought to control the anger that surged through him. 'I have spent almost a year longing to see my child,' he ground out savagely, his eyes as cold and hard as slate, and Emily shivered as she realised the full extent of his fury. 'Did you really expect me to wait passively, hoping you would show up? Do you have any idea what it felt like to learn from a letter you'd sent your solicitor that I had fathered a son? *Sacré bleu!*' he ground out, his jaw rigid with tension. 'You were happy to inform Monsieur Carmichael, but you didn't even have the decency to tell me my son had been born, and for that I can never forgive you.'

'Why should I have done?' Emily defended herself, genuinely puzzled by his anger. 'Why would I have rushed to tell you I'd given birth to our child when you were so vehemently opposed to his conception? You made it clear that you didn't want either of us, Luc, so how can you blame me for wanting to bring Jean-Claude up among people who care for him?'

'If you think I will allow my child to spend his formative years in a hippy commune you are even more delusional that I thought,' he snarled furiously. 'I have lost the first precious months of my son's life and I hold you and your half-baked theories about my supposed affair with my personal assistant completely to blame. Jealousy is not an attractive emotion, *chérie,*' he said, his eyes raking over her trembling form disparagingly. 'You allowed your childish craving for attention to colour your judgement but the one to suffer most is our son. You had no right to deny him a relationship with me, and from now on he will know exactly who his father is,' he told her forcefully, his gaze brimful of bitterness that corroded her soul.

'I would never prevent you from seeing Jean-Claude, if that's what you want,' she muttered as she tried to come to terms with the astounding realisation that Luc seemed to want his son after all. Perhaps it had only been the sight of her pregnant body that had filled him with revulsion, she thought bitterly. 'I assumed you would want nothing to do with him but I'm prepared to be reasonable about access arrangements if you've really lost your aversion to fatherhood.'

'How very generous of you.' Luc's voice dripped with sarcasm and she flushed. He'd always had the knack of making her feel two feet high and once she would have backed down at the slightest hint of confrontation. Now she lifted her chin and stared at him, cursing her body's involuntary reaction to him. How could he still have such an effect on her after everything he'd put her through, the humiliation he'd heaped on her?

She'd been overwhelmed from the first moment she'd set eyes on him, she acknowledged grimly. There was something about his face, the sharp cheekbones and very slightly hooked nose, that gave him the appearance of a hawk, his eyes gleaming from beneath heavy black brows, watchful and calculating. It was hard to believe that those eyes had once softened to the colour of woodsmoke, that the cruel line of his mouth had moulded into a sensual curve as he had explored her lips with a degree of passion and tenderness that had left her weak with longing.

She bit back a gasp as a curious pain uncoiled in the pit of her stomach, self-disgust swamping her as her imagination ran riot. What was desire doing, rearing its ugly head at a time like this, when Luc was studying her with insolent appraisal as if she was something unpleasant that had crawled out from beneath a stone? Swiftly she crossed her arms over her chest to hide her body's blatant betrayal, sickness flooding through her when his gaze settled on her breasts and she saw his lip curl in sardonic amusement.

'But, then, in certain areas you were always very generous, weren't you, Emily?' he drawled. 'Especially in bed.'

'Go to hell,' she snapped, tears of mortification stinging her eyelids. How dared he look at her like that, as if she was some cheap tart and he was considering sampling her wares? 'I'm surprised you even remember. It's a long time since you chose to share my bed but, then, you didn't need to did you, Luc? You were busy elsewhere.' She broke off abruptly, twin spots of colour staining her cheeks. Now was not the time to reveal the depths of the clawing jealousy she'd experienced on those long, lonely nights when she'd waited in vain for him to come home.

'As soon as I arrive in London, I'll have my lawyers contact yours to arrange suitable access to Jean-Claude,' she told him briskly as she looked towards the farmhouse. No doubt Laura was struggling to give her guests a guided tour of the kitchens with Jean-Claude clamped to her hip. The sooner she held her son in her arms the happier she would be, she decided after risking another peep at Luc's inscrutable face. 'If you'll excuse me, I need to go and find him,' she murmured awkwardly. She supposed she should invite Luc into the farmhouse to meet his son and her conscience prickled uncomfortably as he continued to stare down at her with those laser-beam eyes that she was sure could read her mind.

She didn't want to take him inside, she acknowledged as a faint edge of apprehension gripped her once more. San

Antonia was her territory, and for some reason she would prefer Luc's first meeting with his son to take place on the neutral ground of her solicitor's office. Time was getting on, she realised with a glance at her watch. The coach driver was looking impatient and if she wasn't careful she would miss her flight.

'Are you in the habit of losing my son?' Luc enquired, his brows raised sardonically, and she flushed.

'Of course not. I haven't lost him, just mislaid him,' she added, her vain attempt to lighten the situation, receiving no flicker of response from him. 'So, I'll see you in London.' She needed to walk away from him but it seemed as if her feet were trapped in quicksand and she couldn't move as her eyes greedily absorbed every detail of his beloved face. Not that she loved him any more, her mind hastily pointed out, but he possessed a magnetism that even now was wrapping itself around her, making coherent thought impossible.

'As you wish.' The curtness of Luc's tone broke the spell and she became aware of his sudden impatience as he flicked back the sleeve of his jacket to read his watch. The brief glimpse of his tanned wrist, dusted with a sprinkling of fine black hairs, caused her tummy to lurch and she inhaled sharply. 'We need to make a move anyway.'

His words puzzled her and she gave a harsh laugh. 'Let me guess. Robyn is waiting in the car for you. I can't fault her dedication to duty,' she said sarcastically.

He was already walking away from her and paused briefly to glance over his shoulder. '*Oui*, Robyn's behaviour and attitude are exemplary,' he replied in a tone that clearly indicated her own failing in both departments. 'But she is not with me this time. Jean-Claude is in the car and, no doubt, growing restless. *Au revoir, chérie.*'

Incredibly he had already dipped his head prior to sliding into the car and her feet suddenly grew wings. 'Luc! Wait, what do you mean, he's in the car? Jean-Claude is in the house with Laura—isn't he?' she finished uncertainly, and the blandness of his expression only served to increase her fear.

'I took the liberty of stowing my son safely in the car while your attention was…' He paused fractionally. 'Elsewhere. Tell me, *chérie,* are you always so careless about leaving him unattended and in the full glare of the sun?'

'He was shaded by the parasol,' Emily defended herself fiercely, 'and I did not leave him unattended. He was asleep and I was…' She was going to explain how she had taken advantage of Jean-Claude's brief nap to load her luggage onto the coach, but the scathing disgust in Luc's eyes made her want to crawl away.

'You were too busy to watch over him. Anyone could have taken him.' He pushed home the point by glancing into the car and she flushed. It was true that her attention had been focused on the trip back to London, but she had regularly checked on the baby and, besides, the farmhouse was miles from anywhere. A person would have to have been extremely determined, not to mention devious, to snatch him and unfortunately the description fitted Jean-Luc Vaillon to the letter.

She had reached the car and her shocked glance revealed that Jean-Claude was indeed inside, strapped into a baby seat and happily absorbed playing with the brightly coloured toys in front of him. 'But you can't just take him,' she faltered, her shock giving way to stark fury. 'How dare you try to take him from me? I'm his mother.' She rounded on him, her voice bristling with outrage as her fingers fumbled with the door-handle.

Instantly his hand closed over hers, his grip bruising as he surveyed her steadily from beneath his ridiculously long, black lashes. 'And I am his father, yet you thought nothing of keeping him from me. You deliberately hid yourself away and if it hadn't been for your greed, it's possible that I still wouldn't have found you or, more importantly, my son.'

'My greed?' Emily echoed faintly.

'I assume you were banking on a hefty divorce settlement to keep you in the manner to which you've become accustomed,' he mocked, his disdainful glance taking in the rambling farmhouse and various outbuildings, 'although I'm not sure why you need money in this God-forsaken spot. Perhaps you want it for other reasons than providing a secure environment for Jean-Claude?'

'Such as?' She glared at him, one hand on her hip while the other was still trapped beneath his.

'Drugs?' he suggested with a nonchalant shrug that belied the gleam of anger in his eyes. 'Who knows what goes on inside your hippy commune? All I care is that it is not a suitable place to bring up a small child, certainly not my child.'

'Because, of course, you are such a caring parent.' She could hardly speak as her anger choked her. 'San Antonia is not some sort of drugs den. It's a thriving community where everyone works together and where my friend Laura runs a cookery school for middle-aged ladies. The only drugs you'll find here are for rheumatism or the menopause!'

'I have never been given the opportunity to prove my worth as a parent,' Luc snapped, 'but that's about to change. My son is coming with me.'

'The hell he is!' From the corner of her eye Emily saw the coach driver lean out of his window.

'*Señorita,* we have to go.'

'Yes, I won't be a minute.' She tried to open the car door but Luc's hand tightened around her fingers until she was sure they would break. 'For God's sake, Luc!' Tears brought on through a mixture of pain and fear filled her eyes. 'You can't have him.'

'On the contrary, *chérie,* I already have him. It's up to you whether you come, too. Personally speaking, you can rot in hell,' he told her savagely. 'I would enjoy watching you burn in the eternal flames, but for his sake I suggest you get in the car.' Abruptly he released the catch and opened the door while she stared wildly around the courtyard, searching for someone to help her.

'There's no way I'd allow you to take him without me,' she vowed fiercely, and then gave a despairing cry as the coach began to move. 'My luggage is on the coach. Enzo, wait!'

Enzo must have caught sight of her frantic waving in his mirror and braked, but it took Emily precious minutes to drag her cases from the luggage compartment, and when she looked round, the limousine was already rolling forward.

'You bastard, you knew I was coming,' she sobbed as she yanked open the rear door and threw her cases into the footwell while Luc made no attempt to ask his chauffeur to halt. She was panting as she scrambled into the car and pulled the door shut after her. 'I've a good mind to have you charged with kidnap,' she snapped, and his sardonic smile told her he was as aware as she that she stood no chance of carrying out her threat. The trap was sprung. She was entirely at his mercy, she realised and trepidation filled her as, with a barely discernible snick, the door lock was activated.

'Not kidnap,' he murmured coolly as his gaze settled on her flushed face, 'I prefer repossession. And I promise you, *chérie,* this time you will not escape!'

CHAPTER TWO

THE ATMOSPHERE INSIDE the car crackled with antagonism. Jean-Claude suddenly lost interest in his toys, stared unblinkingly at Luc and then back at Emily, his bottom lip wobbling.

'It's all right, Mama's here. No one's going to hurt you,' she reassured him softly, stroking his cheek, and he turned his enormous, velvet grey eyes on her, his tears drying as his face broke into a smile that revealed his one solitary tooth. Luc was sitting on the other side of the baby seat and he stiffened at her words, outrage and bitter, corrosive anger filling him.

'Of course I'm not going to hurt him,' he snarled, aware of the necessity of keeping his voice low so that he did not frighten Jean-Claude. 'What kind of barbarian do you think I am to suggest I would hurt my own son?'

'You don't want to know my opinion of you,' Emily returned, her smile solely for Jean-Claude's benefit, belying the venom in her voice. 'You tried to drive off without me. Don't you think that wrenching a young baby from his mother's arms would hurt him?'

'Don't be so dramatic,' Luc snapped impatiently. 'You weren't even with him. You'd abandoned him. What kind of mother does that make you?'

'A damn good one, and I did not abandon him.' Emily ran a shaky hand over her face as reaction set in. 'He's eleven months old, for heaven's sake. How do you think he would cope without me? He needs me.'

Luc surveyed her silently, his eyes raking disparagingly over her slender figure and she cringed, wishing she'd worn anything but her bright orange gypsy skirt and yellow strap top. With her hair caught up in a ponytail secured with a livid yellow band and the long, beaded earrings and necklace that one of the artists had made for her, she looked funky and modern, a complete antithesis of the sophisticated, elegant women Luc admired. Women like his PA Robyn Blake.

'You're not as indispensable as you like to think,' he said icily. 'He'd soon forget you and instead of a mother he will have a father. However,' he continued, ignoring her fearful gasp, 'I accept that it is in Jean-Claude's best interests that you play a part in his life, for now at least.'

'Meaning what exactly?'

'Meaning that the situation is likely to change as he grows older but at the moment he is a baby and naturally depends on you. It is for that reason alone that I have decided to take you back,' he informed her in his cold, clipped tones, and Emily's eyes grew to the size of saucers.

'Well, pardon me for not jumping for joy, but I don't want to be taken back. I'm perfectly content with my life the way it is—without you in it. In fact,' she stressed, 'I've never been happier.' As she spoke she made the mistake of looking at him and her face flamed as she felt her body's involuntary reaction to his seductive charm. She didn't want to feel like this. She didn't want to be pierced by this overwhelming, almost obsessive sexual attraction, and the worst of it was, he was aware of his power over her.

'I'm sure I can come up with a few ideas to keep you content,' he drawled with an arrogant smile that made her want to scream or hit him, or both. 'I don't remember having any problems satisfying you when we were first married. In fact, *chérie,* after a night in my bed, you used to remind me of a cat who'd gorged on cream.'

The last thing she needed was to be reminded of her total and utter weakness where he was concerned. One look from those flashing grey eyes and she had been putty in his hands, her body desperate to experience the ecstasy of his full possession. She had been little better than a sex slave, she thought disgustedly, and he had exerted his power over her ruthlessly, subjugating her to his will with shameful ease.

Luc had to be playing a cruel game with her, she thought desperately. His insinuation that he knew he could keep her happy by sleeping with her was his despicable way of reminding her of her vulnerability where he was concerned. But she had changed during the year they had spent apart. She had grown up and taken charge of her emotions. With his incredible looks and raw, sexual magnetism, it wasn't surprising that he had once had such a strong hold over her but she had broken free of his spell and she refused to be bewitched again.

Jean-Claude was watching her and the beauty of his smile tore at her heart. He was innocently unaware of the bitterness that existed between his parents, a bitterness that would only fester if they were forced together again. At the moment he was just a baby, but as he grew older he would detect the signs that his parents detested one another and would surely be damaged by their antagonism.

'This is ridiculous,' she whispered huskily. 'For our son's sake, can't we call a truce and aim for an amicable divorce instead of fighting over him? Surely the most important thing is to give Jean-Claude the best upbringing we can?'

'I agree,' Luc replied, his gaze clashing with hers, 'which is why there will be no divorce. Our son deserves to be brought up by two parents who love him, even if they do not love each other,' he continued, ignoring Emily's shocked gasp. 'You will remain my wife, *chérie,* for better or worse. And make no mistake,' he warned her in a tone that gave some indication of his determination, 'it will be a proper marriage, in every sense of the word.'

'You can't really expect me to…to sleep with you,' Emily spluttered, outrage rendering her temporarily speechless as the full meaning of his words sank in.

'Why not? Our marriage may have had its problems, but the sex was always good. You were the most responsive lover I've ever known,' he told her, and she died a little at the way he could discuss something that had been so precious to her with such clinical detachment.

'Well, you've known a lot so I'll take your word for it but I'm afraid it's not an experience I want to repeat.'

'Is that so, *ma petite?*' The sudden amusement in his voice fuelled her anger and she curled her fingers into fists so that her nails bit into her palms. 'Time will tell, although not too much time, I hope. Patience isn't one of my finer virtues.'

'I'd rather kill myself than bear your touch again,' she snapped with a shudder as she contemplated the certain humiliation that would follow if she ever lowered her guard against him. He inhaled sharply, a nerve jumping in his cheek as he stared at her.

'Don't joke about such things, especially as we both know that you're lying,' he ground out, and she jerked her head round, startled by the bitterness in his eyes. 'You might have wrapped that cloak of virginal shyness around you like a nun's habit but you were a whore in the bedroom. Not that I'm complaining,' he added silkily when she turned her stunned, pain-filled eyes on him. 'I may be willing to put up with your presence in my life for Jean-Claude's sake, but I think I'm entitled to some compensations!'

He swung away to stare out of the window and in the ragged silence that followed his shocking statement she could only stare at his harsh profile. He really hated her, she realised as a combination of pain and panic washed over her. During the brief months they'd spent together after their marriage, she'd glimpsed his ruthless streak in his business dealings. Beneath his charismatic charm lurked a merciless disregard for anyone who dared cross him, and despite his insistence that their marriage would continue, he viewed her as the enemy. For a moment she quailed but from somewhere her pride came to the rescue and she lifted her chin.

'You don't really want me back, any more than you want to play happy families with Jean-Claude. I intend to seek a divorce, Luc, and I'll fight you tooth and nail for my baby. You never wanted him and I can prove that while I was pregnant you were too busy sleeping with your bloody secretary to give a damn about your unborn child or me. This has nothing to do with wanting Jean-Claude, has it?' She pressed on, ignoring the ominous tightening of his jaw that gave some indication of his fury. 'This is about your obsession to win, the need to exert your power. You didn't want me and perhaps when you were good and ready you'd have divorced me, but you can't bear the fact that I was the one to walk away. I defied you and now you want to punish me by claiming the child you never even wanted to be born.'

'Enough!' His voice stung like the crack of a whip as he

jerked his head round to face her and Emily visibly flinched, although she refused to drop her gaze. Once she had been in awe of him, her painful lack of self-confidence no match for his brilliant mind and acerbic wit, but she had Jean-Claude to fight for now and she glared across the car, determined not be cowed. '*Mon Dieu!* You have developed the tongue of a viper. I am trying very hard to be fair, which is more than you deserve when you never once gave me the same considera-tion. You stole my son, and like a thief in the night you hid him from me. Let me set something straight once and for all Emily,' he growled. 'I always wanted our child. I longed to hold our baby in my arms, but for all these months you denied me even the knowledge of his existence. Now, finally, I have found him and nothing in this world will ever make me let him go. If you insist on filing for divorce I can't stop you, but I will fight you for Jean-Claude with all the means at my disposal, and financially those means are considerable. If you want there to be war between us rather than peace, go ahead, but I hope you have the stomach for it because it is a war I *will* win.'

The car was speeding along the road, the locked doors pre-venting her escape even if it had been possible to jump out. The plush leather upholstery, the uniformed chauffeur and the discreet but well-stocked bar all indicated a level of wealth that would render any legal fight between them a waste of time. Luc could afford the best lawyers and if he chose to seek custody of Jean-Claude she would stand no chance against him. For the moment at least, she was out of options. Luc had won as usual and she seethed silently. 'I hate you,' she spat at him, and he shrugged indifferently.

'I'm devastated, *chérie,* but I won't force you to endure my company. If you really can't make Jean-Claude and what's best for him your priority, then you'd better get out now. Say the word and I'll ask my driver to stop and drop you off.'

Emily glanced out at the barren landscape, which was as dry and unforgiving as a desert. The empty road snaked past jutting boulders and huge, spiteful cacti, and once again fear gripped her. 'You surely wouldn't abandon us out here, miles from anywhere?' she whispered and Luc gave her a chilling smile.

'Of course not. I've told you, from now on Jean-Claude stays with me. But you are free to go wherever and whenever you like, *mon amour.*'

'Don't call me that,' she said sharply, her body clenching in rejection of the careless endearment that even now had the power to make her long for the moon. She had never been his love. 'Your cruelty is beyond belief,' she whispered, and he gave a harsh laugh.

'That you can accuse *me* of cruelty when you stole my son is also beyond belief but believe this, Emily, I do not forgive easily, and I will never forget.'

The barely concealed bitterness in his voice shook her and she took a deep breath as she concentrated on the scenery flashing past. Slowly her panic faded slightly as she envisaged the bustling airport. Presumably Luc was intending to fly back to England, but he would hardly be able to frogmarch her and Jean-Claude aboard a plane. Hopefully, if she kept her wits, there would be an opportunity to snatch back her son and slip away.

She forced herself to relax and bide her time, but in the tense silence her eyes turned involuntarily towards the man whose presence dominated the car. It wasn't fair that he was so gorgeous, she thought bleakly, feeling a knife skewer her heart as she studied his stern profile. His incredible bone structure could have been fashioned from marble by one of the Old Masters. His olive-gold skin stretched taut over the hard planes of his face. Despite the fact that he was in his late thirties, there was no hint of silver in his thick black hair, and she closed her eyes on a wave of pain as she remembered the feel of it against her fingers when she had pulled his head down to hers. His mouth was to die for and he had delighted in teasing every inch of her body with it, his tongue a wicked instrument of torturous pleasure during their long hours of loving that had left her utterly satiated.

That had been a long time ago, she hastily reminded herself. In those first heady weeks of their marriage when she'd almost convinced herself she had done the right thing by marrying the enigmatic Frenchman and that he might one day even grow to love her as she loved him.

The illusion had been quickly shattered. They had spent the weekend after their wedding in Paris, too absorbed in their mutual passion for each other to do much sightseeing. On their arrival back in London, Luc had swept her into his arms as the lift carried them up to his penthouse flat, but instead of carrying her straight to the bedroom, he had hesitated in the doorway as the most beautiful woman Emily had ever seen moved forward to greet them.

Robyn Blake, once a world-famous model, was Luc's sister-in-law as well as his personal assistant. She was exquisite, there was no other word to describe her, and Emily had immediately felt young and gauche, aware that her chain-store dress had been no match for Robyn's designer outfit.

At first she had been taken in by Robyn's apparent friendliness. Having spent her childhood in the shadow of her sisters, she was plagued by a crushing lack of self-confidence and had followed Robyn around like a puppy desperate to please its master. She had sought the older woman's advice on everything from clothes and make-up to the problems that were emerging in her marriage, and it had taken her a long time to realise that Robyn was the cause of many of those problems.

She could not lay all the blame at Robyn's door, she admitted miserably. Her own insecurity and lack of self-belief hadn't helped any more than the growing realisation that Jean-Luc Vaillon was incapable of loving anyone. He had treated her suspicions about the true nature of his relationship with his PA with scathing dismissal. It was time she grew up instead of behaving like a silly child, he'd told her, but in her heart she accepted that he had never felt more than a faint affection for her and now she had proof that his reasons for making her his wife had been far more prosaic than love.

With a sigh she turned to find Luc watching Jean-Claude. He seemed utterly absorbed, as though he could not drag his gaze from his son, but he must have felt her scrutiny and she blushed as he lifted his head and subjected her to a hard stare. Pride dictated that she should turn away but she was trapped by the brooding sensuality that emanated from him, her eyes focused on his mouth, remembering the taste of him, the feel of his lips on hers. Suddenly she was too hot. The air inside the car seemed stifling despite the air-conditioning, and tiny beads of sweat formed above her top lip. She wanted to wipe them away but her hands were trembling and she shoved them into her lap, her tongue darting out to capture the salty pearls on its tip.

Luc's eyes narrowed as he watched the nervous foray of her tongue and she knew with humiliating certainty that he was aware of her thoughts. What was the matter with her? she asked herself impatiently. He despised her, his contempt clearly visible in the cool grey gaze that speared her. He only tolerated her presence for the sake of his son so why was she consumed with this wild longing to feel his mouth on hers? She hated him, her mind totally rejected his ruthless power, but it seemed that her body had a will of its own and it recognised its master.

With a barely suppressed gasp she tore her gaze from his, biting down hard on her lip until she tasted blood. Luc was a cheat and a liar and he had broken her heart. For the sake of her self-preservation it was crucial that she remembered that fact.

'Don't look at me like that,' she demanded, seeking refuge in her anger. 'You lost the right to look at me like you own me when you increased your *personal* assistant's duties.'

'You're still blinded by your ridiculous insecurities, I see,' Luc murmured coolly, and her cheeks flooded with colour as his jibe hit home. She had always been so unsure of herself, especially where he was concerned, and she hated the fact that he had been aware of her vulnerability.

With her head turned determinedly away from him, Luc was left with the view of Emily's taut shoulders and his eyes rested on the curve of her cheek and one small, pink ear, her long, dangly earring emphasising the slender column of her neck. She looked heartbreakingly young with her glorious chestnut hair caught up on top of her head. A few tendrils had escaped to curl around her cheek and he fought the urge to reach across and brush them back behind her ear, to cup her chin in his hand and turn her face to his.

What was he thinking? he berated himself furiously. This woman, *his wife,* had walked out on him without a backward glance. Not only that, but she had disappeared so conclusively that gossip and speculation among London's society had been rife. He had been terrified for her safety, not knowing if she was alive or dead, but for all those long months she had been living quite comfortable in her Spanish hide-away.

Her accusation that he hadn't wanted their child was ridiculous. His longing for their baby had shaken him with its intensity, but alongside hope had been fear. His secret terror that history would repeat itself had made him appear distant and his perceived disinterest had cost him dear.

He inhaled sharply and forced himself to drop his gaze to the baby who was sitting quietly in his child seat. Jean-Claude, his son. It still seemed incredible that this beautiful, wide-eyed baby was his own flesh and blood, yet there was no mistaking the likeness between them and his heart clenched in primitive recognition. Wonderingly he touched the baby's satiny curls, which were as black as his own hair, and when Jean-Claude lifted his long lashes to survey him solemnly with huge, grey eyes, it was like looking into a mirror. His son, the child he'd feared he would never see. He loved him instantly, a huge wave of adoration sweeping through him, and he vowed that nothing would ever separate him from his child again.

'He looks like you,' Emily said grudgingly as she watched Jean-Claude smile at his father. From the moment her son had first opened his eyes and focused on her, she'd been taken aback by his likeness to Luc. It was as if fate itself was on Luc's side, determined that he would not be forgotten, but seeing them together brought home to her that her baby was all Vaillon, truly his father's son.

Jean-Claude regarded the stranger solemnly. At almost a year old, he knew his own mind, knew whom he liked and whom he didn't, and Emily felt a sharp stab of jealousy when he stretched out his chubby arms to Luc. Would all Vaillon men betray her? she wondered bitterly. And then dismissed the shabby thought. She wanted Jean-Claude to have a good relationship with his father and incredibly it now seemed that Luc shared that desire. Perhaps, once he had calmed down, she could broach the idea of divorce once more. She was certain he did not really want her as his wife and if she assured him of her willingness to share custody of Jean-Claude, their parting could at least be amicable.

'Jean-Claude and I are booked on an evening flight to London,' she murmured. 'It seems silly to waste the tickets but I'll meet you as soon as possible, tomorrow if you insist,' she added when Luc made no reply and simply surveyed her with his cool grey stare.

'I'm not taking him to London,' he replied at last, and she stared at him in confusion.

'Then where are you going?' She had hated Luc's Chelsea penthouse, which had all the appeal of a dentist's waiting room and had never felt like her home, but Luc had seemed perfectly at ease there and she assumed it was still his London base.

'To France, of course. Jean-Claude is a Vaillon, my son and heir. Naturally he will be brought up in my homeland,' he informed her, his brows raised in surprise that there could be any doubt.

'Naturally,' Emily snapped sarcastically, 'but what about my homeland? Hasn't it occurred to you that I'd like to bring him up in England?

'But you weren't, were you?' he pointed out silkily. 'For some peculiar reason you decided that an artists' commune in the middle of the Spanish wilderness was the best place for our son to live. But no longer. From now on Jean-Claude will enjoy all the benefits of his heritage at my château in the

Loire Valley. The Vaillons are an old French family. Surely you would not want to deprive him of his birthright?'

'I didn't even know you owned a château. Something else you failed to mention. But what of Jean-Claude's British heritage?' Emily argued, panic assailing her once more at Luc's resolute expression. 'The Dyers are an old family, too. Heston Grange was their ancestral seat for over four hundred years, until you bought it,' she finished bleakly. 'Tell me,' she demanded with a hollow laugh, 'did you know from the beginning that my parents hoped you would marry one of their daughters so that the Dyers would retain some link with the family's heritage? Did they offer you Heston at a fraction of its value as long as you agreed to marry one of us? And if that's true, Luc, why on earth did you pick me? I was the plain one, the drab Dyer, more at home with horses than people. My sisters are beautiful, clever and sophisticated, any one of them would have made you a far more suitable wife, but I suppose you thought I would be the easiest to manipulate, the one least likely to make a fuss when you resumed your relationship with your mistress.'

At twenty she had been shy and severely lacking in confidence, unable to disguise her massive crush on the handsome, enigmatic Frenchman who had turned all their lives upside down, but to him she must have seemed a pushover. She had been a pawn in a far more serious game.

'You always did seriously undervalue yourself,' Luc murmured dryly, as his eyes skimmed her flushed face and huge navy blue eyes. 'I admit there were a number of reasons why you were suitable…'

'All to do with money and prestige, and none to do with love,' Emily finished for him. She didn't want to hear every cold, calculated detail of why he had decided to marry her.

She already knew it was because her parents had offered him Heston Grange at a massively reduced price if he married one of the Dyer daughters, thereby retaining the family's link with their heritage. It was archaic, she thought bitterly. She felt like a brood mare, sold off with a suitable dowry, but Luc hadn't even wanted her for her childbearing ability. He hadn't wanted children at all, which made his sudden determination to gain custody of their son all the more shocking.

'Jean-Claude is a Vaillon,' Luc repeated stubbornly, 'and from now on the Château Montiard will be his home, not some filthy dump in the middle of nowhere.'

'San Antonia is not filthy. The farmhouse is beautiful and Jean-Claude loved it there.'

'Really.' Luc's brows rose as he murmured sardonically. 'He must be a child prodigy to express his opinion when he's not even a year old. Tell me, *chérie,* what would you have done if he'd been taken ill? The nearest hospital is miles away. For someone who expresses such maternal devotion, you seem to have little regard for his well-being.'

'While you, of course, are an expert on child care,' Emily snapped furiously. 'Jean-Claude was perfectly well cared for, but it's not easy being a single mother and I was grateful for the help of the other members of the commune.'

'You were a single mother by choice,' he pointed out hardily, 'but you never gave Jean-Claude a choice. You forced him to live his life with only one parent and you denied me a relationship with my own son. Now it's your turn to suffer,' he told her darkly, and she shivered at the contempt in his gaze.

'For heaven's sake, can't we be adult about this?' she cried despairingly and he gave a harsh laugh.

'It would be a first for you, *chérie,* that's for sure, but I'm afraid you've pushed me way beyond the boundaries of wanting to be reasonable. Now that I have my son I have no intention of ever letting him go, and there's not a damn thing you can do about it.'

The car was slowing and Emily glanced out of the window, frantically searching for the signs to the airport, but there were none. Instead they drove through the gates of what appeared to be a private airfield and sick fear gripped her. How could she have forgotten that Luc owned his own private jet? There was no bustling airport, no queues at the check-in desk where there might have been an opportunity to grab Jean-Claude and run. Luc's plane was ready and waiting on the runway. He had stated that he was prepared to take her to his château for their son's sake but he couldn't force her to resume the role of his wife, could he?

Suddenly her pride was an expendable commodity she would gladly sacrifice in return for her baby and she stared beseechingly at Luc as the car drew to a halt. 'Please, don't do this,' she begged huskily. 'I can't live without Jean-Claude but neither can I live with you. You must see that.'

'Surely, if you have any sense of fairness you must see that it is my turn to have him now,' Luc replied coldly. 'Jean-Claude is coming home with me, with or without you.'

'But you didn't want him!' she cried, her voice rising with frustration. 'From the moment you knew I was pregnant you made it clear that you had no interest in either of us. You slept in another room,' she reminded him huskily, 'when you bothered to come back to the flat at all. And you were completely uninvolved in my pregnancy. You didn't even show up at the hospital for my ultrasound scan.

'Do you have any idea how I felt that morning?' she demanded bitterly as a wave of memories hit her. 'The fact that you'd spent the night with Robyn was unforgivable but I still thought…hoped you cared enough about our child to want to see the first pictures of him. I sat in that waiting room alone surrounded by excited, happy couples, and I prayed you would come,' she whispered brokenly. Every time they called my name I allowed someone else to go in my place until there was no one left, just me on my own with a very sympathetic nurse who tried to make a joke about men being useless time-keepers.' She scrubbed her eyes furiously with the back of her hand, desperate that he didn't see her cry. 'But you hadn't mistaken the time, had you, Luc? You just didn't care about the baby or me, and that's why I left. I knew I'd outstayed my welcome.'

'That's not true,' he began, his face twisting with emotions she refused to try and decipher any more.

'It is true,' she cried angrily. 'I didn't need any more proof of your indifference. How can you blame me for questioning your motives now?' she finished brokenly.

Luc paused as he opened the door. She looked as young and innocent as on that first day when she had stared up at him and an arrow had pierced his heart. He wanted to hate her—indeed, there had been many times during the past year when he'd convinced himself that he despised her—but she was watching him with those expressive blue eyes. He glimpsed her vulnerability and something tugged at his heart.

He had never been any good at saying how he felt, he conceded, and his conscience prickled as he remembered how his unspoken fears had caused him to appear tense and uncommunicative. His childhood had left scars, a wariness of revealing his emotions. He hadn't forgotten her scan. *Dieu*, he would have given anything to be with her but Robyn had been distraught, he had been torn and by the time he had managed to phone and explain the situation, Emily had already left for the hospital. He had been too late but at that point he hadn't realised the extent of the damage his decision had cost him, and he had never been given the chance to make amends.

'Wait there while I see if they're ready for us,' he growled as he climbed out of the car. 'I have employed a nanny to take care of Jean-Claude. It might be better if he meets her before we get on the plane.'

'He doesn't need a nanny,' Emily pointed out sharply. 'I can look after him perfectly well on my own.'

'*Mon Dieu!* Do you have to argue about everything?' He was already striding across the tarmac and she watched him go, adrenalin coursing through her as she tapped on the car's glass partition to gain the attention of the chauffer. This was probably a hired car, she reasoned feverishly, and it was likely that the driver was Spanish.

'Drive on, please,' she requested in a confident tone that did not match the sick fear in the pit of her stomach. The months she'd spent in Spain meant that she was fairly fluent in the language and she smiled reassuringly at the driver. 'There's been a change of plan and Señor Vaillon wishes you to take me to the international airport.'

The chauffer was young and his dark eyes flashed with a boldness he made no effort to hide as he responded to her smile.

'*Sí, señora.*'

The car rolled forward and she took a sharp breath. 'As quickly as you can, *por favor.*' But it was too late. Luc must have moved faster than the speed of light and already he was wrenching the door open.

'You little bitch,' he swore at her savagely, his face contorted with fury. He yelled at the driver to cut the engine and swiftly released Jean-Claude's safety harness before lifting him into his arms. 'I was prepared to be fair, to treat you with a respect that you clearly don't deserve. But not any more,' he snarled as his fingers curled around her arm.

'Is everything all right, Monsieur Vaillon?' The woman at the bottom of the plane's steps looked calm and professional in her grey uniform. Presumable she was the nanny Luc had hired, Emily thought desperately as she struggled to break free of his bruising grip.

'Shall I take the baby?'

'*Merci.*' Luc transferred Jean-Claude into the woman's arms and immediately turned his attention back to Emily, his eyes dark and dispassionate as he watched a single tear roll down her face.

'You can't do this,' she whispered as he jerked her into his arms.

'Watch me,' he taunted, and before she realised his intentions his head obliterated the sunlight. It was not so much a kiss as a public branding, his lips hot and hard, forcing hers apart and uncaring if he evoked a response. Emily was so shocked that she simply leaned against his chest fearing that her legs would buckle beneath her. Her humiliation was complete when she was forced to cling to him for support. It was as quick as it was brutal and he released her with a savage imprecation while she stared up at him, her trembling fingers covering her mouth. For a few brief seconds she had been on fire for him, her body reacting instantaneously to his raw sexuality, and her cheeks burned with shame at the speculative gleam in his eyes. He knew the effect he had on her, knew that for those few seconds he had made her forget everything, even her son, and with that knowledge came power.

'Take your hands off me,' she demanded, her voice shaking with outrage, and he threw back his head and laughed.

'You're a good actress, I'll give you that. But you don't fool me, *ma chérie*. I know you too well and I have forgotten nothing. I remember vividly what pleases you,' he breathed in her ear and the warmth of his breath on her skin caused a trembling within her that had nothing to do with fear. 'Welcome back, my sweet wife,' he goaded softly as he put his hand in the small of her back and pushed her up the steps into the waiting jet.

CHAPTER THREE

WHAT THE *HELL* had he done?

Luc stared moodily at the glass on the tray in front of him and with a muttered oath snatched it up and downed its contents in one gulp, although he rarely drank alcohol in the middle of the day. Right now he needed something to anaesthetise the effect that Emily had on him—had always had on him, he admitted begrudgingly, although fortunately she seemed unaware that his emotions were veering dangerously out of control.

She was sitting away from him at the front of the plane, nursing Jean-Claude who had taken an instant dislike to his new surroundings and let his displeasure be known in uncertain terms. The nanny he had employed, Liz Crawford, had an impressive record in child care, but she had been unable to pacify the baby, whose cries had only subsided once he was in his mother's arms.

'He needs me,' Emily had insisted, and watching them now, mother and son, Luc knew she was right. She was cradling Jean-Claude against her shoulder, rocking gently as she sang to him in her sweet, husky voice, and Luc felt a curious twisting in his gut as he recognised the familiar French lullaby that evoked memories of his own childhood.

He shouldn't have kissed her, he conceded grimly. He shouldn't have given in to the basic, almost primal need to hold her in his arms once more. He needed to be in control, to take things slowly and persuade her that coming back to him would be the best thing for all of them, not just the baby.

He had convinced himself that he had every right to hate her but from the moment he'd walked across the courtyard at San Antonia the battle being waged in his head had been lost. She had deprived him of the first year of his son's life, and when he'd received notice from her solicitor that she wanted a divorce he had been ready to commit murder. If she no longer wanted to be his wife, that was fine, he had assured himself, because he'd had enough of feeling a fool and he didn't want her back.

Brave words, but unfortunately, as soon as he'd set eyes on her he'd known he could not back them up. He still wanted her, heaven help him. She was in his blood and he'd known instantly that he couldn't let her go, but the flash of fear in her eyes when she first caught sight of him had shaken him. He had never been an ogre, had he? She had no reason to cower from him and as he stared at her it was confusion rather than anger that filled him. She had ripped his heart out, damn it, when his only crime had been to fear for her safety. He wanted her but he was determined to discover the truth about why she had left him before he could even begin to trust her again. It was nothing more than sexual attraction, he consoled himself. The fierce chemistry that had existed from the moment they'd first met still burned for both of them. He wasn't blind, he had seen the way she'd looked at him in the car, had known she felt the same primitive tug of awareness, and when he'd kissed her he had felt her response despite her efforts to hide it.

He set his glass back on the tray and resisted the urge to ask for another drink. He might tell himself that he had every right to despise Emily, but the unpalatable truth was that she had stolen his heart long before she had stolen his child. He resented the hold she had over him but seeing her again had forced him to accept that their lives were inextricably linked for ever.

Jean-Claude's sobs gradually subsided as he fell asleep and Emily reluctantly handed him over to the nanny, who took charge of him with an air of quiet authority. Not knowing what to do, unsure of her role, she glanced round and grimaced as Luc beckoned that she should join him.

'Why did you sing to him in French?' he demanded when she slid into the seat beside him, the expression in his eyes unfathomable as he studied her small, delicate face and the way the strap of her top had slid down to leave her shoulder bare.

'I hoped to bring him up to recognise both English and French,' Emily explained, her cheeks pink as she hastily re-adjusted the strap. 'One of the artists at San Antonia was French and she taught me some lullabies to sing to him.' She bit her lip at the unforgiving hardness of Luc's face.

'I honestly believed you didn't want him,' she said huskily, 'but I still hoped to give you a chance to meet him. I want Jean-Claude to know his father and I was going to tell my solicitor that I was happy for us to share custody.'

'Then why hide away in Spain?' he demanded impatiently and she sighed.

'I was ill after Jean-Claude was born. It was a difficult birth and it took me a while to recover. I was staying at my friend Laura's flat while she set up her cookery school at San

Antonia and she invited me to Spain to recuperate. I was so busy looking after a new baby and helping Laura and the time passed so quickly…'

'What do you mean by a difficult birth?' Luc growled. 'Are you saying there were problems?'

'It was a long labour, thirty-eight hours and he was a big baby. I lost a lot of blood,' Emily admitted, and Luc's face darkened as he fought to control the nausea that swept through him. He should have been there. She should have given him the opportunity to support her during her labour but he had driven her away. She was his wife, the woman he had sworn to protect, but once again, it seemed, he had failed in his duty.

'If you had stayed with me, you would have received the best medical care,' he muttered savagely, trying to disguise his pain. 'You needn't have suffered, yet out of spite, a ridiculous urge to hurt me, you put not just your life at risk but his, too.'

'Hurt you!' Emily stared at her husband with blank incomprehension in her eyes. 'When I mentioned the idea of starting a family you were adamant that you didn't want children. Jean-Claude's conception was a mistake—somehow the antibiotics I'd been prescribed interfered with the reliability of the Pill—but you refused to believe me. I remember how angry you were when I told you I was pregnant. It's not something a new bride is likely to forget,' she added painfully.

'*Sacré bleu!* It was our honeymoon,' Luc said explosively, 'and you did not tell me, *chérie,* you waited until we were on a remote island in the Indian Ocean before you collapsed. It was the emergency medic airlifted from the mainland who informed me of your condition.'

He could not repress a shudder as he relived the moment he had lifted her limp, lifeless body into his arms and had run up the beach, calling frantically for help. It was happening all over again his mind had drummed over and over, dismissing any semblance of calm in a tidal wave of terror. He had truly believed he had been about to lose her and it had been as devastating as the realisation of how deeply he cared. He had been unable to bear the thought of carrying on without her. He wasn't strong enough to survive such pain again, and even after it was made clear that she was in no danger, he had withdrawn into himself as a form of self-protection. He didn't want to love her. Love hurt.

'I hadn't known I was pregnant. It was as much of a shock to me as it was to you,' Emily muttered miserably, but with a savage oath, Luc swung away from her, flipped open his laptop and was instantly immersed in his work.

He obviously did not want to discuss the past, she thought darkly. Perhaps he felt guilty about the way he had treated her. She didn't know and she told herself that she didn't care. She knew from experience that he would resent any disturbance while he was working and she stared bleakly out of the window, wishing she found it as easy to dismiss him from her thoughts.

She must have been the only member of the Dyer household who had forgotten the dinner party planned to honour the potential saviour of Heston Grange, Emily recalled as memories of her first meeting with Luc filled her mind. Rushing in from the stables in her muddy jodhpurs, she had stumbled to a halt, her embarrassment excruciating when she'd viewed her elegant sisters and silently seething mother, but everything had faded to insignificance when she'd caught sight of Jean-Luc Vaillon for the first time.

The world really could tilt on its axis, she thought with a rueful smile, remembering the way she had literally grabbed hold of the back of a chair for support when he'd surveyed her with his cool grey stare. With his amazing facial bone structure and lean, hard body, he had been the sexiest man she had ever met and she had been unable to repress a shiver when he'd trapped her startled gaze with his, the gleam of amusement in those silvery depths warning her that he was aware of the effect he'd had on her.

Conscious of her mother's impatience, she fled upstairs to change into her serviceable navy-blue dress and spent the evening peeping at Luc from beneath her lashes, leaving her sisters to impress him with their sparkling conversation. The head of Vaillon Developments was irresistible with his suave good looks and seductive charm, but despite her sisters' frantic efforts to capture his attention, Emily glanced up several times during dinner to find him watching her. Embarrassment saw her quickly drop her gaze, but throughout the evening he continued to regard her with a mixture of amusement and another, indefinable emotion in his dark grey eyes.

'I have a feeling you are happier in the company of horses than humans,' he remarked a few days later, when he suddenly appeared in the stables. He had accepted her parents' suggestion to stay at Heston and discuss plans for its possible acquisition, but Emily was too shy to respond to his friendly charm and went out of her way to avoid him.

His husky French accent caused a delicious shiver to run all the way down to her toes, and she blushed and half hid her face against the mane of her darling Arab stallion, Kasim.

'I find horses are generally less complicated,' she agreed huskily, and his slow smile took her breath away. He remained chatting for several minutes, displaying an impressive knowledge of horsemanship, although she had been too tongue-tied to respond and afterwards had been furious with herself. She must have appeared a halfwit, but surprisingly he came again the next day, and the next, requesting that she ride out with him, and it was during those blissful excursions through the New Forest that she found herself falling in love with him.

What a fool she'd been, she now thought bitterly, to believe that the charismatic multimillionaire Frenchman would really be interested in a plain little nobody like her. Common sense should have warned her that he must have a hidden agenda, especially when he'd proposed to her so soon after they'd first met. She had ignored her doubts, swept away by his passionate kisses when he'd followed her into the stables and pulled her down into the hay. He'd overwhelmed her senses. She'd loved the way he'd made her feel, loved him and amazingly he'd seemed to want her, too.

Their wedding, in the magnificent grounds of Heston Grange, had been like a fairy-tale, a dream come true, and the dream had lasted for the whole of that first weekend when he had whisked her off to Paris. She had been a virgin on her wedding night, due only to his iron self-control. The memory of the way he had made love to her for the first time still brought tears to her eyes. He had been so tender, so gentle, treating her reverently as if she were made of the finest porcelain. Her untutored body had been eager to learn and his tenderness had given way to a fierce passion that should have shocked her but had only made her love him more.

Unfortunately their arrival back in London had signalled the end of the fantasy. Luc was always busy and always with Robyn, and Emily had resented the elegant American's close relationship with her husband as she'd struggled to fit in to her new life. As her insecurity grew so did the rows, but six months after the wedding Luc suddenly announced he had a break in his busy work schedule and was taking her on a belated honeymoon. It should have been an ideal time to repair the holes in their marriage, but instead the queasiness she had been suffering from for the past few weeks increased and on arrival at their remote island destination, she fainted. A result of dehydration and hormones, the doctor cheerfully informed her before he dropped the bombshell that she was expecting a baby and one glance at Luc's shocked face warned her that the fairy-tale was over. The moment he discovered she was pregnant their marriage died.

'We'll be landing in an hour,' Luc suddenly informed her, his cold, clipped tone interrupting her thoughts, although he barely bothered to lift his eyes from his computer screen as he addressed her. 'I'm sure you remember the way to the bathroom.'

'I don't need it, thank you,' she replied, stung by his indifference. This time he did look up, his brows raised fractionally in disdain.

'You need to tidy yourself up,' he told her bluntly, unmoved by the stain of colour that flooded her cheeks. 'You'll find your luggage in the bedroom. Hopefully you have something to wear in that vast suitcase that is a little less loud.'

'I'm afraid not,' Emily said sweetly, her chin coming up. 'The larger suitcase contains Jean-Claude's clothes, and this is one of my more discreet outfits.'

'Then we need to go shopping as a matter of urgency. You look like a tramp,' he told her, calmly ignoring her gasp of outrage. 'Your gaudy clothes might be suitable wear for an artists' commune but you are not a hippy—you are my wife and I expect you to dress accordingly.'

'You can go to hell. I'd rather run around naked than allow you to buy my clothes,' Emily snapped furiously, and his mouth curved into an insolent smile that still did strange things to her insides.

'An interesting idea for when we are alone perhaps, but I don't think the villagers of sleepy Montiard are ready for such avant-garde behaviour.'

The temptation to wipe the mockery from his face was so strong that Emily folded her arms across her chest. How dared he say she looked gaudy in a tone that patently meant cheap? Her self-confidence took a nosedive and she quailed beneath his contemptuous gaze. She had been so busy helping Laura at the farmhouse that she had regained her prepregnancy figure without even noticing. She looked good, she reassured herself, and the attention she'd received from a couple of the artists at San Antonia had been a welcome boost, but Luc was usually surrounded by beautiful women who were effortless chic and she felt as gauche as when she had first met him.

Furiously she blinked back the sudden rush of tears, aware that meeting Luc again was nothing like her daydreams. She had often fantasised about bumping into him at some glamorous function and had pictured herself looking stunningly sexy, escorted by her equally gorgeous lover, while Luc looked on and cursed the fact that he had let her go. The dream was stupidly unrealistic, of course, especially the part about the lover. The only man she had ever wanted was as indifferent to her as he had been when she'd left him, and it was ridiculous to feel so hurt.

'I'm not planning on staying at your château for a day

longer than I have to,' she told him icily, 'and I certainly won't
be spending any time alone with you, so you can forget the idea
about me sharing your bed. You can't force me to stay,' she
added, aware that for some reason she wanted to antagonise
him, perhaps because a row would guarantee his attention.

'You think not?' he drawled, patently unmoved by her
anger, and the hint of amusement in his voice caused her
temper to ignite.

'What do you propose to do, lock me in an ivory tower
while you travel the world on endless business commitments?
Maybe you'll come home one day to find that I've gone and
taken Jean-Claude with me,' she taunted.

'I wouldn't try it, *chérie,* because I swear I will hunt you
down and when I find you, you'll wish you'd never crossed me.'

The amusement had gone. Luc was deadly serious, Emily
realised with a shiver at the implicit threat in his voice. He
had made it plain that he was only taking her to France
because Jean-Claude needed her, but it seemed that he
intended to hold her as his prisoner.

Muttering something about needing to freshen up, she
jumped to her feet. She was fully aware of the location of
the opulent bedroom and adjoining bathroom and stumbled
down the aisle, desperate to be alone while she came to
terms with the way her life seemed to be falling apart. Luc
had once spent an entire flight to Mexico making love to
her on the vast double bed, she remembered painfully, but
that had been early on, before the rot had set in and
poisoned their relationship. She hated him, she reminded
herself as she splashed cold water on her face and freed her
hair from the yellow band so that it fell in a swathe of
heavy silk down her back. She didn't know why she had
bothered to speak to him. It was useless when he was in

such an unreasonable mood and she should have remembered that in a verbal sparring match his acidic tongue
always left her raw.

What was happening to her? she wondered miserably.
Where was the strong, confident woman who had discovered
her own sense of self-worth amid the artists at San Antonia?
A few hours ago she had been in charge of her life, prepared
to seek Luc out and offer him the chance to build a relationship with his son, but now suddenly he had the upper hand
and she was out of options.

She emerged from the bathroom to find him stretched out
on the bed, his arms folded behind his head as he surveyed
her like a sultan might have inspected his latest concubine.
It didn't help that he was so gorgeous, she thought helplessly
as her eyes were drawn to the muscled hardness of his thighs
beneath his superbly cut grey trousers. He had discarded his
jacket and his shirt was unbuttoned at the throat to reveal a
glimpse of dark hair that she knew covered the whole of his
chest. For a moment she closed her eyes, remembering the
last time she had seen him stretched out on that bed. Then he
had been gloriously and unashamedly naked and she had
revelled in the feel of his body on hers, skin on skin, his rough
thighs rubbing erotically against the softness of hers.

Too much recall, she thought frantically as her eyes flew
open, her cheeks scarlet as she met his sardonic gaze.

'I'd appreciate some privacy,' she told him coolly. 'What
do you want?'

'To prove a point perhaps,' he replied, so softly it was as
if he was talking to himself, 'or maybe it's just because I can't
keep away, which makes me all kinds of a fool,' he added with
a harsh laugh.

'You're talking in riddles.' Unwittingly she had edged

closer to the bed, drawn to him with the deadly fascination of a moth to a bright light, and suddenly his hand shot out to capture her wrist.

'Why did you leave me?' The question surprised her but it was not as shocking as when he swung his legs over the side of the bed and pulled her onto his lap.

'You know why,' she muttered, frantically trying to escape. Already she could feel the warmth of his thighs burn through her thin skirt and she shifted uncomfortably as heat coursed through her. This close she could see the fine lines around his eyes, the faint shadow on his jaw, and his mouth was only inches from hers, a wicked temptation she had to fight at all costs.

'I want you to spell it out,' he said, but the grip of his hands on her waist belied the blandness of his tone and she swallowed nervously.

'I'd had enough of being humiliated by you.'

'When did I ever humiliate you?' he growled savagely, and she winced as his fingers bit into her skin. 'You left me without a backward glance. Do you have any idea what my life was like after you disappeared so spectacularly?' he demanded icily. 'One minute we were an apparently happy couple, looking forward to the birth of our first child and then suddenly you were gone, leaving a brief note to say you were leaving me but no further explanation and no indication of when, or indeed if, you intended to come back.

'The Chelsea set had a field day as the weeks passed and it became obvious that I didn't have a clue where you were,' he snapped, and for the first time she began to appreciate the full extent of his anger.

'You could have told people I was visiting my family in Hampshire,' Emily muttered, and received a scathing look.

'Your selfishness is astounding,' he told her bitterly. 'You didn't spare your family a second thought, did you? You didn't think for a moment that they would also be worried about you.'

'My mother knew our marriage was in trouble,' Emily admitted huskily. 'I told her I was going to stay with friends for a while and she wasn't very happy about it. She warned me that millionaires don't grow on trees and said I was a fool. Apparently it's not uncommon for men to play away while their wives are pregnant,' she added, her scathing glance telling him that she did not share Sarah's view. 'But I had concrete proof that you had spent the night with Robyn and I was so sickened by your deceit I knew I couldn't stay with you, carrying on the act that we had a marriage made in heaven, for another minute.'

'I never slept with her. It was all in your imagination,' Luc replied grittily, but she refused to be intimidated by the flash of fire in his eyes.

'You spent the night with her when you came back from Australia. You'd phoned your housekeeper to say you'd delayed your flight for twenty-four hours, but I never received the message and went to the airport to meet you. I saw you, Luc,' she said bitterly, fighting the stab of pain that the memory still evoked. 'You and Robyn. You didn't see me but I'm not stupid. You had your arm around her and it was quite obvious that you'd lied about your change of flights in order to spend one more night with her.'

'And that's the reason you walked out on me? I lost the first year of my son's life because of a mix-up over flights?' The stark incredulity in Luc's voice caused Emily to try and wriggle off his knee but his grip instantly tightened.

'There were reasons why I…lied about the day I was coming home,' he said tightly, patently making a huge effort to control his anger, 'reasons that I would have explained if you'd given me the chance. Instead, you bolted like an immature child. You, *chérie,* took my son. You put me through months of hell and still you wonder that I'm *angry?*' He looked as though he was about to explode, his face a taut mask of barely restrained fury, and Emily shrank from his palpable aggression.

'I know what I saw,' she muttered stubbornly. 'You shared a closeness with Robyn that excluded anyone else, including me.'

'She's my sister-in-law. I've known her for years and I admit I'm fond of her. She went through hell when Yves was killed, not least because she was driving the car and blamed herself for the accident.' He caught hold of her chin so that she was forced to look at him and she was struck by the fierce gleam in his eyes, the determination to make her believe him.

It was the first time they had ever spoken properly about Robyn, the first time either of them had ever really listened. Before, she had allowed her suspicions about his relationship with his PA to fester until they'd boiled over in a torrent of wild accusations that he had refused to dignify with a reply. Instead, he had withdrawn into himself and treated her with such icy disdain that she had shrivelled while her insecurities had multiplied.

'I swear I have never been unfaithful to you, with Robyn or anyone else,' he told her, and the quiet intensity of his voice caused a little bubble of hope to grow in her chest.

Could he really be telling the truth? Had she misread the signs that she had believed pointed to his guilt? She had been so ready to assume the worst, she thought painfully. At the back of her mind she had always thought he would grow tired of her and she had been waiting, looking for proof that he'd regretted marrying her. Had she jumped on the signs of his supposed infidelity as an excuse to leave him before he'd become bored of her, and if that was true, hadn't she denied him the first year of his son's life because of her pride?

It was not a comfortable thought and she shifted on his lap and then wished she hadn't. Their position was way too intimate and it was hard to think straight when her senses were drugged by the musk of his aftershave. Emily needed to put some space between them and the glint in his eyes warned her he was aware of the reason for her escape bid.

'But the night you spent at her flat?' she demanded feverishly, still unwilling to accept she had been wrong all this time. 'I know you were with her.'

'That's right, I spent the entire night trying to sleep on a sofa designed for a midget, counting the hours until I could get home to you. I knew your ultrasound scan was booked for later that day and despite your accusations, I was desperate to go with you.'

'Then why didn't you?' Emily snapped, her tone plainly disbelieving and he sighed.

'As you know, Robyn was once a top model and like many celebrities she's hounded by the press. The day we flew back from Australia she received a tip-off that some risqué photographs she had posed for early in her career were being circulated on the internet, along with accusations that she had been drinking on the night of the accident. She was distraught,' Luc said quietly. 'She begged me to stay with her and we talked for hours about Yves and how much she still missed him. I wanted to come to the hospital with you the next day but I was afraid to leave her while she was talking about ending her life.' He could not have borne another suicide on his conscience, he thought bleakly, but since he'd been forced to make a stark choice between his wife and his sister-in-law he had suffered the punishment of the damned.

'But why did you lie about changing your flight?' Emily faltered, and he met her gaze with eyes that were as cool and clear as a mountain stream.

'Because I knew you'd immediately jump to the wrong conclusion. I wanted desperately to see you after three weeks apart, but Robyn needed me more than she ever had and, God forgive me, I couldn't let her down.'

He had to be telling the truth. No one could lie that convincingly, Emily thought, and her heart flipped with a feeling that was part joy, part despair that she had got it so incredibly wrong. If only she had confronted him instead of running away to lick her wounds. Luc had accused her of behaving like a silly child and she was filled with shame that she had misjudged him so badly. Was it possible that she had been wrong to think he hadn't wanted their baby either? From the minute he'd arrived at San Antonia he had insisted that he wanted to be involved in his son's life, so much so that he was prepared to install her in his château just because Jean-Claude needed her.

For a few glorious seconds hope began to unfurl inside her that there was a chance they could salvage their marriage after all, but then reality bounced back and with it bitter disillusionment. If Luc really felt nothing for his sister-in-law other than affection, why had he installed her in the Chelsea penthouse soon after the break-up of their marriage, and why had he allowed Robyn to send her and Jean-Claude away the day she had tried to see him?

'Nice try, Luc,' Emily flung at him as she tried in vain to slide off his knee. 'For a minute you almost had me convinced.'

'Are you saying you doubt my word?' The note of incredulity in his voice would have been funny if Emily had felt like laughing, but she doubted she would ever smile again. He was so arrogant, she thought furiously, to believe she was still the shy girl he had married.

'Give me one reason why I should believe anything you say?'

'Because you are my wife.'

That couldn't be a flash of hurt in his eyes, she reassured herself. It was impossible to inflict pain on granite and she hardened her heart against him.

'I may have married you but I never gave you the right to tell me how to think. I know for a fact that you're lying, but you can't fool me any more. I'm not the pushover I used to be,' she finished proudly, but his lazy smile caused a flicker of apprehension in the pit of her stomach.

'Really? Perhaps I should put that to the test, *ma chérie*,' he murmured silkily. 'I could never resist a challenge.' Any more than he could resist her, he thought grimly. How dared she accuse him of lying, in that prim, holier-than-thou tone! He had done his best to explain about Robyn but he would be damned if he would try again. Besides, he was tired of talking. They were going round in the same circles as they had a year ago and talking had never got them anywhere then, either. There was only one place where the lines of communication between them were clear and despite her protestations of maidenly outrage he could see the flare of excitement in her eyes. She might refuse to admit, even to herself, that she wanted him, but there was only one reason why she would challenge him and he wouldn't disappoint her.

He moved abruptly and before Emily could guess his intention Luc flipped her back onto the bed, his hard body instantly covering hers so that she was trapped.

'Let me go!' Her anger was tempered with another, more unwelcome emotion as she acknowledged that the feel of his thighs pressing against hers was sending heat coursing through her body. He was so big, so dominantly male, and it had been so long since she had been held in his arms. Already she could feel her resistance fading as sensation took over, but from somewhere she found the strength to push against his shoulders. 'Touch me and I'll scream,' she threatened, and he had the audacity to laugh, his warm breath stirring the tendrils of her hair that curled around her ear. 'Do you want the cabin crew to barge in?' she demanded desperately as he caught hold of her wrists and lifted them above her head so that she was spread helplessly beneath him.

'I would prefer not to have an audience,' he drawled, and she watched, transfixed, as his smile faded, the heat in his eyes a shocking indication of his hunger. He still wanted her! The realisation should have appalled her but instead a soft moan rose in her throat and was captured by his mouth coming down on hers. She was on fire instantly, no thought in her head to deny him when, if she was honest, this was what she had wanted from the moment he had strode towards her at San Antonia.

His tongue pushed insistently against her lips, demanding access, and she parted them with a groan, the thrust of his tongue an erotic invasion that made her twist her hips restlessly against the throbbing proof of his arousal. Where was her pride when she needed it? she thought frantically when he released her mouth at last and proceeded to trail a line of kisses down her neck. Her yellow strap top was a flimsy barrier he quickly dispensed with before pausing for a moment to stare at the vivid orange bra she was wearing underneath.

'An interesting colour combination,' he murmured thickly, and she flushed as sanity seeped back into her brain.

'I like it,' she snapped.

'I like you better without it.' His fingers had already released the clasp and she gasped as he pushed the lacy cups aside to reveal her small, round breasts that were tingling in anticipation of his touch.

They were going to be disappointed, Emily told herself sternly because she refused to give in to the desire that was threatening to engulf her. Much as her body might want him, she could not let Luc make love to her and she glared at him as she tried to drag her arms down from where he had pinioned them above her head.

'I don't know what you're playing at,' she snarled, 'but I don't want to do this.'

'Why, because my touch sickens you?' he queried, his eyes shadowed by his long lashes so that she couldn't read his expression.

'Yes,' she muttered fiercely, but instead of releasing her, his mouth curved into a sardonic smile.

'You're a liar.' He transferred both her wrists into one of his hands and slid the other down to cup her breast, moulding her soft flesh before he stroked his thumb pad across her nipple and watched in apparent fascination as it hardened. 'And you talk too much,' he mocked when at last he lifted his head to stare down into her stunned eyes. 'What happened to my quiet, biddable little wife?'

Biddable! He made her sound like some mindless idiot and she hated the fact that there was a grain of truth in his words. She had loved him so much she would have done anything he'd asked and he had used her weakness for him with ruthless disregard for her feelings.

'I grew up,' she told him icily, 'but I see your chauvinistic attitude towards marriage hasn't improved.'

'*Non,* I demand exclusive possession of my wife,' he said easily. 'You are back where you belong, *chérie,* in my bed, and this time I intend to make sure you stay there.'

Her angry response was cut off by the simple method of his mouth wreaking havoc on hers and by the time he released her she was a quivering mass of emotions. She shivered, unable to control the trembling of her limbs as he cupped her breast in his hand, his olive skin an erotic contrast to the milky whiteness of hers.

His breath was warm and she gasped as she felt the scrape of his jaw against her sensitive flesh. He used his tongue with devastating effect, drawing moist circles around her breast, moving inexorably closer to its centre. She held her breath, every fibre of her being willing him to continue. Finally, when she thought she could bear the waiting no more, his mouth closed fully around the throbbing peak of her nipple and he suckled her.

Instantly sensation coiled in the pit of her stomach and she clung to his shoulders for support as he transferred his mouth to her other breast and administered the same treatment. How had she lived without him? she wondered desperately as the lash of his tongue against her nipple drove her higher and higher. How had she survived for so long without the tumultuous pleasure only he could evoke, and how could she claw back any vestige of her pride when she was fast spinning out of control?

This had to stop, and right now, before she suffered the abject humiliation of begging him to take her. Her body's shameful betrayal was a result of not making love for over a year, she consoled herself when Luc's hand slid beneath her skirt, skimmed her thighs and moved with unerring precision to the core of her femininity. His questing fingers eased the lacy panel of her knickers aside before parting her delicately, the glitter in his eyes as he stared down at her warning her he had discovered the indubitable proof that he turned her on.

Frantically she tried to squeeze her thighs together, determined to deny him access, but her reactions came too late and his fingers slid in deep, a triumphant gleam in his eyes when he found her slick and wet and ready for him. He moved his fingers in an erotic dance and she clenched her teeth, willing her body not to respond, but it felt so wickedly good and already she was aware of the first spasms of pleasure tightening her muscles. Her body was on fire and instinct took over so that she moved her hips restlessly as a wave of intense pleasure engulfed her. Still he continued with his intimate caress, faster, deeper, and she sobbed his name, her cries captured by his mouth as he initiated a kiss that went on and on, his tongue mimicking the movements of his fingers until she lay limply against the pillows, utterly spent.

'So my touch sickens you, does it, *ma petite?*' Luc's dry tone invaded the sensual haze that enveloped her and she winced and closed her eyes against the derision in his. 'You have a peculiar way of showing it.' He swung his legs over the side of the bed and stood looking down at her, a humourless laugh escaping him when she crossed her arms over her breasts. Her skirt was caught up around her waist and she knew she must look totally disheveled, but he did not appear to have a hair out of place and bore no physical signs of the wild passion they had shared moments before.

It's good to know you've dropped your objections to taking up your role as my wife once more, but we'll be landing in five minutes. I suggest you tidy yourself up before I introduce you to my staff. You look a little…flustered, *ma petite.*'

It was impossible to hate a man more than she loathed and detested Luc Vaillon, Emily decided furiously as she scrambled back into her clothes. She would rather move in with the devil than live with him in his château, she decided as she marched back to her seat, her head held high, and the fact that the members of Luc's staff studiously avoided her gaze only added to her humiliation. She felt like a cheap tart and she was determined not to put herself in that position again, but even as she made the resolution her heart skittered in her chest.

Jean-Claude was awake, sitting on his father's knee and staring up at him with wide-eyed fascination, and for the first time she truly appreciated the extent of Luc's power over her. For some reason he had decided he wanted to be a father to their son after all and she did not underestimate his ruthless determination to get his own way. He had told her she could live at the château for as long as Jean-Claude depended on her, but that would be years. At what age did a child no longer need its mother? she wondered. Nothing would ever induce her to leave her son but the cost to her self-respect could be immense, especially if Luc demanded that she resume her role as his wife for the duration of her stay.

He couldn't force her, she reassured herself, but she'd just proved that he didn't have to. She was her own worst enemy where her husband was concerned, and from now on she would have to be on her guard.

CHAPTER FOUR

THE LOIRE REGION of France was lush and green, in stark contrast to the rocky, arid landscape that Emily had grown accustomed to at San Antonia. The car followed the route of the river before the road began to climb steeply and she drew a sharp breath as imposing grey stone walls rose up in front of them.

'You want Jean-Claude to grow up *here?*' she queried faintly as they drove through an arched gateway cut into the outer defensive wall and into a wide courtyard. 'It looks…medieval!'

'It is. The Château Montiard was built in the fifteenth century although only the outer wall and towers and the wine cellars remain of the original building. And the dungeon,' Luc added and she threw him a startled glance, searching for signs of humour and finding none. 'The main residence has been expertly modernised and I designed Jean-Claude's nursery myself. He will want for nothing,' he said pointedly, and Emily wondered if he was hinting that she would be expected to sleep in the scullery. 'The château has been in the Vaillon family's possession since it was acquired by them in 1506. It is Jean-Claude's birthright, his heritage—something you should understand when your own family has such strong links with Heston Grange.'

'How did the Vaillons acquire the château?' she asked curiously, and Luc shrugged.

'By force, I imagine. My forefathers were brigands, although history has it that René Vaillon had some kind of hold over the original owner and blackmailed him into allowing René to marry his daughter. The story goes that the girl was distraught at being forced to wed the boorish René and refused to sleep with him. To punish her, he locked her in the highest tower but, rather than give herself to him, she threw herself from the top. Lucky for you that you have no such inhibitions where sex is concerned, *chérie.*'

'Poor girl,' Emily murmured coolly, ignoring his jibe. 'No woman wants to be married to a barbarian that she has no respect for.'

Luc's jaw tightened ominously and she waited for his temper to erupt, but instead his mouth curved into a grudging smile. *'Touché, ma petite.* You have developed a clever tongue, but perhaps I should remind you that your position here is extremely tenuous. It wouldn't do to upset me.'

'Heaven forbid, I'm aware that you expect your wife to be obedient and *biddable.*'

'Then we should get along just fine.'

He just had to have the last word, Emily thought viciously as she watched him stride across the courtyard to greet a multitude of uniformed staff assembled on the steps leading to the huge central doorway. His secretaries and the nanny had followed from the airport in a second car, and as she freed Jean-Claude from his child seat Liz Crawford appeared, her arms outstretched to take her charge.

'Monsieur Vaillon asked me to take the baby straight up to

the nursery while he introduces you to his household,' she explained apologetically and Emily's heart sank. During their
brief conversation on the flight from Spain she had warmed
to Liz, who had explained that she had returned to child care
after her husband had died and her daughters were both busy
with their own lives. 'I appreciate that no one can take your
place as Jean-Claude's mother, and of course you want to do
everything for him,' she had murmured sympathetically, 'but
your husband explained that you've been ill and babies can be
exhausting. I'm here to give you a break when you need it.'

On the surface it sounded reasonable, but Emily had her
doubts. Liz was kind and motherly but ultimately she was an-
swerable to Luc and she would follow his orders, even if that
meant unwittingly engineering a separation between Jean-
Claude and his mother.

She was quaking inside as she crossed the courtyard to
where Luc and his staff were waiting and wished she had
followed his order to change into something slightly less colourful. As her bright orange skirt danced in the breeze she felt
like a peacock at a funeral and Luc's jaw tightened ominously when she joined him on the steps. If possible, she was
even lovelier than when he had first met her, he thought,
noting the way the sunlight made her skirt appear almost
transparent so that the outline of her slender figure was displayed.

He wasn't the only one to notice, either, he realised as he
subjected a young groom to a fulminating glare. Perhaps his
ancestor René had had the right idea by locking his young
bride in the tower, away from other admirers, but the thought
did not improve his temper and he stiffened as a sudden gust
of wind blew Emily's hair across his face. It smelt of lemons,
fresh and enticing, and he fought the urge to wrap the strands

around his fingers, tilt her head and take possession of her mouth in a way that would leave the cocky groom in no doubt that she was Madame Vaillon, his wife.

Emily pushed her hair over her shoulders, aware that the members of Luc's household staff were staring at her curiously. No doubt they had expected his wife to be elegant and sophisticated, but beset by nerves she could only drum up a shy smile when he introduced his butler, Philippe, who together with his wife, Sylvie, and their daughter, Simone, organised the running of the château.

'You could at least try to act a little more friendly,' Luc muttered as she followed him into the vast, marble-floored entrance hall. 'Philippe's family have worked at the château for generations. Their history goes back almost as far as the Vaillons' and I expect you to treat them with the courtesy they deserve, not to act like a haughty English princess.'

'I wasn't being haughty,' Emily defended herself, 'but I'm not used to living with dozens of staff. Heston Grange cost so much to run that my parents could only afford to employ our lovely old housekeeper, Betty. I don't know how you expect me to act, or even what my roll at the château is. You introduced me as your wife, but I still can't believe you expect me to resume our relationship as if nothing has happened.'

'Believe, *ma petite,*' Luc suggested grimly, his expression unfathomable, and she sighed and glanced around the wide hallway.

Although the château seemed imposing from the outside, inside it was light and airy, with sunlight streaming in through the tall windows to bounce off the mellow oak panelling and creamy-coloured walls. Far from being cold and austere, much care had been taken to make it a comfortable family residence and she warmed to its charm, feeling instantly at home, which was curious when she had always felt uncomfortable at Heston. There was no point in growing attached to the château, she reminded herself, she wouldn't be staying long.

Her eyes turned to the many portraits that adorned the walls, some of which were obviously very old and no doubt priceless.

'Meet the family,' Luc quipped as he followed her gaze. 'There are paintings of every one of my ancestors, the most recent being this one of my parents.'

Jean-Louis Vaillon and his wife, Céline, stared down at Emily disdainfully and she shivered. Was it simply the style of the painting, or were they really as cold and unfriendly as they looked? Luc bore a strong resemblance to his handsome father but Jean-Louis's eyes were flat and devoid of any emotion while Luc's burned with fire—usually brought on by anger at her, Emily conceded sadly, although there had been times in the past when he had looked at her with an expression that she could almost believe was tenderness.

'Do your parents live here at the château?' she asked apprehensively, but he shook his head.

'They're both dead. As you might have guessed from the painting, it wasn't a happy marriage, more of a business arrangement between two wealthy families. My mother's family owned the vineyards that are now part of the Vaillon estate.'

'But they didn't love each other?' Emily murmured, and Luc gave a harsh laugh.

'Definitely not. My father was a cold, remote man and my mother was sensitive and for the most part deeply unhappy. She was fascinated by the story about old René and his tragic wife, so much so that she felt compelled to re-enact history.'

His words took a few seconds to sink in and Emily frowned. 'You mean your mother jumped to her death from one of the towers?' she queried, unable to disguise the shock in her voice. 'How terrible! How old were you?'

'Fifteen or so,' he replied with a shrug. 'I don't remember exactly.'

But the bleakness in his eyes told a different story and Emily guessed that every detail of the tragic event was etched on his brain.

'That's awful,' she whispered. 'I can't believe a mother would leave her child.' At fifteen Luc would still have needed the love and protection of his parents. Her heart ached for him, knowing in his eyes she'd kept his son away from him, too. Was the tragedy of his past a reason for his reluctance to show his emotions? she wondered, her heart aching for him. 'It must have been grim for whoever discovered her,' she added, and Luc stared at her, a nerve jumping in his cheek.

'Yes, it wasn't a pretty sight.'

'You mean you… Oh, Luc!' It didn't matter that they were sworn enemies. All Emily could picture was Luc as a teenager, a boy on the brink of adulthood with his emotions all over the place. His mother's horrific suicide must have marked him for life, yet from the look of his stern father he would have received little sympathy or understanding for his terrible loss. 'Why did you never say anything?' she murmured, reaching her hand out to him in an involuntary gesture, wanting to comfort him. 'In all the months that we were married, you never mentioned your parents.' And she had been too shy, too unsure of him, to pry into his private life.

Luc glanced down at her hand on his arm, his expression so coolly aloof that she withdrew, her face burning. His body language could not have shouted more loudly that she was invading his personal space. He neither expected nor wanted her sympathy and her blood chilled. She had been an outsider when he'd married her and nothing had changed. She would do well to remember that fact.

'Revealing the curse of the Vaillon wives hardly seemed appropriate on our wedding day, *chérie*. Marriages in my family seem to have the unhappy knack of ending in tragedy. For Jean-Claude's sake, let's hope ours doesn't suffer the same fate.'

'It already has,' Emily pointed out. 'Cupid's arrow was way off target when he brought us together, and now it's damaged beyond repair.' She gave a sigh of frustration when Luc made no reply and simply stared at her as if intent on reading her mind. 'This isn't going to work, Luc. There's too much bitterness and mistrust between us to try and kick-start our marriage. Perhaps I should start looking for a house in the village for Jean-Claude and me. Somewhere close enough for you to visit him easily.'

'Forget it,' Luc told her bluntly, and she watched impotently as he strode towards the wide staircase. 'You can look for a property in the village by all means, but my son stays here, and he certainly won't be alone. I intend to make the château my permanent base, both to live and work. Believe me, from now on Jean-Claude will have my undivided attention.'

'But what about your travels, your endless commitments and meetings in every corner of the globe?' Emily queried, a note of panic entering her voice. 'You can hardly take him into the boardroom with you.'

'I'm cutting right back on my travels. I admit I'm not finding the art of delegation easy but it's a small sacrifice when I have my son.'

'A sacrifice you refused to make for me,' Emily accused bitterly. 'Have you any idea how lonely I felt during our marriage? You dumped me in the middle of a big city where I had no friends and the only time I ever saw you was in bed. We never talked, Luc,' she said miserably. 'We never did all the normal things most couples do, like…I don't know, go to the supermarket together.'

'I employed an excellent housekeeper to take care of the running of the penthouse so that you didn't have to,' he snapped. 'And what's romantic about shopping for groceries?'

'At least it would have been better than those agonising dinner parties Robyn arranged. The few times we could have spent the evening together were hijacked by entertaining your business associates.'

'I thought you would appreciate the chance to socialise,' he muttered. 'You had unlimited access to my credit cards to go shopping for new outfits—and most women like to dress up,' he added in a tone that patently spoke of his frustration that he did not understand her.

And therein was the root of many of their problems, Emily thought sadly. She was nothing like Luc's previous lovers. It was a mystery why he had ever married her and his determination to keep her his wife was even more puzzling.

'You can't force me to stay here,' she warned and he shrugged, as if he was bored with the whole subject.

'No, but I can ensure that you never set a foot outside the château with my son,' he said coldly, and the implicit threat in his voice caused a shiver to run the length of her spine. He knew she wouldn't leave her baby. It was emotional blackmail of the worst kind and she was trapped.

Luc continued with his journey up the stairs, rounded a

corner and disappeared from view, but Emily stumbled after him, halting before a huge canvas that took centre stage at the top of the first main flight of stairs. The portrait was of a woman, the style of painting and her clothing suggesting that the picture was a recent addition to the Vaillon archives, but something about her face captured Emily's attention. She, whoever she was, was the most beautiful woman Emily had ever seen, with classically sculptured bone structure and luxuriant black hair that gleamed like raw silk.

Was she one of the cursed Vaillon wives or a relative from Luc's own side of the family? Certainly she had the air of disdainful hauteur that hinted at her French aristocracy, her dark eyes as cold and lacking in emotion as the painting of Luc's parents. To Emily, the woman summed up everything she was not. She was elegant and exquisite and she looked as though she belonged in the château, which only emphasised the point that she herself, in her cheap, colourful clothes, was a rank outsider. She had no place here, and living in a remote French château would in many ways be even worse than when they had lived in the Chelsea penthouse. She would have no chance to make friends or have a life of her own. She would be totally dependent on Luc and the idea terrified her.

She hurried up the stairs that Luc had taken minutes before and arrived on a long landing where a window at one end allowed sunlight to stream in. It was like a scene from *Alice in Wonderland,* she thought hysterically as she ran the length of the landing, finding that the doors on either side of her were firmly shut. The last one had been left slightly ajar and she pushed it open, her breath catching in her throat as she glanced around the vast room.

With its dark wood floor, panelling and ceiling, the room could have appeared gloomy, but the whole of one wall held the same enormous windows that she had noted on the landing. On the opposite wall was a magnificent fireplace and above it a stunning tapestry that she guessed was a priceless antique from the château's past. It was not the décor or the artwork that made Emily stare, however, but the sight of the huge, ornately carved four-poster bed that stood on a raised platform in the centre of the room. Instinct told her the bed was an intrinsic part of the château and her eyes were drawn to the coat of arms that had again been worked in tapestry and which hung around the top of the bed above the rich velvet drapes.

Had the despicable René insisted that his terrified bride join him on this bed? Emily wondered with a shiver. Had Luc's unhappy mother slept in this room, until she had been drawn to end her life rather than remain at the château any longer?

'Luc!' Ghosts from the past seemed to lurk in every corner of the room and with a cry Emily spun round, catching the sounds of a modern power shower that was a welcome intrusion on her imagination. 'We have to talk.'

The bathroom adjoining the master bedroom was a clever compromise between the château's historical past and modern requirements, and although the enormous bath set on its carved, gold-plated feet dominated the room, the shower cubicle at one end did not seem out of place.

'Are you listening?' she demanded of the shadowy figure whose outline was just visible through the frosted glass. 'As you're so keen to point out, I am your wife and as such I have rights, too. The days when women were treated no better than cattle and were viewed as their husband's possession are over. I'm not the feeble, frightened girl that René's wife must have been and I won't allow you to bully me!'

'Bully you!' There was a volcanic eruption from the shower and Emily took a hasty step backward, away from the door, but she was too late. The glass doors separated and one wet, hair-roughened arm snaked out to drag her into the cubicle where the powerful spray soaked her clothes in seconds. 'My restraint where you're concerned has been nothing short of saintly,' Luc informed her furiously, as Emily backed up against the tiled wall.

Saintly was not a word she would have used to describe him, she thought faintly as her eyes were drawn to his magnificent, naked body, watching the way the soap suds clustered amid the hairs that covered his chest and trailed down over his hips to the powerful muscles of his thighs. He was sinfully gorgeous with a body that would incite the most ardent saint to think wicked thoughts. Hers must have been transparently visible in her wide, shocked eyes as she continued to stare at him, transfixed by the hardness of his shaft that lifted and swelled to burgeoning, throbbing arousal.

'*Mon Dieu,* I don't need this,' he muttered, and her startled gaze swung to his face to see a tide of colour stain his cheekbones. 'Stop looking at me like that, *ma chérie,* unless you are prepared to take the consequences.'

'I'm not looking at you like anything,' she snapped, desperate to disguise her excitement as heat coursed through her. 'You pulled me in here. I can't help it if your body is…'

'Hot? Hard? There's no dispute on that one, is there?' he taunted as he stood barricading the door of the shower, his legs apart, gloriously unashamed of the potent force of his arousal. 'Desperate to finish what we started on the plane? Is that why you're here, Emily? Foreplay wasn't enough and it left you aching for my full possession? You don't have to worry,' he assured her silkily as he moved towards her with

deliberate intent. 'I'm more than willing to help you over-
come your reluctance to resume your role as my wife.' He
gave a harsh laugh, his derision directed solely at himself. You
always did unman me, *chérie*. I have never needed any
woman the way I need you.'

'Luc, no!' with the tiny part of her brain that was still
functioning, Emily fought against the overpowering chemical
reaction between them, which was adding to the steamy
atmosphere of the shower cubicle. As he pulled her up against
his chest he turned off the tap and she gasped, shamefully
aware that her nipples were prominently displayed beneath
her clingy wet top and her skirt was moulded to her thighs.
'I came in here to talk about Jean-Claude,' she muttered, her
eyes focused on his mouth as he lowered his head towards
her. 'I don't want this.'

'*Chérie,* you're gagging for it,' he said bluntly, and she
shuddered at the crudity of his words. Where was her pride?
she demanded frantically, but then his mouth captured hers
in a kiss that stole her sanity and drove every other thought
but her driving need for him out of her mind. He removed her
wet clothes with deft movements, his lips never leaving hers
and she trembled at that first touch of his naked skin against
hers, the hard sinew of his thighs pressing on the softness of
hers as he pushed her up against the shower wall.

She should stop him. Every instinct warned her that she
was following a path she would later regret but the burning
fire in his eyes set her alight. Gone was the cold, aloof businessman she had felt so in awe of, in his place the passionate Frenchman who in the first weeks and months of their
marriage had been unable to keep his hands off her. She
revelled in the fact that his control was teetering on the brink.
It made her feel feminine, desirable, all the things she hadn't

felt since she had fallen pregnant with Jean-Claude and Luc had retreated from her, both physically and emotionally.

'You want this every bit as much as I do,' he breathed as he trailed his lips to her ear where he nipped the sensitive lobe with his sharp teeth before sliding lower to her throat and finally her breasts, taking one throbbing nipple and then the other into his mouth.

Emily wanted to deny his taunt but she was helpless, sucked into a vortex of exquisite sensation so that she dug her fingers into his hair to hold him to his task. She trembled when he moved lower still, the muscles in her stomach quivering as his tongue dipped into her naval, created havoc, and then continued on his relentless path to the junction between her thighs. He wouldn't, she thought dizzily as her legs buckled and he supported her weight while his lips moved over her wet curls until his tongue was able to explore her in an intimate caress that heightened her arousal to fever pitch.

Suddenly he straightened and, before she had time to guess his intentions, lifted her into his arms so that she was forced to curl her legs around his thighs, feeling the solid strength of his erection push against her belly. With his hands cupping her bottom, he stepped out of the cubicle and strode into the bedroom, halting by the huge bed. Emily opened her eyes as reality intruded with a vengeance.

'This is where I should have brought you on our wedding night, where all the Vaillon wives have given themselves totally and utterly to their husbands,' Luc told her, his eyes glittering, and she recognised that he was fast approaching the point of no return. 'If I take you now, on this bed, I can never let you go; you will for ever be mine. You have about thirty seconds to stop me, *ma petite,*' he warned her, but Emily was lost. This was Luc, the man she had once loved, still loved if she had the courage to look into her heart. His hard arousal was pulsating against her thighs and with no other thought than that she needed him, she wriggled lower down his body, her legs still wrapped tightly around him.

Luc muttered an imprecation in his own tongue as he lowered her onto the edge of the bed, his hands beneath her bottom lifting her as he entered her with one powerful thrust that made her gasp. It had been a long time and she closed her eyes as he filled her, waited a second for her muscles to relax around him before he withdrew, only to thrust again, deeper this time, the sensations he aroused in her unbearably intense. It was no gentle seduction. Gone was Luc the skilful, controlled lover, in his place a man intent on assuaging a driving need that had been building for over a year. He took her with a hunger, a savagery that made her tremble, although not with fear, but an answering passion that she was power-less to deny.

She clung to his shoulders as lowered his head once more to take her mouth in a fierce kiss that warned of his ultimate possession, and all the time his body moved within hers, hard against soft, dark olive skin an erotic contrast to the milky whiteness of her thighs. On, on, higher and higher he drove her and she could only hang on for dear life as waves of sen-sation built inexorably, reached their peak and sent her crashing over the edge, her body shuddering as she drowned in pleasure.

He was mere seconds behind her, his brow beaded with sweat, and she stared at him poised above her, his face a rigid mask as he fought to stem the tide of pleasure that threatened to engulf him. 'Emily…' Her name was wrenched from his throat and once again she marvelled at his total loss of control where once his restraint had been so absolute. His aim may have been to humiliate her but there were no winners in this power struggle, only losers, she thought, blinking back the sudden rush of tears.

Their bodies might be satiated, still trembling with the last aftershocks of their mutual climax, but it had been sex at its most primitive, the need to appease a basic urge. At least for him it was, she conceded sadly. He did not confuse lust with love but for her they were inextricably linked and although her body was replete her heart ached and over-spilled with the words he didn't want to hear.

'I think that proves we can dispense with the idea of divorce once and for all, don't you?' The hint of smug satisfaction in Luc's voice demolished the remnants of her self-respect, and she wrapped her arms around her body in a purely defensive gesture. 'I have to admit I found your dedication to duty impressive.'

'I don't give a damn what you think,' Emily told him tightly, her voice thick with tears she was desperate to hide from him. For a moment he stilled and she felt his eyes on her, although she refused to turn her head and look at him.

'Emily…' There was a curious huskiness in his voice but she steeled herself to ignore it. Luc had been hewn from the same stone as his medieval château and any hint of softness was in her imagination only.

'Go to hell,' she told him succinctly. 'You've got what you wanted and so have I. Let's just leave it at that shall we? Quits.'

For one terrifying moment she thought he would join her on the bed and she silently prayed that he would leave her before she broke down. Her tears would be the final humiliation. She couldn't bear him to see her cry and she released her breath on a slow hiss when he eventually moved away.

'As you wish, *chérie*. I suggest you remain here and rest. You look…shattered,' he commented silkily as he strode towards the *en suite,* 'and Robyn has organised a small reception for tonight, a chance for you to meet some of my friends who live locally. Everyone is curious to see the new mistress of the Château Montiard,' he added as Emily stared at him, unable to conceal her dismay.

'You mean Robyn's *here?*'

'Naturellement,' he replied with a shrug that screamed of his indifference to her reaction. 'Where else would she be?'

'Where else indeed?' Emily muttered thickly, shocked not so much by his announcement but by this open display of his cruelty and the level of her pain. Robyn, one of the most stunningly beautiful women of her generation and indubitably Luc's lover, was here at the château and any tenuous hopes she might have harboured about her relationship with her husband drained away.

Luc halted in the doorway to the bathroom and gave an impatient sigh. 'I've explained that my work base is now here at the château and Robyn is my personal assistant. I rely heavily on her organisational skills so try not to let your vivid imagination run away with you, *ma petite.*'

Emily's brows shot skywards and she called on every ounce of her acting ability as she surveyed Luc with cool disdain. 'I'm sure her organisational skills are the least of her charms, but have it your own way. One thing, though, which of us will you introduce as your *mistress* of the château? I suggest you think about it before you cause your friends embarrassment,' she murmured, and winced as he slammed the door with such force that it shook on its hinges. Only then did she bury her head in the pillows and cry until there were no more tears left. At some point exhaustion took over and she slept, unaware that Luc had returned and stood staring down at her tear-streaked face before he covered her with the quilt and finally left her in peace.

CHAPTER FIVE

THIS DAY SHOULD be forever etched on my mind as the day I had first held my son, Luc brooded. Instead, there was only one person who dominated his thoughts.

Emily.

Her name swirled around in his head, teasing him, tormenting him as she had always done. With a muttered oath he strode into the dining room, recalling with stark clarity the way she had writhed beneath him a few hours earlier. Her hoarse cries as he'd driven her to the pinnacle of sexual pleasure and the way she had sobbed his name with the power of her release were not things he would forget in a hurry and even now, with less than an hour to go before the damned dinner party Robyn had arranged, his body was responding to those memories with an enthusiasm that made him ache. How the hell was he going to sit through dinner like this, when all he really wanted to do was go upstairs and make love to his wife with a thoroughness that would atone for the months they'd spent apart?

Not that he would be welcome, he admitted grimly. He had been every inch the barbarian Emily had accused him of, so driven by his own damnable need that he had been rough with her, maybe had even hurt her. It was not a comfortable thought and he walked over to the window to stare out at the spectacular view across the Loire Valley. Hurting her had not been part of his plan but if he was honest, he didn't have a plan other to reclaim what was rightfully his. It was a frightening admission for a man who exerted supreme control over every aspect of his life. He couldn't remember a time when he had acted on instinct rather than following a preordained programme. He didn't like surprises, which was why he had found his reaction to Lord Anthony Dyer's youngest daughter so startling.

Heston Grange represented one of the finest pieces of real estate in England. It would be a lie to deny that his original interest had been solely in acquiring the magnificent country houses with a view to refurbishment. It would represent a huge coup for his development company, he'd acknowledged, but he had felt some sympathy for the Dyers, who had owned the house for generations.

From the start he had been aware of undercurrents within the family, especially from Anthony's pushy wife Sarah, and he had been mildly amused by the hinted suggestion that marriage to one of the Dyers' daughters could result in a drop in the asking price of the estate. Sarah had been desperate to keep a foothold in the door of Heston Grange and her three older daughters were certainly attractive, but as far as he had been concerned, marriage was not on his agenda.

And then he had met Emily.

Even now, two years on, he could not repress a smile as he recalled his first sight of her. With her flushed cheeks and tangled hair she had reminded him of a wood nymph, her beauty completely natural, earthy and unbelievably sexy. The fact that she had been as shy and awkward as a young colt had only added to his fascination. He'd spent that first evening unable to take his eyes off her and although he had accepted Anthony Dyer's invitation to stay at Heston and discuss the most important business deal of his life, he had found himself drawn with annoying regularity to the stables.

He had needed every ounce of his patience as he'd sought to break down Emily's reserve, he remembered, but she had been worth the wait. The first time he'd kissed her he had shocked them both with the level of his hunger, but far from frightening her she had revealed a hidden depth of passion that had left him mad with longing. There had been no plan in his head, no carefully thought-out decision to ask her to marry him. He had reacted on pure instinct, as if his soul had recognised its mate and could not bear to let her go. But presumably she had not felt the same way, which was why she had left him.

'Will there be anything else, Monsieur Vaillon?' Simone's voice interrupted his thoughts and he swung round, dredging up a smile for the maid. She had finished putting the final touches to the table, checking the cutlery and adjusting the position of the centre display of old-fashioned roses. Their exquisite perfume hung heavy in the air, their petals reflected in the highly polished veneer of the table, and he felt his tension ease a little.

'Everything looks perfect,' he complimented in his own language and Simone blushed with pleasure. He had every confidence that the dinner party would run without a hitch, aided by Sylvie's excellent cooking and Philippe's imperturbable presence at the table, but his main thanks would have to go to his personal assistant.

If only Robyn had consulted him first, before arranging a social event for Emily's first night at the château, he thought

grimly. He hadn't expected her to even be here and had
assumed she would remain at her Paris apartment where he'd
phoned to say he was bringing both Jean-Claude and Emily
back to the château.

Why had Robyn immediately driven down? The paperwork she had said was vital had been an excuse, he was sure
of it. She had dealt with far more complex affairs without his
help before. She better than anyone was aware of the tensions
that had existed within his marriage. It was Robyn he had
confided in when he had been unable to reveal his innermost
fears to Emily. Surely she could appreciate his desire for
some time alone with his wife and son?

Perhaps her presence would be a good thing, he mused, a
way for him to demonstrate to Emily that there really was
nothing going on between him and his PA. But he was tied
to Robyn by the past. It had taken her a long time to come to
terms with his brother's death, and she relied on him as her
emotional prop. It was churlish of him to feel restless but
suddenly he wished she would pick up the threads of her life
once more and allow him the freedom to carry on with his.

As Simone made to go he called her back. 'I want you to
take this up to Madame Vaillon,' he requested, handing the
maid a flat box engraved with the name of an exclusive
boutique from the nearby city of Orléans. 'It's a present,
something for my wife to wear tonight,' he explained. 'My
secretary has just returned with it.' Simone nodded, her eyes
shining with an excitement he only hoped would be reflected
in Emily's blue gaze.

'Madame, it is time for you to wake, I think.'

Emily opened her eyes and stared into the anxious face of
Luc's maid.

'It is almost the dinner,' Simone explained agitatedly in her broken English, and slowly Emily sat up. She was in the master bedroom, Luc's bedroom, lying on the vast bed. And she was naked, although fortunately someone had covered her with the heavy silk quilted bedspread. The knowledge did not alleviate her embarrassment and she shuddered as her memory returned. Had Simone discovered her wet clothes in the shower where Luc had stripped her? Had he sent Simone to check on her, perhaps to make sure she hadn't been tempted to throw herself out of the window like two other Vaillon wives before her had done? Heaven knew what the young maid was thinking. Emily groaned as she wrapped the bedspread round her and inched towards the edge of the bed.

'I'll quickly shower and dress,' she explained with a mixture of gestures and her schoolgirl French, and Simone's face cleared.

'Monsieur Vaillon asked me to give you this. His assistant bought it for you,' she said cheerfully, her eyes widening as Emily opened the box to reveal a simple but exquisite sheath of navy blue silk, with delicate shoestring straps and a low-cut bodice.

'*C'est très belle,*' Simone breathed reverently and Emily reluctantly had to agree that Robyn had exemplary taste.

'It's very pretty,' she agreed briskly, replacing the dress between the layers of tissue in the box, 'but I have my own clothes.'

She frowned when she discovered her empty suitcase on a chair and further investigation revealed that her clothes had been hung in one of the wardrobes, her few brightly coloured outfits looking lost and out of place against the backdrop of the grand antique furniture. 'I think I'll wear this,' she said defiantly, selecting her one dress that came anywhere near formal. It was a cerise pink halter neck with a long skirt that looked demure until she moved and revealed a split that reached mid-thigh. Elegant it was not, she conceded, noting Simone's dismayed expression, but it was bright and funky and, more importantly, hers. She refused to wear a dress that had been chosen by Luc's mistress.

'But Monsieur Vaillon—'

'Does not tell me what to wear,' she finished for Simone. 'Did he ask you to hang my clothes in here?' she demanded, and the maid nodded, her confusion palpable when Emily instructed her to transfer all the items in the wardrobe to the empty room across the landing.

'Monsieur Vaillon will not be happy,' Simone muttered, and on that one Emily was forced to agree, but Luc's anger would be vented on her—she could bet on it—not the hapless Simone.

She showered and changed in record time, piling her long chestnut hair into a loose chignon and adding a touch of make-up, emphasising her long eyelashes with mascara and defining her lips with a clear gloss. In the nursery Jean-Claude greeted her enthusiastically and she lifted him into her arms with a sigh of pleasure, rubbing her cheek against his satiny curls.

'I've just given him some yoghurt,' Liz warned. 'He might be a bit sticky and you're all dressed for dinner.'

'I don't care,' Emily returned cheerfully. She would never be one of those mothers who cared more about her appearance than cuddling her baby. 'It's rather late for his teatime,' she commented, and Liz nodded.

'I'm afraid he slept all afternoon and now he's raring to go but I'll play with him while you're busy with your guests.'

'Even better, I'll take him down to meet them,' Emily said

decisively. 'Can you give him the quickest bath on record, while I choose his outfit?'

If Liz was surprised she said nothing, and Emily smiled at her son, her heart clenching with love as she received a cheeky grin in return. She refused to look too closely at her reasons for wanting to take him down to the dinner party. Perhaps it was to emphasise her role in his life to Luc, or maybe it was just because she wanted to show the baby off.

'You are the most gorgeous little man in the whole world,' she told her son a short while later, when Jean-Claude had been bathed and dressed in a smart sailor suit.

'Thank you, *chérie,* but not so little, as I hope I demonstrated earlier,' came a throaty voice in her ear, and her cheeks flamed as she swung round to find Luc close behind her. For a moment she stiffened and then her lips twitched. He was an arrogant devil and she had forgotten how he'd loved to tease her mercilessly, until their shared laughter had slowly died and the chemistry between them had fizzed out of control. Her eyes darkened with an array of emotions she could not disguise and the answering gleam in his grey gaze told her he was aware of her wayward thoughts.

He didn't play fair, she told herself crossly as she swung her back on him and fought to bring her hormones under control.

Resplendent in his black dinner suit and white silk shirt, he looked good enough to eat and she was hungry. Making love with him earlier had whetted her appetite after more than a year apart but it couldn't happen again, she told herself firmly. Luc had to understand that she was an independent woman, not a puppet who would jump when he pulled the strings.

'We must share the same thoughts,' he murmured, and her

cheeks turned scarlet at the very idea of him being party to her fevered imagination. 'I also came to collect Jean-Claude,' he added coolly, lifting the unresisting baby into his arms, and Emily sighed at the look of delight on Jean-Claude's face as he laid his head on Luc's shoulder.

'You're honoured,' she muttered bleakly. 'He doesn't usually take to strangers.'

'But I'm not a stranger, I'm his father,' Luc pointed out quietly. 'Perhaps he recognised me from here, in his heart, in the same way that I recognised with absolute certainty that he is my son.'

Emily was startled by the raw emotion in his voice. The flash of pain in his eyes as he looked down at Jean-Claude was real. No one could act that convincingly. Once again she was filled with guilt that she must have misjudged him. But if that was true, why had he dismissed the chance to see Jean-Claude after his birth? Nothing made sense and she sighed, unaware that he had noted the misery in her eyes.

'Is something troubling you?' he queried politely, as if he were addressing a member of his staff rather than the woman he had made love to so passionately only hours before.

She laughed bitterly. 'Other than being kidnapped and held in your damn great castle against my will, you mean?' she flung at him sarcastically, and his jaw tightened.

'If you insist on leaving, I'll have Philippe drive you to wherever you want to go.'

'But not with Jean-Claude?'

'*Non.*' His reply was cold, unemotional but utterly implacable, and she gave a frustrated sigh.

'You know I'd never leave him.'

'Then it is a prison of your own making, because I will never let you take him again, and if you try…' He broke off and glanced down at the child in his arms, his eyes flaring with a level of emotion he had never awarded her. 'You will be sorry,' he promised flatly, and she shivered at the inherent threat. How had they come to this? she thought miserably as tears stung her eyes.

'Do you ever wish we could turn back the clock?' she whispered, and his harsh laugh scraped across her already raw nerves.

'Every day of my life, *chérie*—and for so many reasons,' he added obliquely, but she was sure he was referring to their marriage, certain he regretted the day he had made her his wife, and all her old insecurities flooded back. 'But unfortunately we cannot change the past. I have missed so much of Jean-Claude's babyhood. Precious time that cannot be replaced, and for what?' He rounded on her bitterly. '*Mon Dieu,* Emily, I am trying very hard to understand where I went wrong, but did my crimes really deserve such a cruel punishment? Do you know what haunts me the most?' he demanded. 'If you hadn't filed for a divorce, I still wouldn't know the whereabouts of my son. Perhaps I should count myself lucky that you only sentenced me to a year of despair. You could have kept him from me for ever.'

'I told you I was coming back to England,' Emily defended herself. 'I wanted us to share custody of Jean-Claude.'

'Only because you were running out of money,' he said scathingly and her head jerked back as if he had struck her.

'That's not true. I don't need money. I don't need anything from you. All I ever wanted was a little of your time,' she muttered thickly. 'I wanted us to build a relationship outside the bedroom but you made me feel as though my only function was to provide convenient sex.'

'Which you hated, I suppose?' he mocked angrily, his eyes flashing fire. She sighed, aware that she wasn't getting through to him. 'I didn't hate it but I was unhappy that it was the only form of communication between us. A marriage can't survive solely on sex, as we discovered once I fell pregnant and you refused to come near me. There was precious little communication between us then, was there Luc?'

'You sound like a spoilt child whingeing for attention,' he ground out furiously as he fought the sharp needles of his conscience that reminded him he hadn't spent enough time with her. He wasn't used to sharing, he acknowledged grimly. He'd got into the habit of compartmentalising his life and when he'd come home from work he hadn't wanted to bore her with details of his day. He'd wanted to lose himself in the sweetness of her body. His role had been to protect her, to provide for her, and he'd been determined to do so to the best of his ability. But instead of appreciating his efforts, she had been so unhappy that she had walked out on him.

Women were totally incomprehensible, he decided bitterly. It seemed that whatever he did he couldn't win, but children were a different matter. His feelings for his son were uncomplicated. He loved him unreservedly and he was determined not to make the same mistakes his own father had. Jean-Claude would never have reason to doubt his love, he vowed fiercely. According to Emily, he had been a useless husband but he was going to be the best father ever.

He swung round and headed for the door of the nursery, pausing for a moment to glance back at her impatiently. 'Did Simone not give you the dress I bought you?'

'She did, but I told you I don't want anything from you.' Certainly not a dress he had requested his personal assistant to choose for her, Emily thought furiously. How insensitive could he get? 'I prefer to wear my own clothes but I don't suppose my cheap dress meets your exacting standards.'

'*Non,* you look like a slut,' he said coldly, and instantly could have cut off his tongue as she paled. Why the hell did he want to hurt her? Was it really because he hated the fact that the dress was more revealing than he was happy with? It had never bothered him when his previous lovers had paraded around in next to nothing but Emily was his woman, his wife and he wanted to lock her away from the world. He was no better than his barbaric ancestor, he acknowledged disgustedly, no better than his father. The thought shattered all his preconceived notions about himself.

'Our guests are already here,' he muttered, tearing his eyes from the dejected slump of her shoulders. Her head came up.

'Good, because the only clothes I possess are shorter and briefer and altogether more *sluttish,*' she told him fiercely. 'Not at all what your designer brigade friends are used to.' She would not give him the satisfaction of knowing his one vicious taunt had demolished her self-confidence, but as she stormed past him he gripped her arm.

'My friends have waited a long time to meet you and are under the impression that, together with Jean-Claude, we are one happy family. Let's not disillusion them,' he warned softly.

'Meaning what?' Emily demanded ungrammatically, and he paused at the top of the stairs to stare down at her.

'Meaning that tonight you will act the part of my adoring wife, blissfully happy that we are reunited.'

Why was he so eager to prove that their relationship was happy? Emily wondered with a frown. He was a fiercely proud man. Perhaps he couldn't bear the idea of his friends knowing that she had walked out on him. 'I'm afraid my acting ability's not that good,' she informed him coolly as she swept down the stairs in front of him and he laughed sardonically.

'Then improvise, *chérie,* like you did this afternoon. You were so adamant that you didn't want sex with me but I would never have guessed it from your wild response when you shared my shower. You're more talented than you think.'

Emily was still searching for a suitable retort when they reached the door of the salon and a tall, elegant blonde stepped forward to greet them.

'Emily, it's been a long time,' she murmured in the cool, faintly amused tone that Emily remembered so well, and her heart plummeted. Robyn was as stunning as ever in sumptuous, floor-length black velvet that was moulded to her body like a second skin, and Emily was immediately conscious of her cheap, brightly coloured dress. What on earth had induced her stupid spurt of rebellion? she wondered dismally. She should have worn the dress Luc had bought her, but it was certainly too late to change now and the familiar sick nervousness tied her stomach in knots as she braced herself to meet his guests. 'Everyone's dying to meet the mysterious Madame Vaillon,' Robyn murmured, so softly that only Emily heard. 'Let's hope they're not disappointed.'

As Luc's friends instantly surrounded him Emily felt as though she were invisible and hung back as he proudly introduced his son. Of course Jean-Claude was adorable, she acknowledged ruefully, and, far from being upset by the attention, he was lapping it up but as she slunk into a corner Luc turned and held out his hand.

'I'd like to introduce my wife, Emily,' he said, his burning gaze searing her as his eyes settled on her face and he lifted her hand to his lips. 'As you can see, I am doubly blessed to have such a beautiful mother for my son.'

Never mind her acting ability, Emily thought frantically, her cheeks burning as he pressed his mouth against her hand. He was surely in line to win an Oscar, but even the knowledge that it was all pretence did not stop her heart from pounding, especially when his lips found the pulse that jerked unevenly in her wrist. She could almost believe that the flare of warmth in his eyes was real and she trembled when, instead of releasing her, his lips travelled along her arm to caress the vein that throbbed in the crease of her elbow joint. His friends would be left in no doubt of his devotion to her but only she knew it wasn't real.

As an ice-breaker, Jean-Claude's presence was far more effective than the finest champagne and her initial awkwardness was forgotten as conversation with Luc's guests revolved around sleepless nights and teething gel. Far from being the social climbing business associates that she remembered from their life in Chelsea, these people were evidently Luc's trusted friends, people he had grown up with and who now had families of their own. Gradually Emily began to relax.

'I adore Jean-Claude's little suit,' commented a pretty, vivacious woman from the group that had circled round to admire the baby. Nadine Trouvier was the wife of Luc's closest friend, Marc. The mother of two small girls, she owned a successful babywear shop in Orléans and had confided that she was about to open another in Paris. 'Where did you buy it?' she queried interestedly. 'It's exquisitely made, especially the hand smocking at the front. Without wanting to appear rude, it must have cost a fortune. Only the best for your son, hmm, Luc?'

'*Naturellement,*' he replied coolly, but Emily knew from

the way his eyes had narrowed that he was speculating on how she had been able to afford expensive baby clothes when she had little money.

'Actually, I made it,' she informed Nadine cheerfully. 'I lived…in Spain for a while.' She felt Luc stiffen but continued, 'And I fell in love with the incredible baby clothes sold in the markets. But I found that although they looked beautiful, they were impractical and the fabric was often stiff and uncomfortable. I searched for better fabrics and redesigned the very formal baby clothes that the Spanish love so that they were more wearable. See…' She showed Nadine. 'The collar of Jean-Claude's suit is detachable and the suit fastens underneath so that dressing him is easier. He doesn't have a lot of patience for lying still while I dress him,' she added with a rueful smile, and Nadine nodded eagerly.

'I had the same trouble with my own two. Emily, this is wonderful. Do you have many other designs?' Nadine demanded enthusiastically. 'Have you ever thought about making them to sell? I would be very interested in stocking this sort of thing in my shops.'

'Well, I'd started up a little business in Spain,' Emily admitted, refusing to meet Luc's gaze. 'My friend runs a cookery school, predominantly for middle-aged ladies who bought my clothes for their grandchildren. They proved so popular that I started to receive orders from around the world. I employed a few girls from the village to help with the sewing and now it's a thriving little business. Fortunately Laura is overseeing things while…' She hesitated, about to say while she was away, but the darkness of Luc's expression made her change to, 'At the moment. It was good to be able to earn money doing something I enjoyed and at the same time care for Jean-Claude. Sewing was the only thing I was any good at when I was younger.'

'Along with riding,' Luc interrupted, taking her by surprise as he strolled across the room and slipped his arm around her waist. 'My wife is an excellent horsewoman,' he proudly told his guests. 'She's quite fearless aren't you, *chérie?*' His smile had the sickly sweet quality of an old movie but everyone seemed to be taken in by his attentiveness and no doubt believed they shared a marriage made in heaven, Emily thought grimly. Only she knew the truth, that Luc's loving looks had been a ploy to turn the conversation from her life in Spain without him. For some reason he wanted to project an image of a blissfully happy couple but she didn't know why and if she didn't stop smiling soon her jaw would surely crack!

'Seriously,' Nadine said, when Emily had handed Jean-Claude over to his nanny and they filed into the dining room, 'you'll have to persuade your husband to set up a workshop for you in the château. There's a ready market for the superb-quality hand-stitched clothes you can make. Parisian mothers will love them and I'm prepared to offer you an excellent deal if I can stock them in my shops. We'll save our discussion for another time,' Nadine added quietly as Robyn stared over at them, unable to disguise her annoyance for a few seconds before her tight smile slipped back into place. Emily smiled gratefully at the Frenchwoman, glad to have found an ally. She had a feeling she was going to need one.

It was late by the time the last of Luc's friends drove out of the gates of the château and the dull ache across Emily's temples had become a shaft of throbbing pain. Robyn was, of course, staying at the château and had joined her and Luc on the front steps to wave goodbye to the guests. Quite a cosy little threesome, Emily brooded darkly as she trailed across the entrance hall after her husband. Robyn had barely spoken to her all evening and that suited her fine. They had nothing to say to each other. She wasn't blind. She had noted the furtive, almost desperate glances Robyn had given Luc throughout dinner, but curiously he hadn't responded and had seemed oblivious to his personal assistant's attempts to gain his attention. Emily was ready to believe he had been telling the truth when he had denied an affair with Robyn, ready to believe that Robyn had lied to her, but it didn't change anything, she thought sadly. It didn't mean that Luc loved her.

'I'm going to bed,' she announced bluntly as she reached the sweeping staircase and viewed it with dismay. There suddenly seemed to be an awful lot of stairs and she was shocked by how tired and drained she felt. It felt like weeks since she had begun the day at San Antonia.

'Emily, are you all right, *ma petite?* You look so pale.' Luc murmured his concern and for a brief, mad moment she imagined that they were the happy couple he had been so desperate to portray. In the fantasy, he would sweep her into his arms and carry her up the long staircase to that vast bed where he would make love to her with such tender passion that she would never want him to stop. That wickedly sensual mouth would explore every inch of her body, coax each nerve ending to vibrant, throbbing life until, utterly satiated, they would fall asleep in each other's arms.

'Let me help you, *chérie.*' His voice broke through the sensual haze that enveloped her and for a moment she forgot that they were at war, forgot that the game of happy families had been for his guests' benefit only. She smiled at him, her heart in her eyes, and heard him inhale sharply before Robyn's sharp tones shattered the spell.

'If you could just spare me five minutes to run through this

report,' she murmured, 'it's urgent. I'm sure Emily under-
stands the importance of heading a multimillion-pound company.'

'Can't it wait until morning?' Luc replied tersely, and
Robyn edged closer, her hand resting lightly on his sleeve.
For the life of her she would not fight with Robyn over her
husband like a couple of curs over a bone, Emily thought
savagely, and she moved abruptly away from him.

'I promise not to keep him for too long,' Robyn assured
her sweetly, and Emily discovered she possessed acting skills
she hadn't known she had as she flicked them a disdainful
glance.

'Have him for as long as you like,' she murmured in a tone
that screamed her bored indifference. 'I don't want him.'
With that she marched up the stairs, aware of Luc's furious
gaze burning like a laser between her shoulder blades. Robyn
was welcome to him, she told herself sternly. She had already
consigned their marriage to the graveyard of broken dreams.
She had Jean-Claude and now, it seemed, a chance to build
a career that would give her not just financial independence
but also a feeling of self-worth.

As she was about to place her foot on the next step, it disappeared. The walls tilted alarmingly and she found herself
lifted and held tight against the uncompromising solidity of
Luc's chest. 'You are perilously close to having me demonstrate here and now just how little you want me, *chérie,*' he
breathed against her ear.

The rigid muscles of his arms around her warned of his
simmering anger, but Emily was aware of other, more subtle
sensations—the warmth that emanated from him and the
musky scent of his aftershave that did strange things to her
insides. She fought the longing to press her face against the

tanned column of his throat where he had removed his tie and unfastened the top few buttons of his shirt. Being held this close to his chest drugged her senses and dulled her wits when she needed them to be razor sharp.

'An interesting idea, but Robyn might not approve,' she murmured with a coolness that masked her inner turmoil.

'Damn Robyn!'

'For once I couldn't agree with you more.' He was nearing the master bedroom and a wave of panic assailed her so that she wriggled wildly until he was forced to set her down. 'I want to check on Jean-Claude,' she whispered, brushing past him into the nursery. She crept over to the cot and as she stared down at her son's innocent, sleeping form, Emily's resolve hardened.

'I want to be free to live my own life,' she whispered fiercely. 'I can't stay here as your prisoner, waiting for the day Jean-Claude no longer needs me. There are things I want to do.'

'Such as set up your own business?' he suggested scathingly, and she rounded on him angrily.

'Yes, damn it. What's so wrong with that?' Her voice had risen along with her anger. Jean-Claude stirred, and with an oath Luc caught hold of her arm and steered her through the connecting door to the master bedroom.

'Your role is here, as Jean-Claude's mother and my wife,' he told her as he swung her round to face him. 'Isn't that enough? *Mon Dieu,* it's not as if we need the money.'

'Sometimes I think you're trapped in a time warp,' Emily ground out, her frustration tangible. 'It's not about money. I've finally found something I'm good at after a lifetime spent being the untalented daughter and the unsuitable wife. I want the chance to make my mark on the world—a tiny mark, I know,' she added self-deprecatingly, 'but as Jean-Claude grows older I want him to be proud of me.'

'And you think that will happen if you are completely absorbed in your career?'

'Obviously he will always come first,' Emily muttered, the resoluteness of Luc's expression warning her that this conversation was going nowhere, 'but I should have known you wouldn't approve. You never wanted me to work or have the chance of meeting people my own age, even before I was pregnant. Look what happened when I got a job at Oscar's.'

'You were waiting tables,' Luc exploded.

'At one of London's top restaurants. It was hardly a greasy burger bar.'

'It was still not a suitable occupation for my wife.'

'And didn't you make your feelings felt?' she muttered sullenly. 'I still can't believe you marched in there while I was on duty and carried me out over your shoulder. You totally humiliated me,' she added, recalling the furious row that had followed his high-handedness. Their furious argument had ended as they always had, with her absolute capitulation in bed. She groaned inwardly at the shaming memory of her weakness where he was concerned. 'Laura said you were a control freak,' she told him bitterly, and his eyebrows rose quizzically.

'The same Laura who persuaded you to hide away in Spain I assume. You must remind me to thank her if I ever see her,' he drawled sarcastically. 'Let's just hope she doesn't take up a career in marriage guidance.'

'Its all academic now, anyway,' Emily said wearily. It had been the longest day of her life and she just wanted to go to bed, alone. 'A few weeks after you forced me to give up my job, I discovered I was pregnant and the rest, as they say, is history.'

Luc raked a hand through his hair as he paced the bedroom floor. His slightly dishevelled state gave him a raffish charm that Emily found irresistible.

'I accept that I was not there for you as much as I should have been during your pregnancy.' The admission seemed to have been dragged from him and Emily gave a bitter laugh.

'You weren't there, full stop. Suddenly your business interests in New York, Rome and every other part of the globe were far more important than spending time with me.'

'There were reasons…'

'Number one being that you were revolted by my body as my pregnancy progressed.'

'*Sacré bleu,* that is absolutely not true.' Luc's voice hissed between his teeth like a geyser letting off steam. 'I don't know how you could say such a thing.'

'It is true,' Emily insisted miserably. 'My mother explained that some men find pregnancy a turn-off. She told me not to worry and assured me things would return to normal after the baby was born, but she was unaware that our marriage wasn't normal to begin with.'

'Why, because I was busy at work and didn't give you enough attention?' Luc suggested angrily. 'I thought the world had gone mad in those months before you left,' he told her grimly. 'There were problems within the company, the suspicion of fraud at a high level, which meant I couldn't delegate to anyone but a few trusted staff. The timing could not have been worse.' he said thickly. 'I was worried about you. You were so young to be facing the rigours of childbirth and the constant sickness left you drained. I used to look at you sometimes and feel overwhelmed with guilt. I should never have married you,' he finished huskily. 'I should have let you remain innocent and carefree with your horses.'

For a moment Emily thought her heart had actually cracked open as pain tore through her. Luc had finally admitted that he believed their marriage had been a mistake and she felt numb with misery. 'Yes, well, it's a pity for both of us that you didn't, but even if our marriage is something we both regret, I could never regret having Jean-Claude, which you patently did. You can't blame me for believing that you didn't want him when you rejected him.'

The faint glow of the candles cast shadows around the room and Luc's face looked as if it had been carved from marble, his eyes glinting like molten steel as he glared at her. 'When did you ever give me the choice?'

'The day I brought him to see you.'

His eyes narrowed, his tension palpable. 'You're lying!'

'Why would I?' she snapped impatiently. 'It was December, bitterly cold, and Jean-Claude was about six weeks old. It had taken me a while to get over his birth,' she continued falteringly when he simply stared at her in a silence that spoke volumes. 'I went to the penthouse. I thought, even if you weren't there, I could show Jean-Claude off to your housekeeper, Mrs Patterson, but it was Robyn who opened the door.'

She broke off, recalling the unmistakable triumph in Robyn's voice as she explained that Luc was too busy to see her now, or any time in the foreseeable future. Robyn had stood in the doorway, tall and impossibly elegant, barring Emily's entrance to what had once been her home and uncaring that the freezing temperature outside was unsuitable for the baby.

'She told me what you've just admitted, that you thought our marriage was a mistake and you had no desire to be saddled with a child.'

In a flash Luc strode across the room and caught hold of her, bruising the tender flesh of her upper arms. 'This can't be true! I thought I was unshockable where you're concerned, but to stoop so low that you could accuse one of my most trusted aides, my sister-in-law, of deliberately engineering a split between us is too much to forgive, even for me, *chérie*. You disgust me,' he said savagely and she winced as his fingers gripped harder. 'Robyn was as concerned about your disappearance as I was.'

'Of course she was,' Emily muttered sardonically, wincing as his fingers bit into her skin. 'Luc, my arms. You're hurting me.' To her relief he released her immediately and she sank onto the edge of the bed as her legs buckled beneath the force of his fury.

'Why would she do such a thing?' he demanded in a low whisper that sounded like the rumble of a volcano about to erupt. 'She knew how desperate I was to see my child. Why would she try to keep me from him?'

'Because she wanted you for herself,' Emily said wearily, 'and still does. Presumably she feared that if you were as anxious to see Jean-Claude as you say you were, you might have been prepared to give our relationship another go. She really needn't have gone to so much trouble,' she snapped. 'It would be easier to raise the *Titanic* than resurrect our marriage.'

'I don't believe you,' Luc said, but this time there was a note of uncertainty in his voice and the hand that he raked through his hair was not quite steady.

'Then ask her.' Emily threw down the challenge. 'Because I swear to you, I'm telling the truth.'

CHAPTER SIX

HE WAS NOT a control freak!

Emily's accusation resounded in Luc's head as he stormed into his study and poured himself a liberal cognac. It was true he hadn't wanted her to work in the restaurant, but what husband would be happy to see his wife rushed off her feet until late at night? It had all been the fault of that damned chef whose vicious tongue had been feared among the other staff at Oscar's Diner. For reasons he could never understand, Emily had struck up a firm friendship with Laura Brent, although it was only now that he appreciated Ms Brent's role in Emily's disappearance.

Had she really been as unhappy in London as she had revealed tonight? His conscience nagged that it had been an incredibly busy and stressful time for him workwise and it was true they hadn't spent much leisure time together apart from those interminable dinner parties Robyn had organised. Perhaps she had been lonely, a young girl in a big city, but he had tried, he assured himself. How many times had he rejected the comfort of a hotel in favour of driving through the night just so that he could spend a few precious hours with her? And she had always been pleased to see him. Despite his best efforts to slide into bed without waking her, she had stirred and snuggled close, her hand straying a familiar path to wreak havoc on his self-control.

How the hell had it all gone so wrong? he wondered bleakly as he downed his drink and refilled the glass. He freely admitted he had been irritated by her unreasonable jealousy of Robyn, but he'd hoped the holiday would give them a chance to unwind and rediscover the joy they'd shared in the early days of their marriage. Instead, it had been an un-mitigated disaster.

Even now the sight of her paper-white face haunted him when he recalled the way she had slid to a crumpled heap at his feet. A virus, some unusual tropical disease she had picked up, would have been terrifying enough, but the realisation that it was history of the most tragic kind repeating itself had rendered him almost beside himself with fear. He hadn't been angry at the news of her pregnancy, he'd been scared witless at the thought of losing her. Even after she had sailed through the first few months safely, he had been unable to relax and as time had moved inexorably closer to her due date he had distanced himself, emotionally and physically, following a defence strategy learned from his childhood.

The damage he carried from his past was not Emily's fault, he conceded grimly, especially as he had never confided his fears to her, or the reasons for them. It was his fault he had failed her and now he was behaving no better than his father. He couldn't realistically hold her prisoner at the château. She was young and vibrant and wanted to live her life to the full, but the knowledge that she didn't want to live it with him hurt immeasurably, almost as much as her accu-sation that he had rejected her and his son soon after Jean-Claude's birth.

She had to be lying, he decided wearily, because the alternative was that the woman who had been his most trusted confidante for the last few years had deliberately deceived him. But in his heart there was no doubt where his loyalties lay.

Emily stood watching her sleeping son long after Luc had stormed from the nursery. Poor, innocent Jean-Claude, she thought sadly, caught up in the crossfire between the two people who loved him most. And Luc did love his son. She'd witnessed firsthand the mutual bond of adoration that had sprung between them from the moment he had lifted Jean-Claude into his arms.

Was it possible that Robyn had lied a year ago when she'd insisted that Luc wanted nothing to do with either his wife or child? Perhaps if Mrs Patterson had been there, Emily would have tried harder to enter the flat that was technically her own home. But there had been no sign of Luc's friendly housekeeper, no sign of Luc, and Robyn had appeared so self-assured, so stunningly beautiful compared to Emily's pale, sleep-deprived state, that she had been more than ready to believe her husband had chosen the ex-model over her.

With a sigh, Emily slid off the bed. The headache that had started during dinner had settled to a nagging sensation above her eyes. Usually she disliked taking painkillers but tonight she needed something to dull the ache around her heart. She'd noticed the medicine cabinet in the bathroom adjoining the master bedroom and quickly searched for a couple of painkillers before Luc found her. The last thing she wanted was for him to think she was preparing herself for a night of passion when she was utterly determined she would never share his room or bed again.

With that thought in mind she swallowed the painkillers, removed her make-up and freed her hair from its chignon so that it fell in a heavy swathe down her back, before making a swift exit. The room across the landing where she had asked Simone to transfer her clothes was smaller than the master bedroom but it was pleasant enough and she was so tired she doubted she would be awake long enough to admire the décor. Wearily she snapped on the light switch but the room remained in darkness, apart from the sliver of moonlight that streamed in between the crack in the curtains. She cursed as she stubbed her toe, but it was too late now to change the bulb, even if she knew where to find one. She closed the door and for good measure dragged the heavy dresser in front of it. Luc no doubt assumed that his *biddable* wife would be sleeping in his bedroom, but if he thought he could flit between her and his mistress, he was in for a shock.

'It's all right, *chérie,* I'm a willing captive. You don't need to barricade me in!'

A bolt of fear caused her to cry out, her heart pounding in her chest as she stared at the tall, menacing figure just visible in the doorway leading to the *en suite.* 'How did you get in here?' she demanded, her disbelief turning to a mixture of fury and embarrassment when she realised he had watched her struggle to pull the dresser across the door. 'You must have lost your way—your room's across the hall,' she added sweetly, striving for the brand of sarcasm he used with such deadly effect. 'And do you know where I can find a spare light bulb?'

Instead of replying, he strolled across the room and flicked on the bedside lamp so that the room was bathed in a gentle glow, his cold smile sending a frisson of apprehension along her spine as he held up the bulb he had removed from the ceiling light fitting. His silence unnerved her yet she could not drag her gaze from him. Tall, dark and devastatingly sexy, *he* unnerved her, she acknowledged wryly. Her tiredness seemed to have vanished and she felt strangely energised, every nerve ending tingling with a sense of expectation that refused to be quashed.

'I'm sure you have your reasons for snooping about in the dark, but I'm tired and not in the mood for playing games,' she told him shortly, and his jaw tightened.

'I'm not the one playing games and it's you who's in the wrong room. As my wife, you have certain duties to perform,' he reminded coolly, and the sheer arrogance of his statement fuelled her temper.

'I'm taking early retirement but I'm sure you'll have no problem filling the vacancy in your bedroom. As for performing, I did that this afternoon. You don't really think I enjoyed myself, do you?' she queried tightly, praying he wasn't remembering her eager capitulation in his arms.

'*Non, chérie,* I would never have guessed from your energetic response between the sheets that you hated every minute of making love with me,' he drawled, and her face flamed.

'Well, I did and I'm not planning an encore.' With the dresser wedged across the door and Luc barring her way to the bathroom she seemed to have reached stalemate and she gave an exasperated sigh. 'I would really appreciate being left in peace,' she said huskily. 'It's been a hell of a day.'

How did she manage to look so achingly fragile? Luc wondered savagely. Her air of vulnerability never ceased to affect him. Her eyes had darkened to the colour of midnight and appeared far too large for her pale, heart-shaped face. Her hair fell almost to her waist and he fought the urge to wind his fingers into the chestnut strands and pull her in. She was his woman, his *wife,* damn it, and he wanted her with a hunger that bordered on the obsessive, but she had tried to barricade herself out of his reach.

Was she afraid of him? The thought made him pause fractionally, but every instinct told him it was not fear that made her shrink from him. He knew her too well, recognised the fierce sexual tension that gripped her so that her pupils dilated and she was forced to moisten her lips with the tip of her tongue. She wanted him as badly as he wanted her, but convincing her of that fact was going to take more patience than he currently possessed.

'I am your husband, the man you agreed to love, honour and obey, if I remember the wording of the old service that *you* decided on. For ever, *chérie.* Until death us do part. Isn't that the promise we once made?'

'We also promised to stand by one another in sickness and in health, but you broke that one the minute you learned I was pregnant,' she said shortly, dragging her gaze from his hard-boned, handsome face.

'When I failed to give you enough attention?' he murmured silkily. 'Rest assured I won't make the same mistake again, *ma petite.* There will be no separate rooms, nothing to fuel gossip among the staff. Simone has already spent half the day transferring your belongings between rooms.'

At that Emily flung open the wardrobe, her temper heating to boiling point when she found it empty.

'You are my wife and you will share my bed,' he stated, and the implacable determination in his gaze was the last straw.

'Lucky me,' she quipped, striving for sarcasm to hide her trepidation as he shoved the dresser away from the door and headed in her direction. 'Did you ask Robyn why she kept

quiet about my visit to the penthouse?' she demanded, unable
to hide the hint of desperation in her voice as he suddenly
pounced and scooped her into his arms, ignoring the blows
she aimed at his chest with insulting indifference.

'I didn't need to. I already know you were lying.' His
voice was so flat, so certain that her hands stilled and she
stared into his face that was only inches from hers. 'I checked
back in my diary,' he explained coolly. 'At the time you say
you took Jean-Claude to the flat, I was in South Africa, partly
on business but also to spend Christmas with friends who understood my desperation that I still had no knowledge about
the whereabouts of my child.' His fingers tightened their grip
and she winced as he kicked open his bedroom door and
strode across to the huge, ornate bed. 'My housekeeper had
gone to Yorkshire to visit family and Robyn flew from our
meetings in Durban to stay with her parents in the States. The
penthouse was shut up for the whole of December,' he told
her hardily. 'There's a chance, I suppose, that you did go
there, but why make up the rubbish about seeing Robyn? Why
make her out to be a liar?'

'Why would I invent the story at all?' Emily defended
herself as he threw her onto the bed with enough force that
she bounced on the mattress. He shrugged, his indifference
warning her that he was growing bored with the conversation.

'Perhaps because if you insist on leaving me, you'll have
to fight a custody battle over Jean-Claude, and you think it
would show you in a slightly better light if you said you had
tried to contact me and allow me see my son?'

'I did go to the flat and I did see Robyn,' she yelled, dismay
that he refused to believe her mingling with fear and a slow-
building excitement as he began to unfasten his shirt. The
room was illuminated by discreetly placed uplighters and

dozens of thick church candles grouped on the fireplace, their flickering flames casting shadows on the walls. It was intensely romantic, a room designed for lovers, but there was nothing loving about the hardness of Luc's expression and the gleam in his grey eyes warned of his determination to fulfil his rights.

'I'm not a liar,' she said thickly, despising the way her voice had softened, the way her eyes fixed of their own accord on his bare chest. In the candlelight his skin gleamed like bronze and she clenched her fingers into fists so that she could not give in to the temptation to run her hands through the covering of wiry black hairs that arrowed down from his chest and disappeared beneath the waistband of his trousers.

'Do you want me to make love to you tonight, *ma chérie?*' he murmured softly.

'I'd rather have all my teeth extracted without an anaesthetic.'

'Then you are a liar.' It was his arrogance, the supreme self-confidence of his smile that set her teeth on edge. His hands moved to the zip of his trousers and she closed her eyes on a wave of despair as they hit the floor, closely followed by his underwear. Her breath snagged in her throat when he had to tug his silk boxers over the rigid hardness of his arousal.

Dear God, he was gorgeous she thought numbly. Earlier, in the shower, she had been so caught up with the exquisite sensations he had been arousing in her that she hadn't had time to study him properly. Now he was standing before her, his stance almost indolent, unhurried, and she was able to appreciate the full throbbing power of his erection. She should escape now, before it was too late, but instead her body quivered, betraying the primitive need that pinned her to the bed with a force she was unable to fight. It was only when he reached out a hand and threaded it through her hair that her instinct for self-preservation kicked in and she tried to scrabble off the bed, only to be lifted and deposited back on the mattress as if she were a rag doll.

'You had what you wanted this afternoon,' she muttered, although speech was difficult with her face pressed against his chest. Already she could feel herself weakening, molten heat flooding through her as the scent of him, a subtle blend of his exotic aftershave and male pheromones, assailed her senses.

'I want more.' His lips feathered along the line of her jaw and moved up to hover at the corner of her mouth, tantalisingly close so that it was all she could do not to close the gap and feel the full force of his kiss.

'But why me?' The words escaped as a wail of despair. 'You don't even like me and you certainly don't trust me,' she whispered on a note of pain. 'Isn't Robyn enough for you?' He had vehemently denied a relationship with his PA but all her old doubts had resurfaced with the knowledge that he believed Robyn's word over hers.

He ignored her, but his mouth settled on hers in an evocative caress that stunned her with its gentleness. She had braced herself for his fierce assault, had assembled her defences, but the sweetness of his kiss, the way he parted her lips with delicate precision so that his tongue could initiate an unhurried exploration, shattered her tenuous control over her emotions. This was Luc, the love of her life and the only man she had ever wanted. How could she deny him, how could she deny herself when her entire being was focused on assuaging this desperate, primal need for her mate?

She was unaware that his hands had slid beneath her hair

to unfasten the halter neck of her dress until he eased back a fraction and unpeeled the fabric from her breasts, leaving them exposed to his hungry gaze.

'Exquisite,' he breathed, his accent suddenly very pronounced, so innately sensual that she shivered and tiny goosebumps prickled her skin. 'I have never forgotten the scent of you, the feel of your skin like satin beneath my fingers. You are in here,' he whispered, frustration at his own weakness evident in his tone as he held her hand against his heart, 'and I can't seem to evict you, however hard I try.'

He didn't trust her, he refused to believe her story about going to the penthouse and he certainly did not love her, but right now Emily didn't care. He overwhelmed her senses, trampled on her pride so that all that was left was desire, piercing her soul and making every nerve ending zing with expectation. She drew a sharp breath as his hands slid down to cup her breasts, his thumb pads brushing across her nipples until they hardened into throbbing peaks that begged for his total possession. Slowly he lowered his head and she murmured low in her throat when his lips closed around first one peak and then the other, drawing it fully into his mouth as he suckled her. Sensation seared her, so that she arched her back to offer him unfettered access to her breasts but already his hands were sliding lower, tugging her dress over her hips while she knelt on the bed.

She gasped as he stroked the sensitive flesh of her inner thighs but was beyond any idea of rejecting him when he hooked his fingers into the waistband of her underwear and drew the scrap of lace down to her knees. Only then did he push her gently so that she fell against the pillows and he swiftly stripped her completely before coming down beside her, his body warm and male and urgently aroused. She

wanted to say something, to tell him once more that she
hadn't been lying about taking Jean-Claude to him, but her
words were lost beneath the pressure of his mouth as he took
her in a slow, sensual caress that drugged her senses and
drove everything but the man and the moment from her mind.

When he dipped his hand between her thighs she parted
them willingly, trembling as he stroked the sensitive nub he
had revealed before he slid his fingers in deep to explore her
intimately. She was ready for him, slick and wet, and she
heard him groan low in his throat as her fingers strayed down
over his hips to hesitantly touch the throbbing hardness of his
arousal that pushed insistently against her belly. His hair-
roughened thighs were abrasive against the softness of hers
as he moved over her, his hands beneath her bottom lifting
her so that she was angled to his satisfaction. He entered her,
slowly, taking his time so that her muscles stretched to accommodate him. He filled her and she gasped as he began to
move, sensation building on sensation, his rhythmic thrusts
sending her higher every time he drove into her. Suddenly she
was impatient, desperate to reach the pinnacle that she knew
was ahead, and she wrapped her legs around him, urging him
on, her pleasure mounting with the increasing speed of his
movements.

Just when she thought she could take no more, her body
splintered and she cried out as wave after pleasurable wave
dragged her under, leaving her boneless and utterly spent. He
was mere seconds after her and she heard him shout her
name, his voice harsh as if it had been dragged from the
depths of his soul, before he relaxed and she gloried in the
weight of him pressing her into the mattress.

'You see, that wasn't so bad, was it, *ma petite?*'

On the edge of sleep, the unmistakable note of triumph in

his voice commanded her attention and her eyes flew open, sick humiliation filling her. Of course he sounded triumphant when she had made it so easy for him. Once again her defences had crumbled at the first touch of his hands on her skin. It wasn't bad, it was terrible, and she cringed away from the warmth of his body that even now had the power to arouse her.

'Are you hoping for a mark out of ten for technical ability, or simply waiting for a round of applause?' she demanded coolly as she sat up and dragged the huge silk-covered bolster into the centre of the bed. 'It wasn't that bad, but it wasn't that good either, and if it's all the same to you, I'd rather not repeat the experience.' With that she dived beneath the covers, hiding her hot face and praying that he wouldn't touch her because she would surely crack.

'Think very carefully, *chérie,* before you put a barricade between us,' he warned softly, 'because, I promise you, *I* won't be the one to remove it.'

'Excellent. Then I should get a good night's sleep without the fear of your hands straying into my side of the bed. Goodnight,' she added stiffly into the silence, and ground her teeth in impotent fury as he gave a low chuckle.

'*Bonne nuit, mon ange.* Sleep well!'

Sunlight slanting across her face caused Emily to open her eyes and she frowned as she stared around at the unfamiliar surroundings. Not the whitewashed walls of the farmhouse but the opulent décor of the master bedroom at the Château Montiard, she noted, her memory returning with a vengeance. She turned her head sharply but the space on the other side of the bolster was empty. Her gaze travelled to the clock and shock saw her scramble from the bed and into the *en suite*.

How on earth had she slept until ten o'clock, and why hadn't anyone woken her? Her thoughts turned immediately to Jean-Claude and she prayed he was happy with Liz. Her first opportunity to impress Luc with her maternal skills had got off to a bad start.

She showered in record time, wincing as ill-used muscles made themselves known. Her cheeks flooded with colour at the memory of just how she had exercised them. What madness had turned her into a wanton creature in Luc's arms last night? She had no one to blame but herself because he hadn't forced her. His methods of persuasion had been a far more subtle incitement of her senses that had left her begging for his possession.

A scant glance through her wardrobe revealed she had nothing suitable to wear for her role as the lady of the château and an imp of devilment saw her slip into faded denim pedal pushers that clung to her hips like a second skin and a bubble-gum-pink T-shirt with the slogan LITTLE MISS NAUGHTY emblazoned across the front. Elegant it wasn't, she conceded with a grin as she caught her hair into a ponytail and headed for the stairs, but her outfit was fun and funky and if Luc disapproved, too bad!

'Where's Jean-Claude?' she asked hesitantly, her bravado slinking away beneath Luc's cool stare as she crept into the dining room, to find no sign of her son or his nanny.

'Liz has taken him for a walk in the garden. He was growing impatient,' Luc added pointedly, and she blushed.

'I can't believe I overslept like that. Usually I'm awake at dawn.'

'Aha.' From his tone he patently believed she never woke up before lunchtime and her face tightened. She had spent the first six months of their son's life waking up every four hours to feed him because he was such a demanding baby. It was only in the last few weeks that she had persuaded Jean-Claude to sleep through the night and her body clock was frantically trying to make up for lost time.

'You've obviously never paced the floor at three in the morning trying to pacify a baby with colic,' she snapped, and he surveyed her steadily over the top of his newspaper.

'No, I was never given the chance.'

Hostilities had been resumed, she realised as she took her place at the table and smiled gratefully at Simone who placed a cup of steaming coffee in front of her.

'There's bread and croissants, or Sylvie will happily cook you something,' Luc murmured, and she quickly shook her head, her stomach rebelling at the idea of food.

'Coffee will be fine.'

'You must eat,' he argued, and then paused. 'Although perhaps not too much or you might actually burst out of your clothes, and they leave little to the imagination as it is.' His lips twitched as his gaze settled on the slogan across her chest and to her horror her breasts immediately swelled so that her nipples were prominently displayed beneath the thin cotton. 'And my imagination is in overdrive,' he commented dulcetly, to which there was no reply she could utter in polite company.

The silence stretched between them, so intense that the ticking of the clock seemed to reverberate around the room. 'Um, is there a spare car that I could borrow?' she asked at last, and he glanced at her speculatively.

'I'm afraid not,' he replied pleasantly, but she didn't trust his smile. He reminded her of an alligator, slumberous and watchful in the seconds before it snapped its great jaws around its unsuspecting prey. 'Where do you need to go? Everything you or Jean-Claude could possibly need is here at the château.'

'I'd still like to go into the village, or visit the nearest town occasionally. If it makes you happy, I'll leave Jean-Claude with his nanny,' she snapped impatiently, 'but you can't honestly expect to hold me prisoner at the château indefinitely.'

'I'm curious to understand why you're so anxious to leave,' he murmured, 'unless it has something to do with this mad idea of setting up your own business.'

His words stung and Emily felt her temper flare. He didn't think she could do it. Perhaps he didn't think she was clever enough to embark on a business venture but she was determined to prove otherwise.

'I'd certainly like to start looking for a workshop or some sort of premises where I can work. It doesn't need to be anywhere special,' she continued as he frowned, 'but big enough for a couple of cutting tables and sewing machines.'

'You're definitely going ahead, then?' he said shortly. 'Let's hope Jean-Claude is not unsettled when you abandon him.'

'I have no intention of abandoning him!' Emily jumped up furiously and scooted round to his side of the table. 'Anything I take on will fit around his routine. I've told you, he'll always come first.'

'In that case, shouldn't you concentrate you efforts on settling into the château so that the three of us can spend time together as a family?' he asked, his voice suddenly as soft as velvet. She swallowed at the lambent warmth in his eyes. In his faded jeans and a fine knit black sweater he looked deliciously sexy and she fought to restrain a shiver of pure pleasure that the sight of him induced.

'Aren't you going to work? I'm sure there must be something urgent on the other side of the world that needs your attention.'

'I told you, I'm learning to delegate,' he replied lazily. 'Having just been united with my son, I'm hardly likely to want to leave him—or his mother,' he added softly, and her stomach lurched.

'You're just saying that to…to get round me,' she muttered awkwardly, but could put up no resistance when he caught her hand and tugged her onto his knee.

'You're quite right. I intend to do my best to make you happy here.' His mouth hovered above hers and she closed her eyes to ward off temptation while her brain tried to assimilate his astounding statement. She couldn't let him kiss her, not when she needed to be on her guard against him, but somehow he had crept past her defences and she gave a little gasp when his lips brushed gently over hers. It was the lightest caress but it immediately made her want more and she lifted her lashes to find him staring down at her a curiously intent expression in his grey eyes.

'Why…why do you want to make me happy?' she asked huskily. 'We despise and mistrust each other. Why sentence us to remain in a loveless marriage?'

'I wouldn't describe our marriage as loveless, *chérie*,' he said quietly and for a brief, awesome moment her heart soared. What was he saying—that he loved her? 'We both adore Jean-Claude. For the sake of our son, I think we should try to put the past behind us and repair the cracks in our marriage. He deserves a stable and happy childhood, loved and cared for by both his parents.'

'For cracks read Grand Canyon,' Emily replied thickly when she could trust herself to speak. Of course he didn't love her. He'd only gone to the trouble of tracking her down because he had wanted to find his son. 'Naturally the only reason for us to stay together is for Jean-Claude's sake, but I'm not convinced it'll work. There's too much bitterness, on both sides,' she finished sadly.

'But we could try? Please, *chérie.*' He had lowered his head again and she knew she should turn her head to evade his mouth. Instead, she could not help but lean forward to close the gap between them, a soft moan escaping her when he captured her lips.

He took it slowly, as if he wanted to savour the moment and by the time his tongue dipped between her lips she was helpless to resist, curving her arms around his neck to draw him closer. She felt his hand slide beneath her hair, angling her head to his satisfaction as he deepened the kiss, the slide of his tongue sweetly erotic and deliciously intimate.

'You see, *ma petite,*' he whispered against her throat when at last he lifted his head, 'it's not over between us, it never could be. We owe it to ourselves, not just Jean-Claude, to call a truce.'

Wordlessly Emily nodded, her heart too full to speak. He didn't just want her at the château for Jean-Claude; it seemed that he really wanted their marriage to work, and hope filled her. She was prepared to meet him halfway.

'So, no more talk about setting up a business, hmm?' His words sent alarm bells ringing in her head. 'We need to devote all our time to each other and, of course, our son.'

'Luc…' She bit back her frustration as Liz carried Jean-Claude in from the garden and the baby's face lit up as he spied his father.

'Papa,' he shouted, justifiably proud of the second word he had mastered, and Emily turned her head away in despair. Luc had said he wanted to give their marriage another chance, and not just for the sake of their son. The news should have filled her with joy, it was more than she had ever hoped for, but it seemed that Luc didn't want an equal relationship—he wanted to own her body and soul. Could she do it? she wondered fearfully. Could she forget her dreams of combining a career with motherhood and make her role as Luc's wife the most important thing in her life?

'It's not over between us,' he had murmured, and she could not deny the truth. He was more important to her than a career and she would gladly sacrifice everything if only he would care for her. She would make him love her, she vowed fiercely as she slipped from the room. He wasn't immune to her, his passion the previous night was proof of that. She would win his trust and with it his heart, and she could not suppress a surge of joyful anticipation as she ran up the stairs to remove the bolster from their bed.

CHAPTER SEVEN

'SABINE REALLY WAS extraordinarily beautiful, wasn't she?' Robyn's cool voice echoed through the hall and Emily's heart sank as she dragged her eyes from the portrait that hung over the stairs. Robyn was poised on the landing above, looking effortlessly chic and understated in white blouse and matching linen trousers whose superb cut screamed their exorbitant price tag. With her blond hair curling about her shoulders, she looked as though she was about to star in a soap-powder commercial, Emily thought sourly, but Robyn wasn't whiter than white, she was a liar and it was agonising to think that Luc trusted her.

'She is—was,' she amended hesitantly, 'incredibly lovely, but who was she?'

Robyn's finely plucked brows arched in surprise. 'You mean you don't know? Sabine was Luc's wife, the first Madame Vaillon. I assumed he'd told you,' she added when Emily continued to stare at her in stunned silence, unable to disguise her acute shock.

'He's never mentioned that he was married before,' she admitted thickly, disbelief giving way to humiliation that Robyn was privy to secrets that she knew nothing about. She felt as though her heart had been ripped from her chest. Why had Luc never told her? His first wife had been breathtakingly beautiful, her haughty demeanour emphasising her suitability for the role of lady of the château, and Emily was aware that any comparison would find her seriously lacking. 'How did she die?' she whispered, fighting the wave of nausea that swept over her.

'Sabine Bressan was a model—the muse of a famous designer at one of the top French couture houses—who went on to have a successful career as an actress,' Robyn told her. 'Luc fell in love with her at first sight. He adored her and they were France's golden couple, which made her death all the more tragic.'

'What happened…?' Surely Sabine hadn't taken her own life like two other Vaillon wives before her?

'She suffered an ectopic pregnancy. I'm not sure if she even knew she was pregnant until she collapsed in agony while they were holidaying on a remote island off Thailand. By the time medical help arrived, it was too late. Sabine was dead and Luc was utterly distraught. I don't think he ever really got over it,' Robyn confided. 'He loved her so much and he swore he would never marry again.'

'But he married me,' Emily pointed out huskily and Robyn threw her a scornful look.

'Yes, but that was different. He had his reasons…' She paused fractionally before murmuring sympathetically, 'Oh, dear, I'm afraid I've said more than I should. I admit I was surprised when you turned up again. I would have thought you'd got the message by now.'

'What message? Luc brought me here, I didn't ask to come, and he wants us to give our marriage another chance.'

'Well he would say that, wouldn't he?' Robyn intoned

softly. 'He has his son to consider. He'd do anything for Jean-Claude including keeping you around until he's gathered proof of your unsuitability as a mother that will swing a custody hearing in his favour.'

'I wonder what sort of proof he was gathering last night?' Emily snapped, her simmering temper disguising the sickness she felt inside. The knives were well and truly out and she was beyond trying to maintain even basic civility with Robyn.

'I wouldn't bank on using sex to hang onto him. You tried it once before and it didn't work. Luc is a man of superlative tastes but I suppose even a connoisseur needs a bit of rough now and again.'

'Which is presumably when he turns to you.' She might be dying inside but she refused to go down without a fight, Emily vowed fiercely, pride her only defence against Robyn's poison. 'You deliberately kept quiet about my visit to the Chelsea penthouse, didn't you? What do you think Luc's reaction would be if he discovered that his ultra-efficient assistant had actively prevented him from meeting his son?'

'I think you'll have one hell of a job proving it,' Robyn replied coolly, a slight smile playing on her lips. 'Luc and I go back a long way. He trusts me. Can you say the same, Emily?'

There was no simple answer to that, except for the humiliating confession that, no, he did not, and Robyn's smile widened.

'I'm on my way to find Luc now. You'll have to excuse us but we've hours of work to get through. Where are you off to?' she queried, her gaze slithering over Emily's funky T-shirt. 'Kindergarten, by the look of it!'

Emily had to move before she gave in to the temptation to push the bitchy blonde down the stairs. She hurried upstairs, desperate to lock herself away while her mind assimilated this latest blow.

Of all the secrets Luc had kept from her, the fact that he had been married before was the most shattering, she acknowledged as she curled up into a ball in the middle of the bed. Was it the reason he had decided they should live in London after their marriage rather that at the château, which had been his home with the stunning Sabine? Surely every time he looked at her he compared her with his beautiful first wife. Did he wish that Sabine was here now or, God forbid, did he close his eyes when he made love to her and pretend she was his first wife?

The idea made her feel physically ill and she pushed her knuckle against her mouth to hold back her sobs. Suddenly his aloof attitude and the fact that he had never intimated in any way that he loved her made sense. How could he love her when he was still mourning the woman he had adored? Sabine was an impossible act to follow Emily recognised despairingly, and it seemed even more likely that Luc only tolerated her because she had provided him with his son.

With her face buried in her arms she was unaware that Luc had followed her into the bedroom until she felt the mattress dip and she jerked her head round to find him sitting next to her.

'*Mon Dieu,* Emily! What is it, *ma petite,* are you ill?'

'Yes, I'm ill, I'm sick to my stomach,' she flung at him as she scrubbed her eyes with her hand and noted the traces of mascara on her fingers. She had never learned to cry prettily. No wonder he was staring at her with such dismay when she must look even more of a mess than usual and the knowledge increased her anger. 'Get away from me,' she snarled, recoiling from him as he reached out to stroke her hair from her damp face. His frown deepened.

'What happened to the smiling woman who half an hour ago agreed to give our marriage another go?' he queried, patently bemused by her transformation into a screaming harridan. Her hurt exploded in temper.

'Sabine! Sabine happened. Robyn took great delight in explaining about your first wife,' she yelled at him. 'Do you have any idea what a fool I felt? I'm your wife, damn it, but even members of your staff know you better than I do.'

Luc had visibly paled at the mention of his first wife's name and now he stood and raked a hand through his hair. 'So I was married before. It's no big deal,' he said coolly, and she stared at him wildly, unable to stop the tears that streamed down her cheeks.

'No big deal! It changes everything,' she sobbed. 'I thought I was special, I thought that the fact you'd married me meant I was important to you.' All the memories she'd clung to of their wedding day and brief, glorious honeymoon in Paris were worthless. He'd done it all before. 'The only ray of hope I had for our relationship was that you had chosen me for your wife, but once again I'm second best. I feel like the last prize in the raffle,' she whispered brokenly, 'the useless item that nobody wants.'

'Don't be so ridiculous,' Luc snapped, his grey eyes cold and so unemotional that she felt her heart splinter. 'Of course I want you.'

'Yes, for convenient sex when you happen to be around and haven't got anything better to do.'

'That's a lie.'

'Then why didn't you tell me about her? And don't tell me she slipped your mind,' she added bitterly. 'I've seen the painting of her. Hell, I could hardly miss it when it hangs in pride of place in the château. Robyn told me how much you loved her. Is that the reason you kept quiet? You thought I'd be jealous of her?'

'If it was, then I was right wasn't I?' he taunted, his eyes glittering as he stared at her tear-stained face. He was responsible for causing such devastation and the knowledge didn't make him feel good. He'd never meant to hurt her, he had wanted to protect her, but as usual she had completely misread his good intentions. 'Sabine died in terrible circumstances,' he said more quietly. 'It's not something I find easy to discuss and I could hardly reveal that it was her pregnancy that killed her when you'd just discovered you were carrying a child.'

'You should have told me,' Emily said stubbornly. His explanation made sense of sorts but she refused to be appeased. 'Why don't you just be honest and admit that you don't consider me important enough to share things with me? We've been married for two years but I hardly know you at all.'

'We've spent half that time apart, and whose fault was that?'

'Yours. It was your attitude that drove me away and nothing's changed, has it, Luc? You still don't regard our marriage as a partnership. As far as you're concerned, the only place I'm useful is in the bedroom.'

'If that's what you think then you'd better start earning your keep,' he growled savagely, the furious gleam in his eyes warning her she had pushed him too far.

'Luc, no.' He thwarted her attempt to scramble off the bed. 'Don't you dare touch me,' she yelled, her anger already turning to a fierce, unwanted excitement as he grabbed the hem of her T-shirt and yanked it up over her breasts. She tried to buck against him but his mouth came down on hers, his

lips hard, hungry, demanding her response. She couldn't deny
him, even now when she felt sick with betrayal that she had
been the last to know about Sabine. When he kissed her,
touched her she could forgive him anything, but the cost to
her self-respect was too much to bear and tears slid from the
corners of her eyes.

He must have felt them against his skin and lifted his head
at last, his expression unfathomable as he stared down at her.

'Sabine was in the past. You are my wife now,' he told her
as he rolled off her and pulled her T-shirt into place. 'For Jean-
Claude's sake, if nothing else, I suggest you start acting the
part.'

Pale rays of sunlight filtering through the curtains heralded
another new dawn and Emily opened her eyes. Autumn was
fast approaching. It was hard to believe she had been at the
château for almost a month. Sometimes if felt as if she had
been there for ever and she could barely remember a time
without Luc.

It had not been an easy month, she acknowledged. In the
days after she had learned about Sabine the atmosphere in the
château had been fraught with tension. Luc had treated her
with haughty disdain and she had refused to back down. He
was in the wrong, she had reminded herself each night when
she had hidden her face in the pillows and cried herself to
sleep. He was the one who kept so much of his past a secret
from her but until she felt that he trusted her there was no
hope for their marriage.

The only glimmer of brightness was the fact that Robyn
had left the château immediately after the upset over Sabine.
Had Luc been angry that his PA had revealed Sabine's
identity? she wondered. He had made no reference to either

his first wife or Robyn, but in the last week she had noticed a distinct thaw in his attitude towards her. Perhaps the small birthday party they'd held for Jean-Claude had helped. It had been a joyous day as they'd celebrated his first year and Luc had been unable to disguise his pride as he'd showed off his son to his friends. Watching them together, father and son, Emily had felt a sharp stab of guilt that she had kept them apart. Luc loved Jean-Claude more than she had ever believed possible and his anger with her was understandable, but she had honestly never known he would care about their child so deeply and she had been unable to stifle a little pang of envy that Jean-Claude's place in Luc's heart was so secure.

With a heavy sigh she stared up at the billowing drapes that surrounded the bed, her breath catching when a familiar, indecently sexy voice sounded from the other side of the bolster.

'Why the sad sigh, *chérie?* Are you unhappy at the château?'

'No,' she admitted honestly, after a long pause during which she came to grips with the fact that Luc had not gone for his usual early morning ride but was lying only inches from her. 'Just confused.'

'Oui.'

The gentle understanding in his tone was her undoing and she bit down hard on her lip. The bolster seemed as insurmountable as the Berlin Wall had once been, a symbol of division that she had put in place and he had vowed he would never remove. He had stuck firmly to his promise and every night climbed into his side of the bed, bade her goodnight in a tone that licked over her like thick honey before he doused the lamp and within minutes appeared to be fast asleep.

Patently he was not tormented by the same aching desire that saw her toss and turn restlessly until the early hours. Even then her sleep was fractured by memories of his hands on her body, her dreams so wickedly erotic that she woke hot, flustered and desperate for him. It didn't help matters, she thought dourly, when every night he stripped in front of her, his lack of inhibitions all the more noticeable when she could not walk from the bathroom to the bed without her armour of a thick, all-concealing robe, her face burning as she leapt between the sheets with more haste than dignity.

Her one defence against her crumbling emotions was the knowledge that he only wanted her as his wife for the sake of their son. What other reason could there be? she wondered bitterly, when Sabine's exquisitely beautiful face taunted her every time she passed the portrait that took pride of place at the top of the stairs?

'Why didn't you go for a ride this morning?' she asked, desperate to break the silence between them. Her eyes widened as his face appeared over the bolster.

'I decided to wait for you. I thought you might like to join me.' With a night's shadowy growth on his jaw and his black hair ruffled from sleep, he reminded her of a pirate, his raffish charm too much for her to deal with first thing in the morning.

'Another time perhaps, although it was kind of you to ask,' she replied stiltedly, and his low chuckle filled her with longing to fling the bolster to the far corner of the bedroom. She loved the sound of his laughter, loved him, she accepted bleakly, but his sudden friendliness was an illusion, a trick, Robyn had assured her, to lull her into a false sense of security while he planned how to win custody of Jean-Claude.

'You'd be surprised at how kind I can be, *ma petite*,' he teased, 'and once you loved riding. In fact, you spent most of your time on Kasim.'

'It was a long time ago,' she whispered thickly as she

curled up into a ball beneath the bedcovers. It was stupid to
cry over a horse, she told herself angrily as her mind relived
the day Kasim had been sold, along with all the other horses
from the stud at Heston Grange. A cost-cutting exercise her
father had explained impatiently, unable to cope with her
misery when he'd dropped the bombshell. He had never understood that she had turned to her horse for the affection she
had never received at home.

Emily had fled to the stables, utterly distraught, and that
was where Luc had later found her, pulling her firmly into
his arms as he sank onto a hay bale and cradled her in his lap.
His strong arms had offered comfort and she had clung to his
wide shoulders as her tears had gradually subsided and she'd
explained between hiccups that the deal had already been fi-
nalised. Kasim would be shipped out of the country by the
end of the week, she had told him, her blue eyes filling once
more. He had brushed an errant tear with his thumb pad
before lowering his head to trace the same path with his lips.

She couldn't remember the exact moment the tenor of his
caress changed, deepened to something that no longer offered
comfort but instead revealed a burning passion that had been
simmering beneath the surface. The first touch of his lips
softly brushing over hers was a revelation and a fierce trembling started deep inside as his tongue traced the contours of
her mouth. Hampered by her painful shyness, she'd had few
boyfriends and her sexual experience was next to nothing, yet
she knew instinctively what he wanted her to do and received
a low murmur of approval when she tentatively parted her
lips.

Suddenly all remnants of restraint were blown away as he
crushed her to him, his mouth an instrument of sensual
pleasure as he teased and coaxed her response in a blatant se-

duction of her senses. She had no thought to deny him, no thoughts of anything but him. Even her heartbreak over Kasim faded, obliterated by the myriad new sensations Luc was evoking within her. When he tipped back into the hay, taking her with him, she made no demur, her excitement reaching fever pitch when he unbuttoned her shirt, his hands warm and deliciously male on her midriff.

'You are exquisite, *ma belle.*' His voice stroked over her skin with the same dedication as his hands and she heard him inhale sharply as he eased her bra cup over one breast, his fingers finding its rosy nub and inciting it to swell until it throbbed unbearably. It was so new, so gloriously exciting, and far from feeling shy she was impatient for more, her hips arching beneath him and her soft cries of rapture filling the barn when he replaced his fingers with his mouth.

Who knew what might have happened if voices from the yard had not intruded on their sensual world? Even then, knowing they could be caught at any moment, she was loath to end her first experience of sexual pleasure, and it was Luc who gently eased away from her, sliding her bra back into place and refastening her shirt buttons when it became obvious that her hands were shaking too much to be of any use.

She had been like putty in his hands, Emily thought dismally, recalling his amused smile at her obvious disappointment that he was calling a halt to their love-making. She had been lost from the moment he'd first kissed her, a willing slave to his desires that more than matched her own. She had made the fatal mistake of confusing sexual attraction for love, because although he had undoubtedly fallen in lust, love had never entered his head or his heart.

'Come with me this morning?' His voice broke into her

thoughts, a welcome interruption from memories that still haunted her and she dragged her gaze from the sculpted beauty of his body as he strolled towards the *en suite* with a nonchalant disregard for his nakedness.. 'We'll show Jean-Claude the horses and there's a quiet little mare who might be suitable for you.'

'So what do you think of Mimi?' Luc asked later as they stood in the yard, stroking the pretty bay mare the groom had led out from the stables. 'I admit she's getting on a bit but she's gentle and safe for you to ride.'

'Why don't you just order me a mobility chair and be done with it? I'm not a geriatric and I don't want to be safe,' Emily argued. She didn't want to seem ungrateful but neither did she want to plod around at the pace of a snail. 'Riding is all about thrills and excitement, the burst of adrenalin I used to feel when I took Kasim on a cross-country hack and we approached a five-foot hedge. It was brilliant,' she finished, her eyes shining, and Luc glanced at her, a curious expression on his face.

'It was dangerous,' he pointed out firmly. 'I know you're an excellent horsewoman, *chérie,* but I could never understand why your father allowed you to ride such a powerful animal.'

'Dad was always too wrapped up in running the estate to care about what I got up to,' Emily revealed cheerfully. 'I was a lasting disappointment to my parents. I should have been a boy, you see, an heir for Heston, but instead I was a fourth daughter and not even a pretty or talented one, like the other three. Nobody really cared as long as I kept out of the way,' she told him honestly, 'and I was more than happy to spend all my time with Kasim.'

Dear God, no wonder she suffered from such a crushing

lack of self-confidence, Luc thought grimly as he stared at her upturned face. She had spent her life feeling second-rate and she had needed someone to put her at the centre of their world, not abandon her in the middle of a big city and promptly leave her for weeks on end. Suddenly the reason for her jealousy of Robyn became clear. She had felt threatened by the older woman's sophistication, had perhaps compared herself unfavourably, as she had done with her sisters. But he had never once taken the time to reassure her that her innocence and gentle beauty were the reasons he had fallen in love with her. He had taken everything she had offered so freely and given nothing in return, not his time, his exclusive attention, and perhaps most damaging of all, not his trust. He had never found the courage to share his emotions. Was it any wonder, then, that she had believed he didn't care?

'Well, I can see you're not impressed with Mimi,' he murmured huskily, a mixture of guilt and confusion making his throat raw. 'There is one other horse you might be interested in,' he told her as she began to push Jean-Claude's buggy out of the yard. 'The groom's just bringing him in from the paddock.'

Even from a distance the proud toss of the horse's head was stomach-clenchingly familiar to Emily and she stiffened, disbelief draining the colour from her face. 'Luc? It can't be Kasim,' she whispered faintly, as the horse came nearer, his hooves clattering on the tiled yard, his breath sounding in loud snorts as he tugged on the lead rein so that it took all the groom's strength to control him. 'Oh, my God!' She stumbled forward, her eyes focused on Kasim, whose coat gleamed like polished ebony in the sunlight, his tail twitching restlessly as he stood, still trying to jerk the rein out of the groom's hand.

'Kasim, is it really you?' she asked wonderingly, and the horse stopped tugging and lowered its head so that soulful brown eyes were on a level with her own. For a moment she thought her heart would burst. She'd forgotten just how much he had meant to her, or rather not forgotten. She'd just buried the memory of him deep in her subconscious because losing him had hurt so much. Now she pushed her face into his neck, trying vainly to hold back the tears as he nuzzled her. 'My darling boy.' Her voice cracked with the emotions she couldn't hide and Luc swung away from the scene, feeling as though he was intruding. He wanted her to be happy, wanted it so much that he ached with it. She deserved so much more than he had ever given her but for so long he had failed her and her reaction to finding out about Sabine had brought home to him how cavalier he had been with her emotions.

'Oh, Luc, I can't believe he's real,' she whispered, and he blinked fiercely before turning to face her. He hadn't cried since he'd been a boy, since he'd looked down at his mother's shattered body and realised that his efforts to make her happy hadn't been enough. Failing the people he cared about the most was a regular feature in his life, he thought bleakly, and the utter joy on Emily's face pierced his soul. He didn't want to fail her.

'He must remember you. I haven't seen him this calm since he arrived,' he remarked diffidently. 'Can I take it that your tears are of happiness?'

'You know they are,' she said, scrubbing her eyes with her knuckles. Her smile caused a sharp pain in his chest. 'How did you find him? I thought he went abroad.'

'He did, and his new owner was loath to part with him, but fortunately I was able to persuade him to sell.' He did not add that it had taken all of his considerable charm and persuasive skills, not to mention a figure that was three times the value of the thoroughbred, before Sheik Hassan had agreed to a deal, but it was worth every penny to see the joy on Emily's face.

'But you can't have bought him for me?'

'Well, no one else can ride him, he's too damned feisty. Why shouldn't I buy him for you, *ma petite?*' he asked gently. 'I know how much you love him.'

'Oh, Luc!' Her heart was surely going to burst and with a cry she shot across the yard and threw herself against his chest, 'I love you. I mean…' She broke off, her eyes suddenly shadowed and her cheeks flooding with colour. 'Obviously not. What I meant was, I love what you've done…it was a lovely gesture.' She stepped away from him, her embarrassment painful to witness, and his heart clenched.

'You used to tell me all the time that you loved me,' he murmured quietly, and she refused to meet his gaze.

'Don't remind me. You must have found my eagerness very…tiresome.'

'*Non,*' he replied honestly, 'I found it very lovely. I liked to hear you say it.'

'But you couldn't say it to me.' She stepped back from him and blinked hard, desperate to banish her tears. She'd made enough of a fool of herself without suffering the humiliation of breaking down in front of him. 'It's all right,' she assured him when he reached out a hand to her. 'I know why, and I understand.' He couldn't tell her he loved her when his heart was with Sabine. 'Finding Kasim for me is the most wonderful thing you have ever done and I don't know how I can ever thank you.'

'Try,' he suggested softly, and the warmth of his gaze stunned her before his lips claimed hers, his kiss so sweetly evocative that she was forced to blink back the tears. He explored her mouth with tender passion and she closed her eyes as he dismantled her defences with an ease that should have appalled her. She'd missed him, she acknowledged honestly. For the past month she'd only been half-alive, waiting, longing for him to break down the barriers she'd erected against him, and now she was in his arms she never wanted to leave. The gentle probing of his tongue between her lips took the kiss to a new dimension and when she opened her mouth fully she heard him mutter something beneath his breath before he hauled her up against the solid wall of his chest, ready to crush any signs of resistance. But he need not have worried, she was all his.

'Your riding gear's in the tack room,' he murmured at last when he lifted his head to stare down at her, his body clenching as he studied her softly swollen lips. He was tempted to simply carry her off into the barn, lay her down on the sweet-smelling hay and make love to her until there could be no more doubts or mistrust between them. Instead, he reined in his desire and ignored the driving need that left a permanent ache in his guts. He had already blackmailed her into his bed once and although her resistance had been minimal, the next time he wanted her to come to him willingly, without duress and certainly not because she felt she owed him for her damned horse. 'Are you ready to try Kasim out?'

'Jean-Claude?' Emily glanced around, guilt assailing her as she belatedly remembered her son. Fortunately he was sitting in his buggy, seemingly fascinated by Kasim, and with excellent timing Liz walked across the yard.

There followed one of the most glorious hours of her life as she saddled up Kasim and joined Luc on his powerful palomino. Luc insisted they take it easy. Kasim was still un-settled by his new surroundings, he warned, and Emily was secretly surprised by the stallion's strength. She hadn't ridden for nearly two years, she consoled herself, and Kasim had always had a will of his own. It was one of the reasons she loved him, but her arms were aching by the time they returned to the stables.

'I want you to promise me you won't take him out alone,' Luc demanded as he helped her to dismount. Where she was hot and breathless from the ride, he didn't seem to have a hair out of place in tight jodhpurs that moulded his muscular thighs and a black lambswool jumper. 'In all honesty, Kasim is too big and powerful for you and if it wasn't for the fact that you love him so much, I would have bought you another horse.' He had spent the last hour on tenterhooks that she would be thrown. In his mind he could envisage her lying broken and bloodied on the ground and he was bitterly regretting his decision to buy the horse. How could he live with himself if she was hurt? It would be his fault.

'I'll soon get used to him again,' Emily began, and was subjected to a hard stare that brooked no argument.

'I mean it, Emily. You're only to ride him when either the groom or I can accompany you. Disobey me and I'll have no option but to sell him,' he finished grimly. 'I won't stand by and allow you to endanger your life.'

'What do I have to do to prove that I'm not a six-year-old?' she snapped in exasperation, her hands on her hips as she glared at him. His lips twitched.

'You've done that admirably already, *chérie,*' he murmured dulcetly, 'but I won't complain if you want to jog my memory!'

Their new-found harmony lasted the length of the walk back to the château. The Loire region of France was so beautiful, Emily mused as they strolled hand in hand along the lanes. Suddenly the countryside appeared even lusher and more vibrantly green, the cloudless sky an even denser shade of blue. It was as if her senses had gone into overdrive, the sound of birdsong sounding acutely sweet to her ears as her heart swelled with happiness. Luc had found Kasim for her. Not only that but he had hunted across several Middle Eastern states to find him and bring him to France. It had not been the action of a man who despised her. Perhaps he was starting to forgive her for keeping Jean-Claude from him and was even beginning to trust her. There was still a long way to go, she acknowledged as the memory of Sabine caused her heart to lurch. Maybe he would never love her the way he had his first wife, but suddenly the future seemed rosier than it had for a long while.

Life had a curious way of refusing to run to plan, she decided a few minutes later when they climbed the steps of the château and were met by Philippe.

'Monsieur Laroche is here to see you, Madame,' he murmured. 'The manager of the bank,' he added when she stared at him in obvious confusion. 'I asked him to wait in the salon.'

'Curious,' Luc murmured in her ear, his expression suddenly unfathomable, although the sexy smile had disappeared. 'Is it a social call, do you think, or business?'

'Business, I imagine,' Emily replied, horribly aware that her cheeks were flaming, proclaiming her guilt. How could she have forgotten the appointment she had requested Philippe to arrange with the bank manager to discuss her plans for setting up her own business? Without access to a car she had been forced to ask Monsieur Laroche to visit the château and had prayed that Luc would be busy in the nursery with Jean-Claude. In her excitement over Kasim the meeting had completely slipped her mind, and with a swift glance at Luc's furious face she pinned a smile on her lips and stepped into the salon to greet the dapper Frenchman.

'I hope you haven't been waiting long,' she murmured, aware of Luc's brooding presence by the fireplace as she offered Monsieur Laroche a seat. It was clear that Luc had no intention of awarding her privacy for her meeting and her baleful glare was met with a bland smile and a shrug of feigned misunderstanding that she wanted him to leave.

'Not at all. I fear I am a little early,' the bank manager replied gallantly. 'I understand that you want to discuss proposals for a business venture, Madame Vaillon,' he pressed on, valiantly trying to ignore the simmering tensions in the room. 'I am most impressed by the business plan you sent me.'

'Thank you,' Emily murmured, her eyes focused on Luc who had strolled over to join them and was leaning over to study her ideas for the babywear business. She wanted to snatch her folder from his hands and only a desire to spare Monsieur Laroche embarrassment forced her to retain a dignified silence. 'I'm certainly considering starting up my own business—'

'But not at the moment,' Luc finished for her, ignoring her gasp of indignation as he stood and offered his hand to the manager in a gesture that clearly indicated the meeting was at an end. 'My wife still has many things to consider before she goes ahead,' he murmured, the disturbing softness of his tone sending out a warning that he did not expect to be contradicted.

'I can't believe you just dismissed the poor man like that.' Emily rounded on him as soon as they were alone. 'It was so rude, especially when he had come all this way.'

'Whose fault is that?' Luc queried shortly, and her temper ignited.

'Certainly not mine. I couldn't drive into town because you won't lend me a car.'

'A decision that is obviously justified when you sneak behind my back at the first opportunity,' he said grimly. 'We discussed this and you knew I didn't want you to work.'

'Exactly, that's the reason I didn't want you to find out just yet. I'm fighting for my independence here, Luc,' she cried despairingly. 'I don't just mean financially. I need to be my own person. You can't simply expect me to live here in your country, in your grand house. I refuse to live my life as a poor imitation of the wife you lost,' she yelled at him, and then gasped and covered her mouth with her hands. It was too late, the damning words were out and she bit her lip as Luc's expression turned thunderous.

'Why do you insist on dragging other women into everything? My first wife bears no relation on our life now,' he growled, and Emily shook her head.

'She has everything to do with it. She haunts me constantly,' she admitted brokenly. 'Sabine was so incredibly beautiful. She must have been the ideal wife and mistress of the Château Montiard and I really can't compete. I don't understand how you could even bring yourself to sleep with me, you must have found me a poor substitute.'

'You understand nothing,' Luc flung at her savagely as he stormed over to the door and almost wrenched it off its hinges. 'But I'll tell you one thing, *chérie*. Sabine never installed a damned great bolster in our bed!'

CHAPTER EIGHT

IT WAS PAST midnight when Luc entered the bedroom and instantly disappeared into the *en suite*. Emily huddled beneath the covers, listening to the sounds of him showering and tried to banish the memories of the time he had dragged her beneath the spray with him. He emerged with a towel hitched round his waist, his hair still damp, and she noted the beads of moisture that clung to his chest hair, his skin gleaming in the soft glow from the bedside lamp. The powerful muscles of his abdomen rippled as he moved to sit on the edge of the bed. She squeezed her eyes shut, vainly trying to steady her breathing so that he would assume she was asleep.

'You're a hopeless actress, *ma petite,*' he drawled when the mattress dipped and she felt him slide between the sheets, although he kept to his side of the bed and the bolster remained firmly in place. 'I know you're awake, in the same way that I know how little sleep you get each night.'

'I don't know how, when you always fall asleep within minutes of your head touching the pillow,' Emily snapped, grateful that he had doused the lamp and her burning cheeks were hidden from his view.

'I've been awake, too. Sexual frustration's hell, isn't it, *chérie?*' he added softly.

'I wouldn't know,' she muttered, aiming for a bored tone but sounding annoyingly breathless. 'Goodnight.' She rolled onto her side to glare at the offending bolster and from the other side she heard him sigh.

'I owe you an apology. That last crack in the salon earlier was uncalled for.'

'But true,' Emily said miserably. 'Robyn told me how much you loved your first wife and how devastated you were by her death.'

'Did she?' Luc stared up at the canopy above the bed and gave a silent groan. He could hear the hurt in Emily's voice, the self-doubt. Would she feel any better if he revealed that he had fallen out of love with Sabine long before her tragic death? He had been afraid to tell Emily about his first marriage. It had not been the most edifying chapter of his life, he conceded grimly, and he had failed not only to be a good husband but also ultimately to save Sabine. Emily had hero-worshiped him, certainly at the beginning of their relationship, and he had liked the way she'd looked up to him. It had made him feel good about himself. Now she was looking at him as if she would never trust another word he said and he could hardly blame her. 'I didn't tell you about Sabine because she was in the past and not relevant to our future together. Obviously I was wrong,' he said heavily, 'and I wish you hadn't learned of her in the way that you did.'

'Robyn has always been determined to cause trouble between us,' Emily said wearily, but to her amazement Luc did not jump to his PA's defence.

'It seems so,' he admitted quietly, and she held her breath, not daring to hope that at last he was listening to her.

'Then ask her to leave. There must be plenty of other suitably qualified staff you could appoint as your personal assistant.'

'It's not that simple,' he replied heavily and she sat up and glared at him over the bolster.

'Why, because she was once married to your brother? You told me Yves died four years ago, and although I appreciate how devastating it must have been for Robyn, isn't it time she moved on with her life?' The silence stretched between them and she sighed. 'You said you wanted us to give our marriage another chance,' she reminded him huskily, 'but it's doomed to failure while Robyn remains between us—especially when you believe her word over mine every time,' she added bleakly. 'Does she have some kind of hold over you?' she demanded, her impatience growing at his continued lack of response.

'In a way.' His quiet confession shocked her to the core and she stared at him, wishing she could see his face properly, but his expression was shadowed in darkness. 'It's difficult to explain,' he added, wondering how he could possibly ask Emily to understand Robyn's fragile state of mind. She had adored Yves and his death had left her virtually suicidal with grief.

He had become her emotional prop, Luc acknowledged, and for the first time he realised how much Robyn must have resented losing his exclusive attention when he'd married Emily.

'How can you expect me to stay here with Jean-Claude when there are so many undercurrents that I don't understand?' Emily demanded angrily. 'Is it any wonder that I want to start up my own business and gain some independence, instead of being dragged into the murky underworld of secrets that you seem to inhabit?'

At that he sat up and snapped on the lamp so that she blinked at him owlishly. 'The Château Montiard is not a murky underworld,' he growled furiously. 'I thought you liked it here.'

'I do.' She gave up and flopped onto the pillows. She was talking and he was listening but somehow the messages were being scrambled and neither of them knew the code.

'I appreciate that you may feel cut off here but the city is not far away.'

'It is when you won't allow me the use of a car, and don't think I haven't guessed your reasons. You're afraid that I'll disappear with Jean-Claude, aren't you?'

'Trust has to be earned, *ma chérie,*' he said harshly, 'and going behind my back to discuss your business plans with the bank manager is hardly the way to impress me.'

Was it possible to beat a man senseless with a feather-filled bolster? Emily wondered. 'I've already explained that I wanted to research all the possibilities before I discussed them with you but I don't suppose you'd have listened even then, would you?'

'I don't know.' His control over his temper was more tenuous than she'd realised and his sudden shout of frustration made her jump, her eyes widening as she watched him rake his hand through his hair. She had never seen him so disquieted and despite everything her heart went out to him.

'I'm sorry,' she offered huskily. 'I know you don't understand and maybe even think I'm being ungrateful. From a financial point of view you can see no reason for me to work when you've provided me with such a wonderful place to live, but it's something I want to do, Luc, something for me. I never excelled at anything when I was younger,' she confided. 'My sisters were blessed with brains as well as beauty and I was always made to feel a failure. Designing and making clothes for Jean-Claude was a revelation. I'd finally found something I could do well and it developed into a successful little business in Spain. With Nadine Trouvier's help I know

I can start up again here. Nothing big. I'm not talking mass production,' she explained, leaning across the bolster in her eagerness to share her plans, 'but there is a place at the top end of the market for exclusive, hand-sewn babywear.'

'And it really means so much to you?' There was a new softness in his tone and his eyes were no longer hard bolts of steel but glinted with a curious emotion she couldn't define.

'As much as being reunited with Kasim,' she told him huskily and caught her lip between her teeth. 'You don't know how wonderful it was to see him again. I was…speechless.'

'I noticed,' he murmured dryly, 'possibly because it doesn't happen very often.'

'And then afterwards we argued and I never did thank you properly.' It was hard to think straight when he was looking at her like that. Her fingers itched to remove the bolster but something held her back. Sex between them would be as mind-blowing as always and she didn't doubt for a second that he was aware of the sparks of electricity that were practically arcing across the bed. Their physical compatibility had never been in doubt but where once she had settled for any small scraps of his attention he was willing to give, now it was not enough. She had grown up during their time apart, and although her love for him hadn't lessened, her self-respect had gone up several notches and she refused to let him destroy it.

Perhaps he understood the battle that was waging inside her better than she realized. Certainly he seemed to want to make it easy for her as he leaned across the bolster and cupped her face with his hand. 'Is it really so wrong to want to recapture what we once had?' he whispered, his mouth millimetres from hers so that she could feel the warmth of his breath on her skin. 'Is it really so hard to trust? You put in place this barricade to separate us and I swore I wouldn't breach it, however much I believe you want me to,' he said, his lips brushing as light as a feather against hers. 'But if you move it you'll find I'm more than willing to meet you half-way.'

It was more tempting than he could ever know, and for a few seconds her fingers curled around the bolster that had come to represent a wall as thick and unbreachable as the defences of the château. He kissed her with the pent-up hunger of a starving man, drawing her response as he used all the seductive skill at his disposal to part her lips and plunder the inner sweetness of her mouth. It was bliss and she couldn't bear for him to stop as heat coursed through her veins. It would be so simple to push the bolster out of the way and pull him down on top of her, wind her arms around his neck and hold him captive, but something held her back.

If she weren't the mother of his son, would she be here now? Would he have tried so hard to find her if Jean-Claude hadn't existed? She wanted to be wanted for herself, not because continuing with their marriage was in the best inter-ests of their son. And what about Sabine? she thought despair-ingly. And Robyn? She accepted that he hadn't been unfaithful but she still mistrusted his emotional attachment to his personal assistant. Without trust, their love-making was reduced to a basic, primitive urge, devoid of any emotion.

She was breathless when at last he lifted his head, and the pulse at the base of her throat thudded unevenly. Her lips felt soft and swollen and she traced them with the tip of her tongue as if to capture the taste of him while he watched her through hooded eyes that masked his hunger.

'I'll move the bolster on the day you appoint another

personal assistant,' she said steadily, and he stiffened, outrage and desire fighting their own fierce battle.

'You can't expect me to fire a woman who I both like and respect, and who has proved herself to be an excellent employee, because of a whim. She was my brother's wife!' he snapped.

'And as your wife I expect you to put my wishes above those of a member of your staff.'

'It's hardly fair to make Robyn a scapegoat for the problems within our marriage.'

'Without Robyn, we wouldn't have any problem. It's her or me, Luc,' she warned. 'Your choice as to whether our marriage lives or dies. And until you've made a decision, this stays put.' She thumped the bolster emphatically and received a glare of such bitter fury that she withdrew to the furthest side of the bed and burrowed under the covers while he swore long and hard and she was grateful for once of her poor grasp of French.

Another week slipped past. Luc made no further reference to her demand that he dismiss Robyn but tension simmered between them. Gone was the laughter and friendship that had begun to develop between them and the ghost of Sabine continued to haunt her. If it hadn't been for Jean-Claude the atmosphere in the château would have been unbearable, Emily thought miserably. The weather, perhaps sympathising with her mood, had changed from glorious sunshine to long grey days of relentless rain and the château seemed dark and gloomy as winter approached. Luc's brooding presence in the nursery didn't help, although she noted that the only time he smiled these days was when he was playing with his son, and it reinforced her belief that he only tolerated her presence at the château for the sake of his son.

Perhaps he was frustrated, she thought bleakly, remembering his taunt about sexual frustration being hell. He possessed a huge sex drive. She could not forget those early months of their marriage, when his desire for her had been almost insatiable. Often he had made love to her for the whole night, leaving her exhausted while he then went off to put in a full twelve hours at the office. It was impossible to believe he had spent the year of their separation celibate, although it would certainly explain his foul mood, she acknowledged grimly. But she had problems of her own and suddenly Luc's sex life was the least of them.

Her period was only a few days late, she reassured herself as she noted the date on Luc's newspaper. Five days at most. There was no need to panic but she had quietly requested Liz to bring back a pregnancy test kit from the village.

'What is it?' Luc had lowered his paper fractionally and speared her with a hard stare as he took in her pale face. 'Has something in the news upset you?' he queried, flicking the front page round to scan the headlines. 'Your French must be improving, *chérie,* if you can follow an article about government fraud.'

'It's not that. It's nothing,' she muttered, trying to quell a feeling of nausea as Simone set a cup of rich, aromatic coffee in front of her. 'I'm not feeling all that well this morning. I've probably picked up a bug.'

'Hmm.' Luc looked plainly unconvinced and she shifted uncomfortably beneath his all-seeing gaze. Sometimes she felt he could read her mind and right now that would not be good. If, and it was a big if, she was pregnant, she didn't want to share the news until she'd had time to come to terms with it herself.

How could she have been so stupid? She castigated herself.

One accidental pregnancy was bad enough, but at least when she had fallen pregnant with Jean-Claude it hadn't been her fault. This time it was purely down to carelessness. She hadn't given contraception a thought, and although a small voice in her head argued that neither had Luc, he wasn't the one who would have to carry another child. It wasn't that she did not want another baby, she mused, a soft smile lighting her face as she watched Jean-Claude pour yoghurt over the tray of his highchair and then play in it. He was the best thing in her life and a little brother or sister could only increase her joy, but she doubted the same could be said of Luc. He had always maintained that he didn't want children, and despite his obvious adoration of his son, she shuddered to think of his reaction if she broke the news that he was to be a father for a second time.

'I have something I want to show you.' Luc's voice broke into her reverie and she blinked at him, wishing that the sight of him in jeans and a black polo shirt, open at the neck, did not play such havoc with her hormones. He had been away for the past two days. An urgent business meeting, Philippe had explained, but despite the tension that simmered between them whenever they were in the same room, she had missed him.

It was a pity the trip hadn't done anything to improve his mood, she mused, unaware that he had returned to London or that his conversation with his housekeeper at the penthouse was responsible for his brooding stares across the breakfast table. If it wasn't such a ridiculous idea, she could have sworn he was hiding behind his newspaper.

'It can wait until tomorrow if you're unwell,' he added, and she shook her head, willing to do anything to prolong the moment when he would retreat to his study for the rest of the day.

'I'm fine,' she replied brightly, surreptitiously pushing the coffee away from her. With her attention firmly set on mopping up Jean-Claude, she did not notice Luc's frown.

Luc took the steep steps leading to the west tower of the château two at a time, needing to find a release for his pent-up aggression. What the hell was he going to say to Emily? How could he admit that he had been wrong about her, that he had misjudged her and had done so on the word of the woman she had always suspected of trying to wreck their relationship?

He had trusted Robyn's word above Emily's, he acknowledged bitterly. True, he had begun to have serious doubts about Robyn's motives and now he had definitive proof that she had lied to him, but he was at a loss to know how he could repair the hurt he had caused.

He glanced back to find Emily struggling to keep up with him and his emotions crumbled at the sight of her flushed but determined face.

'Why have you brought me to the top of the tower?' she demanded as she joined Luc on the small landing and glanced out of the window at the incredible view of the Loire Valley spread below her. 'I hope you're not planning to push me off,' she quipped with a nervous laugh.

'Why do you think I would want do that, *chérie*?' The curiously husky tone in his voice brought her head up and she stared at him, noting for the first time the lines of strain around his eyes and the deep grooves that had appeared around his mouth. He would never be anything other than utterly gorgeous but he looked so tired and on edge that she longed to go to him. Instead, she shoved her hands behind her back, out of temptation's way.

'We haven't been getting on very well lately,' she offered quietly. 'I have a feeling that you're still angry with me.'

'I'm angry, *oui*,' he admitted harshly, 'but not with you, *ma petite*. My anger is directed solely at myself.'

Without giving her time to reply, he opened the door and ushered her into a large, circular room with windows all the way round so that light streamed in.

'What a spectacular view,' Emily murmured as she moved forward to admire the stunning scenery of the valley. 'What is this place, Luc?'

'It's your workroom—unless you would prefer rooms in another part of the château,' he added as silence stretched between them. 'I thought you would like it here. The view is, as you say, spectacular, and the light is good for you to work. Say something,' he demanded, his control slipping. He raked a hand nervously through his hair as he caught sight of her tears. 'Why are you *crying?* I thought you'd be pleased.'

'I am pleased. I'm…stunned,' she admitted thickly, scrubbing her eyes with the back of her hand. The betraying gesture made him want to drag her into his arms and plead for her forgiveness. It was too late for that, he conceded grimly as he swung round and shoved his hands in his pockets. There were things he had to do first, events he had to set in motion before he could even begin to beg for atonement, and kissing her senseless would not help his cause.

'I think you'll find everything you need here,' he told her, keeping his eyes firmly on the view rather than her face. 'Your sketches are there, along with the fabric samples you brought from Spain. The table should be big enough to use as a cutting table and, as you can see, your sewing-machine is on the bench under the window. I've arranged for two girls from the village to come and see you. They've both studied textiles and design and could possibly become your assistants, although the final decision lies with you, of course.'

Emily glanced around the room, her eyes filling once more. It was the unexpectedness of Luc's change of heart that had knocked her sideways and she didn't know what to think, what to say.

'I don't understand,' she murmured at last. 'You were so against the idea of me trying to start up my own business.'

'I realise now how selfish I was being,' he said slowly, as he swung round to her. 'This is important to you and, despite what you think, I want you to be happy at the château. I understand that Nadine Trouvier has invited you to visit her babywear shop in Paris and I'm prepared to allow you to go.'

Did that mean he finally trusted her? Emily wondered dazedly. Or did he assume she would leave Jean-Claude at the château and simply did not care whether or not she came back? 'It's all so much to take in,' she said shakily, sinking onto a stool before her legs gave way. 'You've gone to so much trouble, yet my idea may not even work. I might just be kidding myself that I'm any good and there's a chance that no one will want my designs.'

'Nadine would not have suggested marketing them in her shops unless she believed they would sell. Beneath her smile lurks a shrewd businesswoman.' He paused and then murmured, 'I think you should go to Paris with Jean-Claude. It will do you both good to spend a couple of days in the city.'

'But I thought you didn't trust me?' she faltered, her eyes wide with confusion as she stared at him. 'Aren't you worried I'll disappear with him?'

'*Non,*' he replied steadily, closing his mind to the fear that she would do exactly that. He hadn't offered her much incentive to want to stay with him but perhaps the workshop would go some way towards mending the wounds he had inflicted on their relationship. 'I don't believe you would deliberately try to hurt me and you would never do anything that would be detrimental to our son.'

'Well, you've certainly changed your tune.' The hint of bitterness in her tone faded as hope flooded her. 'Care to explain your sudden change of heart?'

'I hope to do so soon, *ma petite*,' he assured her, and the smoky quality in his voice caused her pulse rate to accelerate alarmingly. Luc trusted her enough to offer her her freedom and she felt as though a great weight had been lifted from her shoulders. Did that mean he finally believed her story about taking Jean-Claude to the penthouse? Suddenly it didn't seem to matter any more and she gave him a tremulous smile, her heart in her eyes.

'Maybe we could all go to Paris?' she suggested lightly. 'I have wonderful memories of the last time we were there.'

She walked over to him and ran her hand lightly over his chest. It was obvious that he had created the workroom for her as an olive branch and she was eager to accept it. He was prepared to view their marriage as a partnership and she was desperate to show that both he and Jean-Claude would always come first in her priorities, but even so her hand was visibly shaking as she laid it against his shirt.

'I'm sorry, *chérie*, but I have an urgent meeting in Orléans,' he murmured, and she quickly dropped her hand, her face flaming. 'Philippe will drive you to Paris.'

'Philippe? But I thought—' She broke off as the realisation hit that he did not trust her quite as much as she'd first believed. 'I can drive myself. I'm perfectly capable.'

'You're not used to driving in France, and you know how busy the roads are around Paris. You'll be safer with Philippe.'

'It's not my safety that bothers you, is it?' she demanded. 'Your only concern is for Jean-Claude.'

'It's natural for me to worry about him. Having just found him, I would give anything, including my life, to ensure his well-being,' he said, his voice unexpectedly fierce. She stared at him. 'Do you blame me for that?'

'Of course not.' Emily swallowed back the sudden tears that clogged her throat. Jean-Claude's safety was paramount to her, too, but Luc could not have sent out a clearer message that he was only interested in his son. Nothing had changed and although she certainly didn't resent the fact that Jean-Claude came first in his list of priorities, it hurt unbelievably to know that she came last. It was continuing the theme of her childhood, she thought miserably. She had always been made to feel she was a spare part. Was it so wrong to long to be loved totally and unequivocally for herself? She hung her head, desperate to hide her misery, but he cupped her chin and tilted her face to his.

'What is it, *ma petite?*' Don't you like the workroom?'

'It's wonderful,' she answered truthfully, 'but it doesn't change anything.' She could not live her life loving him so much that it was like a sickness inside her, while he treated her like a favourite cousin. It wasn't his fault that he did not love her, she accepted sadly, but for the sake of her own self-preservation, she couldn't stay with him.

'It's not going to work,' she told him bluntly, and his eyes narrowed.

'The workshop, you mean?'

'I mean us, you and me. I can't stay with you, knowing that you don't trust me.'

'It's not a question of trust,' he said heavily, and she sighed her frustration.

'It's a question of emotions, or rather your lack of them.'

'I love Jean-Claude,' he shouted furiously. 'How can you doubt it?'

'I don't,' she said, her anger draining as swiftly as it had come. She felt like she was hitting her head against a brick wall and she was too bruised to care any more.

'I won't allow you to throw away what we have. I give you my word that our marriage has my full commitment.'

'As long as I stay at the château and only take Jean-Claude out escorted by a glorified jailer, while we remain as distant as ever, only coming together for occasional sex,' she muttered. 'It doesn't sound like much of a life, Luc.'

'The only life you'll have,' he ground out. 'I won't let you go, Emily.' He followed her across the room as she sought to put some space between them, closing in so that her spine came up against the long table that ran the length of the room. 'If sex is the only way I can bind you to me then so be it. I never asked if you're on the Pill and in the heat of the moment I didn't use any contraception when we made love. You could be pregnant,' he told her huskily. 'Have you thought of that?'

She had thought of nothing else for the past few days but now was not the time to admit her suspicions. Luc was too close, too overpowering and she gasped as he suddenly lifted her onto the table, his hands clamping like a vice around her hips.

'You don't want more children,' she said nervously, her tongue darting out to moisten her dry lips. His eyes narrowed as they homed in on her mouth. 'You didn't want the first one.'

'I always wanted him, and if I hadn't wanted more I would

have taken more care to ensure you didn't conceive,' he told her coolly. 'I would like nothing better than to see you swollen with our child.'

His hand moved to her flat stomach and she could not repress the quiver of awareness that ran through her. This close she could detect the exotic musk of his aftershave mingled with another, more subtle male scent that was essentially his. His hand had moved from her stomach to the swell of her breast and as he cupped the soft mound she felt her nipples harden until they were straining against her thin T-shirt, begging for his touch. He captured her mouth in a fierce assault, hot and passionate, demanding her response, and she gave a moan of despair as her lips parted, allowing his tongue to delve between them in a fierce exploration that left her trembling.

'Please, Luc,' she begged. She couldn't allow him to dominate her like this. One touch was all it took to set her on fire and she twisted restlessly as he pushed her legs apart and stood between them. His hand slid beneath her skirt and she held her breath as he dipped beneath and discovered the shaming evidence that she was desperate for him. His low growl of triumph was too much to bear and the tears poured down Emily's cheeks while her lips still clung to his as she kissed him with all the pent-up emotions inside her.

'Please, don't do this,' she whispered brokenly, and he stiffened, his eyes glazed and heavy-lidded as he stared at her.

'Because you don't want me?' he challenged furiously. 'Because you want your freedom? You are my wife, *chérie*. For all our sakes I suggest you accept that fact.' He jerked away from her and strode towards the door while she tried to bring her body under control. It was all she could do not to call him back but she swallowed the words.

'Where are you going?' she cried instead, and shrank from the anger in his gaze.

'To hell! That's where you'd like to send me, isn't it?' came the terse reply before he disappeared. And as she heard his feet on the stairs she buried her face in her hands and wept.

CHAPTER NINE

EMILY SPENT THE REST OF THE DAY nursing Jean-Claude, who was cutting a tooth and determined that everyone should know about it. Luc had disappeared and her mood see-sawed from misery to anger and finally to a faint tenuous hope that there was still a chance for their marriage. She had overreacted earlier, she berated herself. She had behaved like the silly, immature child Luc had once called her, but hopefully he would listen to her apology.

That hope swiftly died when she entered the dining room for dinner and noted that only one place had been set at the long, mahogany table.

'Will Monsieur Vaillon be joining me?' she asked Philippe.

'I regret not, Madame. He has gone to Orléans and does not expect to return until tomorrow.'

'I see.' He had left already and her dismay was clearly evident in the huskiness of her voice. 'In that case I think I'll have my dinner on a tray in the television room,' she murmured. 'I'll just go and change. I'm rather over-dressed,' she added with a vain attempt at humour.

The butler's usually impassive expression lightened into something akin to a smile of sympathy, which only made her feel worse, and she fled upstairs, wondering for the hundredth time why she had decided to wear the blue silk evening dress Luc had chosen for her. She had wanted to please him, she acknowledged as she hung it back in the wardrobe and pulled on her jeans. She'd wanted to thank him for listening to her ideas about the babywear company she hoped to establish and which initially he had been so much against. He had vowed that he wanted to give their marriage another chance and creating the workshop for her was proof of his commitment, but once again they had been driven apart by misunderstanding and her wretched insecurity.

Philippe wheeled the serving trolley into the television room. Sylvie had prepared her favourite *bouillabaisse,* he announced, but as she lifted the lid of the dish nausea gripped her and she fled from the room. This was no ordinary stomach upset, she thought grimly some ten minutes later when she had staggered from the bathroom to lie limply on the bed. The sickness had passed, probably because she had nothing left in her stomach, but she felt weak and tearful and her breasts ached.

There was only one way to put her mind at rest, she decided, jumping up from the bed and returning to the bathroom to retrieve the pregnancy test kit from where she had hidden it at the back of the cupboard. She had to know if she was carrying another child. Five minutes had never passed so slowly but even so, she was unprepared for the shocking truth.

A baby! Luc's second child! She didn't know whether to laugh or cry and managed both as her emotions swung from joy to despair. What would he say? Would he be pleased or angry? Would he accuse her of falling pregnant on purpose, as he had when she she'd conceived Jean-Claude, and would he withdraw from her as he had done the first time?

She had to know. She could not wait patiently until he returned from Orléans to tell him her news and gauge his reaction. It was still early in the evening and ignoring the small voice of caution she ran down to his study. It was ridiculous for her heart to beat so fast, she thought irritably, to feel that she was intruding in his inner sanctum. She flicked on the light. Her attention was immediately caught by the array of photographs on his desk and tears burned her eyes as she studied them. They were not of Jean-Claude, as she had assumed, but of her. One showed her in the stables at Heston Grange, her hair all over the place and a shy smile on her face as she posed awkwardly for the camera. The others were from the magical weekend they had shared in Paris at the start of their marriage, and she was stunned by the emotion evident in her eyes. She brimmed with love, glowed with it, and she was shaken to see how badly she had failed to hide her feelings for him. Had he kept the pictures to gloat over her weakness? she wondered. Or was there another reason why he surrounded himself with her image?

As she replaced the framed photos on his desk she noted a name scrawled across his notepad. La Fayette had to be the name of a hotel, she surmised, praying that the receptionist would be able to speak English as she dialled the number.

'*Oui.* Monsieur Vaillon is booked into the Plaza suite,' the receptionist confirmed, 'but he is in a meeting and left strict instructions that he does not wish to be disturbed.'

'I'm his wife,' Emily swiftly explained. 'He'll talk to me.'

'Monsieur was very precise,' the receptionist murmured doubtfully, and Emily's temper frayed along with her nerves.

'It's an emergency. I insist you put me through.'

There followed several minutes of silence that played havoc with her stomach before there was a click and Luc's terse voice sounded down the line.

'Emily, what's wrong? The receptionist said it was an emergency. Is it Jean-Claude? Is he ill?' There was no disguising the fear in his voice and she hastened to reassure him.

'Jean-Claude's fine. I just wanted to talk to you…' She came to a halt as his impatient sigh growled in her ear.

'I'm busy, *chérie*. Can't it wait?'

'Yes, it can wait,' she whispered slowly, her excitement draining away as reality kicked her in the teeth once again. 'I'm sorry. I shouldn't have bothered you.'

'I'll be home tomorrow,' he said more gently, as if sensing her distress. 'We'll talk then, I promise.'

'Fine.' She cut the call and sat staring at the photos of herself. What a stupid, deluded fool she had been, she thought bitterly. All she had ever hoped for had been a little of his love, but it seemed it was too much to ask.

The stairs were as steep as a mountain and Emily's legs felt like lead. Sabine's perfect features seemed to mock her as she passed by the portrait of Luc's first wife, but when she reached the bedroom the sight of the vast bed and the bolster that divided it was the last straw and she curled up into a ball and sobbed. She was trapped in a loveless marriage, bound by the ties of her son and the new fragile life within her, and right now she felt miserable, afraid and desperately alone.

'Why don't you let me take care of Jean-Claude for a couple of hours?' Liz asked next morning, her friendly face creased in concern as she watched Emily struggle to force down her breakfast. 'He'll be quite happy with me,' she added, and Emily's heart lurched.

How could she even contemplate taking Jean-Claude away from the château? This was his home and he loved it here, she acknowledged, watching the way he was giggling with

Simone. Every member of Luc's staff adored him and it wouldn't be fair to uproot him yet again. She was caught in the middle, unable to leave him and unwilling to go without him, but how could she remain in her soulless marriage?

The rain had cleared to leave grey clouds scudding across the sky and for once she was glad to leave Jean-Claude in Liz's charge while she took refuge in the place she loved best—the stables.

'I hate him,' she told Kasim fiercely, anger her only defence against the ever-present tears that threatened to spill. She refused to cry over Luc any more and a sudden impulse saw her tack up the horse and lead him outside.

'Wait! Madame, it's not safe to go out alone.' As she crossed the yard the groom sped after her and she glanced down at his anxious face impatiently. What he meant was that Luc had forbidden her to take Kasim out alone, but she was tired of following orders and Luc wasn't there.

'It's all right. I won't be long,' she shouted as she reached the field and urged the horse into a canter. 'Stop worrying. I can handle Kasim.'

An hour later Luc strode into the stables, his thunderous expression giving some indication of his mood. 'What do you mean, she's gone?' Fresh from the worst night of his life, his temper exploded with the force of a pyroclastic flow and he had to restrain himself from grabbing the groom by his neck and shaking the information out of him. 'I gave strict instructions that Madame Vaillon should not take her horse out alone.'

'I tried to tell her, but Madame, she just went.' The groom shrugged his shoulders expressively and for a second Luc felt a twinge of sympathy for him. He did not underestimate

Emily's determination to get her own way and apprehension gripped him as the first spots of rain began to fall. 'You should have gone after her,' he muttered as he mounted his horse. 'Which way did she go?'

'Monsieur!' Something in the groom's voice made him glance back and apprehension turned to full-blown fear as Kasim galloped, riderless, into the yard. The rain was falling harder, driving into his face, and with a savage oath Luc kicked his horse into a gallop and headed across the field as if the hounds of hell were pursuing him.

After spending days cooped up because of the rain, Kasim was even more high-spirited than usual and it took all Emily's strength to hold him back. The ground was waterlogged and several times she felt his feet slip, but that only seemed to increase his frustration. Of all the stupid things she had done in her life, this was the worst, she thought as common sense returned and she carefully dismounted. How could she have put the tiny scrap of humanity she was carrying inside her at risk, even for one second? Whatever Luc's reaction, she would love this baby with every fibre of her being.

Kasim was snorting and tossing his head and the sound of a motorbike hurtling along the lane increased his panic so that he reared up and the reins were snatched from Emily's hands.

'Kasim, whoa, boy,' she called frantically, but he was already halfway across the field. As she stumbled after him she tripped and fell into a pile of brambles. Crying wasn't an option right now, she decided as she gingerly pulled herself to her feet. The rain had increased and Kasim had disappeared into the mist. She could only pray he would head back along familiar paths to the stables, but ahead of her lay a long walk across muddy fields on an ankle that hurt like hell when she put weight on it.

It was a good thing Luc was away, she thought dismally when she peered through the rain to find that the edge of the field seemed no nearer. He would be furious with her for disobeying his orders. Maybe he would even sell Kasim, as he had once threatened. The thought spurred her to hobble faster but as she approached the gate a figure appeared out of the mist and her steps slowed.

From a distance he looked as though he had stepped from one of the tapestries that adorned the walls of the château— a medieval knight whose incredible facial bone structure hinted at a family ancestry that had links with ancient kings. As he urged his horse forward, she could see that instead of chain mail it was his thick black sweater that glinted with sparkling beads of rain. His hair was slicked back from his face to reveal the hard planes of his face. It was unfair that despite being soaked to the skin, he still looked devastatingly sexy, and she was painfully aware of her mud-spattered clothes and hair that fell round her shoulders in rats' tails.

'What the *hell* are you playing at?' he growled when she stopped a safe distance from him. It was sheer bravado that made her fold her arms across her chest and glare up at him.

'I could ask you the same thing. How was your meeting? It must have been vitally important to keep you from speaking to your wife. But perhaps not,' she added bleakly. 'I come a long way down your list of priorities, don't I, Luc?'

'Don't be ridiculous. Of course you're important to me. Were you hurt when you came off Kasim?'

'He didn't throw me,' she muttered hastily, her spurt of bravery trickling away beneath the glowering fury of his frown.

'Then what happened? Kasim turned up at the stables over half an hour ago. Are you telling me you chose to walk back through the rain with a sprained ankle for the sheer fun of it?'

'It's not sprained. I just tripped and landed heavily on it. Is Kasim all right? You won't sell him, will you?' she pleaded, her eyes enormous in her pale face. He muttered a profanity under his breath.

'The horse is fine, although I've yet to decide whether I'll keep him. I knew he was too strong for you.'

'He isn't—'

'Shut up and give me your hand.' He cut her off, his grey eyes glinting like molten steel, and Emily felt her own temper rise. Last night he hadn't been able to fit her into his busy schedule and the concern on his face probably had more to do with the fact that she had placed an expensive horse in danger.

'I can manage, thanks.'

'*Em-il-y!* I could kill you, if you weren't so intent on doing it yourself.' He leaned over, gripped her arm and hauled her into the saddle in front of him as easily as if she were a doll. Instantly his arms came round her, clamping her against the wall of his chest so that she could hear his heart thudding beneath her ear. He smelled of the rain, earthy and sensual, and she closed her eyes despairingly as her senses leapt, awareness flooding through her so that tried to hold herself rigid and not give in to the temptation to turn her face into his neck.

He flicked the reins and they walked on, the pace slow and steady through the rain, but all Emily could think of was the hardness of Luc's thighs pressing on hers as she sat between his legs. The motion of the horse meant that his body pushed against hers in a rhythm that grew ever more erotic and her breathing quickened. Emily tried to calm her wayward thoughts. Luc had made it clear that he only wanted her on his terms, when it suited him, but right now he was fiercely aroused and instead of disgust she was overwhelmed by another, far more elemental emotion, her instincts warning that his hunger for her was close to breaking point. Heat radiated from where his hand lay heavy on her waist and every nerve ending prickled unbearably when it slid lower and came to rest between her legs.

'Take your hands off me. You can't pick me up when the mood takes you and you're not too busy. Last night you couldn't even be bothered to talk to me,' she accused, aiming for anger. Instead, her voice sounded broken and full of misery.

'I spent most of last night driving around Orléans trying to pluck up the courage to face you.' His soft, seductive accent trickled over her skin, his breath fanning her neck so that she shivered, her senses heightened to an unbearable degree.

'I don't believe you and as soon as we get back to the château I'm leaving you. I refuse to be...*humiliated* by you any longer.'

'I won't let you go, *chérie.*' The implacability of his tone made her shiver and she fell silent as they entered the stable-yard and he dismounted before lifting her down. Instantly she swung on her heel, intent on marching back to the château. 'Wait! I want to talk to you.' His voice flayed her like a whip and she swung round, indignation bristling from every pore. But he ignored her while he spoke to the groom.

She would not sit panting at his heels like a faithful dog, she thought furiously. He still had his back to her and she slipped into the barn. He might want to talk to her but she wasn't in the mood to listen. She was still puzzled by his admission that he had needed to pluck up his courage before he returned to the château. Perhaps he was going to announce that he wanted a divorce after all, and she was suddenly glad that she hadn't told him she was pregnant. It was her secret and she was determined to withhold it until she knew where their relationship was heading.

The minutes ticked by and she lay back in the loose hay, wondering if it was safe to emerge from her hiding place yet. He must have started walking back to the château, believing that she was in front of him, but her heart sank as the barn door creaked open. Damn it! He couldn't find her here. She huddled deeper into the hay and squeezed her eyes shut in an effort to stifle a sneeze, but it was no good and the sound of his mocking laughter grated on her already raw nerves.

'I couldn't have chosen a better place for a private conversation, *chérie*,' he murmured as he rounded the hay bale and stood in front of it, barring her escape, 'I want to talk to you about Robyn.'

'Then prepare yourself for the shortest conversation on record because of all the subjects I'd like to talk about, Robyn isn't one of them.'

His smile did strange things to her insides and she dragged her eyes from the way his wet jeans clung lovingly to his thighs. Suddenly her teeth were chattering—reaction to everything that had happened in the last twenty-four hours, she told herself, and the fact that she was sitting in wet clothes. It had nothing to do with Luc's close proximity or the way his eyes were skimming her wet shirt, tracing the outline of her breasts with barely concealed hunger. 'Why do you suppose I would want to talk about her?' she flung at him, and to her consternation he stretched full length beside her, propped up on his side so that he could lean over her to stroke her cheek with a wisp of hay.

'I know that she lied,' he offered quietly, pausing for a heartbeat to assess her reaction before he continued. 'I know you came back the Chelsea penthouse with Jean-Claude soon after he was born. I met her last night in Orléans. She was the reason I couldn't talk to you.'

'My God, you bastard!' Emily gasped as she forced air into her lungs. 'You spent the night with her. And to think I actually believed you when you denied having an affair with her. Will I ever learn?' she whispered despairingly. 'And will you ever stop breaking my heart?' She made to roll away from him but he gripped her arm.

'I did not spend the night with her. I asked her to meet me at the hotel because I couldn't bear to have her at the château,' he explained, the nerve jumping in his cheek giving some indication of his tension. 'After you told me about your visit to the penthouse I decided to check a few things with my housekeeper.'

'Mrs Patterson wasn't there,' Emily pointed out quickly.

'I know, but she told me she had been puzzled because she was sure someone had stayed in the flat while I was in South Africa. It confirmed your story,' he said quietly.

He was watching her, waiting for her to speak, but Emily felt curiously numb. 'So,' she muttered, 'you finally believe that I brought Jean-Claude to you. Robyn lied, but where does that leave us? I can't see happy ever after flashing up in bright lights.' She blinked fiercely, determined not to cry in front of him, and he sighed.

'Robyn lied to both of us, *ma petite,* but if it's any consolation, she's bitterly sorry for the harm she caused.'

'She's in love with you,' Emily said quietly, wondering how he could have been so blind to the signs. She closed her eyes and tried to imagine how different things might have turned out if Luc had been at the flat that day rather than Robyn. Despite his coolness towards her during her pregnancy, she no longer doubted that he wanted his son. He loved Jean-Claude, but she still didn't understand his relationship with Robyn any more than she understood where she featured in his life.

She loved him but he didn't love her. Nothing had changed and she couldn't go on living a lie, pretending to be content when she was falling apart. 'I think I'd like to go back to England for a while, take Jean-Claude to see my family. I'm not taking him away from you but…' She hesitated fractionally. 'I think we need to spend some time apart.'

'You're leaving me!' Luc said heavily, a nerve jumping in his cheek. 'I don't deserve anything less but you have to believe that I am desperately sorry for believing Robyn over you and I swear, *chérie,* I'll do anything to make it up to you.'

The urgency in his voice startled her but, of course, she reminded herself, he was afraid that if she took Jean-Claude to England, she would never bring him back.

'It's not just Robyn,' she said miserably. 'I accept that you never slept with her and I understand how easily she fooled both of us, but that's the point, isn't it? If we had trusted each other more, we would have uncovered her lies before any real harm had been done. I need some time to think,' she admitted slowly, but as she moved to stand up, he pulled her down into the hay and trapped her beneath him.

'I can't let you go,' he muttered hoarsely. 'You belong here at the château, you and Jean-Claude.'

The subtle change in his tone was enough to alert her defences and she pushed ineffectively against his shoulders, suddenly desperate to escape him before she did something stupid, like beg him to make love to her.

'You were mine, Emily, from the moment you first gave yourself to me, and I guard my possessions jealously. Maybe it's time I demonstrated that fact.'

His low taunt fuelled her defiance and she would have twisted her head, but he reacted faster, his mouth finding hers with unerring precision. His kiss stole the breath from her body and took with it the last remnants of her pride as he proved beyond doubt that he was her master. She wanted him with an urgency that was all the more shocking because she no longer cared that he didn't love her. All she cared about was assuaging this driving need to feel him deep inside her and desire rendered them equal. This had been building from the moment he had dragged her onto his horse. It would be the last time she would ever make love with him, a final goodbye. He would never want her once he knew she was pregnant and she couldn't stay and allow his indifference to tear her apart again.

When he eventually lifted his head her mouth was swollen and he stared down at her, his eyes glittering, warning her that this time there would be no reprieve.

'You said you wanted to talk,' she reminded him thickly, and he gave a harsh laugh as he dragged his sweater over his head before coming down on her once more.

'We've tried talking and it gets us nowhere. This is the only lasting truth between us, *chérie,* the only form of communication where we don't argue. You want me as much as I want you,' he whispered, his breath warm on her skin as he unbuttoned her shirt and tugged the fabric apart. She shivered, unable to deny the truth.

He dispensed with her bra with a deftness that warned of his determination and cupped her breasts in his hands, moulding them before bending to lather first one nipple and then the other with his tongue.

'Luc.' She groaned his name and slid her hand behind his head to hold him to his task, but he moved lower to drag her sodden jeans over her thighs with a force that should have frightened her. Her underwear went the same way and she gasped as he shoved her legs apart, exposing her to his gaze as he knelt over her.

'No!' Her whimper of denial fell on deaf ears and if she was honest she didn't want him to stop. His tongue was a wicked instrument of torture and he used it mercilessly, exploring her with intimate precision until she was writhing and trembling, her body poised on the edge of ecstasy. Frantically she tugged his hair, needing him to stop, now, before it was too late. But his lips closed around the ultra-sensitive nub of her clitoris and sensation pierced her as he suckled.

'Oh, God! Now, Luc, please.' She couldn't take much more, could already feel the first spasms of pleasure tighten her muscles.

He stood up, shrugged out of his jeans and stared at her for timeless seconds. She must look like some wild, wanton creature, she thought despairingly, but it didn't matter when he knelt in front of her, slid his hands beneath her bottom and lifted her hips so that he could enter her with one powerful thrust. Instantly she wrapped her legs around his waist to draw him deeper and he eased back a fraction before pushing again and again, setting a rhythm that she eagerly matched.

She had been so ready for him that it was impossible to control her reactions and she peaked instantly, her body overwhelmed by wave after wave of pleasure. Gasping, she clutched his shoulders as he rode her, each thrust driving her higher still, and incredibly, as her climax subsided she felt another build. It was impossible surely to experience such a glorious, mind-blowing sensation again and she stared into his face, noting the rigid line of his jaw as he fought for control. He lost it spectacularly at the same time as she came again and she felt him shudder as her muscles closed round him, her name emitted as a low groan when he finally slumped on top of her.

For a short while there was nothing but the warmth of his body covering hers, the sound of their breathing gradually slowing and the sweet scent of the hay that cocooned them in their own private nirvana. Eventually he stirred and she paled at the bleakness in his eyes as he rolled off her. His expression shouted louder than words that he regretted giving in to the primitive need that had gripped them both, and she shivered and reached for her shirt. It was damp and cold on her heated skin but she dragged it across her breasts, wanting to punish her body for its bitter betrayal.

'You don't really want to leave me, any more that I could stand to see you go,' he said flatly, his eyes never leaving her face. 'Look into your heart, *chérie*. It recognised the truth between us.'

She knew exactly what was in her heart, Emily thought bleakly. It was Luc's that was the mystery. She sighed and swung away from him to pull on her jeans.

'*Sacré bleu!* What have you done to your back? You're bleeding.' His face was white with anguish.

She glanced over her shoulder, alerted by the horror in his voice, and saw that her shirt was streaked with blood. 'I'm fine. It's nothing, just some scratches from when I fell into some bushes,' she reassured him, but he pulled her against his chest and ran his hands over her as if desperate to assure himself that she was unhurt.

'You're so pale, and I'm no better than my barbaric ancestor,' he growled, his voice laced with self-disgust. She was so tiny, so fragile, and he had let her down so badly, it was no wonder she was staring up at him with huge, fearful eyes. 'Here, drink this,' he ordered, dragging a hip flask from his pocket. Her face turned a sickly shade of green as he unscrewed the lid and she caught the unmistakable smell of brandy.

'That's not a good idea,' she murmured faintly, and he clamped down on his impatience as he held the flask against her lips. She looked like death and fear gripped him.

'What's the matter with you?' he shouted as her legs buckled. Had she lied? Had Kasim thrown her and she had kept quiet for fear of his anger? '*Mon Dieu!* Emily, you must drink this.'

'No.' She clamped her blue lips resolutely together as her head lolled forward. 'No alcohol, Luc…I'm pregnant!'

CHAPTER TEN

'WHY THE *HELL* didn't you tell me?'

Emily opened her eyes to discover she was in her bedroom at the château. Luc was leaning over her, his face contorted with fury, and she lowered her lashes again, wishing she could return to oblivion.

'Monsieur Vaillon, the doctor is here.' Liz's calm tones cut through the simmering tension and she heard him mutter something in his own language before he stepped back from the bed.

'Call me the minute he's finished,' Luc instructed Liz, and it was only when she heard the door creak on its hinges that Emily dared to open her eyes again.

'He's just upset,' Liz reassured her quickly, noting the stark misery on her face. 'You gave him a terrible fright when you collapsed in the stables. He literally ran all the way back to the château with you in his arms.'

'He's angry with me,' Emily whispered, her eyes filling with tears that spilled down her cheeks. Liz patted her arm.

'Shock does funny things to people and you have to admit it was quite a dramatic way of announcing your pregnancy. He was scared, that's all. He's very protective of you.'

Luc hadn't looked protective, Emily thought bleakly when the doctor had finished his examination and assured her she was a perfectly healthy woman in the first stages of pregnancy. Luc had looked as though he wanted to commit murder.

'How did Luc seem?' she asked hesitantly when Liz returned to the bedroom. 'I'm not sure how he'll feel about being a father again.'

'If you ask me, he'll be over the moon,' Liz replied softly. 'He adores Jean-Claude.'

'Yes, he does.' There was no dispute over Luc's feelings for his son, she acknowledged bleakly as she stared up at the canopy above the bed. But his feelings for his wife were a different matter. He would never let her go now, but he wanted her for all the wrong reasons.

The doctor had advised her to rest but inactivity gave her time to think, so she padded into the *en suite,* filled the bath and added a generous handful of scented crystals that promised to soothe and de-stress. She needed all the help she could get in that department, she conceded, and closed her eyes as the foam worked its magic.

'So, not content with terrifying me this afternoon, you're now trying to drown yourself.' The furious rumble from the doorway caused her eyes to fly open and she jerked upright, horrified to realise that the water had been lapping around her chin. Most of the bubbles had disappeared and she flung her arms across her chest, her cheeks flaming with the acknowledgement that it was way too late for modesty.

'What do you want?' she snapped, and Luc felt the familiar tug in his chest as her hands slid to her stomach in an instinctively protective gesture. *You* was the simple answer, but she was bristling like an angry porcupine and now didn't seem a good time to reveal what was in his heart, even supposing she would listen, he thought bleakly.

'To talk,' he murmured instead as he leaned away from the door and strolled towards her.

His damp hair indicated that had recently showered. His crisp white shirt was open at the throat and his black trousers moulded his thighs leaving little to her imagination that was determined to recall every second of the moments in the stable.

'It wasn't terribly productive last time we tried it,' Emily said pointedly, turning hot and cold at the memory of their *talk* in the hay barn.

'On the contrary, *chérie,* I found it most revealing, although you withheld one vital secret from me.'

She could say nothing in her defence and sat silently in the rapidly cooling water, defying him to come any closer, which of course he did, holding out a fluffy bath sheet.

'I can manage,' she began, her voice trailing off beneath the ferocity of his glare.

'Humour me, *ma petite.*' He patently wasn't going to move and with an exasperated sigh she stood and stepped over the side of the bath, allowing him to envelop her in the folds of the towel. Having him rub her dry with brisk efficiency was taking it a step too far, she decided when her body was tingling all over, but the blandness of his expression warned her he was determined to play nursemaid and she rewarded him with a dignified silence.

Once satisfied that she was dry, he slipped her nightdress over her head and she raised her brows in silent query at the exquisite creation of ivory silk.

'For the sake of my sanity I need you to be covered while we talk, but I couldn't find the unflattering T-shirt you insist on wearing—although I admit I didn't look very hard,' he added beneath his breath.

Before she could formulate a reply he swept her into his arms and carried her through to the bedroom where he deposited her between the sheets and adjusted her pillows. He treated her with something akin to reverence, as if she was infinitely precious to him, but it had to be an illusion, Emily thought as tears welled in her eyes. He didn't care about her, he only cared for Jean-Claude and she couldn't begin to hazard a guess at his thoughts about the new baby.

'Are you angry?' she queried tremulously when his silent scrutiny had stretched her nerves to breaking point.

'Move from that bed and you'll discover the true heat of my temper.' He stared at her downcast face and sighed. 'I'm not angry with you. I blame myself.'

'Good. I blame you too.' It was obvious from the way he was skirting around the issue that he wasn't happy about the baby and she was surprised at how much it hurt. She should have expected it when his reaction to Jean-Claude's conception was so clear in her mind. There was no hope for them now, she thought, and wished he would go so that she could cry alone.

'Don't you want this baby?' he asked, his voice laced with a curious huskiness that she could almost believe was pain.

She glanced at him, noting the deep grooves around his mouth. 'Of course I want him…or her. My views on parenthood have never been in doubt. But what about you, Luc?' she whispered. 'For a man who vowed he didn't want children, it must be a blow to learn you're going to be a father for the second time.'

'It's not that I didn't want children,' he said hoarsely as he jumped to his feet and paced restlessly next to the bed. His air of urbane calm had always been impressive but he seemed to have undergone a dramatic transformation. His body was as tense as whipcord, his jaw rigid, but it was the agony in his eyes that trapped her gaze. She stared at him, desperate to understand. 'I always wanted Jean-Claude, you have to believe me,' he muttered, his accent so pronounced that she had to concentrate on his words. 'But I was so afraid, *mon coeur,* so afraid for you.

'Last time, when the contraception failed there was some excuse, but this time it was sheer carelessness on my part,' he admitted, his voice thick with self-disgust. 'I made love to you because I couldn't help myself. You are in my blood, Emily, in my heart. One look at you and I knew I had to have you again. It's like an obsession, this need to hold you in my arms and experience the ecstasy only you can give. The last thing on my mind when I made love to you was the possible outcome yet I, more than anyone, should be aware of the consequences of such negligence. It is because of me that Sabine died,' he groaned, his face twisting. 'It was my fault.'

'No.' Emily couldn't bear the torment in his eyes any longer and she reached out to him, pulling him onto the bed. 'Luc, Sabine's death was a terrible tragedy but it was nobody's fault. An ectopic pregnancy is a comparatively rare condition. You couldn't have known it would happen and there was nothing you could have done to prevent it.'

'But that's not true, don't you see?' He broke off and ran a hand over his face, his fingers shaking with the force of his emotions. 'I didn't love her. I doubt I ever did. When we met I was young and arrogant and for me it was lust at first sight, but the cracks started to appear early in our marriage. Sabine was obsessed with having a child while I was more focused on my career. There were endless rows, she had other lovers and our marriage was all but dead. The holiday was a last-ditch attempt by Sabine to save it.' He fell silent, his expression unfathomable, and Emily shivered as she recalled the rest of the story Robyn had told her.

'But Sabine was pregnant,' she murmured tentatively, and he nodded.

'Yes, but I doubt the child was mine, which was possibly why she said nothing. When she collapsed I had no idea what was wrong. We were miles from medical assistance and there was nothing I could do. It was over so quickly,' he said rawly, 'and I felt so helpless. Later a post-mortem revealed that Sabine had already suffered one ectopic pregnancy, hence her difficulty in conceiving. I didn't even know she was pregnant and she never told me of the increased risk of another ectopic. It seemed unbelievable that a woman could die as a result of pregnancy in the twenty-first century and I felt so guilty. I vowed I would never put another woman at such risk.'

'Oh, God!' Understanding dawned and Emily closed her eyes as his words hit her. 'That was why you were so adamant that you didn't want children, wasn't it? But by the time it became an issue between us, I was already pregnant with Jean-Claude.'

'It seemed cruelly ironic that Sabine had been unable to conceive despite all her efforts and yet you fell so easily.'

'You seemed so angry and I was so hurt. I needed you,' she whispered, 'but I was sure you didn't want me or the baby and I had no idea what I had done wrong.'

'Forgive me, *ma petite*,' he groaned, and her heart turned over at the pain in his eyes. 'I knew you were unhappy living in London. There were issues with my company that meant I was busier than usual—and issues with Robyn that have only become clear since,' he added bitterly. 'A holiday, a belated honeymoon on a paradise island where we could be alone, seemed like a good idea.' He broke off with a harsh laugh. 'You'd think I would have learned from my experience of remote islands, but I hadn't anticipated history repeating itself quite so dramatically. When you collapsed with the heat, after whispering that you suspected you were pregnant, I...' He shook his head at the agonising memory. 'I thought I would lose you in the same terrible circumstances as Sabine. I was terrified, *chérie,* and in my fear I went a little mad, but I wasn't angry with you. I blamed myself for risking the life of the woman who meant more to me than anyone ever had.'

Did he mean her? Emily felt her heart lurch painfully in her chest and quickly quashed the little flicker of hope. The ghosts in his past she could deal with, especially now she understood that his coolness towards her during her pregnancy had been the result of fear for her safety, not revulsion for the changes in her body. But there were still things she did not understand. 'I wish you had confided in me,' she said sadly. 'It would have explained so much, saved so much misery. Instead, you turned to Robyn and shut me out. I couldn't understand your closeness to her and as we grew further and further apart it seemed likely that she was your mistress.'

'You must know now that we were never lovers,' he began urgently, and she nodded.

'I believe you, but adultery isn't necessarily a physical act,' she whispered. 'I used to watch the two of you together, Luc. I recognised the bond that existed between you and I felt rejected.'

He was quiet for so long that she thought he must have forgotten her, but as she tried to pull her hand free he tightened his grip and she was shocked by the bleakness of his expression.

'I swore I would never talk about my childhood. It was not the happiest of times,' he admitted grimly, 'but I don't want you to think I'm shutting you out ever again. My father was a cold, distant man. I don't ever remember an occasion when I saw him smile, or felt that I had earned his approval. My mother was quiet, sensitive and for the most part deeply unhappy. I've always thought that I must have failed her in some way,' he admitted quietly, and her heart turned over at the emotion in his voice. 'Perhaps she just didn't care for me enough to want to carry on with her life.'

'Luc, severe depression is an illness,' Emily said huskily, holding his hand between both of hers as she sought to comfort him. 'Maybe in her confused state she thought you would be better off without her, but I'm sure she loved you.' Beneath the urbane, successful businessman she recognised the lonely boy within and she ached for him.

'Perhaps,' he murmured with a shrug, 'but at least I had Yves. We were extraordinarily close, especially after my mother's death. As we grew older our friendship continued. We shared everything and I was delighted when he fell in love with Robyn. It seemed that at least one Vaillon marriage would prove successful. Yves's death was a shattering blow,' he confided, his eyes shadowed with remembered pain. 'Robyn clung to me for support and I suppose I confided in her in place of my brother, but I regarded her as a close friend, nothing more.' He stared at Emily intently, as if he was desperate for her to believe him.

'My seeming reluctance to become a father was not because I did not want our child but because I was afraid I would not be a good parent. I didn't have the best role models,' he said heavily, and she squeezed his fingers reassuringly.

'You're a wonderful father. Jean-Claude adores you, as will the new baby.'

'I feared that my upbringing had left me unable to love and my marriage to Sabine only seemed to prove it. I had lost Yves, the only person I truly cared for, and I decided that life was less complicated if my emotions were uninvolved. But now I realise how much I was fooling myself,' he told her, his voice softening as he took in her delicate features and wide, expressive eyes.

'You discovered that you love your son,' she murmured, and her heart leapt painfully in her chest at the expression in his eyes. He was trying to tell her something and she wished she could decipher the code.

'I met you,' he said gruffly, and the tension between them became unbearable. Abruptly he jumped to his feet, his movements clumsy and uncoordinated, and the tight band around her heart suddenly snapped. This was Luc, the man she loved more than life itself, and he was in agony. 'I felt sorry for Robyn and I trusted her as a friend but I never felt anything more for her,' he muttered. 'I hoped that as time passed she would come to terms with Yves's death and her dependency on me would lessen, but I missed the signs that she wanted more from our relationship. I don't know what I can do to repair the damage I've caused, the hurt I've inflicted on you,' he said huskily, 'but even though you must hate me, I can't let you go. Together with Jean-Claude, you are my life. I can't lose you.'

He was already walking away and as Emily called his name he turned, gripping the bedpost so hard that his knuckles showed white.

'Why did you keep so many secrets?' she asked, desperate to understand. 'What I perceived as your lack of trust in me gave Robyn all the ammunition she needed.'

'*Chérie,* you were so pure, so…innocent. I wanted to protect you especially when I realised I couldn't fight my desperation to make you my wife. Vaillon marriages are not renowned for being happy. It's as if they are cursed and I despised myself for my weakness over you. I should never have married you, *mon ange,*' he finished huskily and the tears slid unchecked down her face.

'Then why did you?' She stared at him, her vulnerability exposed, and he groaned and moved forward as if to take her in his arms. Then he changed his mind and shoved his hands into his pockets.

'Because I love you.' The words seemed to be torn from his throat, as if each syllable was alien and unfamiliar to him, and she had the strangest feeling that he was afraid to look at her. 'I didn't want to,' he admitted, his voice cracking with emotion. '*Mon Dieu,* I know better than most that love hurts. When I first met you I thought I would be content with a brief affair. The chemistry between us was white-hot and I knew you felt it, too,' he told her, and she felt her cheeks flame. 'I hadn't counted on you being quite so innocent and it quickly became clear that the kindest thing I could do, for both our sakes, was walk away.'

'But you didn't,' Emily murmured, her mind still reeling from his startling admission that he loved her. She didn't dare believe him but neither could she ignore the raw emotion in his eyes.

'*Non.* I should have realised then the danger I was in,' he told her ruefully. 'I found that I couldn't leave you any more than I could cut out my own heart. Marriage seemed the only sensible option but even then I kidded myself that I was in control. I arrogantly thought I could have you on my terms, taking everything you gave so sweetly and offering nothing in return except a certain amount of expertise in bed.'

'You certainly gave me that,' Emily muttered, unable to hide her embarrassment as she recalled her wanton response to his passion. 'The only time I ever felt close to you was when we made love, and I clung to the fact that you desired me because I had nothing else of you. When I fell pregnant I took your coldness towards me as rejection and I couldn't bear it. I loved you so much,' she whispered thickly, 'but I never knew how you felt about me and I was so unhappy.'

'*Em-il-y*, don't cry, *ma petite*,' he pleaded as he fell onto the bed and hauled her into his arms. 'I have spent a lifetime hiding what is in my heart, but no more. I would rather die than hurt you. *Je t'aime, mon coeur. Tu es ma vie. Je t'adore*.' He found her mouth in a kiss of such tender passion, such *love*, that words were not necessary and she clung to him as if her life depended on it. 'Forgive me?' he begged, a wealth of emotion in his eyes that were as soft as velvet. She wondered how she could ever have thought him cold. He was burning up for her, his glorious pride abandoned in his need to show the feelings he found so hard to put into words.

'There's nothing to forgive,' she said softly. 'All I ever wanted was your love. Nothing else matters.' She ran the tip of her tongue over her swollen lips, noting the way his eyes darkened as he followed her deliberately provocative gesture. 'I have a feeling I'll no longer be needing this,' she teased, as she lifted the bolster from the middle of the bed and threw it across the room. His mouth curved into a sensual smile that promised heaven.

'You have no idea how close I came to ripping that thing apart, along with the collection of unflattering T-shirts you insisted on wearing to bed,' he confided, as he drew the straps of her nightgown down her arms until her breasts were exposed to his hungry gaze. 'Sleep became an unknown quantity as I fantasised about your body that was only inches from mine but separated by a chasm of misunderstanding. From now on there will be no more secrets between us, *mon amour,*' he insisted, his breath warm on her skin as his mouth followed the path of his hands, and she obligingly lifted her hips so that he could remove her nightgown.

'I love you, Luc,' she told him urgently as he struggled out of his own clothes with a complete lack of finesse that moved her more than anything else had done.

'And I love you, *mon ange,* more than I can ever say,' he assured her huskily, his eyes darkening as he hesitated and eased away from her a fraction. 'I'm not sure we should be doing this,' he muttered, his hand moving to stroke her stomach. 'The baby…'

'Will be fine,' she whispered gently, understanding at last his innermost fears. 'You're not going to make me beg, are you?' she teased, and trembled at the adoration in his eyes as he entered her with exquisite care and began to move in a rhythm that was as old as time.

'I am the one who should beg,' he breathed against her skin, 'for your love.'

'You have it unreservedly,' she murmured, and there was no more time for words as he took them to that place where time ceased to exist and sensation overwhelmed them.

'Are you sure you don't mind about the baby?' Emily asked when they lay replete in each other's arms and he caught the faint hesitancy in her voice. He would spend the rest of his life assuring her of his love, he vowed fiercely. Never again would he give her reason to doubt his adoration for her, Jean-Claude and all their future children.

'My heart is full,' he said simply. 'I never knew I could feel such joy. You, Jean-Claude and this little one—you are my world and I will always be there for you. Especially when you're running a global babywear business,' he added with a smile. 'I love you, *chérie*.' Emily wrapped her arms around his neck.

'I've a feeling I'm going to be fully occupied for quite some while,' she said happily, and his murmur of approval was lost as his lips claimed her in a kiss that spoke louder than words of his love.

THE FRENCH
DOCTOR'S
MIDWIFE BRIDE

Fiona Lowe

Always an avid reader, **Fiona Lowe** decided to combine her love of romance with her interest in all things medical, so writing Medical Romance™ was an obvious choice! She lives in a seaside town in southern Australia, where she juggles writing, reading, working and raising two gorgeous sons, with the support of her own real-life hero!

You can visit Fiona's website at www.fionalowe.com.

To Pam, who supports me and my family in so many special ways, and enjoys nothing better than curling up with a great romance. Thank you!

CHAPTER ONE

CHARLIE BUCHANAN, outreach midwife, made it to her next appointment with barely enough time to catch her breath. But this time she wasn't catching a baby.

She sank into the soft leather chair, and immediately regretted it. The cloying tendrils of fatigue took advantage of her the moment she sat still, wrapping themselves tightly around her. Her shoulders ached from changing her flat tyre on the way into town. She'd give anything for hot food, a warm bath and much-needed sleep.

But it would all have to wait.

'Dr Laurent is ready to see you now.' The new chief of medicine's secretary spoke in clipped tones, casting disapproving looks toward Charlie.

She instinctively ran her hands down her skirt to straighten it, as memories of boarding school washed through her. *Charlotte needs to take more care with her appearance.*

Why hadn't she taken a moment to tame her unruly hair into a neat, thick braid instead of frantically rushing to be on time? She resisted the urge to slap her forehead with her palm. Of course the new doctor would be running late!

The new French doctor had arrived in Amaroo a week ago. According to the hospital grapevine, the dust he'd raised didn't look like it would be settling any time soon. The words 'review' and 'budget' had been muttered a lot in corridors and the cafeteria, along with 'economic rationalist' and 'despot'.

She blew out a breath, letting her body relax. Applying logic, none of this should affect her. Her programme was well established with its own approved budget. This meeting wouldn't be any more than a 'get to know you' session.

She opened the familiar door and stepped into the office.

Standing behind a large desk, talking on the telephone but waving her into a chair was, Charlie assumed, Dr Xavier Laurent. All six feet of him, and probably more.

An immaculately cut charcoal suit clung to his body, emphasising broad shoulders and a narrow waist. The open jacket moved as his arm rose and fell, revealing flashes of a vivid crimson and emerald tie lying against a white shirt.

A 3D image of a solid, muscular chest burned into her mind. Horrified at the unexpected mental picture, she moved her gaze up the length of the tie rather than down. Black hair streaked with silver caressed his temples, adding to his aura of model good looks overlaid with natural authority.

His ebony eyes, ringed with thick dark lashes, gazed at her, their look both charming and scrutinising at the same time.

The butterflies in her stomach fluttered faster, her unease going into overdrive on the back of another sensation she didn't care to examine closely.

She forced herself to meet his penetrating gaze. But looking into those eyes was like falling into the great unknown and she quickly glanced away. The very last thing she needed was to be attracted to the new chief. Not a smart move, professionally or personally.

She didn't do relationships. Relationships meant losing yourself. Relationships forced you to be someone you weren't just to make someone else happy, and that never worked. She knew that misery intimately—bitter experience had taught her well. It had taken half her life to work it out but she knew one thing for sure, she was *never* submerging her own happiness again in an attempt at love.

Dr Laurent put a large, lean hand over the mouthpiece of the phone, smiled and mouthed the words, 'I will be with you in a minute,' and returned to his call.

His deep smile carved into his tanned face, an arrowhead of creases framing his mouth of white teeth. The rays from that smile seared her.

Unwanted heat swirled inside her.

It's a courtesy smile, get a grip, you're just tired. She shoved the mental picture of his smile away with some righteous indignation. *Great, glad I rushed to get here on time.*

Breathing out again, she tried to centre herself and push all emotions away, including her uncharacteristic irritation. Phil Carson, the now retired chief, had often kept her waiting in their meetings and she'd always been resigned, not cross. She swallowed a sigh. Sleep deprivation made her grumpy and she really needed a decent night's sleep. Surely the current Amaroo baby boom would slow down soon.

She deliberately glanced around, forcing her gaze away from the tall, dark, handsome and totally unsettling doctor. Surprise jolted her. Gone were the old fishing prints Phil had loved. In their place hung a large original still life—a bowl of yellow pears sitting against a magenta, teal and Pacific blue background, the vivid colours contrasting with the freshly painted ivory walls.

A large photograph caught her eye. Pink, russet and yellow low-rise European-style buildings, their windows defined by wooden shutters, nestled between craggy green-grey moun-

tains and shimmering azure blue water. Wooden fishing boats
bobbed on the sea in front of a pretty but narrow beach. It
looked like the Côte d'Azur in France.

She'd spent a wonderful month there once, doing a conversation French course in a small village between Nice and
Cannes. She'd loved the area but couldn't help comparing the
narrow stone lined beaches to the soft, golden sands of
Amaroo.

To her left, a French Provincial-style conference table sat
solidly, the walnut wood gleaming in the reflected sunlight
that poured in through the large windows. In the centre of the
table stood a coffee-pot and fine china cups, their lips outlined
with a fine gold band.

In front of her, and completely unrecognisable, stood the
desk Phil had used. Instead of the clutter of patient histories
and piles of random papers, a computer purred, its screen-
saver flashing a geometric design.

The room screamed neat. Nothing was out of place. The
pile of files next to the computer sat in perfect alignment, precision in every sharp corner of the brightly coloured folders.
The top one read, 'Community Midwifery Programme.'

Charlie's project. Her baby. The result of her integral belief
in women caring for women in their own environment during
pregnancy and labour.

Quelling her agitation with a deep breath, Charlie sat down
and crossed her legs. She immediately noticed a splotch of
mud on her knee—a legacy from her flat tyre—and hastily
re-crossed her legs the other way to hide the mark. Dr Laurent
didn't look like mud would ever dare touch him. The butterflies took flight again, her stomach churning.

How ridiculous! She was twenty-eight years old, not
twelve. She was meeting a professional colleague, not Terror

Tompkins, her old boarding-school principal. She sat up straighter.

He smiled as he dropped the handset back into the phone cradle and strode around the desk, both actions swift and decisive. 'I am sorry to have kept you waiting.' The Rs rolled gently on the wave of his French accent. 'A hospital is a series of interruptions, *non*?' He shrugged, the rising and falling motion of his shoulders travelling the length of his body.

'I am Xavier Laurent, and you must be Charlotte Buchanan. I am pleased to meet you.' He extended his hand forward in greeting, his body moving fluidly.

She pushed her hand forward, trying to concentrate on a professional greeting. His large hand immediately engulfed her smaller one, almost a caressing motion, leaving her palm tingling. She hastily withdrew her hand, balling it into a fist to stop the warm feeling racing up her arm.

Focus! First impressions are vital. 'I am, but most people call me Charlie.'

He tilted his head for a moment, as if absorbing this piece of information, his dark eyes never leaving her face. 'Charlotte is a beautiful feminine name and yet you use a man's name?'

She laughed. 'It's an Australian tradition. If the name is long, we shorten it, if it's a short name, we lengthen it. Charlie was a better option than Blue.'

Confusion creased his brow. 'Blue?'

She smiled. 'It's what Australians call a person with red hair. Crazy, isn't it?'

'It's the slang that causes me problems. My time has been spent between two countries and sometimes I am confused in two different languages.' His laughter rumbled around the room, its low timbre warming her.

'But you've spent more in France than Australia?'

'I came first to Australia when I was nineteen. My Sydney uni friends tried to teach me the Aussie accent and I can say, "G'day, mate."' He spoke the two words in the broad, flat Australian accent and grinned. 'But I think my accent is again stronger as I have been working in the Côte d'Azur for the last three years.'

She smiled. 'That sounds like a tough gig—all that glamour and money, the jet-set lifestyle.'

'I was working in the *arrière-pays,* the back country, the small villages in the hills. Although I did enjoy visiting Monaco and Cannes on my weekends. Who would not?' He grinned, his eyes sparkling with devilment, a hint of a man who enjoyed the good things in life.

His grin sent a helix of heat spiralling through her. How could one smile from a man she'd only just met make her cheeks burn? She tried to sound professional and regain her equilibrium. 'Amaroo is a different planet from Monaco. I bet there are a few cultural shocks in store for you.'

He shrugged again, the relaxed movement flowing from head to toe. 'It makes for an interesting time and I can practise becoming an Aussie again. May I offer you coffee, Charlotte?'

'That would be lovely. Black, please.' The coil of tension inside unwound completely. All her fears were unfounded. He was charming, could laugh at himself, and this was, as she had expected, a casual 'get-to-know-you' session.

He poured the coffee and carried two cups back to the desk.

'Thank you.' She took the proffered cup, breathing in the spicy aroma of the fresh brew.

Xavier rounded his desk. As he sat down he deftly slid the

top folder from the pile. 'Charlotte, I called you in today to discuss the community midwifery programme.' He pulled open the blue folder. 'I believe you're the midwife in charge of this project?'

'Actually, I'm the only midwife involved in the project. However, the plan is to extend the programme at the end of the financial year and employ another midwife.'

'I see.' He took a sip from his coffee, his lean fingers wrapping themselves around the cup. 'As you are probably aware, part of my brief as the new medical director is to review all the hospital's programmes.'

She nodded. 'It's a great way to become familiar with the hospital.'

'And after reading all these files...' he tapped the top of the stack '...your programme stands out.'

Pride and satisfaction bubbled up inside her. 'Thank you.' She sat forward enthusiastically, always ready to talk about her programme, her passion. 'I'm really proud of what's been achieved. It's innovative and cost-effective.'

He put his fingers and thumbs together, creating a diamond shape, and rested his forefingers against his lips. His head moved in an almost imperceptible nod. 'Innovative perhaps, but these women could come into hospital and have their children here where all the facilities exist, *oui*?'

Magnetic dark eyes, warm with persuasion, gazed at her. For the first time she glimpsed in their depths a flash of steely determination.

The rumours she'd heard about this man suddenly jelled in her mind. A bitter taste scalded the back of her mouth.

Keep calm. 'I don't agree. Have you read the mission statement?' Charlie reached over and slid the folder off the desk.

She quickly located the paper she was looking for and pushed it back toward him.

She didn't have to read it herself. She'd written every word and they were engraved on her memory. 'To provide women with birthing options. To offer a safe childbirth environment in a non-medical setting to women who satisfy the stringent criteria. To reduce hospital costs and reduce in-patient stays.' She crossed her arms against her thundering heart but kept her voice even. 'You seem to have missed the point, Dr Laurent.'

A muscle twitched in his jaw but his face remained calm and the expression friendly. 'I think, Charlotte, perhaps you have missed *my* point.' His rich voice contained a slight coolness that hadn't been there before. 'Your programme is a duplication of existing services. Which means "cost-effective" it is not.'

Her fatigue instantly disappeared. Indignation kicked in. 'How can it be a duplication of services when it isn't copying a service provided by the hospital?'

His hand tensed. 'Women have a service. They have an obstetric unit geared to cope with all the complications that can occur in childbirth.'

'They have a medical model that isn't what all women want!' The words shot out sharp and loud, despite her resolve to keep calm. She must make him understand.

Rising quickly from her chair, she strode across to the large bookshelves that lined one wall. 'Here.' She grabbed a thick volume from the shelf.

Turning back toward the desk, she almost collided with him. The plush carpet had absorbed any noise made by his footsteps when he'd followed her to the bookshelves. Close up his height dwarfed her, her head barely reaching his shoulder. His aromatic citrus aftershave swirled around her, filling her nostrils. She stifled the urge to breathe in deeply.

She quickly stepped around him, needing to put a great deal of space between them. Needing to get her hammering heart under control. She'd never reacted to a man like this before. It had to be exhaustion.

Clutching the bound copy of the report to her chest, she marched back to the desk. 'Are you familiar with the state review of birthing services? I think perhaps you were in France when it was conducted.'

She restrained herself from slamming it down on the desk. Instead, she clung to every shred of reason and logic she could muster, desperate to keep a lid on her ever-growing fears for her programme. 'Much of Michel Odent's philosophy became the benchmark for the recommendations of the report.

'As a fellow Frenchman, I'm sure you're completely *au fait* with his work. Here in Amaroo we started putting the recommendations into action.' She sat down.

Xavier followed suit. 'Charlotte, I can see you are passionate about your project and passion is a wonderful thing.' His eyes sparkled and a hint of a smile tugged at his mouth, giving it a sensual look.

Her gaze zeroed in on his lips, almost mesmerised. She forced herself to blink and swallowed hard. *What the hell was wrong with her?*

Enough! She squared her shoulders. 'I've worked very hard these last twelve months to get this project off the ground. I really believe in it.'

'I'm sure you do.' He leaned back into his black leather chair. 'Was this project a board initiative?'

'No, I approached Dr Carson with the idea and he took it to the board under his recommendation.'

'I see.' He ran his long fingers across his jaw.

Panic started to build. 'I'm not sure you do.' She took in a deep breath and tried to speak calmly. 'Based on the review, interviewing the women of the community and taking into account Dr Carson's workload, this programme filled everyone's needs.'

Her patients deserved this programme. All her hard work, the long hours, everything she did—she did with her patients' wellbeing in mind.

He pulled out a piece of paper covered in figures. 'It does not matter how much you believe this programme is needed if there is no money available to run it.'

Economic rationalist. The hospital gossip ran through her head. 'Dr Laurent, there's a lot more to running an obstetric unit than financial figures on a page. In Amaroo people matter, they are not just numbers and throughput. Since you arrived have you spotted a patient? Spoken to any pregnant women and heard what they want? Or are you so engrossed in your precious figures that you've forgotten the whole point of why the hospital exists?'

She heard his sharp intake of breath. Had she touched a nerve? Good.

He suddenly sat forward and drummed his fingers against the notepad on the desk. The noise echoed around the office, bouncing off the suffocating tension that hung in the air.

He finally spoke, weariness tinging his words. 'I have taken on this job only to discover the hospital has a huge financial deficit. If this community is to continue to have a hospital, we have to rein in spending. I'm sure you agree with me that the loss of the hospital would be tragic.'

'Absolutely.' At least they agreed on one thing.

'You seem so certain in your belief that the outreach midwifery programme is vital to the women of this community.

I am yet to be convinced.' A look of irony crossed his face. 'However, as you so eloquently point out, I have yet to fully investigate the programme.' He leaned forward, his elbows resting on the desk. 'So, as from today, your programme is under review.'

Charlie's coffee turned to acid in her stomach. 'Exactly what does "review" mean?'

He raised his brows. 'It means detailed reports, regular meetings and close supervision.'

Her heart banged against her ribs in agitation. 'And who is going to work the crazy hours I do and supervise me?'

His dark gaze found hers, creating a hypnotic effect. '*Moi*. I will.'

Her breath stalled in her throat, trapping all words.

'Believe me, Charlotte, this is the best way. By the time I have finished examining this *programme*, I'll know everything there is to know. And then I will make my decision about the future of community midwifery. This is a fair solution, is it not?'

Her heart pounded. Her brain struggled, railing against this pronouncement. Hating his logic and yet knowing that it was eminently fair. 'I… Yes, I guess it is.'

'Good. I look forward to seeing you at nine tomorrow morning.' He gave a quiet yet determined smile. 'Unless, of course, there is a baby between now and then.'

'You wish to be called at two a.m.?' Disbelief laced her words.

'*Certainement*. My secretary will give you my pager and mobile phone number.'

He stood up, his height unfolding and filling the room.

She stood as well, trying to match his power play.

He walked around the desk, his arm extended as if to say, 'After you.'

She walked toward the door, her mind racing, trying to anticipate his next move.

'Until tomorrow, Charlotte.'

Suddenly she was on the other side of the door, facing the severe glare of the secretary. Frustration collided with admiration. She'd just been dismissed in the most charming way possible.

She was on the back foot. She hated that.

Xavier watched Charlotte leave his office. He hadn't been expecting a midwife with such determination. Neither had he been expecting a curvaceous redhead with long, mud-splattered legs.

And none of that improved his humour.

He ran his forefinger across his jaw and walked across to the window. The ocean shimmered in the summer sunshine, not a wave in sight. Beautiful.

This rugged coastline seemed almost uninhabited compared with the Côte d'Azur. Although he loved his native home, he found the comparative isolation of this part of the world refreshing and restorative to the soul.

And he desperately needed some of that restoration right now. Not that it looked like it would happen any time soon.

When he'd been approached about this position in Amaroo, he'd jumped on it. His life in France had become untenable and the offer of a job in an area close to his parents and nieces and nephews had seemed almost too good to be true. He'd lost his dream of his own family, so the idea of being close to his extended family gave him a sense of connectedness.

This job had given him the opportunity to come to the other side of the world and start over. Leave the northern hemisphere and the mess that was his personal life behind and get established 'down under'.

But nothing ran smoothly.

The telephone interview had glossed over the fact the hospital board had just been sacked for financial mismanagement. He'd arrived to find a financial mess and a hospital on the brink of closure. So, instead of dividing his time between patient care and administration, he was chained to his desk. He had the Department of Health demanding he make radical changes to pull the budget into line and get the hospital back on track.

He sighed. Having bureaucrats breathing down his throat was galling enough. He didn't need Charlotte Buchanan inferring he was a soulless, uncaring number-cruncher.

He cared. He loved his work—loved delivering babies and watching new families take shape. *Zut!* He wasn't the bad guy here. But he had a budget to fix and he wanted it fixed *now*.

Only then could he get on with his life. His new Australian life.

He picked up his white coat and made his way down to the antenatal clinic. He was looking forward to some hands-on medicine. It made a pleasant change from balance sheets.

And he needed to *do something* after his encounter with the tenacious yet stunning Charlotte. Attraction had arced between them like electricity, jolting him to his core.

Once before he'd been attracted to a woman who had been so tied up in her job that nothing else and no one else had mattered. She'd marched through his heart wearing jackboots. He wasn't taking that road again. Ever.

He strode down the corridor, shaking his head to get rid of the vision of emerald-green eyes that sparkled with passion. It was passion for her job, nothing else. He'd do well to remember that.

CHAPTER TWO

CHARLIE drove into the car park, her daily dose of awe whizzing through her at the fact she got to work in a place where she could see whales cavorting in the ocean. For a moment she sat staring out to sea through binoculars, watching a sleek black mammal fling all ninety tonnes of itself out of the ocean.

Every year the whales came to Amaroo to give birth and raise their calves. She liked the symmetry. While the whales were birthing, she was helping the women of Amaroo do the same thing. Over the years the whales had faced many battles for survival, and now it looked like she faced a survival battle herself.

Putting the binoculars away, she slung her bag over her shoulder and headed toward the midwifery building, stifling a yawn.

Her desperate craving for sleep hadn't been met. Instead, she'd tossed all night, images of piercing black eyes interspersed with a recurring slamming door meaning she'd woken up tired and groggy.

Dr Xavier Laurent wanted to close down community midwifery, did he? Well, just let him try.

She straightened her shoulders. It was needed, it was valid, it was…her.

All she'd ever wanted to do was bring babies into the world to take their place in loving families. Her parents and Richard had never understood that. Never chosen to understand.

She pushed the pain of their rejection away. It achieved nothing.

She knew the deal. She'd had to fight for her career once before. It looked like she'd have to do it again. She'd start by running an efficient antenatal clinic. The clinic would be the perfect place to showcase her skills and the merits of the programme.

She'd dazzle him with her skills and professionalism.

Don't let him dazzle you. She shook her head against the traitorous thought. Yesterday she'd been caught off guard. Today she came armour plated, completely immune to a lilting French accent and magnetic charm. Dr Laurent was nothing more than her boss. She mentally put him in the 'boss box' in her head.

She jogged up the old, worn steps of the midwifery clinic, feeling the coolness from the old bricks against her skin. In summer, the thick walls gave welcome relief from the heat and the large verandas caught any passing sea breeze. The exterior of the midwifery building had an old-world charm, which contrasted with the modern, welcoming interior. A home away from home for pregnant women.

Charlie dropped her bag into the bottom of the filing cabinet in her office and slammed it shut. 'Right.' She started working through her mental list of tasks to be achieved before nine a.m. When Xav—Dr Laurent turned up he would find the consummate professional.

She heard the front door creak open.

Her heart almost bounced out of her chest. Damn, the man was early.

A pale, wan face peeked around the office door. 'Charlie, have you got a minute?'

Relief flooded into every pore. She was always ready for patients. 'Sure have. Come in.' Charlie quickly swung a chair out for Melissa, whose anxiety preceded her into the office.

'Oh, Charlie, I feel just awful.' Melissa moaned, and her eyes filled with tears. 'I can't keep anything down. I've never had morning sickness like this before.'

Charlie patted her hand, sympathetically. 'I know it's awful, but the good news is that you're actually feeling sick.'

Melissa looked up incredulously. 'How can it be good?'

'Morning sickness is a good indication that this pregnancy is a strong healthy embryo. Your pregnancy hormones are high and they're making you feel sick. We just have to help you get through the next few weeks.' Charlie smiled reassuringly at Melissa. 'Can anyone help you out, minding little Jake for a couple of hours in the afternoons?'

'John's mum has offered, but I thought I would be all right.' Melissa blew her nose and wiped her face.

'So take up the offer and have an afternoon's sleep. Morning sickness is always worse when you are tired. Ginger tablets are really helpful for the nausea and so is vitamin B6.'

She reached out and touched her arm. 'Believe me, Melissa, the morning sickness will fade.'

Melissa gave a wry laugh. 'Let's hope it finishes before the baby is born.'

Twenty-five minutes later Melissa left and Charlie quickly assembled the medical histories in order of appointment. She was ready to greet Xav—Dr Laurent.

The loud and piercing beep of her pager sounded at the same moment it vibrated against her. She quickly checked the digital read-out. Accident and Emergency? A surge of adrenaline shot through her. She could count on one hand the amount of times she had been paged to go to A and E.

In her line of work she saw the uncomplicated, straightforward pregnancies. Her programme had rigid guidelines as to who could be admitted and all high-risk pregnancies were excluded.

She quickly scribbled a note apologising to her clients for the delay of the start of clinic. As she pushed the pin into the wood, the ramifications of the page hit her. Xavier Laurent would have to wait before he could start her supervision. Relief mingled with adrenaline, the combination making her feel quite odd. She'd phone him from A and E and delay his visit.

Xavier pushed himself away from his desk, his stomach growling. Breakfast was a distant memory. He'd done his rounds at seven a.m., enjoying his 'patient fix' so he could squeeze in an hour of paperwork before his first appointment.

He checked his watch. 9:05 a.m. *Zut!* Not enough time to make coffee. He was late already to meet Charlotte Buchanan. Her programme looked to be superfluous and with money tight he needed to avoid two services offering the same thing. But convincing her of that wouldn't be easy. The woman's zealous approach to her job seemed almost unhealthy.

So much passion. Too much passion for his peace of mind. An image of her alabaster face swam into his mind, quickly followed by a vivid picture of her toned, shapely legs and narrow waist that begged to be cupped by large hands.

Never again would he confuse passion for work with love. Genevieve had torn the scales from his eyes and a piece from his heart. Her career aspirations had come ahead of everything—patients, their unborn child, him. He hated that it had taken him so long to work that out. That lives had been lost.

His pager beeped, snapping him back to reality. Obstetric emergency. Two lives at stake.

He grabbed his white coat and stethoscope, a charge of adrenaline skimming along his veins. The quickest way to A and E was across the lawn quadrangle. Dodging the timed sprinklers, he ran across the square, arriving at the entrance the exact moment as Charlotte.

She'd been running as well and her chest heaved against her blouse, the fabric moving smoothly across her pert breasts. Her cheeks blushed pink and her pupils, now large black discs against an emerald backdrop, gave her a sensual glow that hovered around her like an aura. She flicked her damp hair back from her face and licked the droplets of sprinkler water from her lips.

White heat blazed through him.

He cleared his throat, pushing the unwanted reaction away, forcing himself to regain control. He pushed open the large Perspex doors. 'After you.'

She ducked under his arm, her perfume filling his nostrils with the scent of wild roses.

Helen Bannister, the unit manager, met them with gowns and gloves, which she thrust at them. 'Sharon Jenkins is on her way in with shoulder-tip pain. I thought you'd want to be here, Charlie.

'We're frantic at the moment with walking wounded. I've cleared the resuscitation room for you and the ambulance will be here soon. Medical Records is bringing her history over, but in the meantime, Dr Laurent, Charlie will fill you in.' Helen briskly walked away.

'Come.' Xavier strode quickly into the resuscitation room

to prepare, his triage training coming to the fore. If he had some time to set up, hopefully the emergency would run as smoothly as something totally unpredictable could.

He turned to ask Charlotte a question but the words died on his lips. The enticing glow on her face had faded, replaced by an almost frightening whiteness, which emphasised a smattering of freckles across the bridge of her nose.

Her pallor, so sudden and unexpected, worried him. She didn't look well at all. 'Are you all right? Do you need to leave and lie down?'

'No.' She nibbled her plump bottom lip.

His groin tightened. *Alors.* His reaction to this woman was insane. Unwanted.

She reached for the intravenous set, her concentration centred on priming the unit. 'I'm fine, really.' Her voice sounded soft and uncertain—a contrast to her firm tones of yesterday.

He dragged his gaze from her kissable mouth, shaken by his reaction to her. He was a doctor. It was time to act like one. 'It sounds like an ectopic pregnancy and a rupture of the Fallopian tube. What can you tell me about the patient?'

She sighed, her breath shuddering out of her lungs. 'Sharon Jenkins is a thirty-four-year-old woman with a long history of infertility due to pelvic inflammatory disease. This is her first pregnancy.'

Blood pounded in his head. Suddenly the pallor of her face made sense. She was one hundred per cent well but her patient was not.

Bile burned the back of his throat. His chest tightened with rage. With PID, Sharon Jenkins would fall outside the guidelines of the outreach programme. Had Charlotte stooped so low as to risk a patient's life to boost numbers for her beloved programme?

He clenched his fist. In France he'd been naïve, totally missing the signs of driving ambition. But never again. Today he saw the signs flashing brightly and harshly, like neon against a black sky.

What was it with some professional women that made them behave like barracudas? How could ambition blind people to their professional obligations? How could they forget their oath of 'Do no harm'?

Anger swirled in his gut, revisiting past hurt. He didn't need a midwife who put her career ahead of her patients in *his* hospital.

He flicked on the ECG machine and tested the electrodes, the familiar action tamping down his anger. Now wasn't the time to deal with this. Right now all his attention needed to be zeroed in on his patient. But the moment the emergency was over, Charlotte Buchanan and her programme would no longer be part of his hospital.

The doors swung open and the ambulance officers hurriedly wheeled in the gurney. Sharon lay on her side, her face grey and contorted in pain. Her skin glistening with the sheen of sweat.

Charlie raced to her side. 'I'm here, Sharon.' Concern filled her voice and she took the woman's hand, giving it a supportive squeeze.

Xavier swallowed the derisive sound that rose in his throat. Charlotte had good reason for concern. She could be struck off the nursing register for defying guidelines and putting a patient at risk.

He turned his attention to his patient. 'Mrs Jenkins, I am Dr Laurent, the obstetrician who will be looking after you.'

Sharon's fear-filled eyes focused on his face. 'My shoulder hurts so much, Doctor. I feel like I'm going to vomit.'

Charlie silently produced a kidney dish, tucking it under Sharon's arm.

'I'm sorry you feel so unwell. I'm going to have to examine you but I will be as gentle as I can.' He smiled at her, hoping it might distract her for a moment. 'At least in this heat, my hands are warm, *oui*?'

He methodically examined her abdomen. Guarded, distended and bloated, it fitted the picture of intra-peritoneal bleeding. Such bleeding caused the referred, shoulder-tip pain.

'Her blood pressure is eighty on fifty. I'll insert the drip.'

Charlotte's voice broke through his concentration, her words mirroring his thoughts. Like most ambitious people she was supremely competent and good at her job. It was the 'take-no-prisoners' approach he objected to.

He gave a curt nod. 'Take blood for cross-matching and put up a Haemaccel infusion once you've got the line established.'

'Right.' She grabbed the Haemaccel from the fridge and then paused before acting, explaining the procedure to Sharon. 'I'm going to put a tourniquet around your arm and then put a needle into your vein so we can give you some fluid.'

Xavier picked up the phone and rang Theatre, organising Sharon's immediate transfer upstairs. While he waited for Kristy Sanders to confirm an anaesthetist, he watched Charlotte. Surprise filled him at the ease in which she inserted the IV into their shocked patient. Sharon was in venous shutdown—it would have been a challenging job to find a vein, let alone achieve in-venation so quickly. Grudging respect for her skills edged in.

'Kristy, tell Phillip I need him in Theatre now.' He hung up and turned to look at his patient. Charlie deftly stripped nail polish from Sharon's fingers. The tang of acetone stung his nostrils.

He couldn't put it off any longer. He had to break the bad news to Sharon. He hated to be the one to confirm shattered dreams.

He picked up her hand. 'Sharon, I am sorry. It's highly likely that one of your Fallopian tubes has ruptured. The embryo was probably growing inside your tube instead of settling into your uterus. We will do an ultrasound upstairs in Theatre to confirm my diagnosis, but I am certain I am right and I need to operate to stop the bleeding.'

Sharon gripped his hand. 'Will I lose the baby?'

His heart contracted at the pain his words would inflict. '*Je suis désolé.*' The French slipped out instinctively. 'I am so sorry.'

The woman crumbled, sobs racking her body, her grip on his hand vice-like. 'Has…has someone rung my husband?'

Xavier found this part of being an obstetrician the most difficult. For the most part it was an extremely happy job but when a pregnancy went wrong he experienced some of his patient's pain.

Charlie spoke quietly to Sharon, her voice gentle and calming. 'We have to get you up to Theatre now, but Bob is on his way in and he'll be waiting for you in the ward after the surgery is over. Dr Laurent will explain everything to him after the surgery and then again to you when you're up to hearing it.'

She glanced at him, her gaze hooking his, almost a plea in her eyes.

The look completely confused him. He shrugged it away. His patient needed all his concentration.

Sharon's crying jag eased to shuddering sniffs. She transferred her grip from Xavier's hands to Charlie's. 'Oh, Charlie…'

'I know.' She blinked rapidly, her eyes deepening in colour with the shine of tears. She squeezed Sharon's hand again as the porter arrived to take her to Theatre. 'I'll see you after surgery.'

Stepping back, she watched the trolley disappear out into the corridor.

Bitter rage imploded inside him as he watched this charade of caring. She'd deliberately put Sharon at risk, ignoring her professional duties, putting her ambition first.

'You're coming to Theatre with your patient, Ms Buchanan.' The words rolled out on a growl.

Her eyes widened. 'But I…'

He ignored the shocked look on her face. 'But nothing. I need a skilled assistant and you are that person.' He needed her technical skills, but just as importantly, *she* needed to see first hand the damage her ambition had caused. Sharon would lose a Fallopian tube, and if the other tube was damaged her only chance of future pregnancy would be in vitro fertilisation.

'Fine.' A thread of determination edged into her voice, the same determination he'd heard yesterday. It completely overrode the emotion he'd seen in her eyes and the tone she'd used when she'd spoken with Sharon.

That didn't surprise him. She'd been caught off guard for a moment, but now she'd pulled herself together.

No doubt her mind raced with how she could save her skin. And her programme. Well, no amount of fast talking would get her out of her own mess. Staff acting in a non-professional manner didn't belong in his hospital.

Ten minutes later he strode into Theatre. 'Ready, Phillip?'

'Ready my end.' The anaesthetist glanced up from his dials and screens.

'*Bien.* Scalpel.'

A pair of emerald eyes flashed at him over a mask. Charlotte silently slapped the scalpel into his outstretched palm.

He made the incision and quickly located the ruptured Fallopian tube. Sharon's pelvic cavity was a mess of blood and adhesions. It took all his concentration to stem the bleeding and try to save what he could.

Every time he opened his mouth to ask for an instrument or suction, Charlotte anticipated him. She organised the scout nurse for silk and extra packs. He had no reason to request anything.

The co-ordination of the surgical team was seamless under her steady guidance. He could feel the respect the staff had for her. Could he have missed something?

He overruled the thought.

They might be blind but he refused to be duped. He knew her type inside and out. Her tunnel-vision focus for her job and programme had made her commit a professional sin.

The moment Sharon Jenkins was in Recovery, Charlotte Buchanan would be escorted from the hospital.

He gently probed the other tube. 'We'll run some dye through this just to check it's patent.'

He studied the screen, watching the dye travelling easily down a straighter Fallopian tube with no sign of obstruction.

'Oh, thank goodness.' The words, barely audible, breathed out from behind Charlotte's mask.

For the first time since coming into surgery she looked at him. Relief and joy mingled in her eyes. He'd expected the relief. But the joy threw him. That look of happiness in her eyes wasn't for herself, but for Sharon.

For a brief moment he held her gaze, savouring the satisfaction of a lucky save and some good surgery. Then he remembered the great danger in which her ambition had placed Sharon.

'Four-O silk.' He almost grabbed the suture from her gloved hand as his anger surged again at her unprofessional behaviour. To steady himself he focused on creating small neat stitches along Sharon's abdomen.

'Thanks, Phillip.' He turned toward the anaesthetist. 'You can bring her round now.' He stripped off his gloves and stepped back from the operating table. 'Ms Buchanan, I wish to see you in the prep room.'

Surprise crossed her now unmasked face. She dropped the mask in the linen skip. 'I'll be back soon to help you clean up, Kristy.'

The scout nurse nodded and watched with interest as Xavier opened the door and ushered Charlie into the adjoining room.

All the anger and frustration he'd worked so hard at keeping under control for two hours exploded. '*Mon Dieu!* What were you thinking? How could you put a patient with a history like that in your programme?' He thrust his hands out in front of him, gesticulating his complete lack of understanding. He struggled to find the English words he needed, his mind racing in French.

'You have overstepped the mark. I have no choice but to close your programme. It is defunct. Finished. People who put their job before their patients do not belong in my hospital.'

He expected raging fury, a barrage of words. But he got neither. A myriad of emotions darted across her face, incredulity the most prominent. When she finally spoke the only emotion he could detect was tiredness.

'Sharon Jenkins isn't my patient.'

The words punched him in the chest, winding him. *Hein?* He shook his head. 'What?'

She raised her head slightly her chin jutting forward. 'Sharon Jenkins isn't my patient.' Her quiet words shot into the strained silence. 'She is a very dear friend.'

Confusion swamped him, his thoughts jumbled and incoherent. 'But they paged you to attend A and E?'

She looked at him as if he were a bewildered child and sighed. 'This is a small town, Dr Laurent. Everyone knows everybody and their problems. Helen knew Sharon would want me to be with her.'

His brain, normally quick to comprehend, wrestled valiantly to come to grips with this new information. He'd been so certain of her negligence, so secure in his conviction of her. So quick to see her as guilty.

He was so wrong.

She stood before him, her head tilted slightly to one side, with the light catching her hair, sending shafts of golden red swirling around her. Luminous. Truly beautiful.

He didn't want to see her that way. Not as a woman. He had enough battles on his hands getting the hospital under control without being attracted to another woman who lived for her job. He would not risk brutal duplicity again.

It would be so much easier if she were gone. Out of his hospital. Out of his thoughts.

But the balance of power had just shifted. How could he have so misread the situation? How had he got it so totally and utterly wrong? He hauled in a deep breath. 'I see.'

In his rush to find her guilty he'd lost perspective. He'd let his pain of betrayal colour his judgement. In his desire to find a quick solution to his budget problems he'd acted hastily.

He'd never stopped to consider her as a person with a network of friends in the town. He cleared his throat. Humble pie didn't taste very palatable. 'I seem to have misconstrued your relationship with Mrs Jenkins.'

She raised her eyebrows and remained silent, her body rigid with tension.

He struggled not to sound so formal, wishing he could apologise in French. He chose honesty instead. 'I acted on emotion, not facts. I let the past interfere in a place it does not belong. I am truly sorry, Charlotte.'

She moved slowly, pushing off the bench she'd been leaning against, her eyes round with resignation and disappointment. For a brief moment her shoulders drooped but she quickly straightened, standing tall. 'I accept your apology.'

The coolness of her voice told him he had not been forgiven. She turned and walked toward the door.

He moved quickly, needing to explain.

They reached the door at the same moment, their hands colliding on the handle.

Fire on ice.

He heard her sharp intake of breath as she quickly withdrew her hand, her cheeks pink.

He caught her gaze, her flashing eyes full of questions and confusion.

'One moment, *s'il vous plaît.* Please, I have something more I need to say.'

'Shoot.' She took a step back, crossing her arms across her chest.

The colloquial expression confused him. '*Pardon?* I am not in the habit of shooting my staff.'

For a brief moment the trace of a smile flit across her face. 'Please, go on.'

He concentrated on his words, hauling his mind back from

chasing her smile. 'I wish to start our working relationship again. I have not been fair to you. I give you my commitment that I will review your programme using the birthing services review guidelines as well as our budget requirements.'

'Good.' Her face remained impassive.

'Good?' He'd expected more than that.

'Good. I'm very glad you are a fair man. Now, if you would please stand aside, I need to go and tell Bob Jenkins that his wife is in Recovery. I expect you will wish to speak to him too.'

She moved passed him out into the corridor, her theatre greens not able to hide the curvaceous lines that lay beneath them.

He slammed the door closed. She drew him like a firefly to light. But if he went down that road he would be scorched. He'd read her reports, detailing her activities of the last six months. The amount of time she spent at work left no room for anything else in her life. Her commitment was total.

Why was he even thinking about her like this? Relationships with colleagues burned and he wasn't putting his hand up for that experience again. And it wasn't just his experience. He'd watched friends' relationships fail as they'd tried to carve out careers and keep relationships afloat.

No way was he acting on an attraction that would take him down a dead-end, heart-wrenching road again. He wasn't that stupid.

He slammed his hands in his pockets, his fingers curling around a piece of paper.

He pulled it out and smiled at the reminder. Phil Carson's party. After the day he'd had the party would be the perfect event to push all thought of work and Charlotte Buchanan out of his mind.

CHAPTER THREE

CHARLIE sank back against the cold metal of the lockers in the theatre changing room, letting the coolness flood into her overheated body. She closed her eyes but Xavier's tanned face invaded her thoughts, reviving the flame of desire his hand on hers had sparked. A flame that had heated every inch of her, igniting parts of her body she'd thought had died long ago from lack of use.

And she hated that.

Hated that her body would betray her at the hint of sophisticated charm and an intoxicating accent.

She drew in a long, steadying breath and focused on the facts. Facts flattened desire. She needed as many facts as she could get.

He'd thought her capable of deliberately putting a patient's life at risk. Her heart pounded at the thought. How could he have thought that of her? What had she done that would make him think so badly of her? She hugged herself, trying to make sense of the situation. His accusation had rocked her to her marrow.

Yesterday she'd defended her programme, asked him to give it a fair go. She'd done no more than anybody else who believed in what they did. No one wanted to see their hard efforts go down the drain.

She rubbed her temples. His accusation made no sense.

'I let the past interfere in a place it does not belong.' The image of his handsome Gallic features paling under his tan as he'd spoken stayed with her, intriguing her. Was the past he'd spoken of the reason he'd come back to Australia? What had happened in his past to make him jump so quickly to an incorrect conclusion? She really wanted to know more.

She shook her head. His past had nothing to do with her. He was an excellent doctor—his treatment of Sharon both surgically and as a caring physician had been faultless. She'd been impressed by how he'd handled the medical side of the emergency from start to finish.

As for his accusation, well, he'd genuinely apologised and requested to start their working relationship again. His contrition and fairness had shone through. For the sake of her patients she'd do everything in her power to work co-operatively with Xavier.

The shimmering sensations that swamped her whenever she was near him—those she would simply ignore.

Charlie hummed as she drove the short distance to the Carson farm, smiling at her golden Labrador, Spanner, who hung her head out the window, tongue lolling, taking in all the smells of summer.

The warm evening declared itself the perfect venue for a party. Hearing Marie Carson's voice on her answering-machine, inviting her to an impromptu barbecue, had been the perfect antidote to a horrid day. Charlie adored the Carsons and had missed them desperately while they'd been touring, celebrating Phil's overdue retirement. Now they were home and in typical style were throwing a party.

Charlie intended to let her hair down and drive away the

vestiges of the day, including all thoughts of work and Dr Xavier Laurent.

Spanner barked as she turned into the long gravel driveway lined with agapanthus, their large white and purple heads swaying gently in the breeze. The Carsons' rambling homestead seemed more like home to Charlie than her parents' house ever had.

Phil and Marie had taken her under their wing when she'd first arrived in Amaroo, offering her friendship. She'd waited for the inevitable suggestions, the subtle attempts at moulding her, directing her life. They'd never come. For the first time in her life she'd found acceptance. She treasured it dearly.

Kids and dogs charged around the home paddock. Charlie opened the door to let her eager dog out. 'Off you go, Span.'

'Hey, Charlie!' Jenny and Robert Martin, both school teachers, called to her from the volleyball court. 'Join us. We need some help.' The ball sailed passed them, landing on the baseline.

Charlie laughed and held up a bottle of wine. 'Be there as soon as I've said hi to Phil.' A small thrill shot through her. She loved being part of this community. She followed the aroma of barbecued onions, her stomach gurgling. Lunch seemed a long time ago.

Standing behind the barbecue in the most ridiculous apron she'd ever seen stood Phil, expertly grilling steak. He waved the tongs in her direction. 'It's about time you showed up, Charlie. Working too hard, I presume?'

Charlie gave him a hug. 'Of course not. Would I do that?' She laughed. 'Where on earth did you get that apron?'

'You need a tacky souvenir of every holiday and this fitted all the criteria and then some.' His smile increased as he caught sight of his wife. 'Marie, look who finally showed up.'

A well-groomed woman in her sixties hurried over to embrace her. 'You look tired, dear. Has there been a baby boom?'

'You know how it is.' Charlie was deliberately vague. A party was not the place to open her heart to Marie about a certain black-haired doctor with dark penetrating eyes whose arrival had caused her chaos, both professionally and personally.

'Come along, then, let's get some food into you.' Marie picked up a plate and started loading it with salad and some of the home-grown steak that was grilled to perfection.

Charlie joined a group of friends under a market umbrella, eating the wonderful food, sipping her wine and letting the conversation wrap around her in a convivial way. The day's tensions slipped away, and she relaxed for the first time since meeting Xavier.

'Charlie.'

She swivelled around. Marie walked toward her with her arm happily tucked into the crook of Xavier's.

Her breath swooshed out of her lungs as her blood rushed to her feet. In a suit he'd had an aura of sophistication and control. In soft linen trousers with a sky-blue shirt and braided leather sandals on his feet, he radiated a devastating careless style.

She tried to breathe.

How could she have been so stupid? Of course, she should have realised. This was Xavier Laurent's welcome party as well. She wanted to sink under the table and out of view. But there was nothing she could do except stand, smile and act as though nothing in her world had changed.

Anything less and she'd face an inquisition from Marie.

She desperately hoped her body's crazy lust-fuelled re-action to the gorgeous doctor didn't show on her face.

* * *

Charlotte. Xavier blinked and swallowed an embarrassed groan as the enigmatic midwife rose gracefully to her feet. It had never occurred to him that the person Marie Carson insisted he meet would be the one woman he wasn't quite ready to face.

His behaviour earlier that day still haunted him. He couldn't believe he'd let his hurt from the fallout of his past cloud his professional judgement. He prided himself on being objective at all times. He'd convinced himself he'd left the past in France, where it belonged. Instead, he'd used it against a co-worker, a woman.

When he'd left work that afternoon he'd believed he had at least seventeen hours for his apology to take effect. Seventeen hours before he had to face Charlotte again, and even then it would be with the safety buffer of work between them.

But perhaps a social situation was the ideal place to really make amends. Show her he wasn't an ogre, establish a working friendship. He'd chat with her and then head back to Alison Richards, the kindergarten teacher he'd been chatting to when Marie had brought him over to meet Charlotte.

Alison had seemed a sensible woman, the type of woman he should be noticing. Someone who didn't work in medicine.

He smiled a welcome and inclined his head in greeting. 'Charlotte, good evening. It's lovely to see you.'

'Xavier.' She matched the tilt of his head with one of her own—her luminous eyes filled with caution.

A twinge of guilt shot through him. He was the cause of that hesitancy.

Marie seemed oblivious to the tension that radiated from Charlie. 'Xavier, Charlie is like the daughter we never had.

And, Charlie, did you know that Xavier's mother and I are very dear friends?'

Without really waiting for an answer from either of them, Marie suddenly turned to leave. 'Oh, dear, Phil's waving madly from the barbecue so he must need a hand. Well, you don't need me—the two of you will have loads in common. Oh, and, Charlie, be a dear and introduce him to the others.' With a quick pat on both their arms she walked briskly away.

Xavier caught a flash of apprehension cross Charlotte's face. The guilt twisted in deeper. 'I imagine that to disobey Marie's instructions to talk would be tantamount to treason.' He grinned, hoping to put her at ease.

Her face relaxed and her eyes suddenly sparkled with laughter. 'You're spot on there. Marie likes to bring people together.'

Her vibrancy surrounded him, drawing him toward her like a moth to a flame. He sought her gaze. 'Then perhaps I should thank her as I am not certain you would wish to have talked to me this evening if she had not insisted.'

She gave him a wry smile. 'Amaroo is too small a town to hold a grudge, Xavier. I can forgive you one lapse of judgement.' She raised her brows, her emerald eyes dancing as she looked him up and down. 'But just one, mind. Next time it happens you could end up helping Phil here on the farm, mucking out the pigpen. I'm sure the pigs would love Armani.'

His laughter joined hers, the two tones mixing melodically, warming him. 'Ah, but I was raised on a farm, Charlotte. I spent many hours discussing my adolescent crushes with the pigs—they are good listeners.'

He laughed at her wide-eyed look, enjoying the fact that he didn't fit into whatever pigeonhole she had tried to place him in her mind. Enjoying the fact they could tease each other in a friendly, platonic way.

'Charlie, we're waiting for you!' Robert Martin, red-faced and panting, ran over from the volleyball match. 'We're down five points and we need your setting skills.'

Charlie hesitated for a moment, glancing behind her at the group at the table, obviously torn between her desire to play volleyball and her promise to Marie to introduce Xavier to the group. 'I'll be there soon.'

'You said that half an hour ago, and we need you now.' Robert bent over to put his hands on his thighs and to catch his breath.

Xavier didn't want to be the reason Charlotte missed out on playing volleyball. He could meet the other guests later. He put his hand on the panting man's back. 'Robert, I used to play volleyball at Sydney University. May I join you, too?'

He heard Charlotte's gasp of surprise behind him.

Robert straightened up, as if propelled by new life. 'Great! Come on, then, you two, Jenny's waiting for us.'

'So you played at uni?' Charlotte walked beside him to the court. A wicked smile lit up her face, matching the sparkling gleam of competition in her eyes. 'Now, that would have been a while ago, wouldn't it?'

He laughed. '*Mais oui,* but it is a game also played in France.'

Jenny Martin urged them onto the court. 'Hurry up, you lot! We're seven down now.'

'Coming.' Charlotte paused for a moment by the side of the court, pulling her blouse over her head to reveal a cropped sports top. The black Lycra moulded her breasts, outlining every curve.

Desire shot through him, the complete anthesis of platonic.

What was it about this woman? Every time he convinced himself he was immune to her, his body let him down. Thank goodness for some physical activity. He'd play the game and then find Alison Richards.

He nodded a greeting to the other players, noticing that Charlotte knew them all by name. Just like in Theatre that afternoon. She belonged here. She had what he wanted, what he sought from Amaroo. A sense of belonging.

Robert issued directions. 'You can both start off at the net with Chris. Charlie, you go in the middle, Xavier on the left, and Jenny, Geoff and I'll protect the back.' He headed to the baseline to serve.

Xavier took his position, his skin tingling in awareness of Charlotte standing beside him. Totally aware of the brief Lycra top, and now bike shorts which had magically appeared from under her skirt, emphasising long shapely legs. He gave thanks she wasn't dressed in the traditional skimpy bikini, beach volleyball outfit. He'd never be able to hit the ball.

Focus on the game!

Robert served the ball cleanly and the opposing team returned it in one hit.

'Mine!' Charlie called it, and expertly set the ball up. It sailed high in the air, close to the net.

Xavier jumped, spiking it down on the opposing side, its speed passing all the hands trying to block its passage.

'Yes!' He turned and pushed his arm into the air.

Charlotte smiled broadly, raising her arm and giving him a high five.

A shower of electric shocks carried heat right through him. He quickly pulled his arm back. 'Only twelve points to go.'

The heat of the evening sun bore down on him as it dropped low in the sky. That was why he was hot. It had nothing to do with long legs, swinging auburn hair and flashing emerald eyes.

Le jeu. Focus on the game!

The battle on the court intensified, the opposing side determined to hold onto its lead. A crowd gathered to watch the well-fought match, the gap in the score steadily closing. People took sides, inventing chants as the excitement built.

For the first time since arriving in Amaroo Xavier relaxed. This was why he'd come to the country. To have a life outside work and to belong to a community.

Charlotte whispered conspiratorially. 'We're doing great. Let's keep it up.' Enthusiasm filled her words.

Her aura danced around him, sparkling, enticing him. Did she embrace everything in her life with this much enthusiasm?

'Remember to back up Geoff.'

'Will do.' She gave him a mock salute and a cheeky grin, and spun back to the middle position.

A sense of lightness streaked through him.

'Yours.' Charlotte set the ball.

'Got it!' Xavier spiked it down and won the point, enjoying their teamwork.

The lead narrowed until the score was twenty-four to twenty-three in their favour. One point to win. Adrenaline flowed through Xavier's veins, the thrill of competition giving him a complete buzz. A buzz that had nothing to do with the redhead on his right.

The opposition served a fast ball, which curved down close to the baseline. Geoff dived to dig it up. Charlie pushed the ball up over to Xavier and he leapt to thump it over the net.

The ball was returned, just clearing the net.

Charlie lunged, coming up under the ball to set it up for a

more controlled spike. This time Xavier had time to direct the ball. He powered it back. It landed at the feet of the front-line players.

'Great shot!' Charlotte raised her arms toward him in triumph.

Elation surged through him. He grabbed her around the waist, spinning her around. 'We did it!'

'We did!' Her laughter enveloped him, her arms curved around his shoulders, their touch sparking the flame he'd worked so hard to extinguish with exercise. Heat burned inside him.

For a brief moment he stared into her flushed face, reading joy, elation and an emotion he connected only with Charlotte.

She broke the gaze.

The moment ended.

Robert thumped him on the back, Jenny reached forward to hug him and Geoff and Chris pumped his hand. Almost as quickly the team turned their attention to Charlie and then to the opposition.

Xavier stood catching his breath, watching the antics of an excited group of people celebrating a worthy competition. His gaze followed Charlotte to the sidelines. Mesmerised, he watched her take a long drink of water, her head tilted back, highlighting her long neck. Desire surged, stronger than before.

He refused to listen to it. He would *not* act on it. It was her athleticism he admired. Her skill. She played volleyball like she worked, throwing her heart and soul into it.

She seemed to do everything with such passion. *And if that passion was directed at you?*

He squelched the thought immediately. He knew what worked and what didn't. It was engraved on his soul.

No, it was time to find Alison Richards, the kindergarten

teacher who loved children. He scanned the crowd and saw her standing in a group, silently absorbing the conversation. She seemed small, shy and mousy. No signs of vibrant enthusiasm on her face, no aura of fire and heat surrounding her.

Suddenly fatigue hit him. He really didn't feel like talking to Alison. It was time to head home.

The noise of a distant ringing bell slowly penetrated Charlie's sleep-filled brain. She rolled over and reached for the phone. 'Hello? Charlie Buchanan speaking.' The words tumbled out automatically.

'Charlie, it's David McAllister. Julie's started. Her waters broke about an hour ago.'

Charlie glanced at the clock. Two a.m. 'Was the fluid clear, David?'

'Yes, Charlie.' The experienced father spoke with amusement in his voice. 'You know we would have rung you if it was brownish.'

'Of course you would but it's two in the morning and my brain is just starting to wake up.' She stifled a yawn. 'We'll come straight over. Put the kettle on for me.'

'Don't think you're going to need boiling water for a while yet,' David teased.

'No, but I'm going to need a cup of tea.' She laughed as she hung up the phone. This was the third McAllister baby she would be delivering. The first two had been in hospital but this time the McAllisters had chosen a home birth as part of birth options programme Charlie had introduced.

And this time Xavier would be there, too. She hadn't seen him since the Carsons' party four days ago as he'd been in Theatre or tied up in meetings. But even if she hadn't seen him, he'd taken up residence in her thoughts. Her mind seemed to stream footage of him playing volleyball—long, toned legs, rippling muscles as he jumped to spike the ball, and a wicked smile that made her knees go weak and her heart pound erratically.

She could still feel the touch of his arms around her waist at the end of the match, and the tingling wave of sensations that had built inside her.

She pushed the thoughts away. Even if she were in the market for a relationship, which she wasn't, Xavier was her boss. End of story.

She moved into action. A baby was on the way.

This delivery was her opportunity to prove to him she was the consummate professional and that her programme was a vital part of the midwifery department.

She dialled his number. The phone rang three times before a deep voice resonated down the line, his delicious accent emphasised by the phone. 'Xavier Laurent.'

He didn't even have the decency to sound half-asleep. Instead, his voice held the promise of sensual kisses and a long embrace.

You're the midwife, he's the doctor. Nothing else mattered.

'Xavier, it's Charlotte Buchanan.' What? She never called herself Charlotte. Only her mother called her that.

And Xavier.

One day she was going to kill that inner voice. She straightened her shoulders. This was work. Be professional. 'Julie McAllister's gone into labour. You met her at the antenatal clinic and you wanted to attend the birth. If that's still the case, shall I pick you up on my way to their farm?'

'*Merci,* Charlotte. How long will you be?' Friendliness filled his voice.

She tried to sound a little less businesslike. 'Oh, about ten minutes. I just have to throw some clothes on.' The moment the words came out she wanted to grab them back. She sounded as if she was naked, instead of wearing polka-dot shortie pyjamas.

Low, rumbling laughter came down the line. 'Just as well we are not video-conferencing, eh?' He chuckled. 'See you in ten minutes.'

The line went dead. Charlie's cheeks burned and she knew her face would be bright pink. Blushing at twenty-eight! Heaven help her.

He's the doctor, you're the midwife. Two professionals.

Although it was the middle of the night, the summer air was warm. Charlie pulled on a pair of light cotton trousers and a short-sleeved blouse with the hospital logo embroidered on the pocket.

Grabbing her keys, she gave the slumbering Spanner a pat and went out into the night. A full moon lit the sky and the crickets serenaded the peace of the night. In the distance she heard the slow, rolling waves hitting the shore.

Ten minutes later gravel crunched under her wheels as she pulled into Xavier's driveway. She dimmed her lights as he walked out onto his porch, pulling his front door closed behind him.

Her heartbeat picked up.

Dressed in chinos and a designer polo shirt, he looked far too sexy for the middle of the night. In contrast to her own hair, which she was yet to snag with a ribbon, every strand of his lay in place.

She couldn't help but watch as he walked to the vehicle, his long, confident stride quickly eating up the short distance. He swung up onto the front seat, immediately filling the interior with his long body and citrus aftershave.

She took in a deep breath, more to savour the scent than to steady herself.

'*Bonne Nuit*, Charlotte.' He tilted his head to the side for a moment, his dark eyes scanning her face. Looking into her soul. 'Gorgeous night for a delivery, *n'est-ce pas*?' He snapped his seat belt into place. 'The stars in this country seem to go on for ever.'

'They do, don't they?' Oh, she sounded so inane! 'It's about a twenty-minute drive to the McAllisters'. We just follow the Southern Cross.' She pointed to the distinctive constellation only seen in the southern hemisphere, hanging low in the sky.

Charlie passed him a map, her fingers brushing his. A tendril of longing swept through her and she quickly dropped the map. 'But just in case navigating by the stars isn't specific enough, I thought this might help you become familiar with the area.'

He smiled, straight, white teeth gleaming in the moonlight. '*Merci*.' He flicked on the map light and opened the map, spending the next few minutes studying it.

Charlie reversed out of the driveway and tried to focus on the road and not on the fact that this undeniably gorgeous man sat far too close to her for any peace of mind.

'*Colleague and boss, colleague and boss.*'

'Pardon?' He lifted his head from the map, his black brows raised questioningly.

Surely she'd said that under her breath. She smiled brightly. 'We won't get lost, I know the way.' She gripped the steering-wheel.

Xavier returned to the map. The road rolled on.

His voice broke into her thoughts. 'I was surprised that the hospital offered a home-birth option.'

'Yes, the community was lucky to have Phil Carson.' She smiled fondly. 'He was a man before his time. He'd stand up to the bureaucrats for the things he believed in.'

Charlie heard a mumbled noise beside her and turned her head.

Warring emotions played across Xavier's face. 'He was fortunate to have most of his career untainted by the exploding cost of health care. Things have changed a lot. Now we have to justify every cent and every programme we run.'

A desire to defend her mentor bubbled up inside her. 'True, but that doesn't stop you from fighting for what you believe in. And Phil did that again and again. Amaroo has a great health-care system because of Phil's drive and passion.'

His hands rose palms upward along with his shoulders, a Gallic shrug. 'It also has crippling debt, Charlotte. We cannot ignore that for high ideals.' His volume was soft but the tone determined.

'Julie McAllister could have her baby just as easily in the hospital with the midwives on duty.'

Frustration rushed into her. 'But she deserves to have a choice.'

'She deserves access to quality health care. Amaroo risks losing their hospital if hard choices aren't made and the budget pulled in.' His lips compressed into a straight line.

'I understand that, but why *this* programme? It's based on a cost-effective model. It's safe and gives better outcomes for mothers and babies. Midwife care costs less than hospital-based care. The intervention rate is lower.' She heard her voice rising.

Forcing herself to sound calm, she dropped her voice. 'International studies show the outcomes for planned home births are as safe as hospital births and they are cost-effective.

Australia is lagging behind. You must see that, coming from France.'

'Most women in France deliver in hospital, Charlotte, with a midwife in attendance.'

'But it is the home of Odent.' She couldn't believe what she was hearing.

'*Oui*, but it is not embraced by the country as a whole.'

'But women need choice, Xavier.' She heard her voice rise and she breathed in deeply. 'Sorry, I will get off my soap box but I feel very strongly about this.'

'I can see that.' His dark eyes sparkled and she glimpsed a sense of humour. She remembered his quip on the phone earlier.

'It is important to have passion, Charlotte.'

His warm smile softened his cheekbones, giving him a totally different look. A look that turned her insides into a quivering mess. A look she longed to see again.

'But passion isn't enough.' His tone, still soft yet lined with steel, instantly grounded her thoughts. 'It's a tough world and if we want to compete we have to be fiscally responsible. This programme is very small so it is likely to be costing money rather than saving it.' Xavier flicked the map over as if to say, 'subject closed.'

Charlie bit her lip and focused on the road. She wanted to scream, she wanted to rant, 'It's not fair!' But when was life ever fair? She knew she had a battle on her hands.

A battle to save her programme.

A battle to keep her irrational attraction for this man under control.

CHAPTER FOUR

CHARLIE pulled up to the McAllisters' gate, the engine idling. Xavier immediately jumped out of the car and walked toward the gatepost. The headlights picked up the way the fabric of his shorts stretched over the curve of his behind as he moved to unhook the chain.

A flush of tingling raced through her. She should *not* be noticing things like that about him. He was her boss.

Yellow light from the house spilled down the long drive and David walked out to meet them.

'How's Julie?' Charlie called over her shoulder as she started to unload equipment.

'She's still organising me, so I know it's early days yet.' David laughed. 'At least the kids are sound asleep so it's been really great having an uninterrupted conversation, even if it is the middle of the night.'

'It's good you can see the positive at this time of night.' Charlie smiled. 'David, I'd like you to meet Dr Xavier Laurent. Julie met him at clinic last week.'

David extended his hand. 'G'day. Jules said you're from the Côte d'Azur. Welcome to our farm.'

'Thank you for having me here.' Xavier returned the handshake.

Charlie's palm tingled in memory of the first time he'd shaken her hand. Cross with herself for letting the memory intrude, she vigorously pulled at the portable oxygen cylinder. It shot forward, teetering on the edge of the cargo area. Attempting to break its fall, she jammed it in place with her hip, ignoring the pain that signalled a bruise was on its way.

'Got it.' Xavier suddenly appeared beside her, his hands underneath the cylinder, taking the weight.

Heat rushed to her face, embarrassment tagging her. 'Thank you.'

'*Je vous en prie.*' His eyes danced with reflected light. 'You are most welcome.'

Slow heat glowed inside her. *Stop it!*

So the man spoke with a rich, glorious accent that made her feel like her blood had melted into a river of velvety smooth chocolate. So what? She had a baby to deliver.

She flung her medical bag up high on her shoulder and walked inside ahead of the men, who stood on the veranda, discussing the price of beef. Charlie found Julie walking around the kitchen.

The very pregnant woman gave her a wave. 'I've been walking since David rang you. My contractions are pretty weak and irregular, so I'm trying to get them going.'

'Let's have a look at you, then.' Charlie followed Julie to her bedroom. She wrapped the blood-pressure cuff around her arm. 'I'll do a set of baseline observations and listen to the baby's heartbeat.'

Julie settled down against her pillows. 'Funny how the last two were such quick labours and this one feels different.'

Charlie nodded. 'Third babies often do this. Part of it might be you knowing this is your last pregnancy, and you don't want to give the baby up just yet.'

Julie rubbed her lower back and grimaced. 'Believe me, I'm ready to hold this one in my arms.'

She smiled. 'Well, your BP is fine. Now, let's just see how this baby is lying.'

Julie lifted her nightie and Charlie palpated her stomach, feeling the lie of the baby. 'Great, we have a head down here and a bottom up there.'

She laid Julie's hand on the baby's bottom. 'This baby is slightly posterior, which is why your back is aching and why the contractions are a bit hit and miss.' She laid her ear against the black trumpet of the Pinard stethoscope, counting the baby's heartbeats.

She straightened up. 'And that's a textbook heart rate as well. So if you just keep walking, we can try and get these contractions a bit more regular.'

'Back to walking, then.' Julie struggled up and walked to the bedroom door. 'Hopefully David and Xavier have brewed a pot of tea.'

Charlie followed Julie into the lounge room and sat down on the couch. 'I'll just write down the obs and then I'll join you.'

'OK.' Julie waddled toward the kitchen.

Charlie entered the details of the observations and the palpation into Julie's medical history.

'Everything OK?'

She jumped in surprise, her pen scrawling across the page. She licked her lips, steadying her breathing. 'Fine. Everything is fine.'

Xavier looked over her shoulder as she finished the entry. 'Her contractions are irregular, *oui*?'

'They are.' The warmth of his breath stroked the back of her neck. She gripped her pen firmly and kept writing.

'Why are you here so early?' Xavier sat down next to her, the old couch cushions giving way under his weight and tilting her toward him.

She braced herself so she didn't fall against his broad shoulder. 'The last two labours were precipitate. Harry came in three hours and twenty minutes and Bonnie was two hours. That's one of the reasons Julie wanted a home birth. She didn't want to face going through transition in David's ute again.'

Xavier laughed. 'If the ute is the vehicle we parked next to then I certainly cannot blame her for not wanting to drive into town in that. I doubt it has many springs left.' He stood up. 'So what do we do now?'

Charlie glanced up at him, seeing a mixture of eager anticipation for the job ahead and frustration at the current impasse. He'd be more used to inducing labour rather than waiting for nature to take its course.

But to give him credit, he was trying hard to stay in the background, letting her do her job and truly observe her at work. For the first time she sensed companionable co-operation. A vital step toward saving her programme.

'Charlie!' Julie's voice hailed her from the kitchen.

Charlie hauled herself up from the depths of the soft couch and smiled at Xavier. 'I think you just got your answer.'

They found Julie with her nightie up around her waist, standing in a large puddle of amniotic fluid. David stood holding a mop.

'I don't understand.' Julie's brow furrowed in confusion. 'My waters broke a couple of hours ago so what's this?'

'You must have had what we call a hind water leak. That can happen when the baby is not quite in the right position. Then, when he or she moves into place, the main part of the sac breaks and, whoosh.' Charlie grinned. 'I think you might find things speed up a bit now.'

And as if on cue, Julie's face contorted. She gripped the kitchen bench as a contraction hit her. 'Oh, I remember this.'

Charlie checked her watch to time it. 'Sixty seconds and strong. You're on your way.'

'I want to get into the shower.' Julie headed into the newly renovated bathroom, which had a double shower.

Xavier stepped forward, pushing a large red exercise ball. 'You might feel more comfortable sitting on this, rather than standing.'

Amazement spun through Charlie. She hadn't expected Xavier to think of the ball.

Julie sank down gratefully, resting her back against the wall of the shower. David held the hand shower attachment, gently spraying warm water on her back.

Silently they evolved into a team. Charlie kept a close monitoring eye on both mother and baby, while the men kept Julie comfortable.

'I will get some cool water for her.' Xavier stepped out toward the kitchen.

'Thanks.' She hadn't expected him to take on such a hands-on role as part of his supervision. Yet he'd blended in seamlessly, anticipating everyone's needs. It was like they'd worked together as a team for a long time.

Somehow he'd managed to be involved but in a low-key way, completely respecting the wishes of the McAllisters. He whipped between the kitchen and the bathroom, keeping Julie supplied with ice and cold water.

'Please, drink. We do not want you dehydrated.' He held the sports bottle to Julie's lips, an encouraging smile clinging to his lips.

Charlie shook her head in disbelief. She'd never seen an obstetrician behaving as a doula before but Xavier was giving it a good shot.

'I'm cold.' Julie pointed to her stomach. 'Water, here.'

Charlie draped a blanket across Julie's shoulders to keep her warm and David moved the shower nozzle to spray on Julie's tummy. Julie didn't speak, her focus now firmly on her working body and her baby.

It was a great sign. One every midwife liked to see.

The heat of the shower, combined with the heating light and the warm night, turned the bathroom into a humid tropical oasis. As Charlie stood up from listening to the foetal heart, silver spots danced in front of her eyes. 'I'll just grab a glass of water, David, and I'll be right back.'

She stepped out into the hall, pulling her hair back off her neck, twirling it up onto the top of her head. She leaned back against the wall, letting the breeze from the ceiling fan deliciously cool her overly hot skin.

'Are you all right?' Xavier's voice sounded husky and worried. 'You look flushed. Here, drink this.' He pushed a glass of iced water toward her.

Charlie took the water gratefully. 'Thanks. I don't think it will be long now. She's been in transition for the last few contractions.'

'You need to look after yourself, Charlotte.' His concerned tone mixed with a gentle reprimand. 'You are no use to your patient if you faint.'

A prickle of indignation started to form at his criticism. She was a professional, she knew what she was doing, she—

The inner voice interrupted. *He's got a point. You know you push yourself too much.*

'Aagh!' A low guttural moan came from the bathroom.

Charlie and Xavier raced back in.

'I…think…I…want…to…push.' Julie rose up from the ball.

David steadied her. 'Do you want to move, love?'

Julie dropped her head against his shoulder. 'I don't think I can.'

David braced his back against the shower wall while Julie put her arms around his neck. As the next contraction hit her she dropped into a supported squat position.

Xavier handed Charlie a pair of gloves and she was struck by the role reversal.

'Push when you want to and I'll have a peek.' Charlie put her gloves on and knelt on the shower floor.

'Aagh!' Julie pushed.

'Fantastic! I can see a patch of black hair.' She shifted slightly. 'Pant, Julie, pant. You don't want to blast this baby out into the world. Just breathe her out gently.'

Slowly the baby's head crowned and was born. 'Just checking for cord.' She inserted her finger between the baby's head and the vaginal wall, carefully easing a loose loop over the baby's head.

'You're doing so well, Julie. With the next contraction I want you to push gently and I'll deliver the shoulders.'

Julie nodded, her full concentration centred on the contraction.

The next moment the baby slithered out into Charlie's waiting hands. A lusty cry filled the air.

She caught Xavier's glance of pure delight. Something akin to pleasurable pain flared and just as quickly burned out, leaving a small empty space. For a brief moment bewilderment hovered and then the surge of familiar emotion cascaded over her.

She blinked furiously to avoid a tear rolling down her

cheek. No matter how many babies she delivered, the emotion of the event affected her every time. She passed the baby up between Julie's legs into the arms of her mother, staying silent about the sex.

'Oh, David,' Julie's voice caught. 'It's Madeline.' Julie's body trembled and she leaned hard against David for support.

David nodded toward Xavier. 'Mate, can you hold Maddie for a minute while I hold Jules?'

'My pleasure.' Xavier stepped forward with a warm bunny rug while Charlie clamped and cut the cord. Xavier quickly dried Maddie and expertly wrapped her up in a baby bundle, his quick and dexterous actions infused with gentleness.

Julie squatted down and delivered the placenta, which came out quickly and intact. Supported by Charlie, she walked the few steps to her bedroom and settled back onto a triangular pillow. With a look of wonder she reached out for Madeline. Then, with the baby firmly in her arms, she gazed at her, counting her fingers and toes.

David lay down next to her, placing his pinkie inside Madeline's palm, which she gripped firmly. His gaze whipped between Julie and Madeline, love and joy etched clearly on his face.

Charlie glanced at Xavier. He caught her look. A thread of understanding wove between them. Together they quietly left the room so the parents could get to know their new daughter.

Xavier broke the silence as they reached the kitchen. 'Celebratory cup of coffee, Charlotte?'

She smiled at him. 'I'd love it.'

When the coffee was brewed and the milk warmed, they walked out onto the veranda into the freshness of a new dawn.

Across the paddocks the first rays of sunlight caressed the browned summer grass. The promise of another hot day.

Leaning against a veranda post, Charlie hugged her mug of coffee, her body tingling with awareness as Xavier walked across the veranda boards. Her body had developed a radar, telling her exactly where he was in a room at any given moment. A radar that both thrilled and exhausted her.

He stood next to her, leaning forward, his strong forearms resting against the railing as he stared out across the paddocks. 'There is something special about a new life and a new day. It is as if you have a few moments of tranquillity to savour it all before the rigours of the day demand your attention.'

His melodic voice evoked a swirl of yearning inside her. That was *exactly* how she felt.

She stared at him. His once ironed shirt was now crumpled, a lock of raven hair fell forward onto his face and the lines around his eyes betrayed his tiredness. But his eyes sparkled with the absolute joy of bringing a new life into the world— the same feelings of fulfilment she experienced every time she did a delivery.

He pushed up off the railing and turned toward her, closing the gap between them. 'You did a wonderful delivery, Charlotte.'

'Thank you.' She breathed the words out as the now familiar rush of heat unfurled inside her.

He reached out and tucked an errant strand of hair behind her ear. 'I am glad I could be part of it. Thank you.'

His touch was almost perfunctory, the 'neat gene' needing to tidy up.

A strand of hair twined gently around his finger. Instantly, the touch changed.

The tips of his fingers skimmed her skin, their feather-soft caress generating wave upon wave of sweet sensation deep down inside her.

The moment extended, strung out between them, an invisible force keeping them in place. A force keeping his finger against her temple. Keeping her temple resting against his finger. Pulling them together.

She swallowed hard, her breath stalling in her chest.

A low groan escaped his lips, washing over them both.

Their gazes connected. His eyes, now wide and darker than ever before, swirled with a fire she'd not seen before. It called to her. She swayed toward him as if in slow motion, every moment heightened with crystal clarity.

Suddenly shutters slammed down, extinguishing the fire.

The moment broke. He dropped his hand and stepped back briskly, creating a large space between them.

'Can you do the final set of observations on Julie now? I need to get back into town for rounds.'

The doctor was back. Professional distance restored.

Charlie gripped the railing, trying to steady her wildly beating heart and kick-start her stalled brain. *Think.* 'Ah, yes, of course I can. Give me ten minutes and we'll be able to go.'

She walked back inside, her thoughts a chaotic, spinning jumble in her head.

You almost kissed him.

Mortification rushed into her, burning her cheeks. How could her body betray her like that? Swaying toward him, almost begging to be kissed. She didn't do things like that. She was immune to such crazy feelings.

She loved her solo life, she was content with that.

Shivers raced through her and her body trembled, now on retreat from sensory overload. She dragged in a steadying breath. Xavier Laurent liked things ordered. He probably couldn't resist the urge to tidy up her errant hair. The man had fine-tuned 'neat and tidy' into an art form.

There's more to him than you thought. The unwelcome voice in her head boomed loud and clear.

She blew out a breath. So much had happened it was impossible to take it all in. Everything she'd thought to be true about this man had just been turned on its head.

In the early hours of the morning she'd seen a new side to Xavier. She'd met the caring doctor, not the number-cruncher. He'd been respectful of the McAllisters, he'd been respectful of her and her role. He'd even complimented her on her delivery.

He completely perplexed her.

Part of her didn't want to acknowledge this new side of him. Seeing him as the enemy made it so much easier not to like him. She didn't want to like him.

But suddenly lines were blurring. How could you fight when you *liked* the enemy?

Xavier shaved quickly. It was almost seven a.m. and he was expected at rounds. He needed to be at work. Work was safe—it had an expected rhythm, clear boundaries and expectations.

It also had a lot of people around so he wouldn't be alone with Charlotte.

Alors. What had he been thinking when he'd allowed himself the intimacy of tucking her hair behind her ear?

He hadn't been thinking at all. He'd been on such a high after the delivery, blown away by the emotional intensity that came with a couple having their baby together without the usual hospital crowd.

Charlotte had stood on the McAllisters' veranda with her

Titian hair almost on fire from the reflected rays of the rising sun, with no idea how stunning she looked. When she'd glanced up at him with her emerald eyes dancing with the joy of Madeline's birth he'd wanted to hold onto that moment of closeness for as long as possible.

But he could *not* get close to her, would not let himself get close. She was passionate about her job, which she was damn good at. She gave herself totally to her patients, which was fantastic, but it didn't leave much over for anything else.

No matter how stunning, no matter how much she heated his blood with one quick glance from her bewitching eyes, he would keep his distance. Once before he'd let desire overrule common sense. He'd paid dearly for that. He wasn't going down that road again.

The paperwork for Madeline's delivery blurred. Charlie rubbed her eyes with the back of her hand and pulled out another form. She was determined to complete all her paperwork in triplicate and have it finished early now she was being supervised.

An image of golden, muscular forearms with curling dark hairs thundered into her mind. She pushed it away by rereading the form. Xavier was working in Outpatients that morning. At least that gave her half a day's breathing space.

Half a day to find her equilibrium.

A knock on her door made her look up.

Xavier stood leaning against the doorframe, his broad shoulders filling the space.

Every nerve ending jangled. How could one man do this to her? She took in a deep breath, centring her thoughts. Suddenly, she noticed a young woman slightly behind Xavier.

'Charlotte, have you a moment?' His accent emphasised

the 'T' in her name, making it sound totally different from the way her parents pronounced it.

Swirling ribbons of sensation poured through her, delightful and dangerous. She forced out a calm voice. 'I certainly have. What do you need?'

Xavier stepped back and ushered in a woman who looked to be in her early thirties. She wore a worried expression and an air of anxiety clung to her.

'Please meet Anne Brickson.'

Charlie stood up and smiled. 'Hi, Anne. Come in and take a seat.' Was Xavier referring someone to the programme? Yes! She wanted to high-five someone in her excitement.

Anne sat down with her knees rigidly pushed together, clutching her handbag on her lap.

Charlie glanced over at Xavier and raised her brows. He nodded as if to say, Yep, she's one stressed-out woman.

'So, Anne, how can I help you today?' Charlie pulled over a chair and sat down next to her. Out of the corner of her eye she noticed Xavier sit down, too. Uncertainty flicked through her. Was this an observation session or a referral? She wished she knew, but right now she needed to concentrate on Anne and forget Xavier was there. *Yeah, right!*

Anne twisted her handkerchief in her hand. 'You see, I've been trying to get pregnant for a while now and…' Her voice started to break.

Charlie put her hand on Anne's shoulder. 'Would you like a cup of tea? It always makes me feel better when I'm a bit low.'

The woman smiled gratefully. 'Thank you. That would be lovely.'

'Xavier, what about you?' Charlie stood up, plugged in the electric kettle and set out mugs, milk and sugar.

'Tea would be lovely. Do you have Earl Grey?'

She gave him a winning smile. 'The hospital budget doesn't quite run to that, Doctor.'

A smile danced around his strong mouth. 'I thought all nurses kept a secret supply of great tea and special biscuits.'

A laugh escaped her lips. 'They do if they have time to go to the supermarket.' She glanced at Anne, whose face had relaxed into a smile.

'You two get along well.'

Surprise fizzed inside her. Did they get along well? She spent most of her time trying to second-guess him. But there had been brief moments when they'd seemed to be in sync. Like this morning, when they'd delivered Madeline.

She caught Xavier grinning at her discomfort. Fiend. She laughed. 'Sometimes we do, Anne. You're seeing us on a good day.'

She poured the tea and sat down again, directing all her attention to her client. 'So, Anne, how long have you been trying to get pregnant?'

'Matthew and I have been trying for the last year to have a baby.' Anne sighed. 'Dr Carson ran all the tests and we're both fine. He said it's just a matter of time.' She inclined her head toward Xavier. 'But Dr Laurent suggested I learn about my cycle to help things along. He suggested that you'd be the perfect person to teach me.'

Sheer delight ricocheted through her. She wanted to sing. He'd referred someone to her. He was acknowledging the programme. She sneaked a quick peek at him, but his mug of tea masked his eyes.

She flicked open a folder. 'I'd be happy to teach you natural family planning. I'd also like to give you some information on folic acid, healthy eating and exercise.'

'What's folic acid?' Anne sat forward, her interest showing in her face.

'It's one of the B-group vitamins and it's important to take it before you get pregnant. It helps prevent neural-tube defects like spina bifida.'

Charlie passed Anne a pamphlet. 'You and Matthew might like to come to one of my "early bird" classes. These are for people who are thinking about getting pregnant or who are newly pregnant.' She handed the pamphlet to Anne.

'I'll think about that. Right now I find it hard when I hear someone is pregnant because I really want to be.'

Charlie nodded. 'Yes, when we decide to have children we want it all to happen yesterday.'

'Oh, yes, that is exactly how I feel!' Anne put her hankie in her bag. 'So, how long did it take you to get pregnant?'

The question hit her out of the blue, completely distracting her. Most of her patients had been in the district longer than her and knew she was single. 'Ah, I don't have any children.'

Part of her wanted to add 'yet', but there was no point. When she'd left Richard, she'd also left that dream, too. The Buchanan women failed at relationships. Her parents' marriage had submerged her mother's happiness—her father's needs winning every time.

Richard's betrayal had driven away any doubts that she might be better at relationships than her mother. So she'd vowed to stay single and maintain her sense of self.

A seed of sadness unexpectedly turned over inside her.

She quickly squashed it. She'd chosen her life and was perfectly content.

Anne patted Charlie's arm. 'I guess you work pretty long hours, which wouldn't really suit a family.'

Indignation spurted like a geyser inside her. How dare this

woman feel sorry for her? She opened her mouth to comment but Anne continued.

'Still, Amaroo's lucky to have such a dedicated midwife, isn't that right, Doctor?' Anne beamed at Xavier.

Xavier gave a brief nod, but Charlie caught a flash of something in his eyes, which surged and fell away just as quickly. Emptiness—a type of loss?

Puzzlement mixed with indignation. She clung to indignation, the safer emotion. She didn't have to justify herself to this woman. She'd fought hard for her identity. She wasn't giving it up for anyone or anything.

Besides, she delivered babies for a living and she babysat for friends. She didn't have a childless life.

She pulled the conversation back to safer territory. 'Let's focus on these charts, shall we? I'll give you a few charts so you can record your temperature each day. Do you have a digital thermometer?'

Anne nodded and leaned in closer to the desk, looking at the mock chart with interest as Charlie explained the effect hormones had on body temperature and taught her about the biphasic chart.

'Come and see me in two weeks and bring your chart. In the meantime, if you have any questions, just ring me.'

'Thanks so much, Charlie. I can't wait to start.' Anne gathered up her papers. 'Goodbye, Doctor.'

Xavier stood up. 'Goodbye, Anne. Good luck with it all.'

The moment Anne left, he turned to Charlie. 'Come. I'll buy you a cappuccino in the cafeteria to make up for that dust you called tea.'

'If you're shouting, I won't say no.' She desperately wanted to know the real reason behind him sending Anne to see her. It might just come out in a chat over coffee.

They walked down the long corridor. 'Thanks for sending Anne to see me.'

'My pleasure. It gave me a chance to see you at work in a different way. Your skills are excellent.'

His smile of praise sent a trail of wonder through her, licking at the cold, dark places she kept walled off deep down inside her.

'Besides, I thought you would be able to see her faster than the main antenatal clinic, as your numbers are low.'

His matter-of-fact words hit like icy water, instantly dousing the wonder. Her stomach churned. She tried to focus on his praise but the thought that it was only expediency that had sent Anne to her stayed front and central.

She looked up at him, trying to read his neutral expression. This review period was so hard. Being powerless didn't sit well with her, but what else could she do?

Get some help. Why hadn't she thought of that before? She could rally the women in her programme and past patients. She could get them to write letters, send faxes, send emails and show Xavier the heart and soul of the programme. He only knew the figures. He needed to see the soul.

CHAPTER FIVE

AS THEY reached the cafeteria door Charlie's pager beeped loudly. She read the display. 'It's A and E again. Twice in one week, that's odd.'

Xavier's brow creased with concern. 'Do you want me to come with you?'

'I—'

Xavier's pager sounded. 'Looks like I'm coming anyway.'

A minute later Helen greeted them, holding a patient history in her hand. 'Jacinta Gordon is in cubicle one.'

Charlie didn't recognise the name.

She turned to Xavier, to find his questioning gaze centred on her face.

'Your patient?' Their words collided, spoken at the same moment.

Helen gave a wry smile. 'Neither, actually. Although Charlie saw her briefly two years ago for an antenatal check when she passed through town. That's why I called you both.'

She pushed the history into Charlie's hands. 'All I can tell you is that Jacinta is pregnant, in labour and if the noise she is making is any indication, she's about to deliver.'

Xavier opened the door for her. 'We're getting pretty good at being a team.'

His smile washed over her in a delicious wave of warmth as she stepped through the door.

A heavily pregnant woman supported herself on all fours, swaying back and forth.

'Hello, Jacinta. I'm Charlie Buchanan, the midwife, and this is Dr Xavier Laurent.'

Jacinta moaned, 'Can't...stand...up.'

At that moment a gush of amniotic fluid flooded onto the floor.

'What number baby is this, Jacinta?' Xavier caught the latex gloves Charlie tossed at him.

She pulled a pair on herself. If this was a second pregnancy, the baby would be arriving very soon.

'Second.' Jacinta ground the words out as the contraction strengthened.

Charlie threw a ground sheet onto the floor and opened a delivery pack. She took one look at Xavier's Italian suit and wondered if he'd hand the delivery over to her. Obstetricians generally preferred their patients up on the bed, not down on the floor.

Xavier picked up a second sheet, doubled it up and dropped it onto the floor. He threw her a resigned look, knelt down next to her and whispered, 'You'll give me the name of a good dry-cleaner, won't you?'

Amazement rocked through her. He didn't fit the mould she so wanted to put him in. She kept seeing glimpses of him as a person rather than a doctor and together they built an intriguing picture.

'Seeing as you got a delivery this morning, I figure this one's mine.' His boyish grin made her heart skip.

It seemed a fair deal. Picking up the Doppler, she listened to the foetal heart. 'One hundred and twenty.'

'OK, Jacinta.' Xavier's quiet voice soothed. 'We want to guide this baby out so push when I say and pant when I say stop.'

'I'll try.' Jacinta's voice cracked as another contraction hit.

More fluid gushed. The baby's head crowned. 'Pant, Jacinta.'

A pink, bald head slowly eased its way out and then the shoulders and body slithered out quickly into Xavier's hands. His hold on the baby seemed almost reverent before he quickly handed the child to the mother, who had rolled into a sitting position.

'Fantastic effort, Jacinta. This little man wanted to come out into the world pretty quickly.'

'You're telling me!' Jacinta joked weakly.

Charlie mentally estimated the weight to be about two kilograms, which was small for a full-term baby. Instinctively, she put her hand on Jacinta's abdomen. Her fingers met Xavier's hand. Sparks of need showered through her.

She quickly withdrew her hand. 'Sorry, it's second nature to check.'

He smiled. 'It's a good habit. Go right ahead. I'll get the Syntocinon.'

She gently pressed down on Jacinta's tummy, her fingers outlining an extremely bulky uterus. Concentrating hard, she carefully used both hands and explored the abdomen. Limbs.

'Xavier,' she spoke quietly. 'I think we have a twin on board.'

He blinked in astonishment. He dropped down next to her, his long fingers dexterously palpating Jacinta's abdomen.

The action mesmerised her. An image of his fingers against her skin whizzed through her, flushing her with heat. *Stop it.*

'Jacinta, have you had any antenatal care?' His French accent seemed stronger than ever, a sure sign he was worried.

Jacinta looked up from examining her baby. 'Well, I've moved around quite a bit and…' Her voice trailed off.

Xavier frowned. 'So that is no?' His hands quickly traced the outline of the twin. His gaze met Charlie's, his eyes full of admiration. 'A good save, Charlotte.'

His words wrapped around her. She knew exactly what he meant. If they'd given the Syntocinon without detecting the twin in the uterus, they'd have risked disaster.

He stood up. 'Jacinta, you're having a second baby. I need to examine you on the bed.'

'Two?' Her face blanched white with shock and she cuddled her baby close. 'Well, this one came out OK, so the next one should be a cinch, right?'

Charlie exchanged a cautious look with Xavier as she took the baby from Jacinta.

Xavier helped the woman up onto the bed. 'The second twin can sometimes get into a difficult position. I am hoping we can deliver it without you needing a Caesarean section.'

Fear crossed Jacinta's face.

Helen popped her head through the door. 'Everything all right?'

Charlie grimaced. 'Undiagnosed twins, Helen. Please, take the baby to Special Care and ring the anaesthetist now in case we need a spinal block.'

The charge nurse started. 'Can do. What else do you need?'

'A forceps set.' Charlie's voice blended with Xavier's.

Xavier palpated Jacinta's abdomen, his hands locating the lie of the baby. 'Oblique.' He muttered the word as if it were an expletive.

Charlie closed her eyes for a moment and took a deep breath. This wasn't good for either mother or baby.

Xavier's voice belied the growing concern in his eyes.

'Jacinta, your baby is lying across your uterus. I want you to use the mask and breathe in nitrous oxide while I try and turn the baby so it is head down and ready for delivery. The more relaxed you are, the easier it will be.'

Unexpected surprise flowed through Charlie. He was going to try for a normal vaginal delivery first, even though it would be very tricky.

She handed Jacinta the clear mask.

His large hands flexed and caressed, guiding the baby's head across the brim of the pelvis. He checked the position by pressing deeply just above the symphysis pubis—Pawlik's grip.

He caught Charlie's gaze and shook his head, his frown deepening. 'Jacinta, I have to try again so breathe deeply.'

The woman's eyes dilated with fear but determination shone from her face. 'What ever you say, Doc.'

Charlie recorded the foetal heart rate. It was holding steady.

Suddenly Jacinta groaned as a strong contraction hit.

Xavier's shoulders stiffened. 'Gloves.' Urgency poured through the single word.

Charlie quickly opened the gloves, knowing Xavier needed to guide the baby's head into the pelvis without it compressing the cord and depriving the baby of oxygen.

The Doppler sounded loud in the room as she counted. Recording the foetal heart was the only tool they had to assess if the baby was coping well. Or not.

'One hundred.' Her voice sounded firm but her heart hammered at the slow heart rate. Even if they raced her to Theatre now, it might be too late.

Sweat broke out on Xavier's brow, his concentration fully on guiding the baby through the birth canal.

'Amnihook.' He steadied the twin's head over the brim of the pelvis, muttering in French.

'Will the baby be all right?' Jacinta's raw fear solidified.

'Dr Laurent is doing everything he can. You're in good hands.' Charlie spoke spontaneously, trying to reassure the woman.

Realisation poured through her. She believed every word she'd spoken. He was one hell of a doctor.

'Foetal heart again.'

She held her breath as she rubbed the Doppler over Jacinta's abdomen. A whooshing sound like horse's hooves boomed through the room. 'One twenty-five and steady.' *Yes!* He'd done it.

His eyes sought hers, smouldering relief glowing brightly from their inky depths. Something unfamiliar turned over inside her.

Xavier gently removed his hand now the baby's head was safely in the birth canal. 'You're a very lucky young woman, Jacinta. This baby is head down and in the correct position. Now we wait for the next contraction.'

They didn't have to wait long. Four pushes later a baby girl slithered into Xavier's arms.

Xavier stroked the baby's head. 'Well, young lady, you gave us a bit of a scare but you're here now.'

For a few moments the three of them quietly enjoyed the satisfaction of a disaster averted and a new life entering the world.

Stuart Mullins, the paediatrician, strode through the door. 'Got another baby, I believe?'

The next ten minutes passed quickly. The baby girl went to join her brother in Special Care Nursery and Jacinta was transferred to the postnatal ward.

Silence descended and Charlie started cleaning up the room on autopilot, her thoughts completely absorbed by the last hour's events. Xavier's technical skills had been brilliant. Amaroo was lucky to have him.

'Charlotte, do you have any plans this evening?' His low voice broke into her reverie.

Her breathing stalled. *Yes! No!* Thoughts bounced around in her head, confusing her. Was he asking her out?

She didn't want to be alone socially with him, she didn't trust herself. 'I, ah…' her stammering voice sounded completely incoherent.

He gave a wry smile. 'I am sorry, that did not come out quite right. No need for you to panic, I am not asking you out.' Irony filled his voice. 'After my experience in France I am totally separating work and pleasure.'

Curiosity chased away her panic, helping her regain composure. Did this have something to do with his comment in Theatre about the past interfering where it shouldn't? 'Why are you separating work and pleasure?' She tossed dirty linen into the skip.

His shoulders stiffened. 'It does not work.'

Bitterness clung to his words, surprising her with their intensity.

His face tightened, his olive skin taut across his cheekbones. 'Medicine means crazy hours. Two people cannot be dedicated to their career, each other and a family. It leaves no time to build a marriage, to create a real family. It is no way to run a relationship.'

The comment intrigued her. 'Run a relationship? You make it sound like a business.'

'Perhaps if people had relationship plans, like business plans, the divorce rate would be lower.' The muttered words were barely audible.

Astonishment filled her. 'I thought the French believed in passion. Are you saying you think we should be more cerebral in our choice of partners?'

He shook his head. '*Non*, passion is very important. However, you can find passion in many places. I am saying that people should look outside their own pond. Find a person who shares their dream. Right now I am not looking for a relationship at all. But if I was, I would only date outside medicine.'

He silenced any further comments by pulling out his palm pilot. 'Back to tonight. I have a full diary this week and I know you have back-to-back clinics and two imminent deliveries. I need to discuss the clinic figures with you as soon as possible. I thought perhaps we could do it out of hours when the phone will be less likely to interrupt us.'

Her heart slammed against her chest. Spending time alone with Xavier, even though it wasn't a date, wouldn't be safe for her state of mind or her heart.

But going over her programme's budget was important. She visualised her diary and breathed in deeply, forcing out a calm voice. 'Tonight would be fine. My clinic's over at six. But as Sheila Douglas is expected to go into labour any minute, it would be easier if we had the meeting at my house. That way we're ten kilometres closer to her place.'

He added the details to his palm pilot. 'As long as you let me bring dinner.'

She laughed. 'Xavier, I live twenty minutes out of Amaroo. Take-aways aren't really an option.'

His shoulders moved back and his eyes flashed indignantly. 'Let me worry about that.' His pager beeped. 'Birth Suite.' He grabbed a clean gown. 'See you at seven, Charlotte. *Au revoir.*' He turned and walked back toward the door.

Reality hit. She'd just invited him to her home! She spent more time at the hospital than at her house. She'd been so busy thinking about Sheila Douglas and logistics, she'd totally forgotten the state of her domestic life. Total chaos.

She slapped her forehead as she remembered the piles of clothes and dishes that awaited her at home.

Honestly, Charlotte, you need to be more tidy. She stomped on her mother's voice.

She wasn't trying to impress Xavier with her domesticity so what did it matter? Tonight was a business meeting and he'd only have eyes for the figures and the budget. He had a plan for everything, even down to where he should look for a future partner.

What was that all about? What on earth had happened to him in France that made him so insistent that a relationship between two colleagues wouldn't work? His words intrigued her.

She shook her head. Xavier's private life was exactly that. Private. It had nothing to do with her.

But you'd like to know more.

She checked the oxygen and suction, silencing the voice.

Xavier gave thanks for the fact it was still daylight saving time as he negotiated the rutted gravel that doubled as a road leading to Charlotte's house. He'd never have found it in the dark. An old weatherboard farmhouse with a return veranda greeted him at the end of the track. Chickens and ducks wandered about and a sprinkler dribbled out much-needed water to a parched veggie patch.

Surprise slugged him. From her timesheets he knew she spent most of her time at work, so he'd always pictured her living in Amaroo township in an apartment. Just a place to sleep. But this place declared itself a home. A haven from the world.

He stepped out of the car into a wall of heat. A squad of bush flies immediately clustered around his open-neck shirt. Grabbing his supermarket bags and laptop out of the car, he headed toward the veranda steps. He hated the fact that yet again he was extending his workday, wrangling with this budget. At least doing it over dinner made it seem less like work.

Charlotte hadn't seemed to mind. Well, not once she'd known it was a working dinner, not a social one. Her initial reaction to his invitation—a look of pure horror—had seared him. He shouldn't care about her reaction. After all, she was a colleague and colleagues didn't date. But women didn't usually recoil from him.

Her reaction puzzled him. Had a man made her wary?

He sighed, pushing the thought away. He didn't need to know. Didn't want to know. The *only* thing he needed to know was the number of enrolments and the full financial picture of the community midwifery programme. That would place him one step closer to getting the budget in line. One step closer to getting his new job under control.

As his foot hit the top veranda step, a golden Labrador belted around the corner, her paws skating on the veranda boards.

'Spanner, sit!' Charlotte, dressed in shorts and a vivid green sleeveless silk top, which matched her eyes perfectly, walked toward him, smiling.

His gaze zeroed in on her long, shapely legs that her shorts did little to conceal. His mouth dried. How did she manage to look so fresh and vibrant when she'd been up since 2 a.m.?

But as she got closer he saw the lines of weariness etched around her eyes. *Zut.* It was one thing to drive himself hard. He shouldn't be asking this much of his staff.

A self-conscious smile hovered on her cheeks and an embarrassed laugh escaped her bee-sting lips. 'I have to warn you, you're about to enter a war zone. I've been away more than I've been home lately, so we might have to dig to find the kitchen.' She extended her arms, taking one of the three grocery bags from him, her soft skin brushing against his.

A flash of heat roared through him. He steadied his breathing. 'I'm sure you exaggerate.'

He followed her into the kitchen, the wire door slamming behind him, a barrier against the flies. He glanced around. Papers, books, dishes and stray articles of clothing covered every available surface. *Chaos.* Yet at work she was the epitome of organisation.

He groaned inwardly, thinking of his immaculate and tidy kitchen at home. Clearing a swathe through the papers on the kitchen table, he put down his bags. 'You put some water on to boil and I'll make a start.'

Her jaw rose indignantly. 'It's not filthy, just untidy.' The words came out in an injured tone.

Laughter rumbled up and out, a joyful sound he realised he hadn't heard from himself in many months. 'I meant water for the pasta.'

Her tinkling laughter chimed in with his. 'Sorry. I'm a bit sensitive about the clutter.' She picked up a pile of journals. 'But I can't work the hours I do and keep this place looking perfect.'

He started peeling some hard-boiled eggs for the salad. 'Maybe you should get someone to help you with the housework.'

She shot him a long look. 'Doubling as my mother now, are you?'

'*Pardon*, I didn't mean to hit a nerve.' He fondly remembered his sister's desire to be independent and live her life her own way. His mother had smiled and supported her without criticism. But not every family connected in the same caring way. He knew he was fortunate.

Memories of crowded, noisy mealtimes in the farmhouse flitted across his mind. His family surrounded him with love, laughter, warmth and a sense of belonging. Something he had longed to re-create for his own children. But the dream had been snatched away.

He pushed the past down where it belonged and passed Charlotte a cos lettuce. 'Can you find a bowl for the salad?'

'That I can do.' She walked across to a magnificent Baltic pine sideboard, her hips gently swaying. She bent down, her shorts taut against the curve of her *derrière*.

The knife he held hit the cutting board, narrowly missing his finger. He hauled his gaze away, returning his attention to the capsicum.

She carried an expensive-looking crystal bowl to the table, balanced on top of a box of matching wineglasses and solid silver cutlery.

He watched in amazement at the quality china that continued to appear.

She caught his expression. 'Ah, the entrapments of a past life.'

A past life? He should let the comment go. He was there to eat, discuss work and leave. She was a colleague and the only things he needed to know about her was how competent she was at her job and if she was capable of making the community midwifery programme financially viable.

But from the moment he'd parked at the top of her drive he'd been intrigued by the other side of Charlotte, the side that existed outside work. As well as the china, he'd noticed antique furniture. None of it fitted with the salary of a midwife.

He salted the boiling water and added a dash of oil.

She poured mineral water into the glasses, spritzing them with lemon juice. 'You're French yet you're cooking pasta?'

'The Côte d'Azur shares a border with Italy. We eat pasta too, although not as often as the Italians. Tonight I'll combine anchovies, roasted red peppers, extra virgin olive oil and parsley and serve it with Italian gnocchi. The sauce is very Provençal.' He picked up his glass and tilted it toward her. *'Santé.'*

She smiled and raised her glass. 'Cheers.'

He glanced around. 'You have some beautiful things from your past life, Charlotte.'

For a brief moment she met his look and then her gaze slid away and focused on the Parmesan cheese and the grater.

Her silence wrapped around him, uncomfortable and cool. A forbidding silence that yelled out, *Don't go there.*

His need to know about her past life grew. Did it have anything to do with her reaction when she'd thought he'd been asking her on a date? He quickly drained the pasta, gently stirring through the roast capsicum sauce, allowing the silence between them to exist. Silence often yielded results.

Charlie surveyed the table now devoid of clutter but groaning with food. 'It looks and smells delicious. Thank you.'

'You are very welcome. It is my pleasure to cook.' He smiled, trying to relax her.

She forked her food around her plate rather than into her

mouth. Emotions flickered across her face, indecision warring
with resolve.

Eventually she spoke, her voice soft, lost in memories. 'I
haven't used this china, this cutlery or glassware in a very
long time. It seems a lifetime ago.' She raised her gaze to his,
her emerald eyes filled with shadows he'd not seen before.

'Why not?' He kept his tone light.

'My life in Amaroo is very different from my life in
Melbourne. I guess it could almost be compared to the culture
shock you must experience coming from France to Australia.'

'But beautiful things should be used no matter where you
live. Eating with friends and family is one of life's joys.'

She stiffened and muttered something under her breath
before raising her head. 'Believe me, eating with my family
was never all that joyous.'

His gaze hooked hers, locking with the ghosts of her past.
'Amaroo is not your family home?'

She shook her head. 'I was city born and bred. Schooled
in Melbourne, the daughter of William Buchanan.' An ironic
tone filled her voice.

The name meant nothing to him but the way she spoke it
told him he needed to know more. 'Should I know of your
father?'

A fleeting look of disbelief swept across her face and then
she laughed. 'Dad's fame crosses the nation, but of course,
not to the Côte d'Azur. My father is a well-known criminal
lawyer, working for Buchanan, Simons and Carter, a family
law firm that goes back to 1895.'

'Ah, yes, what is called *establishment*.' He pronounced
the word the French way.

She nodded. 'That's right. Establishment both in the
business sense and on the social ladder. He's often in the

press about his work, although more recently he's been there for his social activities.' A brittle hardness entered her voice.

'So you grew up with paparazzi?' Sympathy for her moved inside him. He would have hated to have had his childhood recorded in the public eye. Children needed to play and romp out of the glare of flashbulbs.

She shook her head. 'No, thank goodness. Although I had one very public episode which I suppose I should tell you before someone else does.'

Tell me everything. 'Only if you wish to.' He forced his words out calmly, knowing he needed to tread carefully.

She twiddled the stem of her glass. 'I was engaged to be married to a lawyer from my father's firm. The gossip magazines called it the Melbourne society wedding of the year, the joining of two prominent families.'

She tilted her jaw defiantly. 'I called the wedding off three hours before it was to take place. The magazines had a field day for the rest of the month.' Pain, resolve and relief circled each other on her beautiful face.

'No one should marry unless their heart is totally committed to the other person.'

'Oh, my heart was committed.' She gave a wry smile to cover the tremble in her voice. 'But marriage for the Buchanan family is more to do with business than family and my fiancé, Richard, appeared to agree.'

A surge of unexpected anger blasted through him at the thought of Richard.

She paused for a moment, and concentrated on eating, while composing herself. 'My father is the third generation of Buchanans to work in law. My entire life Dad tried to mould me into something I wasn't. My earliest memories are Dad talking about "taking my place in the firm".'

'And did you?' He thought of their first meeting, her passionate argument, and the way she'd convinced him to review her programme. The debating skills of a lawyer.

She sighed. 'I tried. I got as far as doing my articles. But law just isn't me. Dad refused to acknowledge that. He couldn't separate me from family tradition. Richard was part of the plan. Dad's plan.'

'But what of your mother?' The moment the words left his lips he remembered her earlier comments.

Her eyes clouded. 'At that point my mother was an empty vessel, completely drained by my father. She'd lived her life through him, there was nothing of herself left.'

He ached for her, thinking of his parents' solid marriage. 'So you left the law and your fiancé?'

She nodded. 'I finally realised I couldn't lead the life that was mapped out for me. I told Richard I was leaving law to do midwifery.' She gave a snort of a laugh. 'I was so naïve. I thought he knew the real me, understood me. But it turned out he didn't really want me as much as he wanted a partnership in the firm.'

She straightened her shoulders, sitting up higher in the chair. 'Being a midwife is an integral part of who I am. Dad doesn't get it. The life he wanted for me stifled me, so I left before I lost myself completely. I came here and the rest is history.'

Xavier flinched at the hurt that marred her face. He had a close and loving relationship with his parents. His heart burned for what she'd never had. Unconditional love, which his parents gave out in spades. He could only imagine the grief she'd experienced when her family had rejected her. 'Families are not always what we hope they will be.'

She raised her brows. 'I didn't know the French were the

masters of the understatement—you must have some Aussie blood in you after all.' A smile hovered around her lips. 'I returned all the wedding gifts but soon after I arrived a few of my relatives and parents' friends sent me what they described as "house-warming" gifts.'

She laughed. 'They couldn't imagine living in an old farmhouse without fine bone china.'

The full impact of her decision slugged him. 'That was an incredibly brave thing to do.'

'What, to try and live without china?'

He smiled at her humorous defence but he didn't want her humour to act as a barricade. 'No, to call off a huge wedding three hours before it was all to take place.'

She bit her bottom lip. 'Thank you. No one has ever called it brave before.'

For the first time he glimpsed some vulnerability in the woman who always seemed so in control and sure of herself. It took amazing strength to walk away from family. It didn't come without a legacy of loss. Maybe that's why she worked so hard.

Instinctively he reached across the table, resting his palm over her small, soft hand. The gesture of a caring colleague and friend.

The warmth of her skin dived through his own, firing his blood, tightening his groin.

Stunned, he pulled his hand back. Friendship had never sent waves of longing through him. He needed to keep his distance. They were colleagues. That was all they could be.

Charlie swung her head back, her hair falling around her face like a veil, as if she was shaking the past back where it belonged. 'Richard didn't suffer for too long, and within the year he got the quintessential society wife. She does good deeds and his career has soared, which is good for both of them.'

'And did you get what you wanted?'

For a moment a far-away look entered her eyes. She smiled an ethereal smile. 'Yes, I did. I only ever wanted to deliver babies and I get to do that every day.'

'But your job won't give you the love of a husband and family.' The words flowed out naturally, before his brain could censor them.

She stiffened slightly. 'I'm happy with my job and my patients. I'm accepted for *me*. I've only just found myself— I'm not going to get into a relationship and risk losing *me* all over again. I'm done with relationships.'

Sadness for her crept into him. A beautiful woman like this didn't deserve to be alone. 'It sounds lonely.'

Laughter gurgled up from deep within her, a rich melodic sound that warmed every part of him. 'You can't be lonely in Amaroo. I'm part of this community. I belong.'

He searched her face for any signs that her emotions and her words were at odds, but the familiar mask of competence was back. She was a woman in control who knew what she wanted.

And that was fine with him. He could handle the professional woman.

'Why don't we have coffee on the veranda?' Xavier stood up. 'I noticed you had a table out there. I'll bring the coffee out and we can discuss the budget.'

'Sounds good to me. I'll go and wipe the dust off the table.' She yawned and stretched her arms up behind her head.

His gaze travelled along the smooth alabaster skin to the hint of lace and swell of her breast. Heat exploded inside him, sending shards of desire into every corner of his body. He grabbed the coffee-plunger, his knuckles white around the black handle.

Ten minutes later he carried the coffee and financial papers outside, determined to talk figures and nail the community midwifery programme's budget. He found Charlie curled up on the veranda swing, her long, slender legs tucked underneath her.

'I hope you like strong coffee because...' As he put the tray down he realised she'd fallen asleep. The fatigue he'd noticed on arrival had finally caught up with her.

Alors. So much for the budget.

An aura of vulnerability clung to her in sleep. He thought about the story she'd told him earlier. How could a family reject their daughter? How could a *loving* parent cause so much pain?

He sighed. He'd drink his coffee and then head home. He sat down next to her, and she moved slightly, her head coming to rest on his shoulder. A scent of vanilla mixed with roses filled his nostrils as her hair caressed his face. He breathed in deeply, getting his fill of her intoxicating scent. The tightness in his shoulders and legs, a part of him for so long, drained away.

He sipped his coffee slowly and then put his cup down. He should leave. But if he moved she would wake up, be embarrassed and protest that she was fine to discuss figures. And she wasn't. She was exhausted, not that she would ever admit it.

Non. He would sit a moment longer and let her rest. He leaned into the swing, taking her weight against his chest, gently placing his arm against hers.

She worked too hard. She'd given up a lifestyle and a

family to do this job, putting her job ahead of her personal life. Or perhaps it was fear of a personal life?

What had her father and this Richard done to her? What scars had they left?

Enough for her to want to live her life partner-less.

He struggled to understand. For him, family was everything.

Instinctively he caressed her cheek. Charlotte moved against him, snuggling into his chest, filling him with contented warmth. The crickets started to sing and Spanner wandered over and lay down at his feet. For the first time in months a sense of peace entered him, slowly unwinding, spreading out in coils of relaxed ease.

This was insane. Absurd.

She didn't want a relationship. And did he? Could he ever entrust his love to a woman again? Perhaps one day, but it would *never* be to anyone from work. That much he'd learned.

So what was he doing, snuggling with her?

And liking it?

Urgency ripped through him. He needed to be anywhere but on this swing with her. He had to leave. Now.

He moved his arm away, the heat of her skin no longer soothing. Suddenly burning.

The jerky movement startled her and she woke up, her face filled with sleep-induced confusion, her eyes struggling to focus.

Words tumbled from his mouth. 'I am sorry, Charlotte, but I have to go. You are exhausted. Go to bed. I will see you tomorrow.'

Scooping up his paperwork and laptop, he strode down the veranda toward his car. Each step took him away from the lovely, but absolutely-not-what-he-was-looking-for Charlotte Buchanan.

He put one foot in front of the other, refusing to look back. But, God help him, he wanted to.

Charlie sat on the swing, stunned. Her breath came in jerky gasps. She'd fallen asleep in front of Xavier. But worse than falling asleep in front of her boss, she'd fallen asleep *on* her boss.

Her glorious dream, the one she'd been having about feeling safe, warm and cared for, had been based on reality. She'd lain in his arms. How long for, she wasn't sure, but long enough for the tendrils of belonging and sanctuary to feel so very real.

The image of his discomfort and unease descended on her. He'd been kind and understanding about her falling asleep but it had been obvious he couldn't wait to get away from her. He'd almost run down the veranda.

Having a colleague fall asleep on you wasn't exactly the stuff that dreams were made of. Especially as he'd been so adamant that he would never have a relationship with someone he worked with.

Her cheeks burned hot. What must he think? How could she face him again?

Spanner licked her hand. She ruffled her ears. 'Oh, Span, I'm in a mess again. The off-duty doctor is completely gorgeous, caring and understanding. How the hell am I going to deal with that?'

She stood up slowly and looked out across the paddocks toward town. Amaroo was her sanctuary. A much safer one than a tall raven-haired doctor who set her pulse racing every time he came near.

She pulled in some air in a deep breath. Time to centre herself again. From now on she would only see Xavier during working hours. She could resist the number-crunching, budget-controlling, neat-freak doctor she saw at work. It was the off-duty Xavier who completely undid her.

Work would protect her. But she needed a job for that. She straightened her shoulders and headed inside. Flicking on the computer, she emailed past and present clients, asking for their support for the programme.

CHAPTER SIX

'*BONJOUR*, Jane. How are you this morning?' Xavier neared the end of his postnatal rounds. 'Are you and Master Jack ready to head home?' He caressed the top of the baby's head, marvelling at how neatly it fitted into the palm of his hand.

'Just about ready, Doctor. Jack's got a bit of a sticky cord.'

Xavier pulled the nappy clear of the cord and took a peek. 'Make sure you clean it with a cotton bud twice a day, using some saline, and fold the nappy down so it doesn't rub on it.'

He washed his hands. 'In fact, let the little one have a kick without a nappy for half an hour. Some fresh air will help clean it up.'

Jane looked relieved. 'Thanks, Doctor. Sister Jamieson has made an appointment for me to see you in six weeks.'

'Good. I will see you then. Meanwhile, enjoy this little man.'

Humming, he left the ward and turned toward his office. He loved seeing new families head home to start their lives. He loved getting that last 'goodbye' cuddle and breathing in that 'new baby' smell of fresh soap and breast milk. It sure beat battling with the budget.

'*Bonjour*, Dorothy,' Xavier greeted his secretary. 'Looks like another hot day.'

'Indeed it does, Doctor. Warm days and warm nights. I'm looking forward to a cool change coming soon so I can sleep again.'

Xavier recalled how he'd tossed and turned last night, tangling his normally cool cotton sheets into a long, tight rope. He couldn't blame the summer heat. His restlessness had lain in dreams filled with alabaster skin, long, long legs and sparkling eyes.

He couldn't fathom his reaction to Charlotte. He didn't want to lust after her. These feelings were completely unwanted. Totally confusing.

He might not be able to control his dreams but he could certainly control his daytime thoughts. Today would be a Charlotte-free day. He needed some space.

'Any correspondence?' Xavier rested his briefcase on the edge of his secretary's desk.

'Quite a bit today, Doctor. The letters are on your desk and you need to check your emails. About fifty emails came in, all regarding the community midwifery programme.'

'Fifty? Mostly responses from the health department I imagine.' Xavier turned to go into his office.

'Actually, they're from community members.' Dorothy smiled. 'It seems that Amaroo is well versed in the latest technology. Text messages are building up on the phone as well.'

He paused and turned back to Dorothy. 'Community members?'

'Yes, Doctor. Women who have all been part of the community midwifery project.' She gave him a sympathetic look. 'I also have twenty-five phone messages and six requests for appointments, including a request for an interview by the local radio station.' Dorothy handed him a sheaf of papers.

Xavier's stomach dropped. 'Are these all about the community midwifery programme as well?'

'Yes, Doctor, they are. I'll make you some coffee. I think you're going to need it.'

Xavier walked into his office, punched the button on his computer and sank down into his chair. Usually the plush leather gave him pleasure but not today. Had Charlotte turned an internal budget issue into a political hot potato?

He scanned the emails, all from women who had been cared for in pregnancy and labour by Charlotte, all extolling the virtues of the programme. The phone messages reflected similar sentiments.

He punched his intercom button. 'Dorothy, find Charlotte and request her to come to my office immediately.'

'*Alors!*' He pushed his seat back and jumped to his feet, his frustration rising. He didn't need this. He had a budget to balance and he had to provide comprehensive health care to Amaroo. And that couldn't happen without some changes. The community couldn't afford to lose their hospital.

This was supposed to have been a straightforward process.

The intercom buzzed and Dorothy's voice crackled through the speaker. 'Ms Buchanan to see you.'

Xavier strode to the door and whipped it open, resisting the urge to pull Charlie in by the wrists. 'I'm glad you were able to come over so quickly.' His clipped tone barely held his frustration in check.

'Is something wrong?' Concern hung heavy on the words. Her eyes scanned his face, searching for clues, while her teeth worried her bottom lip.

The vulnerable action derailed him. His chest tightened, air shuddered into his lungs. He fought the urge to haul her into his arms and bury his face in her hair.

He struggled for control, reminding himself he was furious with her. 'Sit down, please.'

Confusion lined her face but she sat, never taking her eyes away from his.

He seated himself behind his desk, needing the barrier between them. 'Have you started an action group to save community midwifery?' The words cut through the silence.

'Pardon?'

'An action group—you know, people who rally and rage against what they see as injustice.'

She straightened her shoulders, an almost defiant movement. 'I *know* what an action group is. No, I haven't organised an action group. Why?'

He picked up the sheaf of papers and waved them. 'Then can you explain why my email box is jammed, why the phone rings constantly and why the KROO breakfast announcer wants to interview me about the petition to keep the community midwifery programme operating?'

'A petition—really?' She relaxed slightly and smiled at him, as if he were a confused child. 'I guess it's because people care. Women care. Rural people constantly have to fight for services and they're strongly attached to their hospital.'

He clenched his fingers into a fist. 'I am attached to this hospital, too. I am trying to save it.' He thumped the papers back down on the desk.

Charlie started in her seat. She laced her hands. 'Xavier, if people feel they're about to lose something, they fight. The French have a great history of protest—this is surely nothing new to you.' She crossed her legs. 'I sent a few emails. It looks like things have gained a bit of momentum.'

'A bit of momentum!' He riffled through the papers. 'There

is a petition to the minister and press releases.' He pushed them toward her. 'Charlotte, I have directives from higher up to pull the budget into line. I have to live in this community too, and you casting me as the bad guy is not helping.'

A brief look of contrition flared, quickly followed by determination. She folded her arms across her chest. 'I have *not* cast you as the bad guy. You're doing a good job of that on your own.'

Her temper hit him full in the chest.

Unfair. He'd inherited this financial problem and the baggage that went with it. He spoke through gritted teeth. 'You know the hospital debt has to be dealt with, Charlotte. You are sticking your head in the sand if you think otherwise.'

She leaned forward. 'I'm doing everything I can to show you women need this programme. I asked ten women to write to you so you could hear the stories behind the programme and move beyond the numbers. Granted, it seems to have got out of hand but I'm not going to apologise for that because it proves what I have been saying all along. This programme is needed.'

She sat in front of him, so convinced of her programme. *I only ever wanted to deliver babies.* Her words from last night boomed in his head, merging with the sting of her words about him being the bad guy.

Anger steamed inside him and words poured out of him uncensored. 'Is this programme needed by the community or needed by you? Have you ever considered that this job is sheltering you from living your life to the full? From taking emotional risks?'

Her face drained of colour—white on white.

Regret poured through him. He'd had no right to say what he had.

She stood up. 'Xavier, I'm sorry you're having a bad day,

but don't take it out on me.' She turned abruptly and walked toward the door.

'Charlotte, please, wait.'

She didn't turn, but strode out of his office, her back ramrod stiff. The door slammed closed behind her.

He hurled a French invective into the silence. Over the years he'd learned to keep his Mediterranean temper in check, especially out of Europe. Australians didn't understand the spark and the regret.

But Charlotte had pushed every button, she had crossed the line, she...

Has got you completely bamboozled.

He spun around and stared out at the shimmering ocean, his thoughts in turmoil. She frustrated him, intrigued him, filled his thoughts, sparked his professional admiration and fired his blood.

She made his emotions swing from complete exasperation to a deep longing. And that bit of insight didn't help him at all.

He ran his hand through his hair. The *only* thing he did know was that right now he owed Charlotte an apology.

Charlie vigorously tugged at the weeds in her vegetable patch, ignoring the scorching heat of the afternoon sun. As she pulled each weed out from the dark earth she pictured a black-haired, black-eyed doctor who'd caused her more turmoil in two short weeks than anyone she could remember.

She loved her work. Women deserved her programme. She hated the idea that everything she'd worked so hard to achieve could just vaporise.

She flung a weed into the bin. Then another. And another. But the physical satisfaction quickly waned. Her conscience pricked her.

She'd lost her temper, which wasn't like her. But the man generated such a surge of different emotions inside her that she'd spoken before she'd thought. Still, that was no excuse. She needed to apologise for calling him a bad guy.

She pushed her hands into the soil, the pain of his words coming back. Was her job sheltering her from living her life? Could he be right? Was she hiding behind work?

She rested back on her heels. No! She loved her job immensely. She enjoyed the acceptance she got from the Amaroo community. But that didn't mean she was *hiding* behind her job.

His words meant nothing. They were just a response to her hurtful words. He'd fired back—who wouldn't?

Except his words kept beating in her head like a slow drum and her answer didn't seem quite so convincing any more.

She squished the unsettling thoughts back down where they belonged. Life was what you made of it. She hadn't found it a hardship to fill her life with a job she loved. It was a heck of a lot easier than relationships.

She loved her independent Amaroo life. Just because Xavier had arrived—tall, dark, and handsome with a voice that sent shimmers of liquid heat radiating through her—it was no reason to start rethinking her life.

She'd created a full life here. A gorgeous Frenchman, who filled her dreams, didn't change a thing.

Enough. She planned to enjoy the pleasures of a quiet, country afternoon. Tomorrow, and apologising to Xavier would come soon enough.

Grabbing the hose, she turned on the water and sprinkled the cottage garden. Serenity trickled through her. She always found watering the garden soothing. The ducks waddled over, quacking enthusiastically at the sight of the cool, clear water.

Spanner raced around, trying to round them up. Charlie delighted in squirting them all with water, the cacophony of noise enveloping her.

'Charlotte?'

Startled, she turned with the hose in her hand. Shock rooted her to the spot. Xavier. Why? How? She hadn't heard his car.

'Charlotte!' He hopped up and down, trying to dodge the water that cascaded from the hose straight at him.

She swung the hose to the side.

He stood in front of her completely soaked—his Armani shirt clinging to his broad chest, outlining every muscle, every sinew.

Her stomach flipped, lust fired every nerve ending into a tingling whirl. 'Sorry.' The word sounded strangled and hoarse. 'You gave me a fright and I didn't expect...'

She watched, fascinated, as his hands pulled at his damp shirt. The neat-freak doctor who was always so well presented looked bedraggled and out of place.

She started to laugh. It bubbled up from deep inside her and no matter how she tried to stop it, the laughter rang out loud and clear.

'What's so funny?' Xavier fumed, looking like a fretful little boy who hadn't got his own way. 'I came up here to apologise to you and before I can get a word out you soak me.'

Charlie sucked in her lips to try to stop her laughter. 'Lighten up, Xavier. I've just found a second calling for you. You should consider entering a wet T-shirt competition.'

He took a step toward her, his eyes darkening into polished onyx. 'Is that so?'

'Yep, you might come in third or fourth.' She giggled at her own joke.

'Really? And how about you, Charlotte?' His rich voice

sent sweet sensations tingling through her. 'Where would you place?'

Her mind blanked. The world stilled.

He closed the gap between them, holding her gaze. 'Got you!' In an instant he'd grabbed her wrist and wrestled control of the hose, sending the spray back over her.

'Low blow! This is war.' Laughing, Charlie half turned, reaching for the hose, but he changed hands over her head, encircling her with his arms. She reached up to pull his arms down in an attempt to get the hose back, her palm circling corded muscle.

His laughter joined hers, a deep-timbred laugh that resonated through her. 'What a shame you can't reach it.'

Never able to resist a dare, Charlie took a lunge at the hose, knocking them both off balance. The sodden garden under her feet gave no resistance and she tumbled backwards.

Gripping Xavier's forearms, trying to steady herself, she brought him down with her into the muddy garden.

She opened her eyes to see his mud-splattered face leaning over her.

'Are you OK?' He spoke softly, concern filling his voice.

'Yes.' The word came out on a breath.

He moved slightly closer. 'I'm sorry I upset you this morning. I was out of line. In my anger I thought you'd been politically agitating to cause me grief. Which, of course, you had not. I lashed out at you and I'm really sorry.'

His breath caressed her cheek, his closeness surrounding her like a cloak. Warm. Comforting. 'I'm sorry, too. I shouldn't have called you the bad guy. We both said things we shouldn't.'

'We did, *chérie*.' His finger ran down her cheek.

'Yes.' Her heart hammered wildly against her chest.

His mouth came down gently onto her lips, a soft grazing kiss, a slight hesitation, almost a question.

She answered the question with a kiss of her own, running the tip of her tongue along his lips, exploring the unexpected softness, savouring his taste.

The noise of the ducks and the dog faded into the background. Nothing existed but the singing sensation of his lips under her tongue. Gentle warmth glowed deep inside her, fanning out and rolling languidly through her veins. She wanted the sanctuary of his arms again.

She wanted this kiss.

She ran her hands up into his wet hair, her fingers exploring, massaging and memorising the contours of his head, pulling him closer to her.

Xavier groaned, deepening the kiss, his tongue probing and thrusting, exploring, demanding, coaxing and giving.

The heat of his body fanned her languid warmth, igniting it into a raging fire. Desire thundered through her, stunning her with its intensity. She matched his kiss, thrust for thrust, wanting to explore him, feel him, touch him, absorb a part of him into herself.

His hand found her breast, his thumb grazing her nipple. She shuddered as waves of longing crashed through her, releasing the cap she'd forced down on her emotions long ago.

Hot, hungry need exploded inside her. She wanted him so much. She wanted his caring, his safe arms and his hot, demanding kisses.

She arched against him, willing him to extend his touch, to explore her body as she explored his. She pulled at his shirt and ran her hands along the length of his back, feeling his muscles taut under her fingers.

'Waah-waah-waah.'

The noise sliced into her haze of desire like a knife. She pulled backed. Cool air rushed into the space between them. 'Listen! Is that a baby crying?'

Xavier raised himself on his elbows, straining to hear.

The cry sounded again.

'I think it is.' Xavier's hoarse voice rang with disbelief. 'Where's the cry coming from?' He pulled Charlie to her feet.

She scanned the home paddock but couldn't see any cars other than Xavier's. There were no signs of any other visitors. 'I'll check the four sides of the veranda and you check the shed.' She pushed him in the right direction.

She ran to the veranda, looked under chairs, in doorways, in every nook and cranny. But there was no sign of a baby.

Racing inside, she grabbed towels, picked up her emergency medical bag and headed back outside, running toward the shed.

As she reached the small structure Xavier rounded the corner, carrying a baby, his face taut with worry and disbelief. 'I found her! I thought we were going mad, hearing a baby crying out here, but someone has abandoned their baby behind your shed.'

'Thank goodness we heard her.' Charlie gently rubbed the infant, drying the amniotic fluid and some of her mother's blood from her skin, while Xavier held her in his arms. She focused on the task, suppressing the pain that surged inside her at the thought that a new life could start this way.

Xavier wrapped a second towel around the baby, hugging her close. Tenderness filled his face as he gazed down at the little girl. 'She's not an hour old and she's hungry.' He put his finger in her mouth and the baby latched on, sucking furiously.

'I bet she's cold.' Charlie reached into her bag and pulled out a thermometer. She expertly tucked it under the baby's arm. 'I hope she's not badly hypothermic. We'll know in two minutes. Let's take her inside.'

They ran to the house. As they waited for the thermometer to beep Charlie glanced at Xavier. Anger, despair and pain etched his face as he examined the baby.

'Her cord has been tied off with a shoelace. At least that happened before she was left alone.' His voice cracked. 'The mother must have felt abandoned herself. How does this happen? How do these needy people fall through our network of care?'

Charlie shared his pain and squeezed his arm. 'Often they don't feel they can come to us. Hospitals can be scary places for many people.'

She looked at the sweet face of the newborn. Conflicting emotions collided inside her. Joy at a new life. Immense sadness that a woman had gone through labour alone.

The thermometer beeped. 'She's cold, you're wet and the wet shirt won't be helping. Give her to me.' Charlie pulled off her shirt and placed the baby against her chest, wrapping a dry towel around both of them. 'Skin-to-skin contact works better than heated blankets.'

Xavier nodded. 'We need to get this little one to hospital and organise a search for her mother. She could be bleeding heavily. Who do we call from the State Emergency Service?'

'Call Helen in Emergency and she'll contact the ambulance and the SES.'

The baby snuggled against Charlie. A surge of protectiveness welled up inside her. With one small movement the baby brought to the surface all the feelings she'd pushed down deep when she'd left Richard. Leaving him had meant leaving behind the dream of a child...children.

She bit her lip and dragged her mind back to what needed

doing. She couldn't think about that now. The baby needed her care. Rummaging through her workbag, she found a disposable nappy. With trembling fingers she fastened it onto the baby's skinny bottom.

She grabbed a cotton hankie and fashioned a funny hat to trap the heat of the baby's head. Then she pulled on a baggy overshirt and buttoned it up around her and the baby.

She heard Xavier's deep voice on the phone to the hospital. The man was soaked to the skin and needed to change. Holding the baby tightly with one arm, she flung clothes out of her wardrobe with her free arm until she found an old pair of painting overalls that might fit Xavier.

He hung up the phone. 'The ambulance is coming for the baby and Helen is contacting Andrew Dennis for the search.'

'Great. Here, put these on.' She tossed the overalls to him.

'*Merci.*' He quickly hauled his wet shirt off, shucked his trousers and pulled on the overalls.

Charlie glimpsed corded muscle on taut thighs. Heat pooled inside her. She moved her gaze to the baby.

He walked over to her. 'Very fetching hat.' He ran his hand gently over the baby's head and sighed.

Her chest tightened at the caring, protective action. Xavier would make a wonderful father one day.

'Should one of us go with the baby?' If she focused on the baby then crazy stray thoughts about babies and parents couldn't take hold.

'No. We don't have a lot of daylight left. Helen is contacting Stuart so the baby will be in caring hands. We have to find her mother. Every minute counts.'

A siren pierced the air and they ran outside. The ambulance officers jumped out of the rig and Charlie met them at the steps.

'The baby seems fine, just hungry and a bit cold.' She unbuttoned the overshirt.

James Rennison took the baby from her arms. 'We'll warm her up in the isolette. Good luck with finding her mother.' He closed the doors of the vehicle and his partner drove away toward Amaroo.

Coldness invaded the space where the baby had snuggled against her. Emptiness flooded in. She was used to holding babies and handing them back to their mothers. But this was different. This time there was no mother.

Frustration jagged through her. She knew circumstances forced some women to take drastic action, but... Should she ever have a baby, she'd hold her so tightly she'd never let her go.

Xavier stepped forward, taking her hand. 'Come, Charlotte, you'll see her later. Are there any buildings on the property that the mother might be in?'

'The Purcells have a haystack about half a kilometre away. Then there's the Harris farmhouse, but generally Sue Harris is at home.' She turned around and swung her arm out. 'This direction is the beach and the caves.'

'Let's start with the haystack.' Xavier strode decisively toward the car.

Charlie grabbed her bag and followed.

He vigorously threw the gear stick into reverse and swung the car around, his face a mask of determination. The rutted track tested the suspension of the luxury vehicle. Charlie gripped the doorhandle for support.

The haystack came into view, its corrugated-iron roof shimmering from trapped summer heat. Xavier hauled on the handbrake and jumped out of the car, making straight toward the shed.

Charlie grabbed her medical bag and ran after him. As she approached the doorway she heard him calling 'Hello.'

She glanced around as her eyes adjusted to the dimness of the hay shed. Hay stood ten feet high and mice ran along the rafters. An involuntary shiver ran through her when she thought about snakes.

'I don't think she's here.' Xavier jogged back to the entrance. 'It's full of hay. There's no place to hide.'

Charlie put her hand out. 'Give me your phone. I'll ring the Harrises and ask Sue to start looking around their outbuildings.'

He passed it over to her. She checked the display as they walked outside. 'Damn, no signal. Come on, we'll walk up the hill.'

Xavier paced next to her, frustration, agitation and worry rolling off him in waves.

She put her arm on his. 'We'll find her, Xavier.'

'*Oui*, but we both know what can happen.' His voice was grim. 'She could have dropped three litres of blood by now in a post-partum haemorrhage.'

'I know but we're doing everything we can. The SES will start searching in the caves and we can join them if we draw a blank here.'

He gave an unintelligible grunt and spun on his heel, heading further up the rise.

Charlie concentrated on plugging in the numbers for Sue Harris, willing the phone to find a signal. On the third attempt it rang.

Suddenly, Xavier yelled out, pointing to a small building on the other side of the hill. 'What's that?'

Charlie turned, shielding her eyes with her hand against the blinding sun. 'It's the Harrises' pump-shed but there'd barely be enough room…'

Xavier sprinted down the hill toward the dam, his athletic stride never faltering despite loose rocks.

She bit her lip, watching him disappear around the far side of the shed. He'd gone on a wild-goose chase for sure. The pump-house barely held the pump—there would be no room for a woman. And Ron Harris would have it padlocked.

'Charlotte.' He reappeared, waving frantically. 'She's here!' He immediately disappeared from view.

Adrenaline burst through her, putting every muscle and nerve on full alert. She ran down the steep slope, her bag banging against her leg. She rounded the pump-house.

Xavier was squatting down next to a pale young teenage girl. She was backed up against the shed wall, her face lined with fear, her body language screaming that she'd bolt if she could.

'It is all right, I am a doctor.' Xavier spoke quietly with his hands loosely by his sides in a non-threatening position.

The girl looked at him, her eyes full of disbelief. She took in the paint-splattered overalls, and his mud-stained face and hair. 'You don't *look* like a doctor.'

Charlie laughed in relief and dropped down next to her. 'You're right, he doesn't. But he really is. I'm Charlie and this is Xavier. What's your name?'

The girl studied them for a moment, sizing them up. 'Jade.'

Charlie put her hand on the young girl's arm. 'We found your baby, Jade, and she's fine.'

For a brief moment the girl's shoulders slumped and her face crumpled. But then she threw her head up. 'I dunno what you're talking about.'

Xavier leaned back. 'It must be our day for finding people in sheds. The baby we found was gorgeous. A little bit cold but fit and healthy. And now we've found you, and we want to make sure you're fit and healthy, too.'

Suddenly the girl's façade fell away and she moaned, grabbing her stomach. 'I thought once I'd had the baby these pains would stop, but they haven't.' Tears brimmed and overflowed, streaming down her cheeks.

'It's OK, Jade.' Charlie gave her a hug. 'Xavier and I are here to help you. But we're going to need to examine you.'

The girl sobbed. 'Blood keeps running down my leg and I feel real dizzy.'

'Lie down on me.' Charlie guided the girl's shoulders onto her lap and at the same time checked the carotid pulse. She shook her head in concern. 'Xavier, her pulse is one hundred and two and thready. There's Syntocinon in my bag.'

Xavier frowned in concern. He snapped open the ampoule with a crack and drew it up. 'Jade, you're losing a lot of blood. This injection will stop the bleeding so we can deliver the placenta, the afterbirth.'

'No!' Jade tried to rise up off Charlie's lap.

He put his hand gently on Jade's leg. 'I know you are scared, but this little injection is nothing compared to what you have just been through. You've had a baby all on your own. This will be a tiny scratch in comparison.'

Jade nodded unwillingly, her lips compressed in a firm line.

Charlie stroked her patient's hair while Xavier expertly administered the injection via a butterfly needle into Jade's arm. 'In a minute you're going to get a big contraction and then Xavier will gently deliver the placenta.'

Jade pulled her legs up. 'Aagh-h!'

'Jade, I have to put my hand on your stomach.' Xavier applied counter-pressure to her abdomen while pulling carefully on the cord. The placenta slithered out, followed by a gush of blood.

'Well done, Jade. That was excellent.' He gave her leg a squeeze. 'You did so well with that injection, and soon you will be an expert. One more needle, OK, so we can give you some fluid so you don't feel so dizzy.'

'I s'pose.' Jade's buried her face in Charlie's lap as Xavier quickly slipped the cannula into her arm.

He stood up. 'We have to get you to hospital, Jade. How about a ride in an ambulance?'

The teenager's pale face flushed with a hint of exhausted excitement. 'Cool.'

'Charlotte, I'll ring the hospital from the hill.'

Charlie nodded and handed him the phone. 'Tell Helen we're at the Harris dam, the paramedics will know where to come.'

Jade snuggled into Charlie as they watched Xavier run up the hill. 'Coolest doctor I've ever met. I could listen to him talk all day. Kinda makes up for those daggy overalls.'

Charlie smiled. 'Yeah, he's pretty cool.' Her gaze followed him up the hill, the daggy overalls exposing broad shoulders and solid biceps.

She pulled her mind back to her patient. 'I have to check your pulse and blood pressure.' She busied herself with the observations and monitoring the drip, happy to see a rise in Jade's blood pressure.

Soon they heard the siren of the ambulance as it drove down the corrugated track. With an expertise born of experience they quickly loaded Jade into the ambulance.

Xavier started to climb into the rig and then stopped, turning back to Charlie, gently touching her arm. 'I'll go with Jade. Can you drive the car back for me?'

'Sure. I'll bring it to the hospital.'

'*Merci.*' He gave her a grin. 'Be careful of the suspension.'

The ambulance door closed on her before she could think

of a cheeky reply. She walked back to the car, the events of the evening running through her head. How did a fifteen-year-old manage to hide her pregnancy from her family? Jade was a child herself and she'd given birth to a baby. At least they were both safe and well.

Thank goodness Xavier had found her before she'd bled to death.

He'd been like a bloodhound on the trail, determined to find the baby, almost frantic. The pain on his face and his air of desperation haunted her. She hadn't expected that.

There was so much more to this man than designer clothes, a fixation on neatness and a take-charge attitude. He'd been brilliant with Jade. Most consultants had no idea how to talk to teenagers, but he'd treated her with the same respect he gave his older pregnant patients. And he'd gained her trust, which was no mean feat.

She climbed into the driver's seat. The scent of leather, mingling with citrus and soap, assaulted her senses. Xavier's scent. She breathed in deeply. The memory of his kiss replayed vividly in her mind—the touch of his lips against hers, the feel of the length of his body pressed against her, the caress of his fingers on her hot skin, creating rivers of delicious longing.

Her heart pounded faster at the thought.

She leaned her head against the steering-wheel. In one moment, one kiss had changed everything. One kiss had exacerbated her loneliness, and hinted at what was missing in her life. What *she* was missing.

One kiss had proved that she wanted to be in his arms, feel his weight against her, and have his warmth surrounding her.

But she couldn't have that.

Right now I am not looking for a relationship at all. Xavier had been crystal-clear about that. He'd even said that if he changed his mind about a relationship, it would not be with someone from work.

Why on earth was she even thinking like this? The thought of a relationship terrified her. A pain edged in under her ribs. More importantly, even if she would consider it, Xavier didn't want her.

The CD in the nursery played quietly in the corner and Xavier hummed along as he fed Jade's baby. He'd sent the nursing staff away—this was *his* time with the baby. She needed love and caring because she'd had a tough start in an even tougher world. No one deserved to be abandoned.

One of her tiny hands escaped from the bunny rug, her little fingers finding and gripping his shirt. His heart turned over, longing tugging at him so hard it hurt.

Painful memories flooded him—his child, the baby he'd never held. A life cut short before it had started. The life he'd imagined, rubble at his feet.

He pushed the thoughts away. It all belonged in the past, back in France. It was pointless revisiting it.

Australia meant a new start.

Charlotte's oval face floated across his mind. He pictured her standing in her garden, her auburn hair cascading down her back, her face alive with the joy of living. The memory of her laughter sounded in his ears.

She had tasted of sunshine and freshness, as her glorious mouth, warm and hard against his, had sent her energy flowing into him, creating a need deep inside him that he could no longer deny.

But she didn't see a partner or family in her future.

And no way was he repeating past mistakes.

So where the hell did that leave them?

CHAPTER SEVEN

CHARLIE pulled into the hospital car park, the twenty-minute journey from the farm passing quickly in the smooth ride a European luxury car offered. She parked Xavier's pride and joy, blipped the car alarm and headed toward Special Care Nursery.

She wanted—no, she needed—a cuddle with the baby. Her arms had ached with emptiness since giving the baby over to the paramedics.

Charlie reached the nursery door and pushed her palm against it. Suddenly she pulled back, the unexpected change in momentum making her sway. Her gaze zeroed in on the image through the glass. Xavier sat reclined in a rocker, crooning softly and expertly tilting the bottle as the baby sucked hungrily. The image of a father with his baby.

The ache inside her intensified. *Your job won't give you the love of a family.* Xavier's message tore through her.

Tears filled her eyes. She'd fought so hard to get away from her stifling family, to carve out an independent life so different from her mother's. And she'd achieved that. She enjoyed being her own person.

The emptiness inside her expanded. She bit her lip. Everything she believed about her life suddenly seemed hazy.

Things that had been crystal clear now blurred in a fog of bewilderment. Everything she'd clung to now seemed unsteady, ready to slip out from under her.

But knowing that just confused her more. If she didn't want a relationship, and her current life was no longer satisfying, then what did she want?

She grabbed a towel off the linen trolley and wiped her face, the remnants of the mud turning the white towel brown. Terrific. She felt emotionally wrung out and she probably looked like hell. Didn't matter, she'd come to hug a baby.

With a deep breath and years of practice she schooled her face into an impassive mask, hiding the swirling blackness that threatened to swamp her. She plastered a smile on her face and walked into the nursery, across to Xavier.

'How is she?' Charlie caressed the baby's head.

Xavier glanced up and smiled. '*Adorable.* Fit, healthy and as hungry as a horse.'

'And Jade?' She focused on keeping her voice light, while his smile made her heart beat in crazy jerks.

His brows drew together in concern. 'I'm keeping an eye on her bleeding. She might need a curette, even though the placenta looked intact. I think a bit got left behind.'

'Let's hope she won't have to go to Theatre. She wouldn't be keen on that idea.'

He shrugged. 'I think she was so scared out in the back paddock that a trip to Theatre will be a walk in the park.'

'That's true.' Charlie watched Xavier adjust the bottle so the milk filled the teat. 'You look like you know what you're doing.'

He raised his brows, his eyes sparkling. 'You sound surprised.'

'I am. Most blokes without kids are all fingers and thumbs.'

She looked at his shoulder, rather than risking the glorious, mind-numbing effects of his gaze. She needed to stay detached.

He smiled a wide smile. 'I am an uncle six times over. I have changed many nappies, walked the floors at night and been dribbled on more times than you can imagine.'

'Ah, an expert.' She sat down next to him and put her finger onto the baby's palm, enjoying the vice-like grip that followed. Trying to ignore the warmth that came when she thought about Xavier as an uncle.

'*Non*, it's just children and family has always been a big part of my life. I have four brothers and one sister. Our parents gave us a wonderful childhood on the farm. I remember Maman greeting us after school with mountains of food.' He sighed. 'I'd always imagined I'd be a father by now.' A wistful tone entered his voice.

Something deep inside her turned over 'So what's stopped you?' She wanted to know. Desperately.

He lifted the baby high onto his shoulder to burp her.

She waited out his silence.

'I spent two years with the wrong woman. I thought we were on the same level family-wise, that we wanted the same things out of life.' Bitterness filled his words. 'It turns out I was totally wrong.'

She wrinkled her nose in understanding, thinking about Richard and how she'd totally misread him. 'I can relate to that.'

His chiselled face hardened. 'Our future plans, it seemed, never meshed. Ambitious under-describes her. While I was busy planning our life together, she was busy planning the next step in her medical career. I was one of those steps. Once she'd achieved what she wanted, she discarded me and our unborn child.'

His pain speared her, trapping her breath in her lungs. 'Oh, God, I'm so sorry.' She reached out instinctively, touching his arm.

He raised his head and gazed into her eyes. For the first time she saw raw and naked hurt. How did a person get over such a betrayal?

He cleared his throat. 'I was so excited when she told me she was pregnant. I missed the signs that she was distracted and distant. I made excuses for her.'

She squeezed his arm, wanting to erase his hurt. 'Sometimes we just don't want to see.' She sighed remembering her own situation with her family.

His black eyes fixed on her in a long, penetrating gaze. 'You're right. I did not want to see and I did not want to look. I'd invested in my dream of a family, a future. She had invested only in herself.'

He stood, laying the now sleeping baby gently in the cot, tucking the bunny rug over her.

His actions tore at her. She hauled herself to her feet, aching for him and the loss of his dreams. All that love waiting to be bestowed on his child. A child that had been torn from him. 'So you came to Australia and to Amaroo?'

'*Oui.* Here I am.'

'With a life plan?'

He shrugged. 'No plan. I planned in France and it all exploded in my face.'

She tilted her head, needing to confront his statement. 'You told me once that you would date again, but only outside medicine. That sounds like a plan, although perhaps today when you kissed me you got confused.'

His guilty look ripped into her.

Her heart bled a little.

He stepped closer. '*Chérie*, I don't regret kissing you. There's been something between us since we met. Neither of us can deny that.' His eyes met hers, willing her to agree. 'You're a stunning, vibrant, desirable woman.'

She swayed toward him, her heart racing, a delicious bubble of joy floating through her body.

'But neither of us are ready for a relationship. And even if I was, I will not have a future with someone I work with.'

The bubble burst. Reality cascaded over her.

Creases furrowed his brow. 'It does not work. I have seen too many fail.'

She shook her head, thinking hypothetically. 'It could work, if both people really wanted it to, if both people were willing to give a little.'

Discomfort radiated from him. 'Charlotte, I'm sorry, but I'm reviewing your programme, things could change and I'm…'

Panic almost paralysed her. Embarrassment burned her cheeks. Oh, God, he thought she was talking about the two of them being a couple. Words rushed from her mouth. 'Xavier, I'm not suggesting *we* would work. Hell, I doubt we would. I just want to know where we stand after that kiss.'

He moved closer to her and every nerve ending shimmered with anticipation.

'Where do you want to stand?' He tucked loose strands of hair behind her ear. 'We are both refugees from failed relationships.' He stroked her face. 'Perhaps we are each other's transitional partner. The person who readies you for the next serious relationship.'

Her mind struggled to absorb his words, deal with what he was suggesting. 'So, you think we should have an *affair* until you find your ideal partner outside work?'

He leaned toward her, his dark hair gleaming under the warm nursery lights. 'Or until you realise you can risk loving again. Why not go with this overwhelming attraction instead of losing hours agonising over what we should do?'

Her heart missed a beat. 'You've agonised?' Wonder fanned out inside her.

His hand rested on her shoulder. 'I have lost more sleep than I can blame on the heat.'

She smiled, hugging the knowledge to herself. He wanted her as much as she wanted him.

But knowing and doing were two different things. An affair? Give into the lust, passion and desire, and to hell with the consequences? She'd never done anything like that.

Right, and what you've tried in the past really worked well—not. Trying to be someone she wasn't for Richard certainly hadn't worked. And today had shown her that shunning all relationships had only left her with an empty space inside her.

She tried to get her mind around his idea. 'So we go with the flow? Accept each other as we are?'

'Exactly. We go into it knowing it won't last for ever. And we walk away when one of us says it's time.'

His hand wound into her hair, showering her in sparks of yearning. She breathed in deeply, trying to organise her thoughts. 'We walk away, no questions asked?'

'None.'

An affair meant she could be her own person, no strings attached. His thigh rested gently against hers, his heat scorching her skin, fuelling her need to be in his arms again. *What have you got to lose?*

'Do you want this, *chérie*?' Desire blazed brightly in his eyes.

She wrapped her arms around his neck, claiming him. 'I do. But I have to tell you, this is my first affair and I have no idea what to do.'

A wicked grin streaked across his face. 'We'll have fun working it out.' He cupped her chin in his hands, his fingers stroking her cheeks. Slowly, he lowered his lips to hers, caressing them with his own, stoking the smouldering coals of her need into raging flames. Sealing their decision.

She returned his kiss, drinking him in like drought-parched soil absorbing water. Using his mouth, hot and demanding against her own, to drive away lingering doubts and fears that scuttled around the edges of her consciousness.

Her tongue explored, seeking his energy and heat, his primal need of her. Her hands flicked under the cotton gown, her fingers burning as they explored the solid muscle of his back.

She tossed her head back, her breath shortening as his mouth explored her neck, his tongue branding a trail of fire from her chin to the hollow just above her collarbone. She clung to him, her knees suddenly weak.

The jangling ring of his phone doused her in reality. She jumped back.

He ran his hand through his hair as he read the display. 'Jade is still bleeding. I will have to take her to Theatre.'

He ran his finger down her cheek. 'You need to go home, Charlotte, to your bed. But tomorrow is Saturday and I want you to pack your swimming costume and be ready at eleven. I promise you an uninterrupted kiss and a day of delights. *Au revoir.*' He dropped a kiss on the top of her head and strode out of the nursery.

Trembling, she watched him disappear down the corridor. She'd just taken a huge step into the unknown, with no map or compass. And tomorrow couldn't come quickly enough.

* * *

Xavier whistled as he drove up Charlie's rutted drive. He'd done his rounds early and had been home to collect the picnic hamper. He'd packed runny Brie, a fresh baguette, home-made olive tapenade, goat's cheese, round red tomatoes and roquette. He sighed at the lack of real French pastries but he'd packed champagne instead. Chilled and ready to go.

Phil Carson had given him directions to a quiet stretch of beach only accessible to those who knew where to find the track. He had food, he had a venue and soon he would have Charlotte.

Spanner raced to greet him as he parked.

'Hey girl, where's your owner?' He scratched the dog behind the ears.

Spanner barked in appreciation of the touch and then belted off around the house.

Xavier took the veranda steps in two leaps, anticipation of the day sizzling in his veins.

Charlie called out through an open window. 'Come in. I'll be with you in a minute.'

He pushed open the front door and stepped into a wide hall and then into the lounge room. A stack of CDs tipped rakishly on a small coffee-table. Numerous books and papers lay scattered on the window-seat and some very dead flowers wilted in a vase. His mind went back to her kitchen the other night. As gorgeous as Charlotte was, housekeeping wasn't her forte.

'Hi.' Charlie came breathlessly into the room, pulling on a shoe. 'Sorry to keep you waiting, but the phone rang just as you arrived.'

He moved toward her and took her in his arms. 'No problem. You are here now.' Her wild rose perfume enveloped him as he nuzzled her neck.

She leaned into him, her sigh of pleasure almost undoing

his resolve. But he had a plan for this seduction and it wasn't going to happen in Charlotte's untidy front room.

He stepped back, grabbing her hand. 'Come, I have a great day planned for only us.'

'Xavier.'

The tone in her voice stopped him dead. 'What?'

Contrition fluttered across her face. 'That was Jessica Leeton on the phone. She's not feeling well and I need to check in on her. Can we do it on the way to the picnic?'

Disappointment rammed him. 'Of course. Let's go.' Still holding her hand, he walked her to the car.

Charlie pulled on her seat belt. 'How's Jade?'

'She is fine. But Jade was just the start of a very long night.' He did a three-point turn and headed toward the main road.

Charlie half turned in her seat. 'What happened?'

He looked at her. Her head was tilted to one side, genuine interest and caring written on her face. Genevieve had never wanted to know about his work unless it had pertained to her.

'Erica Chambers started bleeding and we had to airlift her to Melbourne. It was touch and go there for a while. And the history retrieval system fell over. We almost had to send her without her file. The medical records temporary secretary was hopeless and could not file or find a thing.'

Charlie laughed, a warm tinkling sound, completely unsympathetic to his woes. 'Oh, dear, an untidy temp. That would be enough to send a neat freak like you into therapy.'

'I am *not* that neat.' Indignation rolled through him.

'Oh, please.' She gave him a sly look. 'In four years I never saw the wood on Phil Carson's 0desk. You are hard-pressed not to straighten up everything you come in contact with. I'm surprised you don't ask your patients to lie straight in their beds.'

'Actually, that is not a bad idea…' Laughter bubbled up inside him, warming him, relaxing him. He wanted to touch her, lie with her, wrap himself around her. He gripped the steering-wheel. 'How much further to the Leetons'?'

'Next right.' She rested her hand on his thigh.

Heat burned into his skin. Into his blood. 'It's just a quick check-up, right?' His voice came out as a rasp.

She gave him a long, slow smile. 'Thorough but quick.'

Xavier swung the car in next to the house and five children ran out to meet them. As Charlie stepped out of the car, the two youngest children threw themselves at her legs while the older ones all started talking at once.

She scooped up the youngest, tousled the hair of the others in greeting and gave her attention to the eldest girl. 'Becky, this is Dr Laurent. He's new to town so he came along for the ride.'

Surprise filled him at the ease in which she greeted the children.

Becky gave him a shy smile. 'Mum's lying down and told us to keep a lookout for you.'

Charlie moved the toddler more comfortably onto her hip. 'Well done. Can you keep the kids occupied for another ten minutes while we examine your mum?'

'Sure.'

'Thanks, Becky.' She turned, winked and beckoned him to follow.

Heat coursed through him. He breathed deeply and walked inside.

Jessica Leeton lay on her side in a darkened room. He'd met Jessica before. She'd looked tired then and now he understood why. Five kids with a sixth on the way would exhaust anyone.

Charlie squatted down by the side of the bed and touched her patient gently on the arm. 'Jessica, how are you feeling?'

She sighed. 'Tired and a bit light-headed. It's probably the heat.' She sat up slowly and immediately noticed Xavier. 'Why are you both here?' Panic filled her voice. 'Do you think something's wrong?'

He stepped forward, giving a reassuring smile he'd found worked well with patients. 'Actually, Jessica, I came along for the ride as part of my "get to know Amaroo with a local" programme.'

Jessica smiled. 'Technically Charlie isn't a local yet, she's only been here five years.'

Charlie gave a mock huff. 'Thanks very much, Jessica!' She unwrapped the blood-pressure cuff. 'We're going to check you out and see what your blood pressure's doing. Your job is to take a few long deep breaths.'

Charlie listened intently, a small frown etching itself into her forehead as she slowly released the air out of the sphygmomanometer. 'One forty-five over ninety.'

'Is that bad?' Jessica looked anxious.

Xavier sat down next to her. 'It is not terrible, but it is not great. You can stay at home *if* you get someone in to mind the children so you can rest. And by rest I mean you only get up to use the bathroom.'

Jessica sniffed. 'I can ring Mum but she couldn't get here until tomorrow. Brad's still at the stock sales in Gheringya and he won't be back until mid-afternoon. The kids haven't had lunch and…' Tears trickled out from under her lashes.

'Jessica, it's OK.' Charlie passed her a tissue. 'Xavier and

I will look after the kids until Brad gets back, won't we?' Her eyes implored him to agree.

Xavier stifled a long groan. What could he say? *No, we can't because I have a picnic in the car and plans for a hedonistic afternoon?*

'Absolutely, Jessica. You rest and we will organise everything else. Don't worry about *les enfants.*' He grinned. 'Just to make sure they get fed, I will do the cooking.'

Jessica sank into the pillows. 'Thank you so much. Don't worry too much Doctor, the kids would survive Charlie's cooking—they've had worse.'

'Hey!' Charlie put her hands on her hips but a smile danced on her face. 'I can cook. I just don't do it often.' She tucked the bedclothes around Jessica who closed her eyes in relief.

Charlie straightened up and hooked her finger toward him, tilting her head toward the door.

Desire thudded through him. She could go from professional midwife to sultry temptress in a heartbeat.

The moment she'd stepped through into the hall, she gently closed the door behind them. 'Sorry about this.'

He tucked her hair behind her ears, running his fingers along her skin, needing to feel her softness. 'We still have this afternoon. And it's just as well I came. You'll need my help with the children.' He shot her a teasing grin.

She rolled her eyes. 'Is that so?'

'You can deliver them,' he joked, 'but what do you actually know about them once they're a month old?'

Raising her eyebrows, she smiled cheekily. 'You'd be surprised.' She walked to the back door and called the children inside.

They ran in, the back door slamming shut behind them. 'OK, guys, Mum's got to rest and while we're waiting for your dad to get home we're going to have a barbecue down by the dam. So grab your swimming costumes and towels and fishing rods.'

'Awesome!' The two older boys raced down the hall toward their room.

Charlie turned to Xavier, a sassy spark in her eyes. 'You get Jason organised. He's the two-year-old. Just rummage through his cupboards or ask Becky where his bathers and hat are.'

He laughed out loud, suddenly remembering how she could never resist a dare. He'd thrown down the gauntlet with his jibe about not knowing about children and now she was rising to it. He gave her mock salute. *'Oui, mademoiselle.'*

Jason pushed his bottom lip right out and glared at him suspiciously.

He put on his best Australian accent. 'So, mate, let's get ready for a swim.' He extended his hand down toward the child.

Jason stared at it for a moment and then slid his small hand into Xavier's palm.

Warmth and trust encapsulated in one small movement. His heart ached. He wanted a child of his own.

After a bit of a search he dressed Jason in his swimming gear, pulled a top over his head and cajoled him into his hat. Together, they walked back to the kitchen.

Bags of food covered the kitchen table. Charlie stood on a chair, raised up on tiptoe, stretching into the back of a cupboard. A smooth expanse of skin lay exposed as her shirt pulled up.

Soft, enticing, warm. His palm itched to touch it.

'Where's the tomato sauce kept?' Her question hung in the air, asked of no one in particular.

'Try the pantry or the fridge.' Xavier put Jason down on a chair and started to apply sunscreen to his face.

She stepped down from the chair. 'Why the fridge?'

'Ants. They go for the sugar in the sauce.' He grinned, fun and frivolity spinning inside him. 'Ants do not bother going into your pantry because they know there isn't much food in it.'

'Very funny.' She threw the teatowel at him, laughing. 'Not all of us can be a domestic goddess.'

But standing in that small farmhouse kitchen, she shone like a goddess. A frustratingly, unobtainable goddess. He swallowed a groan. His planned picnic lunch looked like turning into dinner. Brad Leeton had better not be late back.

'Come on, Jason.' Charlie handed him a small bag. 'You can help me load the truck.'

'No, stay him.' A pudgy finger pointed at Xavier.

She smiled straight at Xavier over the top of Jason's head, her face alive with vitality. 'You've got a fan there.' She bent down to Jason's eye level. 'Can you show Xavier where the dam is?'

The little boy puffed out his chest. 'Yes.'

'Excellent.' She straightened up and turned to Xavier. 'I'll meet you at the dam with the food and the other children. See you down there.' The screen door banged shut behind her.

Silence descended as the energy in the room faded fast. Charlie had been like a whirling tornado. Stunned, he realised that in less than thirty minutes and with a minimum of fuss she'd organised him, the children and an impromptu picnic.

Ten minutes later he and Jason arrived at the dam, Jason riding high on his shoulders.

'What took you so long?' A smile raced across Charlotte's face as she walked up to greet them.

She stood before him wearing a turquoise sarong slung

low on her hips and a bikini top of matching swirls of blue and green. Heat surged through him. His gaze skimmed every curve of her body, mesmerised by the contours of smooth skin.

She met his gaze, her eyes smoky with desire.

He swallowed hard. 'We couldn't find Jason's floaties.' How could she do this to him? How could she expect him to keep his hands to himself in front of the children while she wore clothes designed for a tropical island for two?

Time for a cold swim. 'So who's for a swim?' He swung Jason down and fitted his floaties around his skinny arms.

'Me! Me! Me, too!' A chorus of voices surrounded him.

'Come on, then.' He ran down to the water, Jason tucked under his arm. Together they swam to the middle of the dam.

A splash ball hit him on the shoulder and he turned to see Charlotte swimming over with the other children in hot pursuit. A barrage of water rained down on him.

Jason laughed with delight.

'OK, mate, time to hit them back.' Xavier handed Jason a ball.

Jason threw but it fell short.

Xavier gathered up three soggy balls and fired them back with a precise overarm throw.

Squeals of delight and indignation rent the air. Suddenly he felt arms on his back and on his legs. Becky and Sarah tried to climb onto his back while Will and Ben pushed at his legs from underwater. A combined effort to dunk him.

'You're a bit outnumbered.'

Charlotte's laughing voice met him as he came up for air.

'I can't imagine who put them up to this.' He gave her a wet grin before quickly grabbing each child and tossing him or her backwards off his shoulders.

They immediately swam back for more.

'I think you've started something.' Charlotte floated quietly on her back, watching the antics, a smile of wicked contentment firmly in place.

'My turn.' Jason kicked his short legs over to Charlie, dumping a wet ball on her face.

She laughed in surprise and rolled over, wiping her eyes.

'Jason, my friend, that is the way.' Xavier swung him around in an arc, revelling in the excited yells of joy.

Charlotte swam over, steadying herself by putting her arms on Xavier's shoulders, encircling Jason. 'You devil, Jason.' Her eyes danced with fun, sparkling in the noon sun. She dropped a kiss on Jason's wet curls.

An odd sensation wove through Xavier. A fleeting moment of tranquillity and belonging.

'Hungry.' Jason poked Xavier in the shoulder.

'It must be time for lunch.' He cupped his hand to his mouth and yelled. 'OK, lunch, everyone!'

Charlotte grinned. 'I guess that's my cue. You cook the snags and I'll butter the bread, OK?'

'Deal.'

She swam quickly to the bank, beating the children, and distributed towels as they came out of the water. As Xavier cooked the sausages he watched her with the kids—opening packets of chips to keep them going until the sausages were cooked, pouring drinks and talking to each of them.

'Who's hungry?' He put the platter of sizzling sausages down on the picnic table.

'Me!' Five voices chorused.

'Right you lot, line up.' Charlotte wrapped sausages in bread and drizzled them with sauce, handing them out as the children passed by.

For five minutes silence reigned as eating took all of the children's attention.

Jason climbed into Xavier's lap. 'Hot. You feed me.'

'OK, mate.' He held the sausage up to Jason's mouth and sauce dribbled down his arm. As he licked the sauce off he looked toward Charlotte.

Six-year-old Sarah was cuddled up next to her, and she had her arm casually slung around Becky's shoulder, leaning in toward her, listening intently to what she was saying. Since she'd promised to mind the children she'd been acting like a mother. Organised, caring, fun.

She looked like a mother.

His chest tightened. He struggled for breath. He'd spent weeks battling his feelings for this woman because he'd convinced himself he could never be with someone he worked with.

Now she sat in front of him looking like Madonna and child.

She'd taken the role of emergency babysitter in her stride, not missing a beat. Nothing fazed her. The children were relaxed and comfortable in her company, and somehow she managed to give each one her attention when they needed it.

She'd gone from midwife to mother before his eyes.

Suddenly pictures floated through his head: Charlotte in his house; Charlotte holding a red-haired baby; Charlotte in the garden, spraying children with the hose. A week ago it would have seemed ludicrous, two hours ago even, but now it seemed natural. As if the missing piece in the jigsaw of his life had been found.

She works with you. He pushed the cautioning words away, focusing instead on Charlotte.

She ran from relationships, replacing love with work. Could he convince her there was another way to live her life?

CHAPTER EIGHT

CHARLIE waved goodbye to the Leetons and ran to Xavier's car through pouring rain. Brad had finally returned from the sale yards and Jane's mother was booked on the morning train.

'Our work here is done.' Xavier planted his foot on the accelerator.

'Sorry about the picnic.' She looked at the rivulets of rain streaming down the windscreen.

'*Oui*, even the weather has conspired against me. It is time to go home.'

Disappointment rammed into her gut. Wasn't an affair supposed to be secret meetings and passionate love-making? Had he changed his mind? For the last couple of hours he'd been uncharacteristically quiet. His teasing had stopped and he seemed lost in thought. Was he regretting last night's proposal of an affair?

Please, no. She wanted this. Needed it.

Xavier passed her gate and headed back into Amaroo. 'At least at my place we can walk on the floor without stepping on anything.' He gave her a teasing grin and ran his fingers gently over the back of her hand.

His touch burned into her. She wanted his fingers exploring more than the back of her hand. 'I wasn't planning on doing a lot of walking.'

His eyes darkened. 'Glad to hear it.'

He took the corner slightly too fast and pulled into his driveway, the car's tyres crunching on the gravel. Jumping out of the car, he quickly jogged around and opened her door.

'Come on.' He grabbed her hand and together they ran through the rain to the front porch. Keeping her hand firmly in his, he pushed the key into the lock, opened the door and gently pulled her inside, out of the rain and into his arms.

She melted against him, her hands cupping his cheeks. She tilted her head, gazing at him, taking in all of him—his ink-black eyes that called to her with their unexpected shards of colour, eyes that saw into her soul. His thick black hair that curled up at the back of his neck and the lines around his eyes and mouth that merged when he smiled at her.

His arms tightened around her. She needed to be in these wondrous arms, feel them cocooning her, cherishing her, no matter how fleeting it might be.

His hands cupped her buttocks, pulling her closer to him, flooding her with his heat. A guttural groan sounded in his throat. '*Chérie*, all day I've wanted to touch you and it's driven me crazy.' He stroked her hair. 'I had a perfect seduction planned.'

Smiling at the knowledge that he wanted her, she brushed his lips with her fingers. 'Over-planning can get you into trouble.'

His eyes flashed at her teasing words, desire blazing in their depths. He plundered her mouth with his, hungrily taking what he'd waited for all day.

A fire of hot, unsated need streaked through her, overwhelming her. She met his kiss, savouring his taste, his feel, his scent. Absorbing a part of him, filling a void.

His moan rumbled deep from his soul, thudding through her veins, testifying to his need of her.

Her knees sagged as longing consumed her.

His words poured out low and gravelly. 'Plan or no plan, I am not making love to you in my hall.' Scooping her into his arms, he carried her to his bedroom, laying her gently on the bed.

He lay down next to her, his gaze fixed firmly on her face. 'You're so beautiful you're driving me crazy.'

'Really?' *I drive him crazy.* A thrill fizzed through her.

'Really.' He leaned forward, caressing her forehead with light, gentle kisses. Between kisses he spoke softly in French, his delicious accent pouring over her like fragrant massage oil.

He rained kisses along her nose, across her cheeks, down her jaw and into the hollows of her neck. Slow, deliberate kisses, imprinting his touch on her, branding her as his.

Waves upon waves of glorious sensation built, sending tendrils of aching pleasure swirling deep inside her.

His low guttural moans matched hers as he pulled frantically at the buttons on her dress, welcoming her tingling breasts as they strained against the lace of her bra.

His thumb caressed her through the lace. Rockets of white-hot need gripped her, bringing her arching against him. He deftly unclipped the bra at the front and dipped his head, his tongue rasping against her swollen nipples.

Colours exploded in her head.

'It's my turn.' The words tumbled out on a breath as she gently pushed him back onto the bed.

'Chérie?' His eyes widened in question.

Slowly, she raised her cotton dress above her head and let it slide languidly from her fingers onto the floor.

His gaze never left her.

Tugging at his shirt, she slid her hands underneath the soft fabric, her palms quivering as they moulded to taut muscle.

He'd used his mouth in an agonisingly tantalising way. She wanted to return the favour. Leaning forward, she undid each button on his shirt with painstaking precision, batting his hand away when he tried to help.

She gave him a sly grin. 'I know you value your clothes so I'll be careful.'

She heard him growl and she laughed, suffused with the power of giving. She turned her attention to his trousers. Her fingers brushed his erection. He groaned.

'I'll do it!' He quickly sat up, and as she moved aside he shucked his trousers.

He stood there tall, powerful and naked, the reality far surpassing her dreams. Her breath caught in her throat.

He pulled her down with him, gathering her close, stroking her, pleasuring her, driving her to the edge, wild with wanting.

She explored him, her hands desperate to feel all of him, to find places that made him gasp and hold her tighter. She committed those to memory.

He gently rolled her over and stroked her face. 'Are you sure about this?'

'Oh, yes.' She pulled his head down, kissing him hard, hard, taking her fill.

He moved over her, gently entering her, easing in, establishing a powerful rhythm.

She gasped, her breath coming in short, rapid runs. Ribbons of hot, desperate need shot through her, blasting all the way down to her toes.

She gripped his back, arching toward him, needing to feel all of him against her, all of him inside her.

Together their rhythm spiralled them up and up to the precipice, finally flinging them out into space as they shattered
in unison.

She felt his ragged breathing slow, his arms wrapped
tightly around her and his head nuzzled against her neck.

She snuggled in against him, his energy flowing into her,
caressing her, giving her strength. She could stay here in this
safe, caring cocoon for ever.

For ever.

The idea played across her mind, deliciously tempting.
Tormentingly tempting. She breathed in deeply, bringing
reality back into her life after half an hour of fantasy.

All this was temporary. Making love, feeling cherished, it
wasn't real. She didn't do relationships. Besides, Xavier
didn't want her as a life partner. He believed he couldn't love
her because they worked together.

And at any moment either of them could walk away. That
was the agreement.

Yesterday it had been the perfect agreement.

So why didn't it feel so perfect any more?

An hour later Charlie wrapped Xavier's thick bathrobe around
her and breathed in his scent. She planned to hold the real
world at bay as long as possible. She padded down the hall
toward the aroma of basil and garlic.

Xavier stood in the kitchen surrounded by as much stain-
less steel as in a commercial kitchen. 'Hungry?' He turned
from a large tureen, his smile zeroing in on her.

She smiled back, feeling deliciously warm. 'Starving. That
smells great.'

'*Soupe au pistou.*'

'Yummy, vegetable soup with a sort of pesto stirred in, right?'

He started in surprise. 'You know it?'

She grinned. 'I spent a bit of time in France when I did the traditional Aussie backpack through Europe. I remember eating it at a midnight fête.'

His eyes glazed with a far away look. 'And what did you think of France?'

'I still miss those wonderful pâtisseries where you not only bought a cake but you bought an experience.' She sighed. 'None of this "shove it in a bag", like we have here. They boxed every cake, whether it be one or ten.'

He stirred the soup and sliced a baguette. 'All food is an experience in France.'

She sat down on a tall chair at the island bench and then swivelled around to look at the large open-plan living space. Unlike her antiques, his furniture was modern with clean lines. Unlike her clutter, everything was stacked neatly on shelves. The three remote controls sat lined up on top of the television.

She chuckled. 'So how many times a week do you have someone come in and tidy up?'

'I'm not going to answer that on the grounds it might incriminate me.'

His black eyes sparkled. The glow that seemed so much a part of her now, flared. 'Aha! So more than once.'

'All I am doing is helping the local economy by providing employment.'

'Yeah, right.'

'Here, eat your *soupe*.' He sat down next to her, his lips skimming hers in a brief kiss. A kiss shared by couples everywhere. One of companionship and shared jokes.

The ache under her ribs flared. *Just enjoy the moment while you have it. The future will come soon enough.*

She grated some extra Parmesan cheese. As her spoon broke the surface of the soup the aroma of the fresh herbs floated up toward her. She sipped, the flavours exploding in her mouth. 'This is wonderful.'

'*Merci.* I enjoy cooking. It helps me unwind from the stresses of the day.' A wry smile tugged at his mouth. 'Just lately, with all the budget issues, I have been doing a lot of cooking.' He sipped his soup. 'And I've been thinking about Julie McAllister.'

Charlie's fantasy collapsed around her, the real world piercing her cocoon.

Xavier broke some bread. 'She had a fantastic home birth but she could have come into Amaroo and had the same thing.'

Charlie drew in a breath to steady her for the battle she knew was ahead. 'Come on, Xavier. You were there. You experienced the difference. Hospitals and home births are poles apart. For starters there would have been more people coming in and out. Bound to have been a med student or midwife who needed to observe. And just as likely a midwife sticking her head in, looking for the drug-cupboard keys, the moment the baby was being delivered.'

'So we improve the way things are done in hospitals.' He spoke softly, his voice steady.

'No.' She heard the determination in her voice. 'We look outside the box and find a different way of operating entirely.'

He pushed his empty bowl away. 'That could be the same argument as mine.'

'Not at all. You can't "fix" something when it is based on a totally different premise. Hospitals are for sick people based on a medical model. Most pregnant women are not sick. They should be offered a choice.'

'And that choice has to be cost-effective.' He spoke quietly, the message powerful.

She rallied her thoughts. 'It can be. But sometimes passion and belief have to carry a programme until it gains enough momentum to be truly self-sufficient. Ideology has to play a part.'

His eyes sought hers. 'I am sorry but I'm not sure Amaroo has that luxury any more.'

She closed her eyes for a moment, the pit of her stomach rolling with disappointment. 'Are you saying the programme is closing?'

'*Non.* No decisions have yet been made. I just think it would be a good idea for you to think about what you might do if things change. If the programme folds, this could be an opportunity for you to try something new.'

Her mind grappled with the change of topic. What was he really saying? 'I love what I do, Xavier.'

'I know you do.' He stroked her face. 'You have a passion for your work that many people would envy but you should want more out of life than just your job. You should want more for yourself. This could be a time for you to focus on yourself.'

A wave of discomfort rippled through her. 'Don't tell me what I want, Xavier. I think you're confusing it with what *you* want. You want more than work. You want children and a family life. I'm fine with what I have.'

'Are you?' His brows rose. 'I think you have been telling yourself that story for so long that now you believe it.'

A defensive shield rose up inside her against the pain his words inflicted. 'That's ridiculous. I know relationships don't work for me.'

He reached out and touched her hand. 'Did it ever occur to you that perhaps you chose the wrong man? Or that actually your father chose the wrong man for you? Now you are denying yourself happiness because you're scared of taking a risk?' His voice dropped. 'I saw the look on your face when you cuddled Jade's baby. I saw you with the Leeton kids. I think you want a child of your own.'

His words paralysed her. She struggled to breathe against a hammering heart. With a few choice words he'd cut through everything and seen straight into her soul.

Wanting a child was one thing.

But a relationship was something else entirely.

A relationship meant risking her heart again. The idea scared her to death.

She pulled his robe more tightly around herself and forced out a laugh, trying to deflect him away from the turmoil that roiled inside her. 'Stick to obstetrics, Xavier—psychoanalysis isn't your thing.'

He pulled her gently over to him and into his arms. 'I just want you to consider this—no matter how much you want things to stay the same, change does happen. And sometimes the things we think we want aren't really what we need.'

She turned to look into his face. Care and concern etched themselves around his mouth and in his eyes. She didn't want to see that. She didn't want to be reminded that she was alone and childless. That she was falling for a man who did not want a woman like her as a wife. That her job might fold.

She didn't want to see empathy in his eyes. She wanted to see lust and desire and pretend that everything was fine. That her world wasn't changing. That her heart was safe.

She ran her hands along his face and brought his lips down onto hers, driving away reality, embracing an illusion.

* * *

'So why do we have to do this again?' Jade walked through the doors of the clinic two weeks after Ebony's birth and got straight to the point.

'Hi, Jade, how are you?' Charlie gave the teenager a smile. She found if you ignored the gruffness in Jade's voice and manner, the vulnerable young woman eventually came to the surface.

'Yeah, OK.' Jade picked up a magazine and flicked through it, not making eye contact. 'My breasts are hurting me, though.'

'Are you taking the tablets we gave you to dry up your milk?' Charlie asked gently.

Jade looked up from the magazine. 'Mostly. I forgot yesterday.'

'You need to take them for fourteen days. How about you take them when you clean your teeth in the morning? The same time you take your contraceptive Pill?'

Jade was unusually silent.

Charlie signed inwardly. 'Are you taking the Pill, Jade?'

'I keep forgetting that, too. Can't I have an injection or those rods they put in your arm?'

'Sure, if you think that will work better for you, we can make an appointment with Family Planning today. In the meantime, do you want any condoms?' Charlie opened her top drawer.

The magazine flew across the room, just missing Charlie's head. She caught it and laughed. 'OK, I was just checking! Come on, then, let's check out your tummy.' Charlie stood up and Jade followed her over to the examination couch.

Charlie gently examined Jade's breasts and palpated her abdomen. Jade's uterus had contracted well and was at the level of her symphysis pubis. 'Do you have much blood loss?'

'Nah, that's all finished.' Jade pulled up her pants and slid off the couch.

'Well, physically you're doing well. How are things at home?' Charlie tried to keep her voice casual. The physical recovery after birth was generally straightforward. The emotional recovery of giving up a baby for adoption would take a lot longer.

'Mum and Dad are still pretty dark at me. Mum is either lecturing me or ignoring me. Dad has no idea what to say so he just looks and leaves. Maybe…' Her voice trailed away.

'Your mum's still in shock. Remember you knew about the baby for six months. Mum had no idea.' Charlie cringed inside, remembering the scene Jade's mother had caused in the hospital.

'Yeah, I s'pose.' Jade twirled a scrunchie in her hand. 'The social worker says I have six weeks to make up my mind about what I want to do.'

Charlie waited, letting the silence surround them.

'I dunno what to do. I mean, I love the baby and stuff, but…' She shifted in her chair. 'Charlie, what would you do?'

'Jade, I'm not fifteen so what I would do isn't important.' Jade had been in to visit her twice this week. Ebony was now in foster-care with Sharon and Bob Jenkins, and growing like a weed.

'Bringing up a child on your own at any age is hard work, especially at fifteen with Mum and Dad not being supportive.' Charlie leaned forward, touching Jade's arm. 'Today adoption is open and you'll be able to visit Ebony and be like a big sister.'

Jade sniffed, wiping her hand across her red nose. 'Yeah, I know. I just wish it was different.' She gave Charlie a hopeful look. 'Like you and Dr Xavier could adopt her?'

'We work together, Jade. We're not a couple.' The words

slipped out before Charlie realised she'd verbalised her thoughts.

Jade sat bolt upright. 'I saw you the other day pashing in the car park at Wilson's Beach. You both looked pretty hot.'

Heat flooded Charlie's face. Discussing her affair with a fifteen-year-old wasn't something she wanted to do.

Jade continued, 'you know Dr Xavier visited Ebony every day in hospital. You're both old enough to be parents. You could talk to him about my idea, couldn't you?'

The pleading in Jade's voice pulled at her. 'Jade, I'm really sorry but we can't adopt Ebony.'

'Why not? Don't you want a baby?'

Her heart flipped. How did she explain to a teenager that life wasn't black and white? Yes, she wanted a child. But she needed a relationship before she had a child.

She and Xavier didn't have that. All they had was an electrifying affair, awesome in its own way and devastatingly lonely in another. He couldn't love her.

She'd seen his aching pain, the legacy of betrayal. He held his heart close, guarding it. Hell, she didn't blame him.

And he'd been so honest. He'd told her from the start he couldn't offer her love. He'd been so clear about what he wanted and it wasn't a midwife who worked crazy hours. And she couldn't give up what she loved, so where did that leave them?

Exactly where they were. Having an affair.

Unless… Her mind kicked up a gear, ideas pouring through her. Unless she could show him that two people from the medical profession *could* have a life together. That she was worthy of his trust and would never hurt him. That she shared his dream of a family, too.

She dragged her thoughts back to Jade. 'Yes, one day I do

want a baby. I do want to be a mother. But Social Services have a really strict system. There are families who have already been approved to adopt. Couples who have waited a long time to have a family.'

'The rules suck.' Jade slouched again.

'The rules always suck. Come on.' Charlie put her hand out and pulled Jade to her feet. 'Let's grab a hamburger before we see Mr Martin at school.'

Jade made a face and stuck out her tongue.

'If you want to do my job then you have to finish school. Besides, the programme Mr Martin has going is very different from normal school. It's more like a college.' She'd learned a few things about fifteen-year-olds in the past two weeks. 'I'll even chuck in a milkshake.'

'Chocolate?'

'Is there another flavour?'

Jade smiled, stood up and walked over to the door. 'So, you and the doc…'

Charlie almost choked. Trying to keep a straight face, she marched Jade out the door toward the car.

Xavier took a break from being a host and grabbed a glass of cold water from the hospital function room's kitchen. His inaugural hospital cocktail party was in full swing and his guests mingled outside on the hospital lawn, enjoying the warm summer evening. The flickering light from the citronella flares danced in the light breeze that blew in from the ocean.

People chatted together in groups eating the hors d'oeuvres, drinking the French pinot and generally having a good time. The only thing missing was Charlotte.

He'd been in meetings all day and hadn't been able to

catch up with her. He sighed. He wished she were here beside him with her vivacious laugh and intelligent conversation. Without her this party was no fun at all.

He gave himself a shake. It shouldn't matter if she was there or not. An affair by its nature meant occasional meetings, great sex and no commitments. They'd both agreed to that.

But that was before he'd seen her with the Leeton kids.

He sighed and put his drink down. He best get back to being host.

Suddenly warm arms snaked around his waist and a supple body pressed against his.

He spun around, catching the gaze of sparkling emerald eyes. Tender warmth flooded him. 'You're here.'

She pressed her lips against his in a brief, welcoming kiss. 'You sound surprised.'

Confusion and delight merged. 'I thought you were working.'

'I am, but it's my break. Remember, at the McAllisters', you told me I needed to take care of myself.' She grinned. 'I do listen occasionally.'

She gave him a quizzical look. 'I thought you wanted me to be here and I wanted to come.' She leant around him and popped a seafood ball into her mouth. 'Besides, I knew you'd have great food.'

'I did want you here.' He held her close, breathing in her wild rose perfume, enjoying the sensation of holding her close.

She leaned back slightly, her face serious. 'But you didn't ask me.'

'I thought I couldn't ask.'

She levelled her gaze with his. 'I worked that out.' She ran her hand down his cheek. 'When you talked about the party the other day you mentioned a few times how you needed to host it and then you mumbled something about work responsibilities, clashes of timetables and then you changed the subject.'

Surprise rippled through him. How had she managed to read him so accurately? 'I wanted you here but we're having an affair and I didn't want to put you in a difficult position.'

She raised her brows. 'How is me coming here difficult? People who have affairs can support each other. I want to support you. If I hadn't been able to make it or if I didn't want to come, I would have told you.'

'Yes, I guess you would have.' He looked at her standing there—tall, beautiful with a dazzling aura, yet with an air of concern for him. She'd wanted to come, wanted to be with him tonight in public. His heart sang.

He drew her back into his arms. '*Merci*. It was *miserable* without you.'

'Now, that's what a girl wants to hear.' She laughed, resting her head on his shoulder, her hair brushing his cheek.

His arms tightened around her, the action proprietorial. She was his. He didn't want to share her. He'd missed her so much that evening. He'd gone through the motions of being a host but nothing had sparkled until she'd arrived.

She lit up a room and she lit up his life. He wanted her in his life, in his home, sharing her life with his. Together.

He loved her.

The realisation hit him hard, almost winding him.

In a few short weeks she'd turned his world upside down. She managed to totally infuriate him, drive him crazy, make him laugh, be his lover and his friend. And she'd done all of it at the same time. He wanted to be with her, create a family with her.

Now all he had to do was end this charade of an affair and tell her how he really felt.

CHAPTER NINE

XAVIER'S arms stiffened against her and he stepped back, breaking the contact. She turned as Michael Strachan, Xavier's registrar, stuck his head around the door. 'Charlie, Birth Suite needs you to cover for tea relief as they're a midwife short.'

'Thanks, Michael.' She swallowed her sigh that her break had been cut short and turned back to Xavier. 'Sorry. I'll catch you later, promise.'

He nodded. 'I'll walk over with you.'

'Xavier,' Michael interrupted, his tone serious. 'I need a moment to talk to you about something important.'

She squeezed his arm. 'I'll page you the moment I'm free.' She walked briskly toward Birth Suite.

She pushed open the door to find a heavily pregnant woman sitting upright on the bed, supported by beanbags, her face red with the exertion of pushing.

Kerri, the midwife on duty, wore an anxious expression.

'Everything all right?' Charlie picked up the chart.

'Well, I was going to take a teabreak but now I'm not so sure.' Kerri sounded worried.

Charlie turned toward the patient. 'Hi, Imogen, I'm Charlie Buchanan, a midwife, and I've come to give Kerri a break, but you're sounding to me like you're about to deliver your baby.'

The woman nodded, exhaustion etched in deep lines on her face. 'It's harder than when I had Johnny.'

Charlie laid her hand on the woman's abdomen, feeling the strength of the contraction.

Imogen suddenly leaned forward and pushed again, her perineum swelling as the baby's head came down the birth canal. At the end of the push the baby's head retreated.

'I caught a sight of brown hair.' Charlie gave her an encouraging smile and pulled on some gloves. 'Next push, Imogen, I want you to really bear down and then we'll be delivering your baby.'

'Thank…goodness.' Imogen lay back on the beanbag and Kerri gave her a sip of water and mopped her forehead with a cool cloth.

A minute later Imogen grabbed a lungful of nitrous oxide and pushed. Slowly the baby's head crowned and was delivered.

'Well done, Imogen. With the next contraction the baby will come out.' As the words left her mouth the baby's chin burrowed back into the perineum, looking just like a turtle heading back inside its shell. The turtle sign.

Shoulder dystocia.

The baby's shoulders were stuck in the pelvis. Charlie's heart raced. 'Kerri, page Xavier. *Now!*'

The midwife's face drained of colour as she rushed for the phone.

The mnemonic for the obstetric emergency appeared in her head. HELPERRD. H. She'd sent for help. E. Episiotomy.

She reached for the scissors. 'Sorry, Imogen, but I have to make a small cut here because this baby is being stubborn.'

Somehow she managed to slide the scissors in place and protect the baby's head. *Hurry up, Xavier.*

L. Legs. Imogen needed to have her legs over her head 'Imogen, I'm going to drop the bottom half of the bed and then we need to push your legs over your head.' The lever released with a loud clunk.

The woman looked stunned and scared. 'Why?'

'The baby's shoulders are stuck and this will help to free them.' *I hope.* 'Kerri, help her move her bottom down to this edge then take a foetal heart.' Where the hell was Xavier?

She took in a calm breath, focusing on the task rather than the scared expressions of Imogen and Kerri.

P. Pressure. Apply pressure above the pubic bone to move the anterior shoulder. Charlie placed her hand firmly on Imogen's abdomen. 'Imogen, this is really important. I need you to push as hard as you ever have in your life.'

The door burst open. Xavier and Michael raced in.

'Problem?' Xavier's standard understated question in any emergency echoed around the room.

'Shoulder dystocia. Head delivered one minute ago.' Charlie threw the words out as she applied pressure. She heard the snap of latex as Xavier pulled on gloves.

Relief poured through her.

'Is the baby going to be all right, Doctor?' Imogen's fear-laden voice filled the room.

'That is our intention, Imogen. Your job is to follow every instruction we give you and keep your legs up around your ears. Kerri will help.'

Xavier's glance met Charlie's. 'Apply pressure to the top of the uterus as well as above the pubic bone.'

She nodded in complete understanding.

'Right.' He took a breath. 'Let's deliver this baby.' His

brow furrowed in concentration. 'Deep breath, Imogen.' Somehow with limited room he managed to slowly coax the shoulders around.

Sweat poured off him.

'Two minutes.' Precious time marched on, starkly reminding them that time might win.

The silence in the room bore down on them all. With the baby so low it was almost impossible to find the foetal heart, and with every ticking second the outcome for the baby worsened.

The baby would need resuscitation—it might have a fractured clavicle, even nerve damage to the shoulder. She glanced across the room. Michael had set up the paediatric resuscitation trolley.

'Michael, are you ready for the baby?' Xavier's clipped tone conveyed his anxiety.

'Ready.' Michael spoke quietly.

'Push, Imogen.' Xavier's curt instruction bounced off the walls.

The baby's top shoulder appeared. Xavier murmured in French as he lifted the posterior shoulder and the baby slithered out into his hands.

Thank goodness. But Charlie knew the battle wasn't over yet.

'Imogen, you've had a boy but we need to examine him now.' Xavier nodded to Charlie to take the baby while he delivered the placenta.

She picked the baby up, racing him over to the resuscitation trolley. 'Michael, we need oxygen.'

The limp baby lay under the bright lights, his muscles flaccid, his breathing jerky and his skin tinged blue. Michael stood inert for a moment, staring at the baby.

Charlie grabbed the oxygen mask and bag. 'Michael! Suction. *Now.*' She pushed the laryngoscope into his hand.

'Everything all right over there?' Xavier turned toward them.

'Fine.' Michael picked up the fine-tubed suction catheter and cleared the baby's nose. Then he opened the tiny 'scope and started to aspirate the lungs under the direct vision provided by the laryngoscope.

'Apgar at one minute, four.' Charlie started to rub the baby's arms and legs. 'Come on, mate, breathe properly.'

'How is he?' Imogen's teary voice came from the other side of the room.

Charlie put the stethoscope on the baby's chest. 'More suction.'

Michael re-inserted the tube down the baby's throat.

Charlie prayed only clear mucous would come out. They didn't need meconium-induced pneumonia on top of everything else.

She looked at the clock. The baby was very slow to respond. Michael seemed out of his depth. 'Xavier.'

He immediately came over, responding to the tone of her voice, reading her so well, as only he could. Knowing her and how she thought. Why couldn't he recognise they could have that simpatico outside work?

'What's his heart rate?' His eyes seemed blacker than ever.

'Ninety-five.' Michael's voice wobbled.

'Come on, baby.' Xavier rubbed the infant's sternum gently. He turned to Kerri. 'Call Stuart Mullins.'

'Oh, my God, is he going to be OK?' Imogen's voice cracked on the words.

'We're doing our best. He's just a little slow to start breathing properly.' His accent sounded thicker than usual. It always increased in proportion to his concern.

Charlie continued to bag the baby, the mask dwarfing his small face. *Breathe, please, breathe.*

Slowly, the blue tinge of his skin lightened to a dusky pink and then a bright pink. His chest started to rise and fall.

Michael checked the heart rate. 'One hundred and twenty.' Relief shone in his eyes.

'Excellent, but he needs to go to Special Care Nursery for observation after his mother has had the briefest of brief cuddles.' Xavier carried the baby over to Imogen.

Two minutes later Charlie escorted the baby to Special Care Nursery with Michael. After handing over to the nursery staff, they headed back to the birth suite to debrief.

Xavier had made coffee and handed them both a cup as they walked into the kitchen. 'Michael, tell me, what happened just after the baby was born?'

Discomfort cloaked the registrar. 'I froze. I'm sorry.'

Understanding reflected in Xavier's eyes. 'We all have moments when we freeze. The important thing is working out why. Any ideas?'

Michael slowly stirred his coffee. 'It's to do with what I wanted to talk to you about before the emergency.' He gazed into the hot drink. 'I don't think I'm cut out for obstetrics.'

Shocked surprise rippled through Charlie. 'What do you mean?'

Michael put the spoon down, the action studied and deliberate. He glanced up, looking at both of them. 'Have you ever found yourselves in a job that people encouraged you to do and you suddenly realised it did nothing for you?'

Charlie nodded. 'Oh, yes.' Memories of law came flooding back.

Michael sighed. 'I'm six months away from my final exams in obstetrics. I've spent eight years getting to this point and I don't think I want to be an obstetrician.' The anguish in his voice cut through her.

Xavier's brow furrowed. 'How long have you been feeling like this?'

'Too long. A year at least.'

'That's quite a while.' He shifted his weight against the kitchen bench. 'What are you planning to do about it?'

Michael wrung his hands. 'I wish I knew. I feel like I'm on the edge of a mountain and which ever way I move, I'm going to fall.'

Charlie's mind mulled over what he was saying. 'Have you spoken to Phil about this? I mean, you worked with him for a couple of years so he might be of some help.'

'He reckons I just have pre-exam jitters and that once I've got my qualifications and I'm a consultant, I'll feel differently.'

'I do not agree.' Xavier's deep voice resonated around the room. 'A year is a long time to have been feeling unhappy with what you are doing.'

Charlie spoke from experience. 'Those feelings won't change overnight. If anything, they will intensify.'

Michael nodded, anguish washing across his face. 'I know, but I'm so close to finishing, perhaps I should just sit the damn exams.'

Charlie bit her lip, feeling for Michael as his dilemma washed over her.

Xavier crossed his arms. 'These exams, they are no walk in the park. It is a lot of hard work and energy to pour into something that you are no longer passionate about.'

'But you, Phil, the board, everyone at the hospital has been so good to me I feel I owe it to you all to stay.'

'Ever thought that an obstetrician who is not passionate about what he does isn't doing the best for his patients?'

'Xavier's right,' Charlie chimed in. 'You know how impor-tant the patient-doctor relationship is. Women need a caregiver who is able to meet their emotional needs as well as deliver a baby.' The passion in her voice reminded her of the job she loved.

'So you think I should walk away?' Michael's gaze travelled between the two of them.

She shrugged her shoulders. 'It's not my place to say what you should or shouldn't do. Only you can make that decision.'

'Charlotte's right.' Xavier gave Michael a direct look. 'Only you can make the decision. But you need some help with it, am I right?'

Michael's words came out infused with emotion. 'I feel like I'm suffocating with indecision.'

Xavier dropped a hand lightly onto his shoulder. 'So it's time to focus.'

'What do you want to do now?' Charlie asked softly.

'Last year I volunteered for the Fred Hollows Foundation and spent a month in Vanuatu.' Michael's voice lightened. 'Since then I've wanted to do ophthalmology.'

Xavier spread his hands out in front of him. 'So what's stopping you?'

'You, the hospital, my patients…'

'*Zut*. No, Michael, you are stopping yourself. I am the first to say that if you leave, my workload will double and I might as well just rent a room at the hospital for all that I will see of my home. But that is not important. What is important is that you pursue the path that is right for you, and that you find your passion again.'

Warmth flooded her. Xavier shared her opinion exactly. 'You have to love what you do, Michael. That is what carries you through the day.'

Xavier gave a wry laugh. 'Let's face it, you have thirty-plus years left in your professional life. You must do a job that sets you on fire. Look to the future, to where you want to be, and if it's helping the people of the world see again, then get qualified and get out there and do it.'

Charlie resisted the urge to clap, his eloquent words mirroring her beliefs.

'Thanks, Xavier.' Relief flooded Michael's face and his body relaxed. 'I'll start ringing around tomorrow. I heard Gheringya might have an opening coming up next year.'

'I will give you a reference, Michael. Just let me know.'

'Thanks.' The pager on his belt beeped. 'Excuse me, I'll just take this call.' Michael walked out into the corridor.

Charlie shook her head in amazement. 'That was a brilliant speech you just gave. I've never heard you on your soapbox before.'

'Well, it makes a change, seeing I'm usually listening to you on yours.' His smile softened his words as he reached for her.

'*Touché*. So part of your job is to sort out your staff's life for them?'

'No, Michael's doing that for himself. I just pushed him so he could move from limbo to action. I've known he has not been happy ever since I arrived.'

'That's pretty amazing.'

'What?' For a moment Xavier looked confused.

'To encourage your registrar to leave when he's so close to finishing and when the hospital has invested so much in him.'

'But if he isn't happy, is the hospital really benefiting?'

'I know. But it's still pretty amazing.' Her father's face floated into her mind. If only he'd understood what Xavier seemed to intuit. People had to be true to themselves and follow their calling. She had to be a midwife, and could never have been a lawyer. If her father had seen that, it would have saved a lot of heartache.

'Deep thoughts?' He stroked her face.

She reached up and touched his hand, her fingers tracing the length of his fingers. She sought his gaze and wondered about this gorgeous man who'd come into her life. She hadn't known him very long, but the more time she spent with him, the more she needed to be with him. Needed to be a part of his life, experience his love and care.

To be with this wonderful man who believed people should be true to themselves.

A man who set her blood on fire and filled her waking and sleeping thoughts.

She loved him.

Her breathing stalled. She loved him. She loved this man who would support her dreams.

She wanted a future with him. A family. Their family. Her, Xavier and a baby. Could it be possible?

She dug deep and found her voice. 'Xavier, Jade came to see me the other day. She wants you and I to adopt Ebony.'

Xavier's arms wrapped around her waist. 'She's got good taste. We'd make great parents.'

Her mind raced along with her heart. What was he thinking? Great parents as a separate unit or great parents together? 'Would we?'

'Absolutely. We would make wonderful parents.' He gave her a searching look. 'Is that something you've been thinking about?'

Her heart hammered against her chest. 'I… We're having an affair and…'

'Is that something you've been thinking about?' His voice was low and insistent.

'Yes.' The word came out on a breath.

'Me, too.' He cradled her face in his hands, and gave her a smile full of promise that sent her heart quivering. 'I've been thinking about it for quite a while.'

He lowered his head, capturing her lips, kissing her hard. A kiss of commitment, a kiss of shared dreams.

The shrill of Xavier's phone shattered the moment.

'*Alors.*' Xavier punched the 'on' button. 'Xavier Laurent.'

Charlie watched him take the call, trying to absorb what had just happened.

He snapped his phone shut. 'Heather Birchip is about to deliver.' He picked up Charlie's hand. 'I have to go but we will talk about us soon.'

Charlie nodded and stroked his cheek. 'We will. After you've delivered this baby.'

She watched him leave and hugged the knowledge to herself that he wanted to be with her and raise a family. Her life, which had been like a pile of dust a week before, was rising again like a phoenix. Only this time she had a partner who understood her. She wouldn't be alone again.

CHAPTER TEN

CHARLIE sighed wearily and pushed her arms up over her head, desperately needing to stretch. She sat surrounded by financial spreadsheets, patient histories and the fifty-page document from the maternity coalition. Half-empty cups of cold tea made an arc on her desk and a pile of scrunched-up paper trailed across the floor.

In ten minutes she had the official appointment with Xavier to hear the ruling on the programme. She'd gone over every last detail, memorising all the important statistics.

She couldn't wait to see him. It has been a long two days, their only real contact being stolen kisses as they'd passed in the corridor. Both of them had been flat out with a baby boom brought on by a raging summer storm and a huge drop in barometric pressure. So busy that they hadn't found a quiet hour to have the conversation they needed to have about the future.

Their future.

He saw her as part of his future. Her heart soared again, just as it did every time she thought about it. She'd been walking around with a silly grin on her face and hugging the knowledge close ever since he'd spoken the words, "We will talk about *us* soon."

Today's meeting was the last one for the day so the moment it was squared away they could talk. After that, the evening opened up in front of them. She could hardly wait.

Standing up, she placed the empty cups in the sink, then tucked her notes into the appropriate files. She'd explored every corner of the programme and knew it inside out. Last night she'd had a long phone conversation with Rebecca, the convener of the Perth programme, which was the longest-running community midwifery programme in the country. She'd had some new and convincing arguments.

Any question Xavier asked, she had the facts and figures to give a full and detailed answer. She planned to have the community midwifery programme still functioning at 5.30 p.m.

As she headed out the door with her colour-coordinated folders clutched close to her chest, a bubble of laughter escaped into the air. She'd realized that, just once, she matched Xavier in organisation and neatness.

She pushed open the doors into the administration building and took a deep breath.

'Good afternoon, Charlie.' Dorothy Bailey, Xavier's secretary, gave her a warm smile. 'He won't be long, he's just finishing up talking to the endocrine unit manager.'

'Thanks.' The sooner the meeting started, the sooner she would know the outcome. Adrenaline played havoc with her body. Her heart thumped too quickly, her mouth dried, and it took every ounce of self-control not to drum nervous fingers against the folders on her lap.

Liz, the endocrine unit's nurse manager, walked out of the office smiling, giving Charlie a thumbs-up sign. 'He's extended community nursing for diabetes, which is fantastic. Hope your news is as good as ours. Good luck!'

With trembling legs she stood up and walked to the door. Her fingers curled around the cool metal handle. Pausing for a moment, she breathed in deeply, then pushed open the door.

Xavier stood staring out the window toward the sea. Sunlight played across him, his hair gleaming black with traces of silver streaks.

Familiar heat encircled her and she fisted her hand, forcing away the overwhelming desire to run her hands through his hair.

The door clicked shut behind her.

He turned, his face lined with tiredness, taut with tension. The moment he saw her he smiled.

She melted under the wattage of his smile. She wanted to drop everything and throw her arms around him, feel his body moulded against her own, fitting into her curves as if by design. But she couldn't. This was work. But the moment the meeting was over she would lose herself in his arms for a very long time.

She placed her folders on his desk and sat in the chair, clasping her hands on her lap. 'So here we are.' Her voice sounded strained to her own ears.

'*Oui*, here we are.' He sat down, his gaze riveted to hers, exploring every part of her. 'In some ways it has been a long six weeks, but in others it has been the fastest of my life.'

She nodded, understanding perfectly. Her time with him had been pure magic, surpassing anything she'd ever known. But now wasn't about the two of them—that would come later. 'Xavier, today's been the longest day of my life. I need to know your decision on the community midwifery programme.'

'Yes you do.' He tapped his folder. 'I have been right through this programme, I've seen you at work, I've spoken to the patients. You do a fantastic job with limited resources and clearly the patients adore you. You are a dedicated staff member, an excellent midwife and an asset to this community.'

Charlie scanned his face while she listened to his words. She wanted to glow in his praise but she wouldn't allow herself that luxury. Butterflies pummelled her stomach. What came next?

He pulled out a financial spreadsheet and placed it on top of the pile. 'I have also been through the figures, Charlotte, and at this point, because midwives do not attract a Medicare rebate from the government, the programme is not financially self-supporting.' He took in a breath and caught her gaze. 'I'm very sorry, but the programme has to close.'

Her stomach plummeted. *Please, no.* Blood roared in her ears, and her breath shuddered into her lungs in ragged jerks. 'But I have funding until the end of the financial year.'

He sighed, his regret hanging in the air. 'I know that was the plan but it was also based on the programme paying for itself.' Tiredness clung to him. 'Charlotte, I've been up nights, trying every permutation and combination to make this work for you, for the hospital, but right now the programme is not breaking even.'

Her brain clicked into gear. 'But it could if it had the full twelve months.' She pulled out her projected financial sheet. 'I have increased bookings for the next quarter.'

Xavier nodded, his expression emphatic. 'On paper that looks to be a wonderful thing, but the reality is that with those increased bookings you will need another midwife. Her salary would take the programme back into the red.'

'I wouldn't need another midwife.' Her voice started to rise.

Distress creased his brow. 'Charlotte, you are efficient and competent and a sensational midwife, but you cannot be in two places at once. You are already working long hours. With increased numbers you would need help. You cannot compromise patient safety or your own.'

'In Perth the midwives—'

His hands opened palm upwards, in a familiar gesture of contrition. 'In Perth they are dealing with a larger population than we are in Amaroo. Even the National Maternity Coalition admits that in some rural areas community midwifery programmes are not financially viable without support from another agency. Which is why they are starting to lobby the government for midwife Medicare rebates.'

He ran his left hand through his hair, bringing it along his jaw line, and rested his chin in his palm. 'The bottom line is that as much as I would love this programme to continue, there is no money in the budget to support it. We are barely managing to fund the entire hospital. The Department of Health has given me an ultimatum. I'm sorry, but my hands are tied.'

Her mind grappled with his words. 'But money was allocated to my programme for another quarter. Why cut it now, three months early?'

He bit his lip. 'The money is not there. It comes out of the global budget. Everything has been re-allocated to support viable programmes under direction of the department. In another three months the picture won't have changed. The programme still won't be self-supporting. Stopping it now gives the women time to come to terms with another system.'

Tears pricked the back of her eyes and she blinked furiously. Her project, her baby, which had been so much a part of her, was no longer. She took in a long, trembling breath.

Xavier walked around the desk and knelt down beside her,

quietly handing her an ironed, neatly folded white handkerchief. 'I know this hurts, Charlotte. I understand you've just
lost something very special. I'm really sorry but right now the
hospital cannot afford to run community midwifery. If I could
change things, I would.'

Through tear-filled eyes she saw regret etched on his face.
She couldn't hold herself back from him any longer. Leaning
into him, she dropped her head onto his shoulder, breathing
in his scent of citrus and soap. An overwhelming sense of
coming home streaked through her.

He stroked her back, his calmness permeating her distress.
Six weeks of being on high-alert anxiety to save her programme, drained out of her, exhaustion taking its place. She
wanted to stay on his shoulder for ever, sheltering in his care,
avoid thinking about what happened next. What her working
future held.

'Charlotte,' his voice soothed. 'I know it seems dark right
now and you cannot see the light, but sometimes when we're
forced to take a new road we end up realising the new road
is the one we belong on.'

His words bounced off the haze in her brain. What was he
saying? She raised her head. 'Sorry?'

He cupped his hands around her face. 'I'm talking about
us. Now that the programme has closed, that gives you more
time.'

She dabbed her face with his hankie and cleared her throat.
'I need another job.'

'I know you do. I have the perfect job for you.' He hugged
her. 'Midwife in charge of the antenatal clinic.' He announced
it as if she'd won the lottery.

She moved his hands away from her face. 'You want me
to take on the management of antenatal outpatients?' She

spoke quietly and slowly, trying to understand why he'd even suggest that job.

'You will be wonderful down there.' He smiled, his gaze fixed lovingly on her face.

She stared into his eyes, trying to get a hint of what he was really thinking. 'Well, sure, but I could be great in Birth Suite.'

'But Antenatal needs your skills to modernise it. It's lagging behind other regional hospitals. It also has the added bonus of regular hours, more sociable hours. You have to admit, that would be an improvement.' He smiled encouragingly, as if they were of one mind.

A shiver of unease ran through her. 'Xavier, shift work has never bothered me in the slightest. Yet you want me to take on a nine-to-five administration position because it has more sociable hours. Sociable for who?'

'For us.' He reached for her hand. 'It is the perfect situation. You will still be nursing, doing what you love, and we can concentrate on starting our family. The family we both want so much.'

An arrow of anger pierced her heart, her controlling past rearing its head. 'I don't have to work regular hours to do that.'

His brow furrowed in confusion. 'Right now we both know we have something special but we are never in the same place long enough to fully explore that. Look at the last forty-eight hours. With only one of us working crazy hours, we have more chance of finding time to be together. You'd be doing this for us.'

The small wound in her heart broke open and haemorrhaged. This was her family all over again. Her needs and wants counting for nothing, being completely submerged in other people's desires. Again she was being asked to change to please someone else. Love with soul-destroying conditions, a replica of her mother's life.

It was Richard all over again. Working the job to suit the man. Oh, God, she'd been so stupid to let this happen again.

She took in a deep breath. Surely she must have misunderstood what Xavier really meant. She must have missed something. 'I don't want an administrative position.' *Please, understand. Know that I live to deliver babies.*

'But you are over-qualified to join the nursing bank, which is the only other vacancy at the moment.' He shrugged. 'We don't have to decide right now. I am sure there will be a position somewhere in the hospital that will suit us.'

He pulled her into his arms and nuzzled her neck with his lips. 'Besides, I am hoping there will soon be a wonderful reason for you to stop working altogether.'

His heat surged into her, sending tremors of wondrous sensation through her, her body completely betraying her.

No! Her brain screamed in protest. She pulled away, needing the physical distance between them. *Stop working altogether.* Her blood rushed to her feet. He had no idea who she was, no idea what she needed, what made her Charlie. Hell, he couldn't even call her by her preferred name.

He wanted her to change so she suited him more. *Us.* There was no *us*. He wanted a lover and a mother for his kids, but he wanted a tailor-made package. She'd been down that road before. That wasn't love.

Fighting back tears, she walked to the window, her arms wrapped tightly around her waist, her body and mind crying out in pain. She gazed at a calm, sparkling, blue ocean, twinkling in the summer sunshine. How could it be so calm when her world had just disintegrated? She turned slowly and faced Xavier.

'And what about you? How about I ask you to work regular hours so we can be together?'

An expression of disbelief crossed his face. 'Charlotte, I am obstetrician. We don't have regular hours.'

'Oh, right, and I'm just a midwife so my job is expendable.' Bitterness filled her voice.

'That is *not* what I am saying.' Confusion laced his words. 'I know your work is important to you, which is why I thought this was a perfect solution for us. For us and our family.'

'This isn't a solution, Xavier. This is token effort. Delivering babies is part of who I am. I can't take the job in Antenatal or any other job you dream up for me so it best suits *your* life.'

He moved toward her. 'It's not for me, Charlotte. It's for us. What's best for us.'

Her dreams imploded at his lack of understanding. 'No, Xavier. It's all about you.' She put her arms out in front of her like a barrier, knowing what she had to do. She couldn't let him touch her or she'd crumble. 'You once told me that you needed to look for a partner outside medicine. This is why, isn't it? You want a partner who will live her life around you, making all the compromises. I can't be that person.'

His eyes clouded as he ran his hand through his hair. 'How can you know if you haven't tried?'

Her heart contracted in such pain her breathing stalled. He didn't want her. He wanted a version of her, one that would stifle her until she no longer existed. 'I saw it destroy my mother and it would surely destroy me. Then there'd be no *us*.'

She forced out the words against a tide of tears, hating what she had to say. 'I'm leaving Amaroo. Last night the Perth Community Midwifery convenor offered me a job if mine fell through.'

Pain and disbelief crossed his face. 'How can you leave? How can you just throw away what we have, what we could have, without even trying?'

Because I can't be who you want me to be.

'I want us to be together.' Desperation soaked into his words.

She bit her lip, steeling herself against his grief. Emptiness filled her. 'I'm sorry, it just wouldn't work.'

His shoulders stiffened and a muscle in his jaw spasm. 'So your career is so important to you that you will leave me over a job?'

His words shredded her heart. She forced herself to really look at him, searching for signs of understanding. But there were none. He had no clue, no understanding of where she was coming from.

Where was the man she'd fallen in love with?

All she could see was a man who knew what he wanted, and was used to getting it when he asked. Shades of her father. Love with conditions.

Her legs trembled, the walls threatened to close in on her. She had to leave. There was nothing else left to say. Nothing left to stay for. No understanding could be reached when he had no idea who she was. The fire in her soul spluttered and died, her dreams of a future turned to ashes.

'Goodbye, Xavier.' Somehow she managed to walk to the door and walk through it. She didn't look back.

Xavier swiped the colour-coordinated folders off his desk, their contents spilling out onto the floor with an unsatisfying thud. He slumped into his chair, anger and disbelief whirling inside him.

How could she look at him with those large, emerald eyes

as if he was the one causing the pain? Those eyes in the past few weeks had radiated warmth and affection and two nights ago he'd thought he'd seen something even stronger.

But in a heartbeat she'd walked out the door, throwing away the chance to build on what they had together. Throwing away his love. How could she just leave?

His brain reeled at the events that had just unfolded. He'd known she wouldn't easily accept the loss of the community midwifery programme and he'd agonised over the best way to break the news to her. But his hands were tied. The budget had no fat, no reserves, and as much as he would love to give her the community programme, he couldn't.

Hard decisions had to be made. He'd thought she understood that. He'd sown the fiscal seeds of doubt ever since they'd met. He never imagined she would leave him over the decision.

Abruptly, he pushed his chair out from the desk and swung it around to the window. The wind had picked up and whitecaps now danced on the top of the ocean. He'd missed the moment of change from calm sea to rough. Just like he'd missed the moment Charlotte had changed.

How could she not understand that their relationship was far more important than a job?

Another pile of folders hit the floor. What did the psychologists say about being attracted to the same type of person over and over? He'd let his ragged heart overrule his head. He was an idiot!

He paced across the office. But he knew he wasn't a fool at knowing what made relationships work. He'd watched his parents in action, fostering their relationship, while his relatives' had floundered.

Relationships didn't work if you didn't see each other, if

one person's focus was elsewhere. He wanted to give *this* relationship the perfect conditions to grow.

His anger surged again. Why hadn't she seen the closing door of her programme as being the opening of a new door? A door that could take them to a special place. A place where they could be together and raise a family. It had been so clear to him, almost as if the programme's closing was a gift to them. A gift she'd thrown away, along with his love and his heart.

He looked at the clock. Six p.m. Time to go home.

He hesitated. For the first time in a long time, going home didn't appeal. Too many memories of Charlotte pervaded the house. Her perfume lingered on his sheets, her hairbrush sat in his bathroom and her towel hung by the pool. Almost every room held a memory of the joy she brought him.

Had brought him.

No, he couldn't go home. Not to shattered dreams and the constant reminder of what he'd just lost. He picked up his jacket and his wallet, closed the door on the mess and drove into town.

The band turned the bass up full blast and the walls of the pub vibrated, along with Xavier's head. He pushed the plate of half-eaten food away. On other occasions he'd wolfed down the rump steak grilled to perfection. Tonight it tasted like cardboard.

For three hours he'd sat in the darkest, furthest corner of the pub, nursing a glass of merlot, scowling at anyone who attempted conversation.

Charlotte's face constantly swam in front of his eyes, heightening his pain into a jagged sharpness that intensified with every breath he took. He wished he were on call—at least he could have buried himself in work instead of sitting here like a caricature of a broken lover.

'Hiding out?' Phil Carson put two glasses of beer on the table and slid into the chair opposite him.

'Phil.' Xavier extended his hand, clasping the retired doctor's hand, resigning himself to having to make polite conversation.

'Heard you were here.' Phil sipped his beer.

He raised his brows. 'Village gossip travels quickly.'

'Actually, I haven't heard any gossip, but both Bob Jenkins and David McAllister told me you were sitting here with a look of thunder. They're worried about you.' He leaned back in his chair. 'Bad day?'

'You could say that.' He watched the head on his beer slowly diminish.

Phil stared straight at him. 'Work or personal?'

He wanted to say, *None of your business.* But something in the older man's fatherly expression tugged at him. He sighed. 'Both.'

'Ah, but work wouldn't have brought you to the pub now, would it?'

'You are going to badger me until I tell you, *oui*?'

Phil grinned. 'You got that right.'

Xavier ran the coaster through his fingers. 'I had to cancel Charlotte's community midwifery programme today.'

'How did she take it?'

He grimaced. 'Oh, really well. She is leaving Amaroo and going to work in Perth.'

Phil's air of casualness instantly disappeared. 'Perth? Why Perth?'

'Because the woman is determined to work in community midwifery, and she's putting her job ahead of the people who care for her.' His bitterness spilled into the words.

Phil leaned forward. 'That doesn't sound like Charlie.'

'*Non?* It is a familiar story to me. I've been abandoned for a job before.' He downed the glass of beer, the coolness almost hissing against the heat of his throat.

'Did you ask her to stay?'

Xavier rolled his eyes. 'Of course I asked her to stay. I pleaded with her to stay, but she's determined to go to her dream job.'

Phil rubbed his forehead as if trying to make sense of the conversation. 'Is the job a promotion?'

'I don't know.' Exasperation filled his voice. 'I don't think so. She didn't mention it.'

Phil drew circles in the condensation on the table. 'I've known Charlie for five years, and she loves this town. She loved her community midwifery programme too, but she knew it might fold.' He met Xavier's gaze. 'We've talked about what she might do if the programme ceased and not once did she mention leaving Amaroo. I'm certain she'd happily go back to Birth Suite where she worked before.'

'I offered her a job in Antenatal. A perfect job—Monday to Friday, regular hours, so we could focus on our life together.' Bile scalded his throat. 'She threw it back in my face.'

Phil shot him a look. 'Ah.'

'Ah? *Zut!* What is that supposed to mean?'

Phil crossed his arms. 'Did you ask her what she wanted to do?'

A prickle of unease washed over him. 'I did not ask her to give up work, if that is what you are inferring.' His defensive tone hung in the air. 'I asked her to work nine to five. I thought we had something really special.' He ran his hand through his hair. 'Something we could build on, that would take us into the future where we could grow old together.'

The older doctor placed his hand on Xavier's arm. 'You and I both know that Charlie's only ambition is to care for women and deliver healthy babies.'

Being a midwife is an integral part of who I am. I only ever wanted to deliver babies and I get to do that every day.

His stomach rolled, nausea flooded him. Phil was right—ambition wasn't a force that drove Charlotte. She just wanted to be who she was.

I'm not going to get into a relationship and risk losing 'me' all over again.

In his excitement at the idea of being with her, he'd tried to take from her the *one* thing she needed.

Mon Dieu. He'd asked her to sacrifice her identity. He'd done exactly what her father and fiancé had done. He'd asked her to change to accommodate him and his needs. He'd been patriarchal, judgmental and, oh, so very wrong. Of course she was leaving him.

But not if he could help it. He stood up. 'Phil, I have to go. I have to talk to her.'

The older man smiled. 'Of course you do, son. Drive carefully—there's a storm brewing.'

CHAPTER ELEVEN

CHARLIE tugged her suitcase, pulling it down from the top of her wardrobe, and ducked as a pile of other gear cascaded with it. Spanner leapt out of the way with a yelp.

'Sorry, Span.' She sat on the floor surrounded by the mess, hugging her dog, burying her face in her golden coat. The tears she'd held back for so long rolled down her cheeks, carrying her misery and anguish, merging into a pool of despair.

She'd risked her heart, only to have it returned to her battered, bruised and broken. It hurt so much that she ached inside and out. Everything stretched out in front of her, shattered and bleak.

She'd lost her future—her dreams of sharing a future with Xavier, in the town she loved. And along with it she'd lost her dream of having a family with him. A dream that had come so close to reality she could almost taste it.

And now she was going to Perth.

Spanner licked her face. A few hours ago, in her anger and disbelief, going to Perth had been the perfect solution. She'd have said or done anything to get out of that office. Anything to separate herself from Xavier, who'd had been so unaware of what he'd been asking her to do. What he had asked her to give up.

His insistence that *his* way was the only way, had brought her past flooding back so fast that the emotions had swamped her. She hadn't been able to breathe properly, let alone think.

She half-heartedly opened the case and threw in a few clothes. Why? Why had Xavier been so insistent that she change jobs? The question went around and around in her head, niggling like a thorn in a finger.

Xavier had gone out of his way to create an opportunity for Michael Strachan. He'd encouraged him to take a chance and go with his dreams. He'd behaved in a way so different from her father and Richard that his behaviour this afternoon made no sense. Why would he support Michael in his career and not her?

In a pile of clean laundry she found the pair of overalls Xavier had worn the day Ebony had been born. She hugged the garment close to her and breathed in deeply.

Disappointment rocked her. She'd lost him completely— even his scent had been replaced by that of laundry powder.

Images of the night they'd found Ebony played across her mind. The night they'd agreed to an affair. The night he'd opened up about his past.

The night he'd told her how much he'd been hurt. *Two people couldn't be dedicated to their careers, each other and a family. He was discarded, along with an unborn child.*

Her heart stalled, hope raced in. Did Xavier believe he couldn't be loved if she worked? That she couldn't love their child if she worked? Had he asked her to give up work not because he wanted to change her but because he was scared he would lose her? Scared that she loved her job more than him?

Agitation fizzed in her veins. She had to find out. She needed to talk to him. Needed to know. *Now.*

Riffling through piles of clothes and general mess, she frantically searched for her car keys, finally finding them under her T-shirts. 'Back soon, Span.' She patted the dog and headed to the door.

Spanner started shivering and raced to hide under her bed, howling as she went.

A moment later wind gusted into the house through the open doors, rattling the windows. Charlie peered outside. Black clouds scudded quickly across the sky as jagged bolts of lightning headed earthward. Thunder cracked so loud her heart seemed to bounce off her rib cage.

Huge drops of rain slammed into the house, ricocheting off the tin roof and coming in through the hundred-year-old cracks.

Above the deafening rain and wind she heard the penetrating deepness of a truck's air-horn. Then the sickening sound of crushing metal.

Accident. She dialled 000, giving the operator directions. Grabbing her medical bag and her waterproof coat, she raced out to her car.

Darkness, usually slow to creep in on summer nights, rushed forward with the storm. The car's wheels spun in wet gravel as she headed down the track to the highway. She squinted to see through the windscreen, the wipers working hard against the punishing rain. The short few hundred metres to the main road seemed to extend to ten times their normal length.

She joined the highway and rounded the first bend. A semi-trailer lay across the road, its trailer having jackknifed, taking out two cars on its skidding trajectory.

Her mind raced. *Triage.* Assess the scene. Prioritise. She ran to the crushed car, flattened between the truck and the embankment.

She stopped short, biting her lip. She doubted she could do anything. The occupants had probably died instantly. Rain pelted her. She shone her torch, catching sight of the number plate.

Xavier's car.

Her legs trembled and her body shook uncontrollably. Her stomach heaved. Leaning forward, she vomited into the ditch. She'd lost him. Gone before she could tell him she loved him. Before she could assure him that her job would *never* come ahead of him.

She pulled on a door, frantic to get to him. *You can't be dead. I won't let you be dead.* The door wouldn't move. She cupped her hands around her eyes, trying to see through the tinted window, but all that greeted her was inky darkness. In sheer desperation kicked she door. Nothing moved.

'Xavier!' She heard herself scream, a disembodied voice ragged with pain.

Arms wrapped around her. 'It is all right. I am here.'

She slumped against him, grabbing him with her hands, making sure he was in one piece. Never wanting to let him go. Confusion swam in her shocked mind, her thoughts clawing to hold onto something to make sense of the situation. 'I thought…the car… I thought you…'

He stroked her hair. 'I know. I was coming to see you. I missed the turn-off and hit something, perhaps a wombat. I was out of the car when the truck rounded the corner. I am OK.' He squeezed her tightly against him.

He was coming to see me. The wondrous thought wove through her.

'Charlotte. I need you. I need your help.' His firm 'doctor-in-charge' voice instantly cleared her brain, grounding her, bringing her mind back to the accident.

'The truck driver's dazed and he has a broken arm and lacerations. But I can't get to the woman in the car.' He gripped her arm. 'The heavy-duty tow truck and Jaws of Life are still fifteen minutes away. You might just be small enough to crawl through the space between the car and the truck to reach her.'

Charlie nodded, her training overcoming her shock. 'Do you know who it is?'

'It's Penelope Watson.'

Fear shuddered through her. 'But she's eight months pregnant.'

'*Exactement.* We need to get to her now and assess her and the baby.'

They ran to the car, which was pinned under the back wheels of the truck. The rain continued to pour down, bringing visibility down to zero.

Xavier held the torch. 'I smashed the back window with a rock. See if you can fit between the truck and the car and climb through it. The rain will have washed away any petrol, but be careful. If the fumes are too strong, you come back out.' He gave her a quick hug, his words carrying his concern. 'I mean it, Charlotte, be careful.'

Instinct overrode her terror. She crawled through the gloom. 'Pen.' She yelled to be heard over the rain. Using her hands, she felt for the back of the car as her eyes became accustomed to the gloom.

'Pen, it's Charlie Buchanan.' Glass tore at her legs as she pulled herself through into the car.

Penelope reached out her arms toward her, her eyes wide with shock. 'Charlie?' Her voice quivered with fear.

'Yes, Pen, it's me.' Charlie's fingers closed around the woman's wrist, giving support, checking her pulse. Thready.

'Charlotte.' Xavier's worried voice sliced through the dark. 'Are you all right?'

'I'm with her. I'm checking her vital signs.'

Penelope's seat belt held her in her seat. Although she looked unhurt, her rapid pulse told a different story. 'Pen, do you have any pain?'

'I've got a tight feeling down here.' She put her hand on the lap sash of the belt that crossed her abdomen.

Charlie undid the seat belt and gently pressed her hand against Penelope's abdomen. Rigid. Internal bleeding.

A shiver of dread cut through her. The impact of the accident would have been enough to cause a placental tear or a rupture in the uterus. Both mother and baby could die.

Panic rose. She forced it down. 'Xavier, I need more light.'

'I am working on it.' His voice reassured her. Help was on its way.

Maintain circulating volume. 'I need to put in an IV, Pen, to help you and the baby.'

Penelope's hands flew to her abdomen, flattening out under the baby in a cradling action. 'Charlie, the baby…I'm not going to lose my baby, am I?'

Penelope's fear ripped into her. Pen needed to be in an operating theatre right this minute, with Xavier weaving his life-saving magic. Instead, she was trapped in a car, in the middle of a rainstorm, with a midwife with limited equipment.

Where the hell was the ambulance?

Where the hell was the light she needed? She couldn't insert an IV by feel alone.

Stabilise her. The tourniquet snapped into place. Her

fingers probed for a vein. Nothing. Penelope's shocked veins had collapsed. 'Let's try the other arm, Pen.' *Please.*

Bright light flooded the interior of the car. *Thank you, SES.*

She could feel and see a vein. 'This might sting a bit, Pen.' The cannula slid in. She held her breath. Blood entered the needle. *Yes.* She opened the drip full bore, pushing normal saline into her patient, attempting to replace the fluid she suspected was pouring into Penelope's abdomen.

'Pen, I'm sorry but I need to feel if you've lost any blood. I need to put my hand between your legs.'

The other woman looked vacantly at her, all her thoughts centred on her baby.

Charlie's hands met dampness—warm, congealed blood. The life force of the mother. And the unborn child. Penelope needed a Caesarean section. Now.

'Charlotte, is she stable?' The concern and caring in Xavier's voice swam around her, giving her strength.

'We need to get her out now. She's bleeding.'

She heard his muffled expletive. 'We're doing everything we can at this end. Keep pumping in the saline. The moment the ambulance arrives I'll pass in the plasma expander. *Chérie*, you're doing great.'

Great wasn't enough. It was impossible to do a foetal heart so she had no idea of the baby's condition. Part of her didn't want to know.

Hope was all they had.

She checked Pen's blood pressure. 'Xavier, BP is holding.' *Just.*

'Good. The rescue tow truck's arrived. We're going to jack the trailer off the car. You'll be out soon.' Xavier's voice sounded forced, overly bright.

Be quick. I can't hold her for too long. Charlie infused lightness into her voice. 'Did you hear that, Pen? We'll have you in hospital soon.'

She held Pen's hand but the woman didn't flinch. She was directing all her energy to her unborn child, willing her baby to live.

The nauseating sound of crushing metal boomed in her ears, sending shivers through her. Anxiety, fear and anticipation built on top of each other, making Charlie's heart pound hard and fast.

Then there were arms touching Charlie, voices surrounding her. And Xavier. She didn't want to let Xavier out of her sight. The memory of thinking she'd lost him for ever stayed sharp and strong.

He quickly squeezed her shoulder. Then he and James Rennison lifted Pen onto the stretcher and loaded her into the ambulance. Charlie climbed in after them, securing the door.

The brief moment of relief she'd experienced when Pen had been removed from the car had fizzled out. Nothing had changed. Pen was desperately ill. The high-pitched siren pierced the night, the ambulance speeding against time to get Penelope to Theatre before she and the baby died.

They raced through A & E straight up to Theatre.

'Xavier, I want to scrub in.' She needed to be in Theatre with Pen. With Xavier. She didn't want to be apart from either of them.

His raven eyes filled with emotion. 'I want you in there, too.' He turned and called across the scrub area. 'Phillip, we need her anaesthetised in record time. Charlotte's kept them going this long but neither is going to hold on much longer.'

He scrubbed up and entered theatre. 'How's she going?'

'She's intubated and ready.' Phillip checked the ECG.

'Right, let's get started.' Xavier picked up the scalpel, deftly made an incision, quickly located the uterus and delivered a purply-blue, extremely distressed baby.

Stuart Mullins raced the meconium-stained, limp baby over to the resuscitation cart.

'*Zut*. I can't see a thing here. More suction!' Xavier's curt command radiated his fear that Penelope might die on the table.

Charlie kept the suction in place, keeping the field as clear as possible. Blood bubbled up as fast as she could remove it, quickly building up in the suction bottle at their feet.

Beads of sweat lined Xavier's brow. No matter what he tried, the uterus wouldn't contract. The bleeding continued.

'Xavier, we're risking disseminated intravascular coagulation with this amount of blood loss.' The concern in Phillip's voice rang around Theatre. 'Urine output down.'

'What do you want to do?' Charlie asked the question—the code for a hysterectomy.

Xavier's body vibrated with frustration. 'Give her more Synto. I want to save this uterus.'

'Pressure's dropping.' Phillip spoke over the incessant warning beeps of the BP machine. 'No more time, mate.'

'Clamp—now!'

Charlie ignored the anger in Xavier's voice. She knew he hated that he had to take away Pen's opportunity to have another child.

The ECG machine screamed as the green display morphed into a flat line. 'Cardiac arrest. Start compressions.'

Charlie pressed down on Pen's sternum, each compression a frantic desire to save a life.

Xavier's brow creased in deep furrows as he applied clamps.

Time stood still.

'Come on, Pen.' Xavier's voice sounded low and urgent behind his mask.

Phillip shocked Pen's heart, urging it to restart.

'The uterine artery is now tied off.' Xavier gave Charlie a look of pure relief.

The cardiac monitor's scream segued into regular beeps. 'Sinus rhythm, thank goodness.' Phillip's head appeared over the drape. 'I don't want to go through that again any time soon. It's always harder when it's someone you know well.'

Charlie nodded, too emotional to speak. It had been far too close to tragedy.

'Baby's doing well.' Stuart Mullins pushed past with the isolette. 'I'm taking her down to Special Care now.'

Thirty minutes later Penelope left Theatre, transferred to Intensive care. Xavier tore off his gloves, the latex ripping with the force. He tossed them into the bin. His foot released the bin pedal and the lid crashed closed.

'*Alors.*' He ran his hand through his hair, the action jerky.

'You saved the baby.' Charlie walked over to him, putting her hand on his shoulder, wanting to comfort him. 'You saved the mother. Focus on that.'

He turned to face her. 'Penelope's not out of the woods yet. The next twenty-four hours are vital. DIC…'

'She'll make it.' She smiled, trying to take away the bleak look in his eyes.

Xavier put his hand over hers. 'You were fantastic out there tonight. Gutsy and brave. *Merci.*'

'I was scared stiff, but you being there helped.' She wanted to drop her head on his shoulder, take refuge in his arms, but first they needed to talk. Solve this impasse between them.

As if reading her mind, Xavier stepped back from her and

undid his gown. 'Two hours ago I was on my way to talk to you. I still need to do that.' He undid the top tie of her gown, his fingers brushing the back of her neck.

Shivers of longing passed through her. She pulled her gown off, dumping it into the linen skip, and then walked over to the now bare operating table. She sat down, swinging her legs, deliberately putting some distance between them.

'Two hours ago I was about to come into town to talk to you.' She stared straight at him, wanting to see his reaction to the question she was about to ask. 'I need to know the real reason you want to push me into a desk job.'

Contrition washed over his face. 'Because I was stupid and insensitive and desperately scared. Scared of you leaving me. *Je suis désolé*, Charlotte. I am so very sorry.'

His contrition and angst washed over her and she longed to comfort him. *Wait and listen*, her rational voice cautioned her. *Let him explain.* 'Why would you think I would leave you?'

He sat down next to her. 'For too long I have been blaming the wrong thing for my failed relationships. I thought work had been the problem. But I now realise that the job had no impact on the relationship at all. All this time I've been blaming the wrong thing. It was not the job or career that was the problem. It was a lack of love.'

She nodded in understanding, a shoot of hope opening up inside her.

He reached for her hand. 'I thought if your focus was so much on your job, you couldn't work and love me.' He shook his head. 'All I ended up doing was behaving like your father, asking you to change and pushing you away.'

He raised her hand to his lips. 'I don't want you to change. I don't want to push you away. I want you to stay.'

His words carried his sorrow into her heart. She wanted to throw her arms around him but nothing was solved. Yet. 'I want to stay too, but how do you see that happening?'

His earnest look entreated and she knew he'd gone through agonies since she'd last seen him. 'You understand I can't offer you what you had for all the reasons I outlined yesterday. But we both know you love a challenge and so, with that in mind, I can offer you something else.'

Her heart turned over. She closed her eyes and breathed in deeply. She had to focus, keep on track. There was too much at stake. 'What is it?'

'Two days ago I got an email from the Health Department. There is ongoing funding for work with teenage girls. If you stay, you will be setting up and running a clinic-cum-health education programme to reduce the number of teenage pregnancies. Also, you'd be supporting kids like Jade when they are pregnant, being their midwife and hospital liaison, delivering their baby and following up well into the postnatal period.'

Charlie's mind tilted on its axis. Xavier was offering her a job. Not just any job. A huge job, one as big as community midwifery. Almost more important in terms of health impact.

Her eyes searched his face. 'You realise the time commitment this programme will take as I set it up?'

He nodded. 'It will be enormous, but if it means you'll be in Amaroo, that is all that matters.'

She blinked back a rush of happy tears. 'What made you change your mind?'

'You once said to me that two careers could be combined if both people wanted it to work. I really want it to work. I love you and I don't want to live without you.'

He really loves you. Her heart soared with wonder. He'd accepted who she was and recognised what was important to her. He'd changed his plans and compromised so he could be with her.

She reached out, laying her palm against his cheek, soaking in the love that radiated from his eyes. She looked deeply into those black eyes full of love. 'Tonight I thought you were dead and all I could think was I hadn't told you how much I loved you. How you've opened my eyes and showed me that living alone is not the way I want to live. No job I ever have will come before you.'

He smiled. 'I know that.'

'And you know that no job will come ahead of our children either.'

'*Oui*. I do.' He slipped off the table and stood in front of her. 'Charlotte, will you accept the job, and accept me too, by marrying me?'

She reached for him, drawing him in close. 'Is it a two-deal package?'

'Only if you want it to be.' The sincerity in his voice pierced her heart.

'I do.' She slid off the table into his arms. 'I do have a condition, though.'

'What is it?' The resignation in his voice played around them.

She ran her hands through his hair. 'No need to panic. I think you'll be OK with this and it won't cost too much of the hospital's money.'

He raised his brows. 'Why do I get the feeling I should be worried?'

She put her finger against his lips. 'I'll set up and run the programme as long as I can train another midwife to take over when I'm on maternity leave.'

He pulled her tightly against him, burying his face in her hair. 'I think that is a wonderful idea.'

'And you need to find ongoing money for that midwife because she'll be an integral part of the programme. Once we're parents, I'll only be working part time.'

Xavier tilted her head, staring deep into her eyes. 'I love you. From the moment I met you, you've changed my world, and made every day a glorious adventure.'

Happiness cascaded through her. 'I love you, too.'

His lips came down to meet hers, two people merging into one, accepting each other, evolving together.

Xavier reluctantly drew away. 'Let's get out of here. Let's go home.'

Charlie tilted her head to the side. 'And where is home?'

He rolled his eyes. 'Your hairbrush is in my bathroom and I have neatly folded towels and a fluffy bathrobe waiting for you.'

She gave him a grin. 'I have a pile of dirty washing on my bathroom floor.'

'Now, why doesn't that surprise me?' He swung her back into his arms. 'I've just thought of a condition of my own.'

'Really?'

'Really. We're increasing Mrs McDonald's cleaning and tidying hours.'

Charlie laughed. 'I can live with that as long as I'm with you.'

'You, me and Amaroo. Now I've got everything I've ever wanted.'

'So have I.' She leaned up, capturing his lips with hers in a brief, tantalising kiss. 'Take me home, Xavier. Take me to *our* home.'

He grabbed her hand, flicked off the lights and together they walked toward their future.

EPILOGUE

XAVIER swung two-year-old Amélie up onto his shoulders and held Luc's hand as they walked home from the park. The sensation of a warm little hand in his larger one always sparked a sense of overwhelming joy.

As they walked they stopped and chatted to friends and peered into prams to see how the babies that he had delivered were growing.

'Papa, I love Wednesday afternoons.'

He glanced down at his four-year-old son. 'Why is that?'

'Because we feed the ducks. Then we go home and you cook dinner. And Mummy always comes home at dinnertime with a big smile. Then she sits down, hugs us and says, "I love Wednesdays."'

Xavier smiled. 'I love Wednesdays, too.' He fished a key out of his pocket but the back door opened unexpectedly.

'Mummy!' Amélie stretched her arms out, almost toppling off Xavier's shoulders.

Charlotte reached out with a wide smile, steadying her. 'Anyone would think I'd been gone for days instead of a few hours.'

Xavier lifted his daughter from his shoulders then leaned

forward to kiss his wife. 'Luc and I have just been discussing Wednesdays.'

She walked inside with him, her arm around his waist. 'I know you love Wednesdays.'

He pulled her into his arms. 'And you do, too. You get to go out into my world and I get to come home into yours.'

'True, I love Wednesdays.' She smiled at him. 'How would you feel if in a few months' time I gatecrashed your Wednesdays for a while?'

He stepped back, looking into dancing, emerald eyes, trying to read her. Five years of married life and she still amazed him, lighting up his world, giving him so much pleasure. He grinned. 'As long as I still get to cook.'

She swatted his arm in a mock huff. 'Luc tells me my cookies are wonderful.'

'*Oui*, but he has French blood and knows how to charm.' He laughed at the indignation on her face. He tucked a few stray strands of hair behind her ear. '*Chérie*, tell me why do you want to share our Wednesdays?'

'Actually, it won't just be me.' She threw her arms around his neck. 'The Laurent family is increasing by one next spring.'

Delight ricocheted through him, expanding the happiness his life already offered him every day. '*C'est magnifique*, my darling.' He wrapped his arms around her, holding her against his heart, giving thanks for his blessings.

Small arms hugged his legs and waist. 'Family hug, family hug.'

His laughter merged with Charlotte's as they opened their arms to their children, hugging them close. His family.

Everything he ever wanted was right here with him in this room. He sighed in contentment. Life didn't get any better than this.

The World of Mills & Boon®

There's a Mills & Boon® series that's perfect for you. We publish ten series and with new titles every month, you never have to wait long for your favourite to come along.

Blaze®
Scorching hot, sexy reads

By Request
Relive the romance with the best of the best

Cherish™
Romance to melt the heart every time

Desire™
Passionate and dramatic love stories

Visit us Online
Browse our books before you buy online at
www.millsandboon.co.uk